Fallen Thorns

Harvey Oliver Baxter

Fallen Thorns

Paperback ISBN: 978-1-7395208-1-6

Ebook ISBN: 978-1-7395208-0-9

Cover and interior illustrations by Harvey Baxter (@topazsunzart on Instagram)

To anyone who secretly has wings

AUTHOR'S NOTE

This book contains topics and themes I believe should be addressed before you begin:
- Frequent depressive and self-deprecating thoughts
- Allusions to suicide
- Body horror
- Self-inflicted injuries
- Attempted sexual assault (non-graphic)
- Manipulation
- Possession
- Physical torture (mostly off-page)
- Ignorance to touch aversion
- Reference to eating disorders and weight loss

"You travelled to seek happiness, but a fatality seems to pursue you."

— Mary Shelley, *Frankenstein*

PROLOGUE

Cobbles, poetry and bells. A stone paradise buried in history and birch. Buildings buzz with smoking fools while larger-than-life bodies float in a drowned haze, stamping their feet out of time with the muffled songs everybody knows but no one knows the name of. The heavy influx of students, all chasing impossible dreams, dominate the streets at dusk. Two shots of whiskey and they're invincible.

In a city so alive, mortality is quickly forgotten. Yet death lives in hidden places, corrupting the shadows and feeding from the light. It's the whispers through dusty cracks; the movements behind every blackened window, and the silhouettes cast under flickering streetlights. Blink, and you'll miss it — but oh, how it thrives.

They gather at night — they always do. Swarming from city to city, they emerge from the arches and light-pooled passageways and hit when black has long cloaked the sky — when lone travellers know all too well not to be out beneath the stare of the all-seeing moon. But some never learn. By some power, they think themselves immune to what they cannot see. And it always starts the same. The one left behind.

This evening it's a man of wise years: a coated shadow underneath the alder branches. Hands placed firmly in each trench pocket, his head angles towards the mossy path ahead with his eyes focusing on each calculated step. He grumbles to himself and clears his throat, breaking the silence. At the crack of a branch from a foreign foot, his pace quickens but not in fear of the impending danger. This was simple human instinct. The body's response to the unknown. This man had walked many a dim passageway after dark and his lengthened stride was merely second nature.

The distant, golden haze of the cathedral seeps through the partings of the leaf-arched path below. The steady stream of the river drowns out the second and third cracks of the shrubbery. He mumbles again, with greater urgency this time. Adjusting his tie as the path behind him closes, and the ancient, watchful light dies.

It's funny how quickly humans react to their own shift in senses; driven by adrenaline and possessing no control over how they choose to fight back.

They know when to strike, enabled by a second nature of their own. Too early and the elation could trigger vital mistakes. Too late and they run the risk of sacrificing flavour.

It took seconds. The man felt nothing but a prick. They flocked around each other like birds, pushing and shoving for a drop of ecstasy. Monstrous growls defied the river gushing below, joined by cackling laughter and the whine of animal chants. They had starved too long to let this go to waste.

They drag his body like a rag-doll; the man's shoes scrape and scuff against the concrete, muddying his ankles while crimson soaks into his collar. The terror bleeding from his eyes is a privilege to witness, and not many have the honour. Frantically, he grasps for something — anything — though his brain no longer understands what. And right before his body finally slackens, the eldest withdraws a knife, no bigger than a hand, but sharp like the devil's tongue. It draws a perfect downward arch from ear to ear, erasing any sign they had ever been there at all.

So as the evening entertainment of the city draws to a close, high on red bliss, they toss the body down into the river, and, unnoticed, they retreat into the abyss.

Too far away to raise any alarm, the oil painted city watches on as the man in the trench coat silently floats away.

Act 1
The Thorns

CHAPTER ONE

I must have drifted off. One moment, I was in the lecture hall, focusing on the clock rather than the ongoing speech on 19th century romanticism, and the next, I was blinking awake in a mild and slightly annoyed panic.

My name is Arlo Everett and I daydream my way through life. Attending events in body but not always mind, coasting through school with commendable but not quite stand-out grades, and miraculously landing myself a place on a course I was only half interested in. Yet the degree was one I believed necessary to create the life I had chosen for myself.

At the age of four, when my mother read me stories before bed, I had already planned my life. I would be an author, and no one would stop me. An author of what, I could never decide, but writing was about the only thing that brought me real enjoyment. I tried sports and music and art, and all the extracurriculars parents encourage you to attend for 'character building', even though all I wanted to do was write.

Growing up in a village in the northwest of England — surrounded by forests, lakes, and an abundance of sheep — fuelled my passion for inventing fictional scenarios: a world to escape to.

I believed I was on the right path. Everything was going according to plan and I was... satisfied. It did not take long before I realised how much of an idiot I must have looked, trying too hard to be someone I was never cut out to be: the picturesque location and poetic lifestyle, precariously parted hair and charity shop camel coats; thick golfer vests and over polished boots, striding the narrow streets of Durham as if I were written by Donna Tartt. You'd think this was deliberate, writing myself into a narrative too cliché to ever exist in the real world. In actuality, I more just fell into it. I didn't want to stand out, nor blend in; I was content on just existing. One thing I did not expect upon arrival, was being instantly judged for being northern in a city that was even further north, and thus I had no option but to assimilate. I thought I was doing a pretty good job at it, though. In the month since I'd arrived, I had made enough acquaintances to be remembered in hallways and greeted in cafés, while maintaining enough privacy to avoid activities that would admittedly peak my ever-present anxious thoughts.

THE LAST HALF hour of the lecture dragged, but I made a reasonable number of notes, and even asked a question, but only to prove to myself that I was paying attention. My severe lack of sleep recently was certainly catching up with me.

As per my Wednesday routine since the start of term, with no other commitments for the day, I headed to the quaint coffee shop in town to read and wait for my friend Rani to finish her respective morning events. We studied the same course, but Rani had other business to attend to that morning. It had become standard procedure by this point, the constant in our messily scheduled lives. We'd always be there, without fail. Our preferred method of keeping ourselves awake for the remainder of the day.

It rained heavily that afternoon, and I cursed myself for still having not purchased an umbrella since my last one blew away.

And with my brain stuck in the mode of over-analysing, I couldn't help but mentally point out the pathetic fallacy of it all — everything so wet and miserable.

I ordered my drink then sat in the last remaining two-seater. The chair was positioned beside a small window overlooking the alleyway, yet the dripping condensation clouded the view.

I pulled out my book while waiting for the tea to cool, discretely glancing around before pulling out my biro to annotate. No one saw, or even cared — but in my head they did.

I shifted momentarily, before switching seats to better observe my surroundings. An old habit. But a page into my book, I realised my brain wasn't processing the words, so with a sigh, I tucked the book away and waited.

Rani spotted me the second she came through the door, shuffling herself past the tight queue to reach me.

"So, the vending machine broke. I am now seventy pence poorer and significantly sadder than I was this morning because I didn't get my mints." Rani threw her bag down dramatically to emphasise her displeasure. I rubbed my brow, disturbed at the sudden rise in volume, then handed over a tin of mints from my pocket and smiled as her face lit up.

"Wow you really are my knight in shining armour," she teased.

I shrugged then took a sip of my drink, now luke-warm. "Morning any good?" I asked whilst she arranged herself on the chair opposite. The cogs whirred in her head as she debated whether to open up her umbrella to let it dry or to keep it retracted — after all, everyone knows opening up a brolly indoors is bad luck. I let her take her time, grinning inwardly.

"I suppose good is one word to describe it, although the word 'good' doesn't really have enough *oomf* now I've studied literature for this long," she joked. She removed her black trench coat and pushed up the sleeves to her cream turtleneck jumper. "I finished my essay and tidied my room, though I regret washing my hair this morning because the rain did it anyway, but overall, yeah... 'good'. You?"

I loved the way Rani started interactions so easily. I always felt more comfortable being myself around people who took charge of conversations and kept the topic flowing without any awkwardness. I was the person who had to assess the company I was in before opening up. Most people who met me presumed I was shy, reserved, and all those other patronising terms. I was shy, until I got to know someone. If talking with them was as easy as it was with Rani, I became a whole different person.

We caught up for nearly two hours and our drinks grew cold. So we queued up for another and then another, laughing about our student loan going down the drain. I completely forgot about how miserable I'd been earlier that day. I never thought about university, or how I regretted starting this course, or how desperately I wanted to go home to see my dog. Nor did I worry about signing up for groups to make temporary friends or going out and getting drunk with strangers to meet someone and lose my virginity, or the fear of pulling all-nighters to study for a degree that was destined to land me in a financially unstable, dead-end job, as I would never find success in the publishing industry and — *breathe.*

All things terrified me, and if I was left alone long enough (which I often was) the doubts invaded my mind and gnawed away at me, piece by piece, until I'd either cry myself to sleep or infrequently but regrettably, do something worse.

But for those blissful two hours, I was free.

"Oh gosh, is that the time?" Rani stood, raking her jet-black curls into a low ponytail. I hurtled back to the present.

"I said I'd meet with Mila and Ava and some of the other girls to discuss some things. Wanna come with?"

Did I? Not particularly. I'd only met Mila and Ava once before; it had been an awkward introduction and I felt bad imposing on a group of close friends who probably didn't want me around. So, like I always did when I felt a rising sense of social panic, I respectfully declined the offer. Rani insisted she'd stay by my side the whole time, but I offered her a grateful smile and assured her I'd be fine. I made up something about finishing the work I had planned. She left me and said she'd message me later, thanking me — as she always did — for a lovely catch up. While I watched Rani hastily charge out the door, I forced down the cold dregs of my third pot of tea. I intended to remain seated and continue reading, but that part of my brain had long since shut down. Instead, I zoned out, staring out the windows across the room: mostly daydreaming, with a bit of people watching, until the thoughts started.

"Excuse me, sir, are you using this chair?" An elderly woman broke me out of another daze. A tray with a pot of tea and a slice of carrot cake trembled in her hands. I shook my head and smiled, instinctively standing up to take the tray from her once I noticed the bag slowly slipping from her shoulder. She commended me with words of gratitude and told me what a gentleman I was as she made herself comfortable opposite me. "Men like you are few and far between these days," she said. "It was so different back in my day. Now all you young'ns are so engrossed in your tiny devices and those ear buds, you forget how to communicate!"

The Arlo in my head rolled his eyes but on the surface, I laughed in agreement, to prove I was one of the good ones. Normally I was opposed to small talk, but as she nattered away, I figured she lived alone. Perhaps this was a regular thing she did for some company, so I welcomed her discussions and added to her points where I could, and when she was close to finishing her drink, I bid her farewell and left the coffee shop with a smile on my face.

Life wasn't so bad sometimes.

FOUR THIRTY. I checked my watch as I ambled back to my room. The sky was a mixture of pink and orange clouds post rain; the Victorian street lamps flickered on in sequence up the bank, and an amber glow lit the sodden path below. Stores pulled their shutters while restaurants filled up, and as much as I told myself I preferred my village back in the west, I picked one hell of a city to move to. It reminded me of Keswick or Ambleside: painted, stony edifices in all shapes and sizes, packed together up and down narrow, paved hills. And of course, there was the cathedral (a place I was shamefully yet to visit despite living so close), which stood proudly at the height of the town, protecting the city from centuries of harm.

As someone with an appreciation for history, I respected the effort that had been put into maintaining such a quaint 'frozen in time' city-centre. Sure, there were plenty of modern additions as well, despite some of the questionable works ongoing slightly outside the centre, yet nothing could mask the beauty of the bridges and the river walks. Degree aside, there were far worse places to live.

I'd taken my wandering observations a little too far when I reached the top of the hill, barging straight into to someone. I stepped back to find a young woman with bold green hair, dressed in a studded leather jacket and ripped jeans. She hadn't been paying attention to where she was walking either; while I was looking up, she was looking down.

"Gosh, I'm so sorry," I said, "did I hurt you?" I raised my hands in an embarrassed panic.

"No, no," she replied, "I'm fine! It was my fault." She offered me a sweet, dimpled smile, then continued on her way.

I hoped she'd forget our brief interaction by the time she reached her destination, but my mind feared she'd go home thinking about the rude man she bumped into. *I need to be more careful*, I thought, and mentally apologised to her the rest of my way home.

HOME WAS NOT QUITE *HOME*, but it was the closest thing I had to it, and was conveniently based in the centre of town, surrounded by quaint 19th-century terraced houses. The building was a little dated, as were the furnishings but I was blessed with a somewhat decent view of greenery. My neighbours were not perhaps the sweetest, having travelled from Oxford with the belief that the university was built for only people like them, but I kept quiet enough to not have to engage with them. They were too engaged in each other — evenings beside my thin walls would kindly remind me — but the little I let them know about me, the safer I felt.

I threw my bag down and sat at my desk in the middle of my room, opposite the window. Though I had ample time to complete my coursework, I sat and twisted a pen between my fingers as darkness consumed the room. I didn't bother checking the time, but judging by the growls in my stomach, I needed to make something to eat. But I didn't. I often didn't, in fact, as I could not be bothered engaging in small talk with the other residents. Despite my mind insisting that I *should* eat — even if that meant ordering a takeaway — my body refused to move. So, I sat staring out of the window, watching as the branches bent and curled over the mock gas lamps while browning leaves swirled across the path. I was glued to the chair, my breaths thickening as the pounding of my heartbeat sounded in my ears. Sweat beaded my brow, despite the freezing temperatures both outside and in. I was *aware* I needed to move and occupy my brain, and perhaps a change of scenery would have helped, but I just *couldn't*. Suppressed doubts from the day broke the dam in my mind, waves of anxiety flooding through. Why didn't I go with Rani? It might have been nice; I might have enjoyed myself and proved my over-thinking was baseless. I needed to stop avoiding people in fear of awkwardness. What about that poor young woman I bumped into? Was she thinking about our unfortunate encounter like I still was? *Why can't I just be normal?* I chewed my gums to oblivion.

Two heavy knocks pounded against the door, powerful enough to stop me spiralling. I stood and fanned my face, steadying my breathing as I invited reality back in. I took off my thick, knitted vest and ruffled my hair. *Why are you like this, Arlo?*

"Arlo, it's me. Rani. Are you in there? Can I come in?"

I glanced at my bedside clock; it was almost seven-thirty.

"Yeah. Hang on." I shook my head and turned on the light. I quickly neatened up my bed, and though Rani wouldn't mind the mess, *I* would mind knowing she'd see it.

I unlocked the door for her and welcomed her in. She'd changed outfits since I last saw her, or was she wearing that cream jumper earlier?

"Cold night?" I asked. That was usually how I started conversations, commenting on the weather. I really needed to work on icebreakers.

Rani made herself comfortable on the edge of my bed, clutching onto her coat, so I casually rested against my desk, thanking some higher power for my long legs that spared me from yet another awkward moment of 'where do I sit?' Sitting at my desk would have seemed too informal, the wall too unnatural, and the bed... well, I was a nineteen-year-old virgin with a pretty girl in my room; my mental timer was set to self-destruct for even considering the thought.

Rani didn't react to my statement. I must have misread the reason for her visit. This was not a happy meeting.

She lowered her head and sighed. "Arlo, I came to apologise."

That was unexpected. *What did she have to apologise for?*

"I know we haven't known each other for very long, but I really do believe we've become good friends, especially since we started here. I really appreciate your company, and I just wanted to apologise for leaving you today; that was a really shitty thing for a friend to do."

I was in shock and had absolutely no idea how to respond. In my eyes, she had done nothing wrong. She invited me to go with her friends and I said no. If anything, it was *I* who had to apologise. I looked at her, my heart full and confused.

"Rani, you have no reason to apologise," I said, brows furrowed.

"But I do," she insisted, gently placing her coat to one side. "I didn't tell you I had plans for later and then cut our meeting short because of it. I saw it in your eyes when I left, and I know you said you didn't mind not coming, but I knew you did. I've known you long enough to recognise that face, Arlo, and I'm sorry."

I *really* didn't know what to say. A giant lump formed in my throat. She was right. I didn't mind, but at the same time, I did. I wanted her to enjoy her time with her friends, but part of me wished she would have stayed longer. Her company calmed me. But how could I expect her to always be there? After all, she was her own person. She had her separate life and every right to live it without me. We weren't *together* and there was no *commitment* in our friendship. I needed to accept that — I always tried to.

"Don't worry about it," I said after a short pause. Rani looked at me with a sad smile. God, I really did take her for granted sometimes. Rani was one of the sweetest people I had ever met: pure through and through, and I didn't deserve our friendship. Why had she chosen me as a friend? Out of everyone she could have picked, she decided on a six-foot-three lump of fake sunshine with a terrible fashion sense.

I was aware I wasn't an easy person to be around. I often preferred to be alone, but that was when I was most most destructive. I never really knew what I wanted out of situations, and often ended up confusing even myself. Rani didn't have to make time for me, but she did. She actively chose to come and see me to ensure I was okay, even apologising for something as insignificant as meeting up with her friends. *Why am I like this?*

As the people pleaser I was, I thought about promising to come out with her next time, but then I stopped myself as I knew it was a lie. I often assured people I would do something before panicking and dropping out closer to the time. No one deserved constant disappointment and I didn't want to brand myself as the unreliable one, or the person you could never trust to be there.

"Come here," she beckoned, gesturing for me to join her on the bed.

Panic.

"I'm not going to hug you; I know you don't like that," she said with a sweet laugh.

I do not deserve our friendship.

I sat myself beside her, maintaining a comfortable gap between us.

"I'm glad I met you, Arlo." Rani flashed a happy smile this time. "Lucky we were thrown together in sixth-form and happened to end up in the same university. Lucky I argued with my parents to let me study this course. Lucky we had each other in the beginning and even luckier now I've gotten to know you more. I just wanted to say that I am always here to talk if you need it."

I was glad I'd met her too — more than glad, actually, and I told her as such. If it were not for Rani in those first few weeks, I dreaded to think where I would have ended up.

A cloud of tension lifted from the room, giving me enough confidence to shuffle back to the headboard and cross my legs. Rani followed suit, backing onto the wall with her well-worn combat boots hanging from the edge and scuffing the sheets. I sucked in my lips and pretended not to notice. Rani did.

"Gosh, sorry." She leaned forward to untie her shoes.

"No, honestly, it's fine." I wafted my hands out in expression.

This earned a grin and a soft finger jab. "Don't lie, Everett. I'm taking my shoes off. It's polite."

We both chuckled. Another tension cloud evaporated.

"So did you have a nice evening?" I asked, transitioning as smoothly as I could.

Rani rolled her eyes. "Well..." she began, taking in a deep breath.

"Oh, do I sense a story time?"

"You do indeed. Prepare yourself for some girl drama."

"I'm all ears." I tucked my knees up and offered Rani my pillow for her back. I froze as the pillow moved and revealed Wellington, my tattered teddy bear that I forgot was there. Rani didn't react so neither did I, returning my full attention to her.

I'd never been one for gossip, and generally avoided all common room conversations back at school. People judged the slightest thing, and some could be so cruel for absolutely no reason — even those I considered friends. Yet I was well enough acquainted with Rani now to know her definition of gossip constituted a more factual and relevant retelling of events.

"Right." She slapped her thighs. "So, you know Mila and Ava, and how they are together but not together — this whole complicated thing." She waved her hands in circles and I nodded, despite not having a clue about any of this. All I knew was that Mila and Ava existed.

She continued. "Well, it turns out they are currently going through a rough patch, and Ava didn't even turn up. So it was just me, Mila, and two other girls from Mila's old school. It was fine, we all got along, but then those two had to leave and I had to spend the last hour or so listening to Mila's relationship crisis. Which I would have been okay with if I wasn't close with Ava, but I am and now I feel guilty and like I've gone behind Ava's back." She rubbed her legs again. "Honestly, you would have thought this sort of stuff would have been left behind in school. But nope! I'm always the neutral ground for the firing squad." She tipped her head back against the wall in defeat.

"Are you going to tell Ava then?" I should *not* have been enjoying this as much as I was, being reminded again how she made conversations so *easy*.

"Would you?"

"Hmm." Thankfully, I'd never found myself in this situation. Where Rani saw herself as the person on the fence, I was never in the field to begin with.

"I don't know," she replied, head rolling to face me. "Probably not, I don't want to be the go-between. Ava will probably ring me with her part of the story soon, anyway. And then in a few days' time, they'll be back together like none of this ever happened. Honestly, I keep telling them how lucky they are to have each other. Us queers are hard to come by."

"You're queer?" My tone sounded too surprised for my liking, but it didn't appear to impact Rani in any way.

She shrugged. "Well, to be honest, I'm not really sure. It's a difficult one. Sometimes I don't even think I care about having a specific label. I'll know when I know, but I'm certain I'm queer and that can mean a lot of things. Which is why I like to say it."

"Nice."

She laughed. "Wow. That's probably the best reaction I've ever received. That's how it should always be. Thanks for that, man."

I sat up and folded my arms. "I've never understood why people make it such a big deal. It makes no difference what you identify as, as long as you're happy." I inwardly shook my head at my preaching, but I meant every word. I never wrapped my head around why we believed we needed to have a label or a default identity. Why should it matter? People spend way too much time getting involved in other people's business when it doesn't concern them in the slightest.

"What about you?"

"Hmm? Oh, right." I'd never been asked that before and therefore had never had a solid answer. Love was a topic I chose to steer away from. Something so far away in my plans, it wasn't even visible. "Maybe?" An honest answer.

"Well, whatever the future has in store for you, I can safely say any person will be lucky to have you." She playfully leaned over and grabbed Wellington, throwing him in my face with a grin.

CHAPTER TWO

I awoke the next morning to news about a tragic accident down by the riverside. In the early morning hours, the body of a middle-aged man washed up amongst driftwood along the outskirts of the city. The police were unsure about the time the death occurred, but by the fact that there had been no reported missing cases matching his description, it was safe to assume he had not been there long. Two days at most. It was horrifying, regardless of the circumstances, but what really made my skin crawl was the fact that in the mere seven weeks since my arrival in what was deemed a relatively safe city, this was not the first incident.

The first death was a history student who had yet to even begin her course. They discovered her body on the first Sunday before the term started and ruled her death a suicide. The newspapers penned it as a 'rowdy night', an insensitive term, yet one that sparked a brief national debate over students' mental health and the pressures placed upon us by those in power — and in some cases — our own peers. As always, nothing ever came of it. We were expected to move on just like the media often did. A handful of people came forward after the light service held at the cathedral, claiming their friend would have never done something like that.

Reporters put words in their mouths, they argued, and wrote false statements like 'maybe they just didn't notice the signs'. These friends, one of which attended the same lectures as me, were adamant something else was the cause. This sparked another brief — and this time localised — discussion about the possibility of it being an accident, or worse. The case very quickly grew cold, however, as there was little evidence to indicate another cause.

One thing that was glaringly obvious was that this incident didn't so much as scratch the reputation of academic institutions. Scholars shrugged and shed fake tears; papers were written and ignored. I didn't dive too deeply into the conspiracy of it all, though, as I often found getting too involved in cases like that spilled into my own health. On many occasions, I have struggled to learn when enough is enough, craving answers instead. On the night of the service, I took a moment to silently respect the poor girl and her family. I am not religious, and therefore did not understand the power of a prayer, but I held this stranger in my thoughts that evening, and hoped her soul found peace.

My mum rang me to make sure I was okay, checking that I was eating properly and being responsible. I assured her I was fine.

A few students decided to go back home, but for the rest of us, life returned to normal. Whatever that meant.

But now this: A fifty-three-year-old business man found floating, face down. Rumours quickly spread that morning with speculations of suicide. Yet only a few hours later, the news confirmed this man's throat had been cut — in one clean slice — from ear to ear. And that's what terrified everyone. A suicide meant internal suffering for others, but a murder? An external reminder that no one was ever truly safe.

People rarely fear what they cannot see, and that has always baffled me. Why was this man's death treated with more severity? Is death not simply death? Sure, knife crime had been low over the last few decades, and no one ever expected something like this to happen. It's one of those things you hear about on national news, or in places too far away to ever concern you. Never do you expect it to happen so close to where you live.

But I saw the bigger picture. We had lost two people in this city, weeks apart.

Police were already out interviewing people, trying to piece together parts of the puzzle and create a list of potential suspects. I had spoken to Rani over the phone that morning. The two of us discussed how lucky we had been to have not been out late that night. A part of me was tempted to bring up the girl to see if Rani had any thoughts on her apparent 'suicide'. I held back, worried it would look like I had been mulling over the case too intensely — which I definitely had been — but she didn't need to know that.

I had no plans that day, so, partly out of curiosity and to make up for my wasted evening the night before, I wrapped up and went out for a walk. I stayed well away from the discovery site; hordes of news reporters had already begun the rounds of picking scenic enough backdrops for their segments, expressing the event with melancholic hand gestures. Instead, I popped into a coffee shop, grabbed a hot chocolate, and headed over to Elvet Bridge. I stood and watched the calming flow of the river below, gazing out as the trees swayed to a slow rhythm and birds soared above. I wondered, as I have frequently in the past, what it would be like to fly. Not like a superhero or even an actual bird; not like we do in dreams, where we flap our arms frantically to simply levitate above the ground for several moments. No. I thought of actual flying, or floating to be more accurate. Letting your arms drop, bidding gravity farewell as the air lifts you upwards — as the clouds kiss your cheeks, and the sun blesses your forehead. To smile in the face of peace until you are weightless.

"I do hope you're just looking for inspiration," came a voice from behind. It took me a few seconds to realise the statement was directed at me, my brain wasn't attaching focus to the conversations of passing strangers. I turned to my left, greeted by a petite woman in a bright red, woollen coat. Her familiar green hair was plaited on each side and half-buried beneath an exceptionally soft-looking train-conductor hat with two brass buttons sewn into either side. My eyes widened.

"Oh." An instinctive reaction.

The woman raised an eyebrow, but her smile was not unpleasant. "I'm sorry, have we met before?"

Of course, she can't remember me. My cheeks flushed. *How embarrassing.*

"I believe I bumped into you yesterday, your hair it's... I'm sorry about that."

She laughed. "Oh wow, that was you? I remember now." Her grin widened. She spoke with delicacy, her words exceptionally articulated and edged with an accent I couldn't place, like that of someone well-travelled.

"I wasn't watching where I was going either, I'm very sorry about that, sorry." It eased my mind knowing I was able to share my full apology with her again rather than let it simmer in my head for days.

"There's honestly no need to apologise, I completely forgot about it to be honest. I bump into people all the time. I'm always so distracted."

Relief washed over me, knowing I'd very much blown the situation out of proportion. She didn't even *remember.*

"Like this moment, for example." She took a step closer. "I was out, admiring my surroundings as I often do, and there, in front of me, pressed against the wall with eyes wandering out of this very world, stands a handsome young man, coffee in hand, dressed in an outfit fit for a novel. I got distracted by him and thought I would take a chance in getting to know him a little." She reached my side, the light breeze blowing her short, choppy fringe from her face as she faced out onto the river.

Oh, I thought, unable to compute the information correctly.

I returned my gaze, so that we mirrored each other.

A stronger gust of wind passed over us before the woman continued talking. Neither of us moved.

"Sad about that poor bloke," she said, crossing her arms and resting them across the thick stone.

"Yeah, awful."

"You never think it could happen in a place as safe as this, do you?"

"No." I swallowed. "You don't."

"And just after that young girl too..." she trailed off as though debating whether to say more, but thinking twice about it.

"That's what I can't get out of my head," I said, sniffling as the cold breeze brushed face.

"How close they were." The woman finished my thought, prompting me to face her again.

"That's exactly it." I didn't blink.

But instead of continuing the conversation, the woman's shoulders relaxed. She faced me once more and sucked in her lower lip, inhaling deeply.

"I'm Lucienne, by the way, or just Lucy. I prefer Lucy." She held out a cream mitten'd hand and threw me another pretty, dimpled smile.

I nodded in mild awkwardness but returned my best 'pleased to meet you' face.

Silence followed, and she tilted her head expectantly. "And you are?"

"Oh, sorry. I'm Arlo. My name is Arlo."

"Well, it is nice to meet you, Arlo." She paused, still looking me in the eye. I shifted my gaze to the side of her face instead.

"So... you like my hair then?" She pulled at one of her long plaits.

Where is this going?

"It's very... memorable," I laughed a little, though not unkindly.

Lucy gave me a slow nod, yet her smile did not fade. If anything, it seemed to grow.

She released another deep breath. "I hope this isn't too forward but... is there any chance we could perhaps meet again? Maybe grab a drink or something later?" She shrugged. "That's if you're free, of course. And... available."

Available. Was I available? Physically yes — I had no urgent work or plans for the day therefore was most definitely free to go out, but mentally? I had no idea. I'd just met her, if we disregarded our brief, unfortunate encounter from the day before, but she seemed rather kind and innocent and she was pretty, too. Except she was a stranger. I could not fathom the idea of walking up to a stranger and asking them out. *Is that what this is?*

In any other situation, I would have worked my way out of this quite easily. I'd make up some white lie about being extremely busy, or asking to rearrange then repeat my excuse until the topic was dropped. Would you not need to get to know a person first? Learn their likes and dislikes, their routines and interests. How can you get all of that from a side profile?

But my mouth said yes.

In that moment, with her beaming smile and soft, fluttering lashes, I couldn't say no. It was as if all other vocabulary ceased to exist.

Yes. The only answer.

Her hand grazed my coat and she pinched my upper arm. I cringed at the sensation as nervous needles gathered in my arms and chest, lingering for too long.

"It's a date, then. Meet you here at seven?"

"Today?"

"Why not?" She winked.

A date. "Here at seven," I confirmed with a nod. *What am I doing?*

"See you then, Arlo."

.   .   .

I HADN'T THOUGHT MUCH about dating. The notion was always tucked away in the back of my mind, a concept I felt was inevitable if you wished to lead an average life, but something I asserted would be too far in the future for my current self to consider. Everyone around me had been getting into relationships, only ever discussing feelings and crushes and breakups, but my brain never wandered there. I had far more important things to stay focused on and I was perfectly content with that. But I had briefly considered that if I *were* to find someone I liked, I would — as society had so violently drilled into us — have to be the one who initiated the relationship. Yet when my mind attempted to venture towards *that* avenue, I felt sick.

But there I was, standing mouth agape, holding a prewritten phone number as Lucy confidently strode away, her coat and scarf billowing behind her. I had just accepted an invitation to a *date* without even pausing to consider it. I just blinked and agreed. And then, it finally hit me. It was so unlike me to do such a thing. I was never spontaneous. I always had to have things planned out and organised in advance, after having taken all factors into consideration.

She'd left me in a state of bewilderment, cemented in place on the bridge as an icy wind pierced the tips of my ears.

All previous thoughts of the morning completely evaded my brain.

PACING my small dorm room was becoming a weekly, sometimes daily, thing. I would just start doing it without even processing it. You often observe people pacing during phone calls in public, and I always considered it rather dramatic, like 'hey, look at me, I'm important'; only then as I did the same thing in private, did I see the hypocrisy in it. *I should cancel. Tell Lucy something cropped up. An assignment. An illness? Gosh, what am I doing?* The instant she left, I had regrets. *I can't do this.*

The clock hand ticked around the face. I froze until the very last minute, fearing if I were to leave any later, I wouldn't make it on time. I did not want to be that type of person. I had to at least look like I cared.

I texted Rani to tell her I was going out for the night, but I wouldn't be back late. I deliberately worded it to avoid an interrogation, especially as I was going on a date with a stranger. I didn't want anyone to make a fuss over it, I just wanted to get it over with. Rani's reply was a short, 'Ok! Enjoy!' which somewhat calmed me. I would try to enjoy it; and it only had to last as long as I wanted it to. *Treat it like you are meeting with a friend you haven't seen in a while*, I forced myself to think.

I showered, shaved my non-existent facial hair, and picked the most generic outfit I could to draw as little attention to myself as possible: a plain white shirt and black trousers. And I needed a jacket — multiple even, as it was forecast to snow soon.

My fingers fiddled with the stupid silver ring on my right middle finger; I had not taken it off in years. I'm not sure why I always insisted on wearing it but it held great significance. My mother gave it to me when I turned fourteen. Maybe it had become a safety blanket, of sorts, without me even realising.

My pulse pounded in my temples and ears and chest as I picked up the pace getting ready. I hated that sensation. I managed to go about my life mostly detached from my physical body, rarely looking in mirrors, or viewing myself as a vulnerable, living thing. But that periodic *woomf woomf* of my heartbeat was an intimate reminder of my fragility. How embarrassing that my body would betray me like this.

I tried to calm myself through deep breaths, reminding myself that this date did not have to be serious at all. But my mind circled back to what this evening could entail, teeth chewing away at my gums. *What if she kisses me? No, that would be too soon. People don't do that on first dates.* But they do. Nowadays, people do so much *more* with those they are not even officially with. Sometimes with people they have barely even spoken to at all. How could anyone do that? I was unable to wrap my head around how someone could possess the confidence to do such a thing.

What if she wants to get close to me, though? What if this evening goes so incredibly well that she wants to take me back to her apartment or house or whatever? People do that at university, having sex so freely and without worry. Should I bring... precautions? Gosh, Arlo. Stop this. You don't want that to happen, so it won't. Why can't you see that?

I never even asked her age. I had initially assumed she was my age but looking back, she had this presence of someone who had travelled and experienced the world, someone who may have already left university and owned an apartment or a house.

I didn't know her job, her surname, her passions. All I could picture was those bright green plaits and her freckled dimples.

But what if she did touch me? Even an arm tap like before, or a hug? She might not have meant anything by it, though. People do just touch for the sake of touching.

I put a jumper on in case, and the extra layer rendered me at ease.

Physical contact had always been difficult for me, but it felt as though it got worse as I grew older — though I believe that was only because I learned the language to express myself. Oddly, the more I knew a person, the less I wanted them to get close.

I was never a physical person anyway; nor one to give out hugs unless it was a social necessity, not one to deal a handshake or seek out close comfort. Unexpected contact caused my limbs to tense, unable to relax beneath a touch.

I never thought I needed fixing or that this would infringe on my life – it was other people who made it a big deal. 'How can you get close to someone if you can't even hug them without curling inwards?' Someone had once asked me at school.

But now, I had to adjust and prepare for the inevitable... I was going on a date and some sort of contact was highly likely.

You will be fine. I encouraged myself, shaking my hair in the mirror and splashing my face with water one final time.

You will be fine.

CHAPTER THREE

Lucy took me to a bar by the riverside, only moments away from our meeting place. I'd passed it many times on my walks but never had the courage to go in alone, but there I was: on a date. The concept of dating terrified me, but the experience was a necessary one; after all, this was what life was all about, right? Get a good education, meet someone, start a family, and live happily ever after, working a nine to five job until retiring with just enough pension funds to live a comfortable yet dull life of watering flowers and going to bed at six thirty. Those were my exact thoughts as we entered, not 'I wonder if these people notice I'm on a date with a pretty young woman?', which was something I presumed normal people thought when spotted dating someone out of their league.

I was a few minutes late. Lucy already stood with her arms wrapped around herself, wearing the same red coat from earlier, yet she had curled her hair and paired the outfit with a studded cross-body bag. I was, for lack of a better word, underdressed.

Once inside, we sat at a two-seater table by the window, overlooking the river. The evening sky was an inky black, and a handful of people sat outside on benches under orange heat lamps, cigarettes in hand. I wondered if any of them were on a date. *Were they happy?*

"How long have you been here then?" she asked me, sipping her drink through a cocktail straw. "You don't exactly sound local." She sat back with confidence, one leg crossed over the other so that her dress rode up her thighs. A giant snake tattoo circled her skin, partly concealed by the fishnet tights. I averted my gaze.

"I moved here just last month for university." I turned to take a drink but felt Lucy's stare. She wanted me to elaborate. I had intended to, but stopped myself prematurely for fear I might over-share — something I did a lot. "I'm from the Lake District, Northwest."

Lucy's face brightened, "I knew I recognised the accent. It's cute. You one of those farm boys then? Mountaineers? *A poet?*"

I laughed. That wasn't the first time I'd been asked that. My present sense of style also didn't help matters, but no, I was not a farmer. I explained I lived in a village with my mother and dog, Bess, in a converted chapel, and though I was prone to the occasional mountain walk, I generally didn't love the outdoors. This generated another beaming smile, which would have put me at ease, if it were not for her hand brushing my thigh under the table. It was subtle and harmless, but my heart contracted. I began rubbing my neck whilst trying to maintain eye contact. I wasn't sure how to react; I would have thought it was too early for this sort of contact. We had barely talked.

She must have noticed my discomfort and removed her hand.

I cleared my throat, desperately seeking distraction from the last ten seconds. "So, where are you from, if you don't mind me asking? I can't place *your* accent."

Lucy started twirling strands of her deep green hair while a smirk formed across her face. She took another big slurp of gin. "All over really. I was born in France believe it or not, but after many disagreeable travels, I ended up here," she gestured to the surroundings with both arms. "I've been here for about six months. Everyone is so polite, and the architecture is *stunning*. Have you been to the cathedral yet?"

"Not yet. Though I want to. It looks...peaceful."

She cocked her head to the left and leaned closer, floral perfume wafting in my direction. I noticed her silver hooped earrings had little red gems in them.

"Are you religious?" she asked.

I wasn't. Not at all, in fact. But every religious building offered a sense of comfort. The cathedral from the outside was spectacular. Heroic stained-glass scenes and proud statues protected every corner, like a knight watching over its kingdom.

"Not really, how about you?"

It dawned on me, then, that I was simply relaying questions back to her rather than starting topics on my own. I was trying hard to keep the conversation flowing, despite my growing discomfort.

She removed the straws and downed the rest of her glass in a rather dramatic fashion. "Don't really have time for it. My mother was a Catholic, a rather devout one too, but thankfully I found my own path."

"Hmm." I wasn't even trying at this point. "Would you like another drink? My treat." The words sort of fell out of my mouth.

"Trying to get me drunk? I see the true Arlo now." She winked at me, but the joke took a while to sink in. All I could think about was how hot the room was getting, how loud people were talking, and how dark the sky was. *Calm down,* I told myself. *You are in control.*

I took off my jumper and went over to the bar to buy her another drink. Reluctantly buying another for myself as well. I took my time back to the table where she sat, her cheeks glistening from the light of her phone screen. She was evidently bored, and I damned myself for how rude I had been.

"Sorry," I said, setting her drink in front of her.

She let out a disinterested huff, almost a laugh, but was clearly not engaged in my presence at all. Realising I'd returned, she quickly slammed her phone face down on the table and sat back upright, eyes wide.

"Sorry, where were we? Oh, thank you." She grabbed her gin glass and pulled it towards herself. "So, what are you studying? Are you first year or...?"

Straight back into the conversation.

"I'm first year. English Literature."

Lucy raised her head, assessing me as if I were a book to read.

"A poet?" She smirked. "I'm right, aren't I."

My shoulders raised a little, embarrassed. "Maybe. I enjoy writing, but I won't claim that title just yet," I laughed.

Lucy squinted slightly, eyes wandering the path into my soul. Her face illuminated. "Read me something."

I leaned back into the sponge of the chair, feet firmly on the ground. "Oh, I'm not sure... I don't have anything on me..." I was not prepared to share my work at all. It was far too personal for a first date. Or any date, for that matter. My poems were mine, and I deliberately did not advertise that yes, I wrote frequently — every day, actually. I did not wish to share that I spent many a night pouring my heart and soul into writing. Pages upon pages sat stashed in my drawers, never to be looked at again. These were spur-of-the-moment scriptures, nothing for the eyes of anyone, including my future self.

I needed to change the subject.

"Do you have any siblings?" That was the only thing that came to my mind, but it was something I deemed important to learn about someone whom you were getting to know.

Lucy smiled fondly then looked to the wall for a fraction of a second. "No. Just me."

"Same for me, an only child. Though I wish sometimes I wasn't." That last part was unexpected and said without thinking. She fixed her stare back onto mine.

After a beat, she leaned over the table in a clear attempt to expose parts of her I very much did not want to see. I maintained as much eye contact as I could manage, offering my best forced smile, in the hope it seemed genuine.

"You are so sweet, Arlo, I'm glad I met you," she said after the prolonged silence.

"Oh, thanks."

"You don't do this often, do you?"

"No, I'm not really the dating type." I sincerely hoped that was what she was referencing.

At this she raised an eyebrow, easing back into her chair. "I wouldn't have pegged you as a 'fuck them and leave them' kind of guy."

My eyes strained wide, and a wave of heat flushed over me. "Oh, dear lord. That's not what I meant."

She playfully hit my shoulder. "Oh, I'm just messing with you. Look at your face!"

I laughed awkwardly.

We finished our drinks, talking a little about what we liked and disliked about the city. She told me she worked a 'pretty average job' and shared a bit about her life in France and her global travels. I shared a bit about my life, ashamed by my *lack* of travels. I discussed what it was like studying away from home, which I learned she had never done; she left school at sixteen and never looked back. I kept the conversation light — simple small talk. I wouldn't have known how to flirt even if I tried.

"Shall we get some air?" Lucy suggested after I closed the tab. She thanked me for paying and stood, placing her hand on my shoulder. It was a very intimate gesture, done in front of everyone. I was a considerable amount taller than her too, inviting even more attention to the action.

I wasn't stupid. I knew fine well what she really meant by 'getting some air', and despite not being sure I wanted what she did (actually, I *knew* I didn't want it), I had been the worst company all night and mild curiosity got the better of me.

Maybe this would be good. We all needed to start somewhere, right? I couldn't hide forever. I was in full control. I could stop whenever I wanted to…

I nodded and followed her out of the door.

It was pitch-black outside, nearing midnight. While a handful of people still congregated around the building, it was a lot quieter than I expected, but I supposed that would work in our favour.

She took me around the corner from the bar, so the only view of us was from the empty river ahead. Slowly, she backed me against the wall, whispering things under her breath as her arms wrapped around my neck.

"You're so tall," she observed, and I glanced down; she was standing on her toes to reach me and I was beginning to panic a little. I'd never even come close to kissing someone before. But she was nice, and we were getting on reasonably well. Not to mention, she *was* exceedingly attractive — pretty, even. All tattoos and piercings, and a striking confidence I'd always dreamed of having.

She leaned in close, her breath warming my cheek. "You look very hot this evening," I believe she said in my ear.

And then she kissed me. It wasn't at all what I expected. I felt no spark or sexual awakening; the kiss was wet and squishy, and as I tried to return it, I knew it was completely wrong and awkward. I was ready to break away, but she pushed harder, tightening her arms and pressing against me so I felt every curve of her body digging into mine. My hands precariously landed upon her waist — an action I believed appropriate, considering I wasn't getting out of this any time soon. She breathed faster, the corners of her lips turning up between kisses.

I wanted to stop. Everything had started spinning around me and I knew it wasn't just the alcohol. I dropped my hands and Lucy pulled back, eyes searing into mine. It was dark, but I could have sworn her eyes were a light blue earlier. Not anymore. Under the dimmed lighting, they looked almost... *red*?

She released a breathy laugh, and before I had a chance to push her away, she pinned me in place with her hips, and began to pull my shirt out from my trousers, forcing her exceptionally cold hands beneath every layer and pressing her palms to my chest.

"Oh, bless you, you are so nervous... This is your first time doing this, isn't it?" she teased in a much deeper tone than before.

It was, and I was very quickly coming to the realisation that I never wanted to do it again. Ever.

Growing up, I'd always thought it odd how I never related to the feelings described by my friends. For a time, I presumed I must have been gay, but picturing myself sexually with *anyone* made me uneasy — and not in a good way.

And then, despite having an undeniably attractive woman throwing herself upon me, I felt nothing. No desire, no butterflies. Nothing. I could have been kissing a wall and it would have felt no different. I tried to enjoy it, I really did, but it shouldn't have taken that much effort.

I was in control. I could have stopped it at any point, and so, I did. With Lucy's hands firmly pressed over my heart and her lips lingering on my neck, I pushed her away. I didn't intend on pushing her so hard, but I wanted no more of this and I needed it to stop before it went any further.

Lucy crossed her arms, red lipstick smudged across her face. I tried to calm my breathing before I spoke, but she beat me to it. "Was I going too fast?"

"A little." I lied.

"Sorry."

"It's okay."

Silence fell upon us.

"I should go," I said, but she had already started moving back towards me with a feline prowl. "You're not going to walk me home?" she whined, squinting.

I should. That would be the gentlemanly thing to do. But I was admittedly growing a little scared of her. The woman that stood before me was not the same woman I bumped into in the street, nor the one who asked me out and brought me to this bar. No, this woman burned me with her eyes and every place where she had touched me had begun to sting.

"I'm... I'm going to go now." Despite the pang of guilt I felt for leaving her there, I was too desperate to get away. I backed up slowly, yet Lucy followed me with her eyes until I was around the corner into the city light.

Some people still sat about on benches as artificial heaters flickered around them. I didn't dare turn back around, though I sensed Lucy wasn't following me. I fixed my shirt and my pulse had finally begun to slow, my breathing normalising.

I made my way back up the stone steps beside the bridge. My skin stung, guilt haunting me. *I should not have left her. I'm overreacting.* She had been nice to me all evening. *Maybe I embarrassed her. I didn't know what I was doing.*

I reached the top, and immediately, my chest eased. I was surrounded by so much life; bars were still abuzz with customers, and people clattered down the bank in merry pride. I didn't have far to walk back to my accommodation, so I remained focused on the journey, weaving in and out of drunken couples. I stopped briefly in a narrow alleyway to tie my shoelace. Seconds away from my apartment block. Something so simple and yet who would have known this would have been the beginning of the end? If only I'd just continued walking just those extra few meters...

"Hey kid."

I stopped short. There was no way this was possible. She had followed me, yet she must have taken a different direction. So she knew where I lived. That was when I really was scared.

"Arlo."

I turned around to see Lucienne's silhouette at my side; a

frightening smile painted across her face. She'd tied her hair back, but this was only a detail I realised much later.

"I'm sorry," was all I said. I wasn't, but I knew I needed to say it. I was in the wrong, or at least I thought I was.

"You embarrassed me," she said, stepping into the light. The unnatural colour of her eyes forced me to step backwards. From my angle, it looked as if her eyes were bleeding. You couldn't distinguish where her irises began. I backed away, further into the alley.

"I'm sorry," I said again, palms sweating.

"Aww." She threw me a patronising look. "Don't apologise. You're only human."

I thought it was rather an odd thing for someone to say, but she *was* seeming less and less human by the second. I can't blame myself for missing the warning signs though; I'd spent more than my fair share of time reading novels of all sorts of weird and wonderful creatures, but I was sane enough to keep fantasy separate from reality.

In that moment with the two of us in the dimly lit alley, I knew there was nothing she could do to hurt me.

How naïve of me.

"I was starting to like you, boy." She closed the gap between us, spitting out 'boy' as if I were a badly behaved child at school, another warning sign about her age.

She pressed forward, forcing me further into the alley. I noted the number of windows at the side of each building, and I remembered thinking that surely nothing could happen because someone would see us... There were so many windows...

"You know, I was going to leave you be. The day we first met, part of me thought about letting you go, forgetting about those silly little moles and your lanky limbs and cherubic curls. But I gave in to temptation, as we all do, and I made you my business. I made it my mission to seek you out again. To learn more about you. I'll even go as far as saying I grew fond of you. But I lost my patience." She was a hair's breadth away from me, fiery red pulsing around her.

I was frozen to the spot — all other sounds but her voice fizzled away. "You." She touched my face and I winced. "You are no longer of any use to me."

I ran. Scrambled for footing, unsure of where the path would lead me as the light faded. I reached a dead end and turned to both sides; each path was blocked by a fence. I eyed the stairs to freedom from behind the bars, but it was no use. She, of course, caught up with me in an instant. Inhumanly fast, she grabbed me by the collar, and I lost all remaining opportunity of escape. My fate was sealed in that moment. Oh, how different things would have been if I had just walked home.

I grabbed her arms as they tightened around my neck, clawing and scraping for release. She was just... so strong. I didn't stand a chance.

"How old are you, boy?" she growled, inches from my face. White canines protruded onto her lower lip. I might have wet myself, but it is hard to recall those final moments. I was going to die.

"I'm... nineteen." She released her grip on my throat momentarily for me to answer. I think she knew I was too distracted by fear at that point to even consider getting away.

"Works for me." She grinned, then kicked my shins. I buckled, and she yanked my head to the side, sinking her teeth deep into my neck.

I had never imagined what it would be like to be bitten, but the pain was fleeting. It was sharp for a second, the same second I tried to pull away, but then a strange numb sensation flooded my veins, and I went limp. Lucy held me up with an iron grip as my vision went blurry and my legs gave way entirely. I didn't even have the energy to cry out. I tried so desperately to focus on the rusting sign on the slanting brick wall in front of me, if only to keep my brain alive. But before long, I saw nothing. I was losing consciousness fast and nothing would stick in my mind. I wish I could remember what I was thinking in those final moments as she lowered me to the ground, shoes scuffing the pavement. My heart forcing out its final, uneven beats as her laughter echoed around me.

"Imagine what this could have been, my boy," she whispered, caressing my face. "Sweet dreams, Arlo." She pressed her bloody fingertips over my eyelids.

I saw a flash of feathers behind her. A cloak of ashy white.

And then I died.

CHAPTER FOUR

Death is such an odd term. We see it all around us every day, and yet the concept still terrifies us. I used to spend many a night pondering the theory of life; what existed beyond *everything*. Is there really a place we go to when we die? Or do we simply cease to exist? Just like that. Everything we've done, the people we've met, the places we've been — none of it matters in the end because even if there was some plane beyond life where our souls float around in perfect harmony, no one has ever been able to prove it for certain.

As it turns out, your life doesn't flash before your eyes when you draw your last breath. In fact, it's the most uneventful last few seconds you will ever experience. There's no time for regrets or worries. No happy memories or smiling faces or comforting embraces with those you love.

It's just really, really cold.

I awoke, sitting upright in what appeared to be a battered, leather armchair. Something you see in the corner of the 'haunted' rooms in stately homes. An itchy tartan blanket rested across my shoulders, smelling of tobacco and old people. I had absolutely no idea where I was. My overwhelmed senses affirmed this was not a dream or a hallucination. My head throbbed as if I'd been dangling upside down for hours, my skull seconds away from exploding and limbs completely numb.

As the haze began to clear, I took in my surroundings. I was in a dungeon of some sort — no, just a cellar.

The room was quite large, with sandstone pillars holding up the low ceiling. A misty slit of sunlight emerged from the corner of the room. There were, as I came to see a few moments later, other furnishings in the room too: a bookshelf, two in fact, packed with nondescript hardback spines and empty photo frames, a cracked, porcelain sink fixed straight into the wall, and to my right, a bed. A four-poster bed with maroon drapes tied to each post. *Where am I?*

I was trying to recall my last thoughts before I... *fainted? Fell asleep? Was I dreaming?* Nothing sprung to mind. It felt like a dream though, I didn't feel *alive*. My body felt *wrong*. Like in nightmares when you try to run but your legs don't work, or during sleep paralysis (which I unfortunately experienced a lot) when you believe you are strong enough to turn your head or lift an arm but all you feel is a phantom strain. I couldn't feel my toes, or any part of my body for that matter. So, naturally, I panicked. At this point, my heart would usually try to force its way out of my ribcage, yet I felt nothing. Not even a slight beat. *Wake up, Arlo.*

Hinges squealed, and before I had a chance to find the source, shuffled footsteps followed and a tall figure appeared to my left, obscured by the shadows.

"Oh, thank the skies! The kid's finally awake," spoke the shadow in a rather expressive voice. "Mars, you actually did it! I didn't think he would wake up, but you did it. You brought him back."

A sleep paralysis demon was my first conclusion. But then my limbs started to tingle, and I could wiggle my fingers, yet the figure remained.

"Of course I did it, Casper. Happy birthday! You doubt me

too much," spoke another, slightly higher-pitched voice and a second, smaller figure formed in the dark-cast archway, playfully patting the taller one on the back.

Who are these people? Am I losing my mind?

One of the faceless voices flicked on a light and I immediately squinted against the sudden brightness until I gradually opened them again to learn the voices were coming from... ordinary people. A tall black guy with short, unnaturally bright red hair leaned against one of the pillars, arms folded, with a leather biker jacket draped heavily over his shoulders that matched the clumpy, buckled boots on his feet.

The other was a smaller, East Asian person with warm brown skin and silky black hair tied half up, analysing me with a... grin? Two gold studs dotted the bridge of their nose, and as they crouched, I noted they wore *vinyl* trousers. Interesting.

"Of course I did it," they repeated, grin widening. "Welcome back, kid." They directed this at me, before reaching their arm out and attempting to brush my hair away from my face. I jerked away before they had the chance.

"Oh, sorry. That was a little forward of me." They stood back up and retreated, their brow tensed. "I'm just glad you're okay."

This was too stressful.

"Who are you?" I tried to ask — *tried* being the operative word. The second I opened my mouth to speak, the words came out like a scraping wheeze, my throat parched and dry.

Both laughed, but not to mock.

"I'm Casper," said the taller one, "and that's Mars," he gestured towards them. I detected an American accent this time. *Southern, perhaps?* I'd never been well versed in accents but the prolonged 'a' sound was a strong sign. He continued. "But that's not what you meant, was it?"

"This is going to take some explaining." Mars' brow quirked. "Casper, go and get our guest a nice glass of water." They winked, and Casper obliged.

"Who..."

Mars stopped me with a raised hand. "Take it easy, you've been drained. You'll feel better once you've had something to drink."

Drained?

They must have sensed the confusion on my face. "Don't worry, you're safe now. I'm going to try my best to explain to you what happened, without you thinking I'm completely insane.

STILL ADJUSTING TO THE BRIGHTNESS, I finally realised a single, shade-less bulb dangled from the crumbling, plastered ceiling to light the room. My brain was drowning in a million different things, and my liquid thoughts buzzed together as one.

Mars pulled up a wooden bar stool seemingly out of nowhere. Pulling one leg over the other, their steel capped boots mirrored the shine of their trousers, and I found myself in awe at Mars' whole ensemble. I glanced down at my plain black shirt and battered shoes. Generic. *And that's not even my shirt. The fabric is wrong. Too harsh...*

Casper returned a second later with a mug of liquid that was definitely *not* water, but I accepted it even so. I wasn't in the condition to be fussy.

"I'll just be outside, shout if you need me," he said cheerily, before leaving us alone again.

I shifted into a more comfortable position, letting the blanket fall to my waist. I stared at the watery, red smoothie in my hands, and my nose turned up in instinct.

"Just drink it. You need it."

I peered up at Mars through my overgrown fringe, unconvinced.

A repressed smirk broke onto their face. "If we were going to poison you, we wouldn't have bothered saving your life beforehand."

If anything, that admission made me even more unsure. Poison hadn't even crossed my mind — I was just a little stunned at the entire predicament still.

I took a sip. For my first taste of diluted blood, it didn't taste as vile as I would have expected. Though at the time, I believed it to be a lumpy, long expired berry smoothie.

"What was the last thing you remember?" Mars asked sincerely, once my turned-up nose relaxed.

My mind was completely and utterly blank. I tried going back further than the night before or even the entire week, but the last thing that vaguely swam to mind was the memory of my mum standing in my accommodation, wiping a tear from her eye and bringing up how much she and Bess would miss me. That was nearly a couple of months ago now and I most definitely had memories since then – I just couldn't think of *what*.

"You went out for the night?" Mars prompted, leaning into their palm.

Did I?

"You are a student at Durham University. Your name is Arlo James Everett. Your birthday is the second of September nineteen ninety-nine..."

My head throbbed.

"I only know that because I had to check your ID in your wallet — sorry for the intrusion by the way, I just had to put a name to the body at my feet."

I froze, wide eyed. *Body?*

"You're talking as if I died. Did I pass out or something? I must have hit my head because I have absolutely no recollection of anything I did last night, and I swear I don't normally drink that much; I must have got carried away."

Mars' shoulders dropped, their expression turning sympathetic. It was the same look I always imagined a police officer wore when turning up at your door to announce the tragic death of a loved one.

"*What?*"

Mars sighed and leaned forward. "You were attacked, Arlo," they said, tone lowered. Another sigh. "Look, I would normally just point it out, but I take it you're not one for close contact with strangers so... check your pulse on your right side."

What an odd request, I remember thinking, but I obliged. Placing the half-full mug on the ground, I raised two fingers to the right of my neck, Mars' gaze following my every move. Not only did I struggle to find the pulse, but I felt two crusty, raised bumps an inch or so apart. I rubbed harder in confusion. And then, it stung. In fact, my whole body stung; all of me ached, overcome with an intense dizziness forcing my head to loll back against the chair. Everything flooded back to me. University, Rani, the coffee shop. The dead man. The bridge.

Lucy.

The bar.

The alleyway.

"She..."

"You remember who did this?"

"I remember everything."

"I'm sorry."

"Why?" I hated when people apologised to me for matters out of their control — even more so when I was certain it was *my fault*.

"You know why. You just don't want to admit it because you think you're going insane. You're hoping this is all a dream and you will wake up in your own, warm bed where everything has returned to normal. But this is reality. You are awake now. As awake as you ever will be. For the rest of eternity. And I'm sorry."

I remained silent and touched my neck again. No pulse. Bite marks...

Dead.

"I understand this is a lot to take in, but I'm here now. We're all here and we're not going anywhere anytime soon. We'll get through this together."

All I did was blink. For a good ten seconds.

"Arlo? Did you hear me? We can help you. You aren't alone here. You never have to be."

"I'm..." I gulped. "So, I really did die then?"

Mars nodded. "Sort of."

"And I'm a..."

"Honestly, I've been one for almost a decade and it still sounds silly to say it out loud, but yes. You are a creature of the night. One who feeds upon life's vital source. An immortal cursed with the burden of an unbeating heart." They flashed their human looking teeth, raising their hands like comical claws.

"But I am sorry." Mars dropped their arms, eyes softening.

"Why do you keep apologising?"

"Because it's my fault. I found you. You were seconds away from death, lying in a gutter, and I took one look at your innocent face, and I wanted to save you. And I did. But I'm also sorry because I did not have your consent. I was selfish and thought only of myself. And now this is your life." They rubbed their bandaged left arm.

I was speechless. I raised my hand to my chest and listened for the beat. Nothing. My body was an empty shell, yet it felt *good*. Should it have? It didn't matter. I would no longer have to tune into that uncomfortable pounding while I was lying awake in bed, or suffer the feeling of the booming drum-beat of my heart whenever I was stressed or anxious. I could be at peace.

"You are probably going to want a list. You know, the Ts and Cs and whatnot. I want you to meet the rest of the gang, too. Well, we're not so much a gang, more of an organisation. We keep the peace while the humans think they're doing all the work. They call us The Thorns, well, we call ourselves that 'cos we think it sounds cool." Mars was trying hard to lighten the mood, and I nodded, surprised their tactic was working.

"And that too was an absolute lie because I named us and everyone hated it for years."

I half laughed through my nose. Whatever they were doing to calm me was definitely proving effective.

"Right." Mars slapped their thighs and crossed their legs. "We're the closest thing to what fiction deems a 'vampire', but in reality, we're more like immortally infected human hosts. That's probably the best way to describe it. It's a parasite that is only transmitted if the person is fatally drained and then transfused somehow with *our* blood. I don't know the science, but the blood flows itself, it's that strong of a parasite."

I slowly nodded along, though I feared their words went in one ear and out the other.

"Sunlight burns. But not like the movies. You aren't going to step out onto the street later and instantly disintegrate into a pile of smouldering ash. The average summer's day here won't so much as tingle, but if you find yourself stranded without shelter in the middle of the Sahara, you'll last a day, give or take, before it really starts to peel away at you. Think blistering sunburn but amplified as though you were sitting in a kiln. Not pleasant, and yeah, fatal."

I raised an eyebrow at the image conjured in my head.

Mars studied my expression and sucked in their top lip, stifling a laugh. "That... got dark. Just be sensible, and you'll be more than fine. I take it you're not one for enjoying sun anyway."

True.

"And we can Manipulate. Quite intensely. It's kind of how we've managed to stay hidden all this time," they continued. "You'll learn that naturally over time but it's essentially the ability to erase a memory, and in some cases, stuff something back in there. You can make humans think and do pretty much whatever you want. Fellow vampires are much harder to get to but it's perfectly possible if their guards are down. You can sometimes smell it in use if you're playing close attention. Although, I doubt I have to warn you it's extremely frowned upon — anyone with a scrap of humanity left wouldn't dare take advantage of an innocent like that. Not without reason."

The tension rose and my brow ached.

I was Manipulated.

Mars stood up and began pacing. "Most other things you'll learn as you go. I've never understood where the garlic myth came from, though. It makes absolutely no sense and I still love garlic bread, so..." Their head twitched back to me. "Silver, or any precious metal, can kind of hurt because our skin reacts differently but they're not going to melt you or anything dramatic. We're all unique and so it affects some of us more than others but I see you've not noticed the fact that you're still wearing that pretty ring so it looks like you must have quite a high tolerance already, which is great." They patted the head of the chair I was sitting in, the closest they could get to patting me on the back.

"Part of the deal is you don't physically age. Yes, you will heal quicker than the average human, but..." they removed their bandage, revealing a vertical pink scar across the centre of their wrist. Still fresh. "You're not immune to wounds."

"That's..."

"How I turned you. Yes."

By this point, I must have been exhausted or disassociated, as I was taking it all in remarkably well. Nodding along, I casually accepted my fate. If you had told me the moon was made of cheese, and the earth was flat, I would have nodded, too. As if it were obvious.

"You can still live a relatively normal life, you know," Mars insisted, tone raised in a questioning manner.

"Yeah," was all I could say. Looking back, none of their words had sunk in yet. I was still a little hazy. "You've done this before then? You know... brought someone back?"

"Hmm. Not exactly. That was my first attempt. I know I said before that I was confident it would work, but I honestly wasn't sure. You were pretty far gone when I..." They shook their head, frantically waving their hands. "But, you know, it did." They lifted their chin in pride. "And I think I'm going to really like you."

"Oh." I didn't expect to hear something so kind. I never did. "Wow. Thanks?"

"You're nineteen, right?"

"Yeah. Just." I swallowed the lump in my throat.

"I was nineteen when I turned," they beamed, almost fondly. "So we'll forever be blessed with the beauty of youth." Their voice turned into a sing-song, their teeth flashing again. Not sharp.

I laughed. We were joking about death — my death, for that matter — and yet I was still laughing. It was an unsure reaction though; normal interactions with strangers don't flow for too long with me.

"You said there were others?" I picked my mug back up again, inhaling deeply before taking another sip.

"Many. You've already met Casper; then there's his boyfriend, Ben, he's such an angel. I think you three will get along well. Eternal goths with hearts of gold. They're in a band, you know? Forever Red? They got quite big a few years back..."

Mars continued speaking, words marked with expressive hand gestures, but though I was looking at them, I was zoning out. The room suddenly shrunk, and I could no longer make out Mars' features. I was dead. Murdered. By someone I thought I liked. I felt betrayed, but it was unlike any betrayal I'd experienced before. No, this betrayal cut deep into my bones. I'd let my guard down, stepped out of my comfort zone, and now I wasn't even... me.

"Sorry. I'm rambling. I'll just let you meet them; I'm sure they will love to meet you." And just like that, I was being led out of the room and into a dimly lit corridor with oil paintings that hung haphazardly along the wall. My legs walked without command, the path paved by the solid form in front of me.

They were still talking, I realised, though I can never recall what they said.

It was the change of rooms that finally broke me from my daze. This time, we were in a much airier room with more decorations and stylish furnishings. There were about a dozen people in the room, some sat around a fireplace, deep in conversation, others milling around. One person instantly captured my attention: reclined over a chaise lounge, they were smoking a cigar in a pleated skirt that flowed elegantly over the side. I then spotted Casper, and whom I presumed to be Ben. He was a few inches shorter than his boyfriend, dressed in similar attire with a mop of thick, black curls on his head and the brightest green eyes. I understood what Mars meant by 'angel'.

"That's him, yeah?" He tipped his head in Casper's direction, yet looked straight at me, a boyish grin across his freckled face.

I wanted the ground to swallow me up. Every face in the room swung in my direction, assessing me with intrigue. Six million eyes pierced needles into my skin. The best I could do was shrink into the shelter of Mars' back, instinctively picking at my itchy shirt sleeves; the height comparison not helping.

"Sorry, I didn't mean to embarrass you," Ben lowered his tone and edged towards me. "I'm Ben, by the way." He held out his ringed hand, nails coated in chipped black polish. I just nodded and introduced myself with a forced smile.

"Look at that, Mars made themself a pet," chaise lounge person piped up. I recoiled.

"Shut up, Lawrence," Mars snarled. All eyes flitted between the two of them now.

"Just kidding," Lawrence took a dramatic, long drag of his cigar. "You saved someone. Good going."

"Ignore him," Mars whispered only to me.

I shouldn't have let the comment get to me, but surrounded by all those inhuman creatures, who all shared the same belief that I was some helpless human boy in desperate need of saving, I felt so weak and feeble — a rag doll, discarded in the street, to be stuck in the window of a charity shop, waiting for new owners to claim me. If my heart was still beating, I would have felt it pounding in my skull.

"Now, that is no way to treat a guest, Lawrence."

A calming but assertive voice travelled from the other side of the room. I was shocked I hadn't noticed her yet; the second she opened her mouth, the entire room fell silent.

I soon learned her name was Marianne. The Georgian Vampress and founder of The Thorns (I wondered briefly what she named them before Mars' input). She stood before us then, donned in lavish 18th century garments. Strawberry blond ringlets were pinned high upon her head, and her face was pasted with white makeup and bright red blush. If not for her serious expression, I would have interpreted this guise as a jest. I would come to learn she frequently dressed herself in period clothing, for no other reason than she could. Though at the time, I viewed it as a welcoming costume; she was asserting her dominance.

"Mars, my dear, care to introduce us?"

Again, I was nothing but an object on display.

"Our lady, Marianne," Mars addressed in an overly polite manner, spanning their arms across the room, "and my dear Thorns, please welcome our newest member, Arlo Everett. He's nineteen, a student and..." they paused. *Was my discomfort that obvious, even from behind them?* "Sorry, I'll let him speak for himself." I know they thought they were being helpful and respectful but it made me feel worse. The damage was done.

"Hi," was all I managed, spoken with a cracked voice and a clogged throat.

The entire room waited for me to continue, but I had nothing more to say. I had been thrust into this brand-new world over night, and the more I stood and took in the surroundings, the less sense everything made.

The smoke of Lawrence's cigar reached my nostrils, as did the perfume of every single person in the room; my senses overloading.

"Welcome to The Thorns, Arlo. Welcome to your new family." Marianne smiled.

Family.

Marianne glided over to us, and it struck me how small she was up close. A petite, porcelain doll wrapped in lace and bows. "So young. I'm sorry, child." She turned to Mars. "Any leads?"

Mars gave a solemn shake of their head. "Arlo said it was a woman."

They were talking about my death; the person who killed me.

"Lucy — Lucienne. She said her name was Lucienne," I interjected.

The name didn't appear to ring any bells between them.

"There has been another rise in attacks recently, as I'm sure you are all aware." The Thorn's leader turned to address the room. "I will treat this as no coincidence. Arlo here was killed by whoever was involved in the previous two recent deaths. But we cannot rest now. This is only the beginning. Whoever this woman is, it is highly unlikely she works alone. Our second victim was not a solo attack, and that I can confirm. They were both *drained*, but unfortunately police are being Manipulated into closing these cases. We need to start coming up with plans and increase our patrols. We need to get to the bottom of who is behind this. We cannot let this get out of hand *again*."

A cacophony of agreements followed. And, despite the frightening sting of the word '*again*', I finally felt seen. Not just as an extra or irrelevant presence, but someone whose death mattered — someone whose *life* mattered.

"My dear boy, we promise we will find the woman who did this to you. She will not get away with this. That is not what we stand for." Marianne stared into my eyes, a calming gesture, and crossed her hands over her chest.

My eyes softened, tears forming in the corners. *Don't cry. Don't cry. Don't cry.*

"We can protect you now, and stop this from happening again," Mars added from beside me. I looked at them in that moment and saw only sincerity.

That was the moment that reality took hold. This was no joke. No fantasy. These people were real. Monsters *are* real.

Nothing would ever be the same again.

"Arlo. Let us find you a room so you can make yourself comfortable. You'll have a lot of adjusting to do and we will be there to support you every step of the way. You are not alone." Marianne continued.

I considered the offer, tried to imagine myself assimilating into this lifestyle and leaving my old life behind, but it wouldn't work. "I... thank you. But I think I'd like to go home now." My hands trembled.

"This is your home."

"No, I'm sorry, but it's not. I need to think things through. Please."

Think things through. The excuse sounded valid, except there was nothing I *could* think through. The choice had been taken from me the second Lucy murdered me, and Mars brought me back. But oh, how desperate I was, and how in denial. I desired nothing more than to pretend this was all fake so I could continue living my shitty life, one where I bought overpriced drinks and debated every single life choice, no matter how trivial. It all suddenly became a lot less complicated. I lived a simple life. But this, this inhuman business, was too much for my brain to handle, and I wanted nothing to do with it. Nothing at all. I wanted to live.

Mars moved beside me. "You probably should stay with us, you know, even just for a few months," they said, words hushed.

I blinked a few times, brain refusing to soak up what they just said. "But my life."

"We can help you sort it all out, you don't have to stop anything. You can attend your course as normal; we'll figure out your loans, too. That's no issue. You'll just need to learn how to cope with your new body and... urges."

Urges.

"Please let me think things through," I repeated through

clenched teeth as pressure rose into my throat. My hands grew restless, and I repressed the urge to scream.

I watched Marianne glance displeasingly at Mars, unspoken words shared between their interlocked gaze. "Okay then," she finally said.

The invisible weight lifted from my shoulders.

"Okay?" I waited for confirmation.

Marianne nodded.

Nothing more was said. Mars escorted me out. Ben, Casper, and a few others formed an unintentional parting around us, and they all shared the same look of sadness. It didn't alter my thoughts, though, or my resolve. I was adamant I could cope with this alone, I just needed breathing space. Time to process. I was not entirely sure I would ever be able to, but I could try.

Oh, the optimism.

Mars returned my coat to me, and I followed them silently through corridors and staircases until we reached the light. I shielded my eyes momentarily, but it was overcast, and, just like Mars had explained, I was unaffected by the sun.

We were in an unfamiliar alleyway but still in the same city. While that was obvious, I was completely disorientated as to *where* in the city. It was freezing — significantly colder than what I remembered the night before.

We didn't stop walking until we reached an area I recognised then Mars directed me into a corner for discretion.

"Listen, before I let you go, I'm going to give you my number. I want you to know that you can call me at any time. And I *want* you to. You need to learn how to feed properly and how to act human. I can't stress how important that is. Please, hear me when I say you are going to need our support. *My* support. I did this to you, and I take full responsibility, but now I need you to take some responsibility, too. You will not be able to go through this life alone."

"I know," I said solemnly, taking the tattered scrap of yellowed paper. And I did know. I was stubborn, but not stupid. I needed time to wrap my head around everything before my life changed forever.

"I put something in your coat pocket. Call me when you take it."

I rummaged in my pocket, weighed down by a tightly sealed packet of reddish, almost black liquid.

Mars studied me closely. "Take it when you are hungry. You'll know when. Mix it with a drink, food, anything you feel necessary. You'll get used to it quickly. I did. That will be enough for tonight and tomorrow, then you will need more. Call me when you're ready tomorrow morning and I will meet you."

I glanced back down at the package. Blood. Human? Animal? I supposed it didn't matter. I was going to have to drink it regardless.

"Thanks." I re-pocketed the bag, the viscous substance sloshing around in my hand. "And thank you. For saving me, I mean."

Mars simply smiled, a twinge of sadness hidden behind their beautiful face.

CHAPTER FIVE

elcome to your new family.

W   I ran onto the main street, navigating my way back through the cobbles towards my accommodation, whilst my eyes focused only on my trembling feet and hands. I lurched in, panting with exhaustion and slammed my door shut. I thumped my back against it and slid to the floor, head in hands.

You are not alone.

Murdered.

Urges.

After five minutes — or an hour, it was always hard to tell when I was trying to calm myself, I leaned back, shifting my legs in front of me.

I refused to say it aloud, but I knew exactly what I was. Dead. Immortal. A monster.

I unbuttoned the top of my shirt and placed my hand over my heart, the pointless organ sitting under my skin. I controlled my breathing and tipped my head back, staying in that position for a while. Nothing. Still no pulse.

I checked my neck and wrist. Nothing.

How was I breathing? Talking? Functioning? Scientifically, it made no sense, but this was completely beyond science. Beyond human life.

I was no longer human.

How will I ever process this? I had forever — an eternity to try.

My room was pitch black before I finally rose and walked over to my desk, and back again, then back to my desk. All subconscious of course, I had no idea what I wanted to do.

I felt different. Stronger. I didn't want to experiment with *how* much stronger, however; the sensation was enough. My back felt wider, and as I stretched my fingers, they felt more flexible. Physically, I didn't *look* any different, but I knew my own body — or more, I knew what my body wasn't.

Teeth. *Would they be longer?* I flicked on the bathroom light and stared head on in the mirror. I played around with the skin on my face; colder and softer to the touch. I pulled at my eyelids, eyes the same hazel as before, except they didn't feel *mine*. Arlo died last night and now this thing stood in his place. An exact copy of the boy it once was: a head of light blond waves, two annoying moles under its right eye, with teeth that appeared the same, except when I pushed my thumb into them and drew blood — they were monstrous.

Sense forced me to wince and I sucked the small wound clean, but as the drop of red soaked my tongue, I panicked and pictured the pouch Mars handed to me.

'Take this when you're hungry. You'll know when.'

I pulled it from the pocket of the black coat I still wore and stared at the thick liquid within. *Is this my life now?*

I looked back up and the reflection frowned at me, eyes imbued with sadness.

Why me?

An abrupt bang at the front door echoed through my ears and the hairs on my arms stood on edge. I couldn't move, my eyes fixed to the glass. I hoped whoever it was would give up and go away, but they didn't. *Bang, bang, bang.* I squeezed my eyes tight.

Bang, bang, bang. The knocking weakened, but then I heard, so faintly:

"Please." A pained plea.

Rani.

My eyes widened. I patted myself down for my phone until I found it, tucked in my back pocket. *I said I would call.*

Twenty missed calls and fourteen texts. All from Rani — spanning from midnight until twenty minutes ago.

Shit.

"I'm... coming!" I shouted, frantically drying my hands. Chucking the packet under the sink, I tore off my coat, buttoned up my shirt, and threw a discarded, unwashed jumper on top. "Coming!"

I unlocked the door and it fell open. A blur of a person lunged towards me, arms locking in a tight in embrace. For the first time in a while, I returned the tight hug comfortably; leaning into it and dropping my face into Rani's soft hair. Her warmth grounded me. *I'm so sorry,* I thought.

As she pulled back, I noticed the mascara smudged beneath her bloodshot eyes. "Arlo," she panted. "You're alive."

My brow furrowed... *did she know? How could she know?*

"I..."

"Don't you ever worry me like that again," she snapped.

"I'm sorry."

"You said you would call but you didn't! I thought maybe you were having a better time than I expected, so I waited, but then I woke up this morning to find out there had been another death down by the riverside and you still weren't answering me. I came here and knocked so many times but you wouldn't answer, so I asked around to see if anyone had seen you because I was thinking the absolute worst and that the body they found was *yours.* I thought I'd lost my best friend because I let him go out with someone I didn't know, but you were here. Were you here the whole time? Why didn't you text me back?" Her eyes teared up again, and then my own welled, too. Not once had I thought of Rani. How selfish and ignorant of me.

"I'm sorry. I am so, so sorry."

She hugged me again and sighed into my chest. "I thought you were dead."

I was. I am. What am I?

"Where have you been? What happened?"

Where to begin.

"Arlo?"

Where. To. Begin.

"When did you come home?"

"Last night." I lied. *Why, why, why?*

"Then why didn't you pick up?"

"I... slept in."

"It's five o'clock."

"I drank. A lot."

"I know you're lying." She released her hold and stepped back, staring straight into my eyes. "Why are you lying?"

"I..." *I can't tell her. There is no way I can tell her.* Phantom hands groped my neck, immeasurable weight pressing down against my chest.

Her face softened. "Sorry. I'm just scared. I genuinely thought you were dead. Why is there so much death?"

Then I properly started to cry. Rani pulled me into another hug. "It's okay," she said after a moment. "I'm just glad you're alive."

"I'm sorry," I choked.

"I know. I'm sorry too."

We held each other for a long moment, until I finally loosened my grip and let my arms flop back to my sides.

Rani wiped her eyes on her fluffy scarf. "I don't want to sound like a crazy friend, but I care so much about you, Arlo, and... please just call next time. Or text. Even if it's just a thumbs up or a kiss. I only need something to let me know I've not been a terrible friend and left you in danger."

"I promise. I'm sorry, Rani, I really am. I got carried away and wasn't thinking. I had no idea someone... someone *died.*" Realisation set in. "Do they know who it is?" I thought back to all the faces I could possibly remember from that night. *Had Lucy attacked others? Killed others? Why was I the one who was saved?*

Rani shook her head. "Not yet, which is why I got so concerned. You practically vanished off the face of the earth."

"Sorry."

"Stop apologising!" she snapped.

"Sor..."

She glared, hiding a grin.

A ghost of a smile twitched across my face as I closed my eyes, the tension lifting.

Rani slumped herself on my bed, pulling Wellington to her chest and wrapping her arms around him tightly. "People are getting scared. This isn't supposed to happen."

"Do they know the cause of death?" *It has to have been Lucy.*

"Suicide, apparently. Those are the rumours anyway. Jumped from a height, they say. The... carpark," she choked out the word, clearly envisioning the scene.

Right next to where we were. My mind spiralled... it wasn't a suicide. It couldn't have been. They were pushed, to cover it up and make it easier to control the police. None of these deaths were accidents or murders inflicted by ordinary people — no, the victims were murdered by the same creatures that killed me. *But why am I still here and they're not? What made me any more important?*

But how could I have expressed my thoughts to Rani in that moment without sounding inconsiderate and delusional? Spouting off the truth like some crazed conspiracist who ambles up to the police station, blaming some other worldly force for the deaths of three completely unconnected strangers. They would believe I'd lost my mind and have me escorted from the premises with a warning for wasting police time. I'd probably end up a suspect too for tying the cases together. I'd be essentially incriminating myself there and then. Two clear suicides and a murder. Victims not linked except they *were.* The two supposed suicides were, as I found out later that day, both from the same course. And the man? The police and investigators will have no doubt discovered a link to him too; they're good like that. I would be locked away.

"Arlo?"

"Yes. Sorry. I was just thinking." I tapped my fingers against my crossed arms.

"About what?"

"Nothing."

That earned me a glare.

"Just about how surreal this all is," I added.

Rani sighed, sitting up and parking my teddy between her crossed legs. "It's a lot to take in, isn't it. I can't quite wrap my head around any of it. I wonder how the families are feeling. It's heart-breaking."

Instinct told me to console her, to sit by her side and drape a comforting arm around her but the notion felt too much. So, I remained standing and kept my arms folded, awkwardness creeping its way back in.

The bathroom fan buzzed away gently in the background, though the off-putting aura settling between us was probably my fault. I've never been good at comforting others, and though I tried so hard, I never had the right words to say or the correct actions to make the other comfortable. To prove I could be empathetic.

"Did you at least have a nice time last night?" Rani finally said.

"Hmm..." *How much should I say?* "It didn't work out. But that's fine."

"Yeah. Oh well, you know what everyone says: There are

plenty more fish in the sea." Rani's nose curled up at the statement.

"Yeah." *If that's even what I want.*

IT WASN'T long after Rani reluctantly left that I fished out my laptop and began searching, looking for any sort of connection between these deaths so far and what happened to me. I needed to see if there were any loose ends or parts where Lucy or whoever she was with had not been so tactful and left a crucial detail of their involvement behind. I looked for anything I could use as proof to help these families and debunk it all. *How would detectives go about this? Journalists?* Surely, they can't have brainwashed *everyone*? There had to have been at least someone out there who still suspected foul play. *How does the Manipulation even work?*

After reading all publicly available accounts and statements, I flicked through photograph after photograph on every news site. There wasn't much to go off, understandably, as these were not, and probably never would be, *big* cases. However, I did manage to conclude that each victim had supposedly been out drinking the night before they were found. *Perhaps meeting someone?* I did some more digging and begrudgingly traced social media accounts (which felt so wrong on so many levels. I hated those apps. Primary school had taught me all I needed to know about how dark those sites could get.) The two students were, as far as I could tell, not in relationships and therefore easily could have been set up as I was. Led into falsehood and *used.* But despite my strained effort, I still had no real links, not a fleck of concrete proof. I was tracking a dead end. They were too good.

Am I going crazy?

I decided I wasn't. Enough had happened in the last twenty-four hours for anything to be possible, and despite what the media said, all these deaths were linked. *Yet why does no one else see this except The Thorns?*

My only hope now would have been to look straight into finding potential murder suspects. There was no way the second victim's death could be passed as anything other than murder — the body had been almost decapitated. But there weren't any suspects, just posts about how the County Durham police department were 'doing everything in their power' to bring justice. It's a pretty small city and it is highly uncommon for murder to occur, let alone in such a dramatic and performative way.

I touched my neck; the two puncture wounds were mere scabs now, barely noticeable. But if a... *vampire* wanted to cover their tracks (I was really starting to reconsider my sanity here), they would remove signs of entry wounds. The neck. Decapitation. Cutting through the bites... I shivered.

Could it have been one of The Thorns? After all, I knew none of them, and they could have been lying through their teeth. No. They were good people. *People?* Marianne clearly stated they were trying to catch whoever is responsible and I remember the truth in her eyes. Nonetheless, I feared Lucy wasn't acting alone, and for all I knew, there was a whole network of undead murderers gearing to attack.

A searing pain shot through my head, like someone had shot a bullet straight through my skull, and it now lodged there, filling my mind with immense pressure. My eyes had begun to burn a few minutes before, but I brushed it off as screen strain. I'd had headaches before, and while some were relatively painful, this was no ordinary sensation. I squeezed my eyes shut and pushed myself away from my desk, head in hands. Sheer blackness enveloped the room, the laptop the only light source.

My breathing quickened, and my limbs grew weak as pins and needles shot up my toes and fingers almost simultaneously. *Am I having a stroke?* Pushing up from my chair, the wheels clattered off the rug behind me, and I could barely keep my eyes open. I tore off my jumper, sodden with sweat that now dripped off me in rivulets. It was no use. I was going to pass out, I knew it. The irony of my anaemia crossed my mind, but I had never felt such intense symptoms like this. As my legs gave way beneath me and I clung onto the bedhead for support, I started to picture what the scene would look like if someone were to come into my room and find me lying unconscious, curled up like an embryo in the pitch dark. They'd think I was dead without a pulse...

I already was dead.

'You'll know when.'

The blood.

I FIXED my eyes on the crack of bathroom light and dragged myself across the cold, tiled floor to reach it, the transparent package visible from under the faucet. *What was I doing? Was I really going to do this? To give in?* These were such human symptoms; what if I'd just caught a cold or a fever? Something I could battle away with rest?

'You'll know when.'

I grabbed the packet and tore it open in one clean tug. My arms barely supported my movements as I raised the packet to my face. This time it really did smell like blood, all metallic and fresh, so very fresh.

And *sweet.*

My canines elongated; this was no human sensation. I was an abomination about to commit an unspeakable act. Tipping my head back, I downed nearly the entire sachet in a few gulps, dropping the packet beside me and letting the remaining contents drip out onto the floor. I slouched my body against the toilet as my vision cleared and breathing subsided. Blood trickled down my shirt and I was certain it was on my face too.

But it tasted so *good.*

Tears slipped down my cheeks and mixed with the drying blood on my lips.

. . .

I SLEPT for a while with my body propped up against the bathtub, recharging. I awoke as the sun crept through the frosted glass of my bathroom window, the fan still whirring and light still on. My back ached, legs slightly numb from the unnatural position I found myself in. I was, for the first few seconds or so of consciousness, completely unaware of why I was there. Then my eyes honed onto the blood splattered tiles, trailing to the sink where two bloody handprints slid down the porcelain. The blood bag lay on the floor beneath it, remnants dried onto the tiles. I glanced down at my hands, palms inked with dried blood, then I touched my face and rubbed my thumb across my teeth. *Normal.*

I was sat in the centre of a crime scene. I was very conscious of the fact it wasn't a *true* crime scene, but if I let the blood dry any longer there would be no hiding the evidence of what I'd done.

I stripped my shirt off and thoroughly washed my hands, avoiding the mirror in front of me. I went to the cabinet to grab every form of cleaning product I could find and began *scrubbing*.

It took forever, my mind abuzz with thoughts and fears of everything I'd found myself experiencing. Still waiting to wake up from the nightmare, muttering words of disbelief.

Once I was satisfied the room looked as it did before, I ran a shower and binned my entire outfit, desperate to erase all traces of *everything*. I stepped into the scorching hot shower and rubbed hard at my face and body, and even after the water stopped running red, I persisted, scraping my bare arms until they were red raw. I needed to be clean of it all.

The room had steamed up and I was struggling to see in front of me, but instead of turning the shower off, I put the plug in and watched the tub fill. I slowly lowered myself until I sat with my head against the side of the tub, where I closed my eyes and breathed.

"You see, I wrote this, but then I had a bit of a breakdown because I think I've interpreted the whole thing wrong. I don't think that's what he meant with that line," Rani said, pointing at her notes over lunch the following day. We were discussing a poem by Shelley, the poet I'd studied at length two nights ago, but was yet to expand upon my knowledge because, well, everything had changed since then.

"You could ask him?" I gestured to the sky, earning an audible eye roll. Successful sarcasm, I think.

"Okay, but seriously, what do you think? You're normally really expressive with poetry."

I uncrossed my legs and leaned forward, trying to engage properly; I was only half listening before. "Well, you could say he is saying we're all useless and empty inside. Untameable and ever-changing vessels that serve very little permanence in the grand scheme of things and simply ruin what the world already has to offer. If you think about what clouds are, in essence. We are not free."

Rani's eyes widened, then she snorted. "Always the pessimist."

"Just seeing our existence as it really stands."

"Is that really a Shelley perspective though?"

"Very Shelley."

"Okay then," Rani adjusted her chair and flicked her book to a different page. "What about this one then? Hope or no hope for humanity?"

I looked down at her notes. "You're forgetting we studied that one at school. Only hope for the common man."

That garnered another laugh, and I joined in, recognising my severity.

"Gosh, I'm glad you're okay today," Rani innocently added.

My smile internally faded as flashes of the night before re-emerged. Memories of me watching in horror as my eyes shifted from hazel to an aggressive, veiny red. My mind flitting back to the murders. The Thorns. Mars. Lucy. Blood. Blood. Blood.

I had binned the blood bag without a second thought, dreading to think about any part of what my future entailed. I was living in the now, and because I felt okay in that moment, I hoped I would be okay forever. Even that morning, I was forgetting how bad the sensation was, as we always do. We tell ourselves, 'oh, maybe it wasn't that bad after all.' Until it happens again.

I hadn't eaten anything, not since breakfast on the morning I met Lucy. *Maybe I'll never have to eat again.* I no longer felt hunger, only an extreme sense of power and weakness all at once. Limbs aching with this unexplainable, immortal body...

I wasn't sure how long this bag was going to last in my system, until I would once again burn up from the inside out. But I decided without hesitation that I would require no help, and that I was going to manage it on my own. I'd be prepared, finding my own ways of dealing. I was sure I would be able to figure it all out. *I'll drink my own blood if I must. Many vampires won't have a community like that and they will have to manage somehow.*

One thing was for certain, I wasn't going back to those rooms, or to any place where normality ceased to exist. I refused. I was determined to live my life with as much stubborn optimism as I could.

"May I join you?"

My gut sank. In fact, my whole body sank. We'd been sat for barely twenty minutes before reality crawled back in.

We both looked up and there stood Mars, in the middle of the day, dressed like a funeral-attending secretary with knee high buckled boots and hair flowing graciously down their back. I stared in awe. *Are they a student here? No. They can't be. Were they* following *me?*

"Hello..." Rani beamed, with a discrete glance in my direction.

"Arlo, are you going to introduce us?" Despite her reluctance, she was already making room on the booth beside her.

"I... this is..." *What is happening?*

"I'm Mars," they stuck out their hand for Rani to shake. She did, looking far too excited whilst doing so. *How can she greet strangers so easily?*

"Mars! What a cool name. I'm Rani. It's lovely to meet you. Arlo, you haven't mentioned...?" She flicked another puzzled glance towards me.

"I only met them..." I stopped myself. "The other day."

"In the bookshop next door," Mars intervened. "I asked for recommendations, and it turns out we have a lot in common." They were either taking a seriously lucky guess based off my pretentious fashion and the book in front of me, or they'd been following me.

"Oh, nice! Are you a student here as well?"

Mars made themself comfortable opposite me, crossing their legs and easing into the booth as though this meet up was pre-planned. "Nah. I mean, I was a few years back, but now I'm just one of those sad ex-students who floats around campus looking for first years to rope into joining weird clubs." They grinned a sort of contagious grin that made me momentarily forget my frustration.

"That was a joke, obviously. Ha ha. No, I'm an artist and the manager of a local band. Forever Red? You might have heard of them," they said this solely to Rani; I'd already been informed of this, of course — minus the manager part. *How many vampires are in this band?*

Rani's eyes seemed distant for a moment, her memory cogs winding in her mind. "Wait... I think I have, actually... sort of alternative indie stuff, right? I think they performed at Leeds last year, right? I didn't realise they were from up here!"

Mars' face lit up, radiating with pride. "Formed right here at this university nearly ten years ago now. Wow, time flies. They're like gods on stage." Another infectious grin revealed a dimple on each cheek. "You should come see them some time!"

Rani nodded in gracious acceptance, whilst I, on the other hand, kept quiet. I was trying and failing at wrapping my head around the notion of a vampire band touring the country. Maybe I needed some stronger medication.

"So you... manage them? Like tour with them and everything?" Rani had no desire to drop this conversation, twisting her whole body around to fully engage with Mars. My collar started to itch.

"Fully manage." Mars nodded, somehow also using their hands to answer the question.

Rani looked star-struck, her mouth forming a silent 'wow'.

"Do you play an instrument?" Mars pursued the topic, realising Rani's investment.

Rani sucked in her lips in an embarrassed motion, side eyeing me before answering. "I played the clarinet in primary, very badly though. I begged my parents to pay for lessons because my friends were doing it and I wanted to skip science on a Thursday. Alas, it didn't last long. I split my lip on the reed four weeks in and my teacher shouted at me for not wearing enough lip balm. I stormed out there and then, leaving the instrument and waltzing back to my science lesson as if I'd just quit a high paying job and freed myself from the shackles of corporate life. True story." She tapped the table.

I snorted, I had heard that story many times before and it never ceased to brighten my day. Just picturing the scene was enough, but the way she told it made it even funnier.

"Arlo tried to teach me piano in the summer, but my coordination said no."

Mars looked up, surprised. "You play?"

I shrugged, not wanting to make myself out to be something I definitely wasn't. "A bit. Mostly just my own stuff though."

"Oh, that's even better. Original. You'll have to play for me sometime."

Are we really friends now?

I mumbled something between a 'yeah' and 'hmm', which thankfully cut that avenue short.

"Anyway." Mars wafted their hand, sensing the conversation was burning out. "Enough about music. I must seem a bit weird just plonking myself amongst you and rambling nonsense. I just get a bit excited sometimes. I really need to cut back on the caffeine."

Caffeine. Hmm.

Rani bobbed her head pleasantly. "Don't be daft. Any friend of Arlo's is a friend of mine. Ramble away."

Mars took in a visible breath of happiness. I feigned agreement with a nod. *Is that really what we are? Friends?*

My right leg started to bob under the table while Rani shuffled through her study notes, stacking them into a neat pile and capping her highlighter pen. This was now a three-way conversation.

"So, Mars, what do you like to read? Tell me what Arlo recommended. He has the weirdest taste." She winked at me, and I watched Mars smirk too. They'd prepared for this question.

Without having to think, they said, "Well, we met in the history section."

Rani covered her mouth with her hand. "Oh, say no more."

"Hey! Am I that predictable?" I cut in.

Rani burst into a fit of hysterics, her deep brown eyes glowing with sincerity. "Arlo, I mean this with all the love in my heart, you are a walking leather-bound textbook."

I feigned an offended expression.

"But that's why I love you. You've definitely taught me a lot with all your interests."

Mars watched this whole interaction play out, looking between us as if finding the right moment to join in.

"So, Rani, how long have you and Arlo known each other?" they asked.

"About two years? We went to the same sixth form, but only properly got to know each other once we learned we both had offers here."

"Rani took me under her wing," I added. She winked in acknowledgement.

"You'd expect it to be the other way around." Rani said, gesturing to my height with an up and down motion of her head. That garnered a laugh from Mars, who I figured was probably a similar size to Rani. I was acutely aware of how much space I took up in comparison to my current companions, but I kept my face the same, swallowing it down.

Rani noticed. *She always does.* "No, but enough of my teasing. Arlo is the sweetest guy you will ever meet." She leaned close to Mars, who listened intently. "He's always there to talk to, always there to cheer you up. He's my best friend." Her leg playfully kicked mine under the table.

I choked a little when she said that. No one had ever proudly announced me as their best friend before. I was always 'everyone's friend,' but never anyone's 'go-to' person. It was a notion I never gave any power to, and I was shocked by how much it meant to me to hear that. Not another painting on the wall.

Rani shuffled her sheets again, zipping something into her pencil case.

"So, you like literature then, Mars? You never answered before," she asked.

Mars leaned forward so that their elbows rested on the table. "I like my fair share of Shakespeare, *'If music be the food of love, play on'.* Although that probably sounds really generic to you guys."

"Not at all. Who doesn't love a bit of Shakespeare? Though you'll have to learn more quotes if you're going to be hanging around with us more often," Rani joked.

"Oh, I won't bother you both too much, I didn't expect to

find myself in such good company today. I was coincidently passing by and just wanted to check in on Arlo. He wasn't feeling too well the last time we met."

"Oh really? When was this?" Rani gave me a worried look.

I was going to have to go along with this gibberish, wasn't I. "Not long ago. Just a headache, nothing too bad. Felt a bit faint, you know what I'm like. Mars got me something to drink and we sat down and talked for a bit. Honestly, nothing to worry about!"

"Oh."

I must not have convinced her enough. I sometimes forgot how much about my health Rani was aware of.

"Nothing like last time," I promised. "Really."

Rani clearly didn't want to embarrass me by declaring my medical history in front of Mars, who, despite their confidence, was still a stranger to her — to us. She took the 'we'll talk about this later' route and shifted her tone. "Well, I'm glad you were there because Arlo here could lose a limb, be lying on his death bed and still declare 'ay, ay, a scratch, a scratch.'"

"Romeo and Juliet," Mars interjected, receiving a slow and proud nod from my friend.

"You would think I'm always in the wars if I complained every time I felt off," I continued, feeling the need to defend myself.

"Ah, but that is why we are friends, Arlo. I would sew you back limb to limb if I had to. You know that, though."

"And I you." I smiled sheepishly.

THE THREE OF us ended up talking for a while longer. My mind somewhat eased but not entirely. I very much wished to leave my seat and run home to comfortable surroundings, but Mars and Rani got along like they'd known each other years. I'll never understand how people can interact with such ease, to not let their minds over dramatise every scenario and create panic out of such situations.

The afternoon turned to early evening and the café had long since emptied, sounds dulling. I drifted into a state of numb consciousness, as if nothing felt real anymore, and it was starting to frighten me. Then finally, Mars announced they needed to leave.

"Oh, it was such a pleasure to meet you, Mars. We will have to talk again soon," Rani said, standing with them and going in for a hug. I took that as the signal we would all be leaving together.

"Yes, indeed! Hopefully, I'll see you both around soon!"

RANI LEAVING in the opposite direction prompted me to catch up with Mars and finally confront them.

"What the hell are you doing?" I asked, tugging them into a side alley.

"I'm just trying to make things normal."

"There was nothing normal about that. Why did you follow me?"

"You probably won't believe me when I say I *didn't*. I genuinely was passing."

I raised a brow in disbelief.

Mars didn't flinch. "I was going to leave you alone, but I asked you to call and when the afternoon passed, I figured you weren't going to. You're going to need my help, Arlo, so I'm integrating myself into your life so you don't need to come looking for me. We're giving you space, but you *will* need support."

"I... Mars, I'm fine as things are. I can deal."

"Can you?"

I nodded. I wasn't going to let myself be controlled. Monitored.

"You have no idea what it's like for us to find our feet in the first few months. You think you can manage it now but just wait until the hunger *really* sets in and takes you over in ways you will never expect. No matter how strong you think you are, nothing can prepare you for what is to come. You need me, Arlo. I'm not going to take over your life, but I'm trying to make this as easy as possible for you. A time will come where you *will* need me. Need us."

Fear laced their tone, eyes darkening and brow tensing. *They're right, Arlo. Listen to them. Let them into your life. Learn.*

I bit my gum, swallowed, and closed my eyes. "Please leave me alone."

They didn't budge. "You had the packet then?"

I took a deep breath. "Yes."

"And what did it taste like?"

Paradise. "Blood."

"The hunger. You felt it?"

I said nothing.

"Did the blood satisfy you or did it leave you wanting more?"

More. So much more.

"Please leave me be."

"Arlo, don't do this. I know exactly what this feels like. I can't stand by and watch this eat away at you."

"Why would you care?" I snapped, anger erupting from nowhere. I regretted my tone before I even finished the sentence.

Mars looked as if I'd slapped them, colour draining from their face. Fear morphed their features, and I quickly learned why. My canines pierced my lower lip, blood dripping from my mouth.

A haunting silence fell between us, interrupted by my own panting breaths as my face cooled and my blurred vision regained focus.

"That's why."

They shoved two large, ice-cold blood bags into my hand then disappeared into the street.

Chapter Six

*When I first breathed in the earth, I could feel the world burning
around me. So much pain and anguish. A millennium of tears.
Acid on my soul.
He will awaken and it will be glorious.*

*My companion does not know who I have chosen. It is too soon for
that, but he will understand.
He reaches out an elegantly ringed hand, his form as exquisite as
always.
"Rise," he says. "You've got work to do."
This is going to be fun.*

I *'ve got work to do*, I thought as I stormed away, my pockets
disgustingly full. *I can't let this get to me, I can't fall behind.*
Up until this point, I'd managed to stay on top of my stud-

ies. Stuck to my routine, as I always did. Never allowing myself to go too slow. And I would let none of this hinder that routine in any way. I would figure it out all by myself, like always. Though I knew I'd burn out soon; my obsessive overworking always caught up to me, but I hated the idea of breaking my streak. Working kept my mind active and reminded me of my goal and how there *could* be a chance of success in the future.

The instant I got back to my room, I slammed my door shut and threw my duffle coat on my bed; ignoring the weight of liquid within it.

One part of my mind was telling me I was being ridiculous. That Mars was right and that there was no way I would be able to manage on my own. But the other, much louder part screamed that I *could* do this alone. Thinking about all those faces I met, how each of them will have most likely been turned as I was, would they have all had help? Or were some of them strong enough to get by on their own? They all looked fit and healthy to me. All sane. All thriving.

I refused to be weak. I wanted to be in control, to do something by myself and be in charge of my body and mind.

If I was going to need blood, I'd use my own. Be self-sufficient. There was no harm in that, surely. At least for the time being, until I worked out another source. I wouldn't allow myself to be discretely handed bags every time I needed to feed, like a baby — spoon fed at feeding time.

Mars meant well, I knew that, but I was an adult, capable of doing my own research and gaining my own experience.

I can do this. I can do this. I can do this.

MY LAPTOP FIRED TO LIFE, all my tabs from the night before reflected in my glasses. 'Local Man Found Dead by Riverside.' 'Teen Becomes Second Student Death of the Year...' 'Mental

Health at Top Universities.' Scrolling through the tabs, my descent into fixation became apparent: conspiracy pages, media articles and news sites — all irrelevant now. I had given up trying. All of this led me on the road to nowhere. I closed each tab before checking my emails: a clean slate, ready to start my essay. The university had sent a message to all, discussing student health and the different mental health services that could be found on campus. Individual lecturers had also taken it upon themselves to profusely remind us that they cared about our wellbeing and poured their hearts out, stating that they would always be there to talk to. I appreciated the effort, but it was just another reminder of my current situation. I muted the group chats I had unwillingly been added to.

Setting timers always helped me. Whenever I needed to get work done but was more drawn to reading a book or scribbling poetic lines, I would set a timer and sit myself away from distraction. My aim this time was not only to get my essay done, but to keep my mind off the hunger. I was preparing for it, but if I kept my brain focused on one specific area and didn't let it wander, then nothing would get in my way.

And it worked. I sat for nearly three hours, street lamps my main light source, and completed my work.

I remember the elation I felt, the glory of conquering my cravings already. *This isn't going to be so bad.* I had thought. *See, you are stronger than people think you are.*

Still on my high, I decided to finish off my evening with a brisk walk to relieve the growing desire. A walk never failed to distract me.

I tried to make this a part of my new routine too, just as it was back home when I would take my dog, Bess, for a walk. Every morning and night, no exceptions. It was our time, to switch off from the world. I missed her terribly. I wondered when I returned home for the winter break, if anything might have changed in the village, but then my stomach sank. Just over a month. *Mum.*

The realisation physically *hurt.* A needle straight into my chest.

"Shitshitshit," I mumbled to myself in the empty corridor, gripping tightly to the hair on my forehead. Amid my confusing and terrifying new life, not once had I stopped to consider how I would go about seeing my mum like this. My mum who devoted her whole life protecting and supporting me, doing everything in her power to make me happy and safe, worrying about me day and night. And I'd do anything for her too, she'd been through so much as a single parent and deserved the world. *Do I tell her?* She would think I'd lost my mind. But could I hide it? How long could I hide this from Rani, even? How was I going to do this? They deserved to know, didn't they?

Cross that bridge when you come to it, my mind said. *You managed one day; you can manage many others. No one needs to know; you can be normal.*

Starting down the hallway, I pushed all thoughts aside as best as I could. I was just going on a walk. I had no more responsibility for the evening. I could do this. I could get through it all. One step at a time.

I left the building, the whispering cold biting at my face in an instant. The thoughts, barely at bay, returned once again. *Tell Rani. What if police find me?* I turned up the path to the cathedral. *What if no one believes me? How can I hide it from my mum? Won't she question my behaviour? Bess will know. How long can I really hide like this?*

"Arlo?"

I stopped short, following the voice with my eyes. There, under a pool of yellow light, with black hair and a trench coat blending in with the Victorian lamppost and city bollards, stood Ben, alone, with a half-dragged cigarette in hand.

"Arlo!" he repeated, more confidently. He casually beckoned to me with his free hand.

Why would he be here? Did he know I would be here? Where I live? I stepped across the road cautiously. "Ben?"

The dead boy beamed. "Fancy seeing you here!"

"Yes…"

Ben cocked his head, eyes quizzical. "You think Mars sent me to keep an eye on you." It wasn't a question.

I sighed. That was exactly what I thought.

"They didn't. I promise."

I gave a snort of disbelief.

"As much as I want you to be safe," he took a final drag of his cigarette before extinguishing it under foot, "this is merely a coincidence. Though I really do hope you'll reconsider our offer of protection."

Before I'd even had the chance to ask my next question, he answered with a gentle laugh. "I'm currently living nearby, just for a few months whilst we record. Sometimes I need some quiet time to myself, and I like the view from here," he gestured to the vast cathedral before us, "it keeps me relaxed."

My shoulders loosened. "Alone time is nice," I said, taking a confident step closer.

"People forget how important it is."

I lit up at that.

"It's not that I don't love company, I do. I love my partner and my band, and of course, The Thorns, but I also love being on my own, to get away from things for a while. Sometimes it all gets a bit too much, you know?"

I couldn't believe I was finally having a conversation with someone who could relate to how I felt.

"You like being alone too, don't you?" Another observation.

"More than anything," I sighed.

Ben smiled a comforting and friendly, diamond smile. "I won't keep you then."

"Oh no, don't worry."

"You sure? I was going to leave soon anyway. I sometimes *say* I don't mind when I really do, I just don't want to sound mean."

"No, it's…" My eyes brightened as I processed what he said. I chuckled. *He just read me like a book.* "No, stay. Let's... talk for a bit." The genuine contentment I felt in this moment was a sensation I wished I could always feel, devoid of intrusive thoughts, questions or distractions. I felt clear and I wanted to talk — I actually felt comfortable enough to talk. "If *you* want, that is," I added.

"I'd very much like that."

"Okay then."

Ben stuck his hand in an inner jacket pocket and produced his packet of cigarettes, no doubt to light another. He raised it towards me, a fresh stick between his teeth. I held up a polite hand to decline.

"It won't harm you now, you know," he said once he freed up his hand. "I smoked *a lot* when I was alive. It definitely would have caught up with me, and it was stupid of me really, but I was just living the rockstar life." He laughed at himself. "All these piercings and shit, but now that we're..."

"Dead," I finished.

"Dead," Ben repeated in clear relief the word hadn't triggered me. "We can kind of just do what we want now. We're not like humans anymore, not in that way. We're essentially immune to human illness. So I stuck with it. Terrible advert for kids." He threw me a look of sarcastic guilt.

I'd not thought about that yet, the extent of our immortality. I was still clinging on to the concept of humanity. Manipulating myself to believe I was still normal.

"Go on then," I said, keeping my hesitations to a minimum – living in the moment.

"Casper will kill me for being such a bad influence," he joked as he handed me one and lit it for me. The first drag took me by surprise and a cough followed but then I realised it wasn't as bad as I'd always expected it would be. It didn't taste like it smelled, either, but I made a mental note of not making it a frequent thing.

We stood in silence for a moment, the wind whistling through the balding trees. Ben took in a breath through his teeth, shaking out his limbs in the bitter air.

"So, you're a student here then, right?" he started.

"Yeah. First year. Literature. Still new to it all, but I suppose it's alright. It's a nice city at least."

"Beautiful city," Ben agreed. "I went here too. I studied music. Though you probably figured that out already."

"That's when you started your band?"

"Yeah, we started in our very first term. Casper had just moved here, and we wasted no time; he was determined to get straight into playing. Luckily for me, he's extremely extroverted, so I didn't even have to put any effort in. He needed a bass player. I obliged." He wiggled his fingers.

"That's so cool." I sounded like a child, mind blown by something so simple. But it was cool. He was happy, I could tell. More than content with where his life was.

I could be like that.

"You have any hobbies?" He took another drag and held the smoke in his lungs for a prolonged time.

"Yeah, a few. I like to write, play a bit of piano... I like photography though I don't have a proper camera yet. I enjoy doing a bit of everything."

"Nice, you're so like me. I hate being tied down to one thing. I've probably dabbled in every hobby you can think of over my life. Many never stuck, though." He drew a circle into the gravel with the tip of his boot. "So, you enjoy writing, then? You wanna get published?" He sounded genuinely interested, pretty eyes full of optimistic attention.

"That's the dream, I suppose. Bit far-fetched if I think about it logically, but you know... it's worth a try, right?"

"Of course! Never doubt yourself. Nothing is ever far-fetched if you believe in it. I'm sure you're super talented. You've got as much of a chance as anyone." He nodded up at me. "I need to read more to be honest. I used to read a lot when I was a kid, and I don't know if it was secondary school or just my change in mentality, but one day I just stopped. Sad really. No one seems to read these days."

"I could give you some recommendations?"

"Really? I'd like that."

"Maybe you could give me some music recommendations? What was your band's name again?" My hands trembled; I'd never survived this long in a conversation with a stranger before. My script was near its end. Time to improvise.

"Forever Red! We're not that big. Well, I don't know really. Maybe we are? But you might like some of our songs, possibly? Do you like post-punk?"

I looked at him blankly, panicked by my lack of education in music genres. I normally listened to random songs I'd picked up over the years, never taking too much care into learning anything about them but simply listened to whatever I felt like. My mum brought me up on the sixties, my auntie on the seventies.

"The Cure? Joy Division? Siouxsie and the Banshees?" He reeled off some names.

"Oh, The Cure! They sang that song about the days of the week, right? The guy with lipstick."

His eyes widened; lips tightly pressed together. "Oh dear, we've got to do something about that. Just wait until you listen to 'Disintegration'. It will change your life." The light on his cigarette died.

WE TALKED SOME MORE, sharing parts of our lives and interests and it was working, I was no longer worried like I was earlier. I managed to fully switch off and engage with Ben. It turned out he had also never met his biological father, which was refreshing and of a great comfort to me; he understood what it was like... the not knowing. But unlike me, he had someone to call 'dad'.

We moved to the bench against the wall as he told me about

how his parents didn't know how to handle it when he came out and how they split up not long after — leaving him to decide to move up to Leeds to live with his grandmother for a few years before moving here for university. I tried my best to sound sympathetic and understanding, and though I honestly was, I struggled with sounding sincere.

"I love my parents, and they always proved they loved me regardless, but they had their own issues to deal with at the time. I blamed myself for a long while, but I realised being an adult is a lot more complicated than it seems. I just wish they'd worded their original reactions better," he told me. "Sometimes, when I'm feeling childish though, I think about rocking up to their doors and flashing my teeth, proving there are far worse things I could be."

I laughed at that.

"You know, despite the fact that what we are has nothing to do with any religion."

"It's not a religious thing?"

"Nah. Think about it, creatures and demons exist in almost every religion or culture — there's always an opposite force, so if you believe in it, then we could fit into that category, however, history and media has made us out to be such twisted and horrible things, bending our origins to fit their cruel ideologies. But we are still souls. We still have a conscience. It's science, we just know very little about it. It's a parasite, it's probably not from earth. So, whether you have a belief or not, it's how you live your life that determines your relationship with your faith. Look," he pulled out a small chain from under his jumper: a crucifix. "This doesn't *burn*. I never renounced anything. I'm not sure what I believe in really but..." He looked down at the silver chain, twiddling it between his fingers, "I'm not a demon. It's not like I chose this."

And then I asked, it just *came* out.

"How did you die?"

Ben jolted his head up, his eyes glistening. *Was he crying?*

"Never mind," I said, panicked. I'd grown too comfortable and stepped out of line. Too personal. Again, I was winging this. My boundaries were all askew.

"No, no," he sniffed, then straightened his back against the bench. "It's kind of a long story," he wafted his hand, "I don't need to bore you anymore but basically, we fell into the wrong crowd. Got involved in a few things we shouldn't have, and well," he gestured to himself from head to toe, "shit happened."

"Marianne saved us. The Thorns existed a good few years before because of the disturbances in the city. To this day, I'll never understand how she managed to save us, but she did, and I'll be forever in her debt."

Us? "You *and* Casper?"

Ben gave me a sorrowful laugh. "Yeah. Poetic isn't it."

I so desperately wanted to ask more, my mind grasping all the pieces together. But we were interrupted.

Two girls around my age and both dressed for a night out, had approached us, or more, had approached Ben. They looked at me for a brief second before realising they had no idea who I was. They were here for the star.

"Hi... Ben? It's you, right?" the taller one said shyly.

I watched Ben's face light up and he adjusted his hands in his pockets, shifting in his seat slightly to face them.

This isn't the first time this has happened to him. I watched the scene play out, like an outside observer detached from my body.

"Sorry to bother you... we're just big, big fans and we heard you were back up here for a while but we never actually thought we'd just *bump into you.* Sorry. I... ahh. Sorry." The girl was visibly trembling, likely from the cold but genuine awe too. She *really* admired this band. What a feeling, to meet someone you idolised.

I wanted to be remembered.

Ben let her talk as she muddled up her words about the first time she watched them perform, and how one of their songs meant so much to her. The lyrics made her feel seen and she even started playing guitar because of them. She spoke of how they gave her the confidence to come out to her family and how she listened to them every day, eternally grateful that they exist.

"Wow, that means a lot. Thank you so much. What's your name?" *He's good at this.*

The girl looked as if she might faint. "Janie. My name is Janie."

Ben looked to the quieter girl who had not spoken a word and was clearly there for moral support. "And yours?"

The second girl seemed to panic momentarily before her face softened. "Beth."

"Well, Janie and Beth. I wish you both all the best with anything you want to do in the future. This is the reason we do this! And to know we're clearly doing something right is the greatest feeling! I'll be sure to let the band know how much of an impact we've had on you. Thank you so very much for your kind words. In fact..." He rummaged into his back trouser pocket and pulled out a guitar pick, handing it to Janie.

"Have fun with your guitar." He extended his hand further, giving it to her. She reached out, taking it slowly from his hands before glancing back at a beaming Beth, as if to say *did you see that?*

Ben hadn't stopped smiling this whole time, the tears in his eyes had long dried away.

"Actually, I think that might be Fran's pick," he said.

Then, I really thought I would have to intervene to catch this girl from collapsing.

"*The* Francesca Young?" Her eyes practically popped out of her skull.

Ben chuckled.

Janie looked back to her friend again then back to Ben. "Oh my god. I have such a crush on her." She instantly clasped her hand over her mouth, a little too late to catch the words.

Ben didn't seem to find it weird though. "Don't we all."

Janie nodded frantically, frozen to the spot.

"Anyway, I don't want to keep you standing in the cold. Go and enjoy your night." Ben waved them off, though not rudely.

"Yes. Of course. Sorry to have bothered you. I know it must be super annoying to have people come up to you. Sorry." Janie panicked.

"No, no! Don't apologise. I wish I was lucky enough to meet all the people I admire just *by chance.*"

Janie nodded again.

Before they left, Ben added one final thing. "You didn't hear what we were talking about before though," he said pleasantly, a sincere smile across his pretty face.

The girls' faces flashed in understanding; an expression so subtle it was easy to miss if you weren't looking for it. There was a slight scent of dried leaves in the air, barely detectable. *Manipulation.* So that was how easy it was.

Once they'd left, I turned to Ben, my mouth open in shock.

He didn't let me speak.

"I hate doing that. But they can't ever know." He closed his eyes, biting his lip.

DESPITE THE DARK TURN, we left on a high. Ben told me not to worry about what happened; he said it was necessary to keep us all safe and as long as it was done properly, with no other effects on the receiver, it was okay.

After that, he said he would 'love me and leave me' and wandered off into the night.

It did feel like a high. I felt like I could finally breathe again, the air cooling my insides. Maybe I *could* get used to this life. Ben made it seem so straight forward.

That's the way my brain worked. The rare social situations I found myself in would distract me enough until I felt like the bad thoughts would never return, almost like these interactions made me a completely different person. And that's exactly what happened here. Ben's calm and collected — *human* — manner eased me into this fresh mentality of conformity. I went back to my room, searching all things demons and monsters and creatures of the night. Most of it was folklore and myths, and though some had religious context, others didn't. I didn't know what I was hoping to find, but I tried to take advantage of this temporary intrigue — and I knew it was exactly that: temporary. *Maybe you* can *ask for help?* My new mind said. *Ben seems nice, genuine. He can help. Maybe Mars can help too. Maybe I'll finally find myself.*

While aimlessly searching for anything of value, I concluded I would try the blood bag when I next felt hungry. Just a small cup to make it last. Yet the more I scrolled, the more my newfound passion dwindled, and my original mindset crept back in. I couldn't find any real information about eternally living off blood, aside from a weird and clearly human blog page explaining the nutritional value of our own blood. I closed the tab in disgust. I knew then I needed to learn more about myself and this life, and to do that I would need to talk to the others. I would need to fully involve myself in this. Why was I naïve to think the answers would serve themselves to me on a silver platter? Talking to Ben had made it seem so *normal*.

I began aggressively chewing the inside of my mouth, biting away without care for injury. *So, you're just going to give in? Stop thinking for yourself? You're above this.* Was I? I wasn't. But I wanted to be.

I stared blindly at the screen, words blurring in and out of focus; I felt my canines lengthen until the bites deepened and I drew blood. The sweet taste of iron dragged me back to my senses and I snapped, throwing back the chair and I ran to the bathroom cabinet for my pain relief tablets. *I'm not doing this.* The drop of blood I'd swallowed was already heightening my senses and I desperately craved for more. "No! No! No!" I slammed my fist into the side of the sink. "I am not *this*. This is not me. I'm me. Me. Just me!" I refused to look at myself in the mirror; to remind myself of the monster within.

I downed the extra strength paracetamol without checking how many pills I popped into my hand. I wasn't thinking of anything other than the fact that I needed to remove this alien feeling, to numb it all.

I staggered back to bed, breathing heavily. Fully clothed, I buried myself under the duvet like a child escaping from the monster under the bed. Eyes squeezed shut, I desperately searched my mind for blank scenes. A lake. Clean washing hanging on a line. Coffee pouring. Anything.

It was no use.

The lake filled with blood. The white linen soaked a crimson red. Instead of coffee pouring, viscus black liquid stained the mug.

Breathe. Blood.

Breathe. Dead.

Breathe. Monster.

After the eternity of five minutes, it hit my system. I felt it. My breathing calmed, my head sank into the pillow, eyes drooped. But the symptoms didn't stop. My head was a bowling ball, limbs liquified. Panic stricken, I staggered with my remaining strength across my floor, dropping into a crawl as I felt a bubbling sensation in my throat. I'd barely reached the bathroom before I violently vomited across the tiles. I scrambled further towards the toilet before the second wave hit. I was tearing out my insides, burning acid and blood. *Blood.* That's all I had inside. I didn't need to eat anymore. Because I wasn't human.

Monster.

I gagged and choked; hands curled like claws around the toilet bowl. I began retching when my body was emptied of substance. I couldn't stop. My entire body trembled, each muscle sparking out of control.

And when the pain did finally ease, for the second evening in a row, I curled up on my bathroom floor and cried.

I sat there for a while, taking in the scene until my body calmed. I knew then, and perhaps even before, that I would not survive the night without food. I could no longer deny it. I couldn't numb the pain or distract myself from thinking I didn't need it, to smoke it away.

My mind went to the blood bags, but once again, I couldn't bring myself to open them. *What would I do if I did? Drain the whole thing? Crave more? Lose myself?*

My only other option was my own blood.

It was the best option, I told myself. I could control the quantity that way, and it could hardly harm me. Wouldn't even harm a normal human.

Am I really going to do this? Would it hurt? Doesn't matter. It's irrelevant. I am in control.

I stood up, legs like a newborn deer, and reached for my razor. I wasn't going to bite myself. I wasn't an animal.

I hovered the blade over my palm, right hand unsteady. *I am in control.*

The first bite of metal stung against my skin, but as the blood welled to the surface, all I could think about was its beauty.

No. Not beauty. It's disgusting.

But it wasn't. I wanted it more than anything.

I brought my palm to my lips, mesmerised by the red slowly trickling down my wrist, then took my first taste. And second. And third. Closing my eyes somehow helped me detach from the situation, feeling the sensations from outside my consciousness in blissful pretence that it wasn't *me* doing this.

It was more bitter than my previous sample, but it worked. My senses returned to normal almost immediately. I was floating. Not literally, but I felt lighter than air.

Untouchable. Unstoppable. *Powerful.*

I did it. *Ha!*

I ran my hand under the tap to seal the wound, flexing a fist, detecting the sudden strength that rolled within me. A smile tugged at the corners of my lips.

I am in control.

CHAPTER SEVEN

I found that last missing puzzle piece.
My Moon is looking at me now, pride dripping from his diamond
eyes.
I promised it would be a surprise.
We stay hidden, as necessary. A thousand years of history dulling our
whispers. We lie low; I observe.
Just like we arranged.
Once I bring my Star home, it can begin.
Soon, the three of us will rise as one.

I woke up to the smell of eggs as a crack of muted sunlight smiled through the curtains. I'd forgotten how small my bedroom was, with just enough room for a bed, wardrobe and my small, battered desk that was tucked away in the corner. It was more than comfortable though, all I needed.

I yawned, stretching out of bed and rubbing my sleep-clad eyes. A familiar voice called from downstairs. "Arlo! Breakfast!" Three loud barks followed and a moment later, my bedroom door shuffled open and my dog, Bess, bounded in, jumping onto the bed, and pushing me back down onto the mattress. I laughed as she frantically licked all parts of my face, smothering me with her golden mane. There's a saying that dogs always have a look of their owners. I remember thinking it silly at first, until I realised how accurate owning a Golden Retriever was for me and my mum.

"Arlo, it's going cold!" my mum shouted again, sterner this time.

"Coming, coming!" I playfully pushed Bess off my chest and let her trail behind me to the kitchen. I always felt mean eating on our high chairs while Bess lay on the floor, constantly pawing at my feet with big, sad eyes. She had grown too big to sit on my knee.

My mum had made us scrambled eggs on toast and was in the middle of retrieving the fresh orange juice from the fridge when I came down to greet her.

"Morning sleepy head," she beamed, reaching up awkwardly to ruffle my hair, as she always did. I bent down to help her. She did it deliberately now, normally following it with the line "please stop growing, I can't afford new clothes!"

I hadn't grown an inch since I was seventeen. Everyone in the village always had something to say about the height difference between us both. Our elderly neighbour John's favourite joke being: 'Is the weather nice up there?'

We never really talked about it alone. I never liked to push my mum; I knew my dad was a difficult topic for her. But she did once mention he was where I got my height from. When I was young and just starting to understand that sometimes parents split up, I asked her if it was because of me. Holding me tightly in her lap, she kissed my forehead and promised it had nothing to do with me. In fact, he disappeared before she even learned she was pregnant with me. Vanished from the face of the earth, she said. An inquest followed his absence, and a few people came forward to claim sightings across the Northwest. The statements were valid enough to drop the case entirely, but my mum had already lost interest by that point. She said she always knew in her gut that he was still out there somewhere, but he had no relevance in our lives because of what he did. And she was right. Even as I grew older, through my own choice, I never went looking for him. My mum was my parent. We managed. We didn't need anyone else. No matter what his reasons were for leaving, he never deserved her. And I was content in that belief.

We had once walked to the local corner shop when I was about eleven years old; the cashier wouldn't stop staring at me, and once we got to the till, she looked at my mum with a grin saying: "By Melissa, that's Jerry's kid right there." My mum wasn't facing me, but she didn't need to be for me to know what she was feeling. We paid for our things and left without saying a word.

She cried that night, and though she tried to hide it, I heard her muffled sobs through the walls. I went into her room to find her holding a photograph, squeezing it tightly in a fist. She wiped her face and pushed the duvet aside to let me in. That was the first time I saw a picture of my dad. September 1997, two years before I was born. I remember the first thing I thought was how pretty my mummy looked: blond curls down to her waist, a beaming smile and a floaty blue dress with delicately embroidered flowers around the neckline. Then I looked at him. My Dad. He had deep, thick red hair, long and wispy, and a face full of freckles. He wasn't at all what I expected, though I never thought about him enough to care. I concluded he looked nothing like me, and I said as such. My mum tilted her head to the side solemnly, tucking me in for a hug. "You're *my* baby," she whispered into my hair, placing three gentle kisses to my crown. "Nothing will change that."

"I HAD to get a different brand of orange juice," my mum announced, pouring us both a glass as I sat down. "It claims to be premium, though I doubt the price really changes the taste," she chuckled.

"Living the lavish life now, are we?" I joked.

"If only kiddo."

We tucked into our eggs while Bess circled the table. Oh, how I'd missed her.

"How's uni life then, son?" my mum asked after taking a big sip of her juice.

"Good, good. You know. Uni."

She laughed. "Ahh yes, I remember the days. Working but not working."

I smiled sheepishly. "I am working I swear!"

"I know, I know. Let me have some fun. I've missed winding you up."

"I missed you too, mum."

She pushed her finished plate to the side, feeding her burned crusts to Bess. "Don't forget about your old mum when you're all big and famous now will you?"

I had another mouthful. "Don't worry, that won't be happening."

"Oh, don't be silly. Stop putting yourself down. I've seen you write, those lovely poems you used to make me. You are beyond talented, sweetheart."

I shrugged and went in for another mouthful, but then I realised there was nothing on my fork and when I looked down at my plate, I noticed I'd not touched my food at all. *Huh.*

My mum continued to talk but her voice grew muffled.

Bess started to bark.

My head went fuzzy.

"Eat up, Arlo!" My mum's booming voice rattled through my mind.

"Yeah, sorry..." I said, only no sound came out of my mouth. I tried again, more forceful this time. Nothing.

"You haven't eaten your breakfast; it'll be cold now."

"I..."

Bess continued to bark, though it wasn't her usual bark. It was more of a growl — too harsh to come from my dog, or any dog in fact.

The room expanded and squeezed in on itself simultaneously, paint dripping from the cream walls.

My mum was looking straight at me now, eyes fixed on my face.

"Why aren't you eating?" she asked.

"I..." Nothing.

I'm not hungry.

"Arlo?" She looked seriously concerned now. Almost worried. *Why is she worried?*

"Arlo?

Sweetheart? You're scaring me.

Talk to me."

More growls ripped through the room — monstrous, terrifying growls. Wailing. Screaming.

Crimson leaked down the walls. Gushing faster and thicker.

Then she just stopped talking, looking at me with bloody tears staining both her cheeks. A pained smile ruined her face. I only saw red. Smelled it. Heard it. Tasted it.

I lunged over the table, glass shattering to the floor. I grabbed her by the collar of her dressing gown and sank my teeth deep into her shoulder. Bess barked, the sound returning to normal: a distress call. My mum cried out, arms thrashing, trying to frantically push me away, but it was no use. I was so very, very hungry.

I JOLTED UPRIGHT, sweat dripping down my forehead.

It was not the first time I had a nightmare like it. Dreams that fooled you into a false reality until everything falls apart at once and skews your brain until it burns.

The nightmares began around three weeks ago, after I decided to work this out myself. It had to have something to do with adapting to the ingestion of my stress-imbued blood. States of sleep paralysis or hallucinations were common to me now, so this dream was nothing new. I was growing accustomed to dealing with these situations. Despite the initial severe disorientation and questions of my own sanity, I would just about manage to pick myself up again to re-enter the real world.

This dream in particular was probably the worst of them all though: a constant reminder of what my future held in store. I survived around Rani and my other acquaintances during the day, managing to ignore my senses and desires. But my mum? How I would be able to act around her was an intensely worrisome thought. *She can't ever know.* Would I even be able to face her at all?

I allowed myself to properly awaken, reminding myself it was only a dream. I could control it. I would never lash out like that or let the creature inside take over. I managed perfectly well in my first month, so what was to say I couldn't always be like this? I wasn't weak.

Every morning before I left my room, I would cleanly cut my palm and drank until I was satisfied I would last the day. I was coping. No excessive hunger pangs or headaches. No more vomiting.

Of course, it wasn't that pleasant, it definitely lacked the full satisfaction of the blood bag Mars had originally given to me, but I was getting used to it and my routine was falling perfectly into place.

I'll admit I was occasionally finding it hard to keep my senses in check, overwhelmed by the constant presence of blood as I listened to hearts beating in lecture halls and on the streets. The closer people got to me, the more unbearable it became. The old me would have been repulsed by these sounds, yet now, I heard a heartbeat and envisioned the veins and arteries where blood flowed strongest, imagining how it would taste. Canines threatening to lengthen. But I dealt with it, slipping away discretely to take a little extra blood if needed. I knew these feelings would pass the stronger I became — teething problems, if you'll excuse the pun.

I had convinced myself I'd survive living like this, but I'd never been good at looking into the future. I used to struggle picturing myself as an older person, and how my life and job would play out. I took each day as it came and felt somewhat content that I *was* managing.

I was allowing myself to assimilate back into an ordinary life, keeping up with Rani and my course mates as much as possible. I occasionally bumped into Mars, though each encounter was no accident. I knew why they were doing it, and I trained myself to stop caring. They continued providing me with blood bags (that joined the growing pile in my bathroom cabinet, rotting from the conditions) and stopped pestering me about them. I continuously reassured them I was using the bags sparingly, and if I had any questions I would ask (though I never did, so I was lying twofold). Instead, Mars talked to me as any friend would, getting to know me, and I them. I was beginning to view them as a friend too, as was Rani. That's all I wanted — normal friendships. When we were talking, I could forget about how we met and just feel human.

NO MORE DEATHS or reported attacks. It was not just me regaining normality, but the entire city as they returned to living as they once did.

I got my work done, adhered to deadlines and engaged with my course to the best of my ability.

As always, I met with Rani every Wednesday and eventually Friday evenings also became meeting times, with Mars joining us as well.

Rani invited me to go home with her to celebrate Diwali with her family, and we had such a beautiful time. Her family were so welcoming, with her older brothers being exactly like her: sweet and charming, with energy that filled the room. I felt guilty not telling my mother I was coming back for a few days, but I just wasn't prepared to face her yet. I could manage with staying with

Rani for comfort, because I would admittedly be lost without her company, but… baby steps.

I would sometimes see Ben and Casper and the other two members of the band: Francesca, the pale and petite lead singer, with frosty spiked hair and arms full of random tattoos, and then to my surprise — Lawrence, the guy I met at The Thorns hideout who seemed to pick on Mars. I soon learned there were no hard feelings between the two; Casper informed me they were merely bitter exes, just as bad as each other. That amused me; after all, the Mars I knew appeared to be one to avoid drama at all costs.

It was no coincidence that in the space of a month, I had met numerous members of The Thorns *countless* times. While I stayed well away from the hideout, they continued to appear. Despite Ben's previous denial, I knew they were all following me and checking in, ensuring I didn't go 'feral', or whatever that meant. I welcomed it eventually though, because to me it was a perfect way to prove I *was* perfectly fine and going about my life as normal, like they promised I could.

I never saw Marianne. She struck me as a 'lurking in the shadows' type of leader who only showed her face when necessary. Part of me hoped I would see her again though. In a regular setting. I wished to know more about her and her exceedingly long life; to learn all she had seen and experienced.

I'd come to a comfortable point of coexistence. Not being in denial of their existence but keeping myself separate from it like a curious outsider.

Three weeks of thinking I was fine.

Three weeks of living.

The last three normal weeks of my life.

"So, they think they finally found who killed that poor bloke," Rani said, glancing up from her newspaper, the front page displaying the clarity of her statement. We sat in a sushi bar while rain pelted the pavement and windows outside. It was mid-November.

I'd been waiting for her to bring it up and had planned my response in advance. I had to remember the public consensus was the two other victims had committed suicide and were not murdered in cold blood. I couldn't let my thoughts slip, but my head wasn't compiling my words properly. My script was all jumbled, crossed out, erased and rewritten.

I remember that morning, and the previous few mornings too, I had started to feel a little queasy, waking up each day as if recovering from a night of heavy spirits. Nothing too drastic, but noticeable enough for it to cross my mind. But, like I did with everything, I brushed it off.

"I still can't believe something like this happened. I hope they make an arrest soon and throw away the bloody key. Poor, poor guy." She ruffled the paper, dropping one end to take a slurp of her drink.

The police were looking in all the wrong places, through no fault of their own; they deemed human suspects responsible. It was a dead end. Lucy and whoever else she had working with her were clever and had plenty of experience covering up their tracks. Switch up the deaths to avoid suspicion of a rampant serial killer stalking the streets.

Maybe I could Manipulate the police into knowing the truth? But that's what Lucy had already done, instilling them with false truth. I couldn't work my skill regardless, nor did I feel right doing so after I saw what Ben had to do. I would hate to have anyone inside my head, especially imbuing false thoughts and feelings in my mind. I shivered at the thought.

The Thorns could help. But how? They couldn't risk exposure and the damage had already been done. Their role was putting an end to future attacks, but they couldn't just *frame* someone.

"Arlo?"

"Yes, sorry, focused on... something else. Gosh, no, yeah, awful. Horrific."

Rani sighed, flopping back against the booth. "Are you sleeping?"

Where did that come from?

"Of course."

"Properly?"

"Yes, what's wrong?" I asked a little too harshly.

"Arlo, I'm being serious. You've been up in the clouds these past few weeks. Especially since we came back from my parents' house. Do you want to talk about anything? I told you I'm always here."

I closed my eyes. "I promise you I'm fine. I just think a lot." *Please drop this conversation, I can't take it.*

We stayed silent for a moment, Rani clearly planning her next words carefully. I sensed her quickening heart rate and shifted uncomfortably in my chair. It was louder than normal, yet I'd not long had my own blood, so I was confused as to why my craving was returning so soon. I shifted again, discretely shaking my head. The craving dulled momentarily but didn't fade, which was why I was glad Rani stood, a momentary distraction.

"Carmen should be here soon. I'll go get the drinks. Same again?"

"Erm, yeah, please. No milk. Thanks. I'll pay you back."

Rani threw me a hand that told me not to worry about it then wandered over to the counter without waiting for my response.

I steadied my breathing, grateful for the sudden quiet. No one was sitting too close. *What is happening?* I thought I had this under control. I *did* have it under control; I noted down every time I fed, and for how long, and nothing had changed. I was doing this properly, so why was my brow heating up?

The faint scar on my left palm began to itch. It had mostly healed up from a few hours earlier but there was no reason why I would need it again so soon. *Control yourself.*

Rani gleefully returned a few minutes later carrying a tray of hot drinks, mumbling something about her new friend I was about to meet. I watched her settle it on the table, trying my hardest to absorb what she was saying, but it was no use, all I could hear was her heart, and that of the person brushing past my chair, and the cashier. I needed to sort myself out.

Palm burning, I abruptly stood up and darted straight for the toilet, slamming the door behind me. I didn't stop to look at her reaction, I'd explain when I got back. I felt sick or was I anxious at the prospect of meeting someone new? No. I needed food.

Blood.

I reached into my pocket for the razor blade I kept wrapped up for emergencies, but it wasn't there; it wasn't in any of my pockets. *I never forget it.*

Fuelled with frustration, I banged my fist against the tiled wall, then slapped myself for being so childish. "Get it together," I hissed through gritted teeth.

I paced the cubicle, staring at the floor as my mind fuzzed over. The only way out of this would be to use my teeth. *Like an animal.*

My brain pulsed against my skull and black dots swarmed my vision as if I was on the verge of passing out. I pulled on my hair, suppressing an aggravated scream.

I lowered myself to the floor, knees crumbling beneath me. There was no time for debate. I needed to fix myself. Rolling up my sleeve, I exposed my milky white arm; blue veins tracing the surface of my skin. I took in a deep breath and clamped down on my wrist. Hard. Tendons snapped and my veins teared. My jaw ached as I let whatever lay dormant within me take over.

Euphoria shook me. I'd never taken this much this quickly before, but I didn't even have the room in my head to care. Arlo wasn't there anymore. All that stood in that cubicle was a whisper in the midnight shadows, a creak in the alley gate, the reason children checked under their beds at night. Nothing human would taste flesh and beg for more.

The pounding door stunned my body, preventing the impending and irreversible accident. Angrily, my body shrivelled back down into its human mind, and I could have sworn I felt the returning weight in my chest, if only for a moment.

"Arlo, are you okay in there?"

Arlo. That's my name.

I looked around the room, panting and bewildered. *What just happened?*

A patch of blood marked the floor and I checked my body for any wounds, only then noticing the already fading bite marks on my arm. Two full rows of teeth lined my forearm. A dull ache followed my discovery, causing me to consciously shake my arm, my sleeve dropping in the process.

I bit my arm? What was I thinking?

"Yes! Give me a second."

I EMERGED A MOMENT LATER, after washing my hands out of habit and wiping up the stains.

Rani had already sat back down, presumably to draw attention away from us. I walked back over to the table, frantically blinking away my confusion. Another head had joined us. Carmen. When I rounded the corner back to my seat, I was struck with a heavy sense of déjà vu. I had met this woman before. Choppy brown waves, piercing blue eyes and curves like Aphrodite. I'd even done this before — face her from this exact distance...

"Nice to meet you, Arlo," Carmen greeted me in a delicate voice, lightly turning to address Rani as well, to apologise for being late. "I couldn't find my keys. Tore my whole apartment apart before I realised they were already in my bag." She and Rani laughed in unison. I'll admit my laugh was delayed, yet not through ignorance. *Where have I met her before? Uni? Where did Rani say she met her? Did she even mention where?*

Rani caught my eye and mouthed 'you good?'. I nodded subtly. A blatant lie. *What had just happened to me?*

"Sorry I just need to..." my voice trailed off. Would I really let the first thing that came out of my mouth to a stranger be the fact I needed the toilet?

"Gosh, you're bleeding." Carmen pointed to my arm, where I peered down to see a small but deep red patch on my sleeve that must have soaked through before the wound closed. I slid my arm under the table to avoid further attention. Rani gave me her usual sad and sympathetic look.

"It's nothing. Old shirt."

Carmen squinted her eyes but Rani broke the tension. "So, Arlo, I was just telling Carmen about that time we both walked into that glass door." She pointed over to the entrance.

"Just nearly did the same thing myself. How embarrassing," Carmen snorted.

"Oh god yeah, how could I forget that?" It was probably the last time I laughed so hard that I actually couldn't stand up properly. "It's really polished!"

That encouraged more laughter, to the point where I joined in myself as the memory replayed in my head.

We then somehow got onto the topic of halls of mirrors and fun houses — things we collectively agreed were a menace to society.

Once I'd settled back into conversation, I decided to discretely press Carmen to try and jog my memory of where I had met her before.

"So, how did you two meet?" I tried to ask casually, taking a sip of my now room temperature tea. I swallowed disdainfully.

"Oh, well it's a funny story actually," Carmen started before Rani added, "kind of similar to the way you and Mars met, one of those weird coincidences..."

That's when I knew.

Carmen.

Those ocean eyes, peering out from the shadows of The Thorns hideout. She was one of them. One of *me*.

But I can hear her heart? She's human. A human working with The Thorns?

Dread washed over me. How could I warn Rani? The Thorns had taken things too far now. It was one thing to monitor me, I could handle that now, but it was another thing entirely to invade the lives of my *friends* — my best friend, for that matter. I could not let Rani get dragged into this world. It would be too dangerous. I could not bear the thought of her being put in danger all because of me. *Are they using her to get closer to me?*

"Arlo, are you okay?" Carmen asked.

"He zones out sometimes. Earth to Arlo..." Rani waved her hand dramatically in my line of sight.

I looked up at her jesting, but I'd clearly embarrassed Rani by ignoring the conversation, lost within the depths of my thoughts.

"Sorry. I — I think I just need some sleep."

"Oh, don't worry, I think we can all relate there," Carmen said. "I was just asking what you like to read. Rani told me you read a lot. I'm somewhat of an avid reader myself."

"Oh, right, yeah. Yeah, I enjoy reading. Erm, mostly literary fiction, contemporary stuff? A bit of poetry. You know, the standard English student stuff. I don't really have that interesting of a taste really. I like a bit of everything. You?"

Keep it simple.

"I love a good horror, you know. Not the mundane stuff, like a really gritty, mess-with-your-mind sort of horror. And fantasy, which is probably a bit of a contrast to you."

I got the reference. Carmen knew who I was.

She wanted to play a game? Fine.

"Monsters?" I suggested.

Carmen grins. "Oh, the worst kinds."

We stared head on now. I was trying to suppress my shaking. "Ghosts? Werewolves?"

"Nah, not real."

My hand tried to still my leg under the table. "Serial killers?"

"Boring."

"Psychological horrors?"

"You're avoiding the obvious."

My blood boiled, but I refused to let her win.

"Nightmares... hallucinations... body horror..." I gulped.

"Just say it, Arlo."

"LITTLE WOMEN."

Carmen and I snapped our heads around to Rani, who sat with a pained smile on her face.

"I like Little Women," she said, slapping her lap. "It has good characters. Timeless."

Silence.

Rani turned to me. "Arlo, didn't you need to be going to that... thing soon?"

She's trying to save me, bless her. I can't let her life be taken from her like this.

Rani could always tell when I was overwhelmed.

Maybe I need to distance myself from her for a while. Perhaps it's for the best.

"No, no, you don't have to do that, Rani," Carmen stood up and patted my friend on the shoulder affectionately. "I best be off."

"But—" Rani began to protest.

"Sorry Arlo, it was nice to meet you... properly."

I was stunned. *What was happening?*

Then she was gone.

"I'M SORRY ABOUT THAT, Carmen can get a little... *intense* sometimes. I think it's just her personality. She's harmless though, I promise. I'll explain to her about you, if you want." Rani shuffled back to the centre of the booth.

Really?

"Don't worry about it." *You have nothing to apologise for.*

"I had hoped this meeting would have been slightly more relaxed. I'm sorry. I'll talk to her. She doesn't know you like I do."

I just waved my hand and shook my head, wanting to drop the issue. My head was spinning.

"Okay but Arlo, can I ask you one thing?"

I nodded, though I was concerned she was about to ask me a number of different things I was not ready to talk about. I was right.

"That's not an old shirt, is it?"

I slowly shook my head, resisting eye contact.

"You..." she leaned in, "you're not hurting yourself, are you?"

My head snapped up. "What? No. Gosh no."

"So, what is it then? You've been so closed off over the past couple of weeks. You think I haven't noticed, but I have. You're out of focus a lot more than the Arlo normal. You've lost weight, so much actually..." She looked at me head on. "You keep disappearing and then returning with new bandages on your hands. You constantly look ghastly pale, paler than normal," she gave a small, strained laugh. "You've just... not been here. Where are you? Can I meet you there? Can you tell me what is going on?"

She reached her hand across the table, close enough to me but stopping before it touched me, then it rested out flat. An invitation. I paused before bringing my arm back up from under the table and slowly meeting my hand with hers. Rani's palm was soft and gentle and I bit back the heavy tingles that were making their way up my back. I could tolerate this.

"I'm not going to ask again, but I want to know what's wrong. You might not believe it but I can help. If you'd let me. Tell me what's on your mind, Arlo. I know more than you think, but I want you to talk to me. I want you to *want* to talk to *me*." She closed her fingers over my palm, though not too tight.

I know more than you think.

If only.

I could tell her. I could tell her everything. Right down to the tiny details. But then there would be no going back. She would be part of it all then, and I wanted the exact opposite. I'd be leading her right into the trap The Thorns were clearly already trying to set. I'd be that catalyst. I couldn't have that.

So I did the best I could.

"I've met Carmen before. Be careful."

I left her alone, walking out into the storm.

CHAPTER EIGHT

It is sad to watch his decline.
His stubborn pride.
It is necessary though. He will feel it soon.
My Star.
Come home.

"D rink it," Mars demanded, hurling a cold sack of blood at me and striding into my room less than a second after I reluctantly opened it. It was late and I was just about to get ready for bed, but their harsh knocks rattled every patch of tiredness I was feeling straight back out of me.

They sat themself firmly on my bed in clear refusal to leave.

"Well, hello to you too," I said, taken aback by my own rudeness. I slammed the door shut and threw the bag onto the bed beside them.

A pause followed.

"I don't know why you would lie."

"I don't know what you're talking about."

"Don't you dare." Fire raged in their eyes.

I shrugged. I was playing this part now it seemed. The role of The Fool.

"Why would you lie?" they repeated firmly.

"You're acting like you've just figured this out." A guess, and a correct one at that. Mars had no poker face.

I continued, charged with adrenaline. "You surely would have been able to sense this, I know you're smart, so why now? Why are you only saying this today?"

"I'm concerned."

"You're concerned." I glared at them and crossed my arms.

"Everyone is." Their tone finally simmered.

"Well, I'm fine."

"Ooh, more lies."

"I'm fine. I'm in full control, so you have no reason to be *concerned.*"

How long was I going to keep this up?

Mars stood and began to pace. "What have you been taking instead?" they asked after a beat.

I gulped. Somehow, despite my arrogance, this question stifled me. I think I always understood my own blood could not have possibly been substantial enough to continue taking forever. "Other... blood," I said finally.

"Your own." Not a question.

I nodded.

"Idiot. You fucking IDIOT!" Their scream reverberated through my core whilst their eyes glared deep inside my soul. Regardless of my height advantage, they still managed to make me feel so very small. My mouth grew dry.

"Why?" Their eyes searched mine, pleading to understand, I looked away.

I was lost for words. I truly had nothing left.

Mars started to pace again. "Arlo, I don't know what you think you're doing, I don't know who let you think this was alright, but you are killing yourself. *Killing* yourself, do you hear? I gave you those bags to *help*. I wasn't joking when I said you'd need us, and you know, for a time I thought you'd listen to me. Yeah, you had a rocky start, but we all do. I really believed you would learn to accept this new reality and do what needed to be done to help yourself. But you're doing the opposite, Arlo. You cannot survive on your own blood. It's not possible, not natural. I know you don't want to admit it, I really do, but you are going to be dead in less than a week unless you STOP this nonsense. Let us help you. Please, Arlo. Please. I am begging you. Let. Us. Help."

"But I'm already dead." I wasn't listening.

"No. Don't you get it? Can't you see, Arlo?" They stared at me head on now, eyes pools of pity. "Us, what we are, we've never been more alive."

My brain shut down and I swallowed again. "I can't see it that way."

"Then learn."

I crumbled, stumbling over to my desk chair and rubbing my hands over my face.

"Why do you care so much anyway? You barely know me."

"Because I..." They didn't let themself finish, instead they took a deep breath, composing themself. "You've felt it? The darkness taking over. The complete disregard for morality."

No point in denying it now.

"I knew a girl once. Nice lass, kind. She was so much like you. So full of desire. She had the passion for success and always wanted more. More to life, to the world. A desperate seeker. She worked so hard to find that missing piece, but in the end, even she did not know what that was. She drove herself to the point of sheer exhaustion, yet she never gave up, not once. Not even when she could no longer think straight. She stopped sleeping, stopped going out, stopped speaking. I tried so hard to reach out to her, but it was no use. She'd already set herself out to do this one thing and I was completely helpless. There was nothing I nor anyone else could do to help her and then..."

Mars had tears in their eyes, tilting their head back to blink them away.

"I care about you, Arlo. I don't know why, but I do. You are my responsibility, and I will not fail again. I know what to do now, and I refuse to stand by and watch."

The walls were moving in, the air thinning around me.

They really do care.

All these weeks we'd spent getting to know each other, all the conversations and meetings... *they really are my friend after all.* How was I so blind?

"I'm sorry," was all I could think to say.

"Don't apologise." They perched themself on the side of my desk, looking down to the floor. "Just take the bag. Drink it. Take your time. You'll feel a lot better. You're not weak; in fact, you're quite the opposite. But stop telling yourself you can do this alone because you know, and I think you've always known, deep down, that you cannot keep this up. I want you to stick around. I don't get to save people often, but I believe I found you for a reason, so live, Arlo. Live."

They picked the packet off my bed and gently placed it on the edge of my desk then left without saying another word.

What a funny thing, friendship. The things you do for people. No matter how much you think you know them, you don't.
If I had a heart, a real heart that is, I feel I'd have quite a lot of friends; people to look out for me, and I, in turn, them.
Watching this scene play out is a rather joyous venture, so complex that not even I, with all my sight, can see how it will ultimately end.
I believe I've earned my front seat view tonight.
My evening entertainment, it seems, has begun.
And this, oh... whoever would want to miss this?

. . .

I KNEW what I had to do. My mind still clawed away at itself; one side eating the other. *Don't listen to them. You're fine. Listen to them. You're going to die.*

It's funny isn't it, how I sat there contemplating the idea I could die, as if I hadn't been left dead in the back alley of a restaurant just over a month earlier. If I had known I was to die that night, would I have done something different? Cancelled my date? Walked the other way? Of course I would have. So why was I now cradling my knees in my stuffy dorm room, thinking about my impending second death as if it were even a topic of debate? I wanted to live. Even if 'living' had adopted a new definition entirely. I still breathed the same air, still felt the same sun, the same ground. *So what am I doing?*

Mars' words rang through my mind on a loop. *'You're not weak.'*

People say that when they think they know what you're thinking as though they believe they're one step ahead. They think they can win you over by proving they can read what's on your mind. And yet, something still shifted in me.

You're not weak.

Mars cared. It was written all over them. Was I really going to let them down?

I eyed the bag. It was a lot bigger than the other ones, the ones I — for whatever reason — never discarded. Maybe I always knew I'd have to come back to them eventually. I never really thought too far into the future, but I really believed I had everything figured out.

Mars had made me realise I wasn't just living for me. People actually did care about me. How could I be so selfish?

I had my mum, Bess, Rani. Hell, maybe even Mars after all. They saved my life — now maybe even more than once.

The darkness. That thing inside me... I could feel it getting stronger, slowly sewing itself into my soul, one painful stitch at a time.

Okay.

I closed my eyes.

It falls silent for an hour or so. The interlude, if you were. Two humans circle the building like vultures, that night creature sitting with their back against the corridor wall with an expression I can only read as pain torn across their face.

"I didn't think he'd be that bad." One of the humans says, nursing a coffee from the nearby building.

"I wish I'd known before; I feel as if this is all somehow my fault." The other states, chewing at her fingernails. A disgusting human habit.

The creature remains silent in the hallway, occasionally tipping their ear to the door, waiting for signs of movement.

I grow tired of watching them after a while.

The great and heroic act of friendship is the exact entertainment I had hoped for this dull evening. So concerned for his wellbeing. Keeping an eye out, never being too far away.

You can't stop a fire with pity though.

MARS SAT OUTSIDE, or at least I presumed it was Mars at the time. It would have made sense. They wanted to allow me the freedom of privacy and yet still be there in case of an emergency. I should have been more grateful, yet spite still pricked in me. *I am not a child.*

But I knew better than to continue what I started.

The bag lay before me, warm and sweet liquid swimming within. I paced my room, building up the courage. *This is the right thing*, I kept telling myself.

I had never allowed myself to think of it properly before, but it finally hit me then, as clear as day. I was so ignorant towards my own existence; how could I have ever thought I'd be able to maintain that lifestyle? But the answer hit me just as easily. I never did think of the future. It all stemmed from that. There was never an end goal in sight — just the present and my existence for that exact moment there and then. I never looked ahead. Ever. Even when I tried, I would be overcome with a wave of nausea and a heavy pit would open up deep in my chest, behind my heart, behind my soul. *You'll never make it that far anyway.*

I slammed my palm out flat onto my desk, a rustle of clothes echoed outside the door.

Deep breaths, Arlo.

I'm not weak.

I picked up the bag.

Not weak.

Held it in my hands, eyeing the corner.

Not weak.

It's not hard. Nothing bad is going to happen.

Then everything changed. My breath caught and I staggered back in shock, choking, as a heavy growl clawed through the back of my mind. **Hungry.**

That wasn't me.

That wasn't me.

Help. What is happening?

It's okay, just drink the bag and you will be fine.

I took a deep breath and closed my eyes. *I'm saving myself.* And Mars was just outside. *They will help me if I need them. It's okay. All good. All fine.*

So hungry.

I shook my head, eyes tight shut. How did I manage to let it get this bad?

Breathe.

Feed.

Save yourself.
Surely this isn't meant to happen... it's not that bad... it's not...
Free.
It's so crowded in here.

Oh, what a sight! I'm so privileged. This, this right here, is a
spectacle. A marvel. I've witnessed my fair share of performances, but
this has to be up there with the greatest. His little face contorting in
despair. I can hear his cries even from my distance. Feed the body!
Those pretty, soulless eyes. The beautiful, powerful presence
manifesting as he tears open the bag and desperately swallows every
last drop. I have never witnessed a change of this kind before. I'm
glad I chose this one.
He gags back the remnants of the bag, tossing it aside and wiping his
mouth.
But oh, that's not enough, is it? He has waited far too long!
Interesting. He disappears from the window and into the frosted side
stage where the movements are so sporadic and extravagant, I almost
let out a cry of joy. A crimson delight. A bath of vermillion light.
But oh dear, is that the door I hear? His little friend pounding their
un-beating heart out. So, what will he do? Let them in? Oh no, that
would be such a disappointment. No, here comes the twist. The
audience gasps as he returns to the room, painted head to foot in
delightful colour. Teeth fully grown and back hunched, he looks back
at the door and hesitates for dramatic effect — audience on the edge
of their seats. He turns to face us all, before pulling up the window
latch and jumping out three stories high, landing in the abyss of
darkness below.
I gasp, eyes wide with pride. He's coming.
It begins.

IT HURT. It hurt more than dying. I felt my soul shredding. *Where are my shoes? How did I get here? It's so cold and dark.*
More.

I was running, stumbling, my legs carrying themselves in sought of something. Something? ***Power.***

My head. Get out of my head!

There was blood and mud on my hands and arms. So much blood. *How did I let this happen? Mars said they would help, that I was doing the right thing—*

Oh, shut up! It pounded my head, and I was silenced again. Every second, I was losing grip of the tether still holding me down.

Mars never said it could get *this* bad. *There's something inside my head.*

I don't think this is meant to happen.

Maybe this is something different.

My body dragged itself out into the street, silent except for the occasional whisper of leaves in nearby trees. Street lamps flickered, the cobbles cold against my bare feet. I tried to stop, but it was no use, I was absent in all but a tiny square of my mind. Arlo's consciousness blacking in and out as the *monster* asserted its dominance.

I cried out once more, the body I was trapped in listened to me a final time then collapsed to its knees, staring at the damp ground. I kept staring frantically to the pavement I found myself on, grasping on to that last drip of autonomy I had. A bloody tear fell from my eye, ragged breaths reverberating through my lungs, and then I was gone.

What a sight that befell them as they finally forced open the door. I will never forget the anguished look painted across their face as they ran over to the wide-open window, curtains billowing in the wind, leaning over as if yearning for a lover to free them from the tower.

The humans are not far behind, both equally full of shock and
hopelessness.
The three of them silently come to the same conclusion at precisely the
same time. They are gone in a second, out into the dead of night.

WHERE IS EVERYBODY? Don't they know this body is
starving? My Sun chose this body for a reason and now it
needs to be fed.

They call his name, though he will never hear them. The thing they
are looking for is no longer there. They should call him by his new
name, his real name. Pathetic humans. And the third one should
know better. A verbal warning does nothing against fear. Hmm.
Blinded by an emotion I will never understand.

THERE IT IS. I hear it. My Sun.

He greets me with open arms, canines masterfully elongated. He is
such a wonder to behold; I will never deserve this privilege. I pull
him close, stroke his brow, his soft curls. I let him feed. Oh, this is so
much better than I had hoped. There, there, dear one. Take as
much as you need. Choosing a vampire host truly has been a
wonder.
He grips on so tight, his eyes consuming me.
"It's okay, you are safe now," I mutter, goading him to drink deeper.
I would freeze us in this moment if I could. This never-ending bliss.
He is in pain, that is plain to see. I must heal him.
I pat his head, holding him close to my neck.

He grows limp after a time, finally sated. I have done my part
for now.
I gently lower him to the ground, yet he still grips tight to my shirt.
His actions having decorated it splendidly. One of a kind.
He panics slightly — a child in withdrawal, his breathing sporadic,
his ruby eyes searching for compass.
"Rest now," I say, stroking his brow and his face once more. They're
coming for him. I can sense their cries. I want to steal him away, to
protect him. But I cannot. Not yet. There is still time.
So, I leave him, sad to see him fade. But I must be patient.
I'm gone before anyone registers I was ever there.

THEY CALLED MY NAME, multiple voices at once. I couldn't see yet; my eyes were sealed shut. Was I alive? What a complicated question. I felt alive, but what does that even feel like? It was hard to tell anymore.

"He's here, he's here!" Cold arms grabbed me. Mars' arms. *Mars?*

"Oh, dear lord." A new voice. No, not a new voice. Human. *Carmen?*

I was lifted up, wrapped in a comforting embrace. This time I sank into it, I had no energy to act otherwise.

"He's breathing," Mars said, pressing their hand to my chest. *I'm so cold.*

"Is that *his* blood?"

"Some of it."

"It's *black.*"

"I don't know what was here but that most certainly wasn't human."

"What was it?" Another voice, rushed and distant. Familiar.

Mars' grip loosened slightly. "Let's just say, it appears the world is a lot bigger than we thought."

I eased my eyes open, a blur of images forming before me. There was barely any light yet I made out my three carers. Mars gazed worriedly into my eyes; Carmen stood behind them with a similar expression. The third I could not see fully, but their posture indicated they were the most panicked of all. I didn't want the realisation to sink in. It couldn't be her. No. I swore I'd never let this happen. I tried so hard.

I looked down at my arms, tears healing, scars glistening, hands coated in a dry mixture of my own blood, the bag, and something else, something much darker. And not just in colour. No, this was a deep routed darkness, the hue of true evil.

I looked up again, the third figure now in full view.

Rani.

What have I become?

"I'm sorry," I cried.

The shadows claimed me once again.

Act 2

The Falling

CHAPTER NINE

The new hour chimes were what finally brought me back to the world.

I should have known I'd end up back in that room: my friendly sandstone prison. What I never would have expected though, was to find my best friend in here with me. Rani slept with her head resting on Carmen's shoulder, the two sitting propped up against the pillar in front of me. Both at peaceful rest. Unharmed.

The other unexpected surprise was the buckled restraints wrapped tightly around my wrists and ankles.

But it's what I deserve, isn't it?

My arms had been cleaned. The wounds had mostly healed themselves, but those faint scars would likely always be there, no matter how much my inhuman abilities tried to disguise them: a reminder of my limits.

I don't remember what I did before I awoke there, not clearly anyway. But the strangling dread that encompassed me answered every question I might have had. I lost control. And... *I think I might have killed someone.* I glanced down at my arms again.

My throat burned as I wretched up my insides; my fingers tingled and my back ached.

"Arlo!" Rani was on her feet in an instant, rushing over and mopping up my mouth with her sleeve. I recoiled.

"Get back!" Carmen shouted. She abruptly pulled my friend away and positioned herself between us.

I stared up painfully at Rani who peered over Carmen's shoulder like a startled fawn.

"You can't be doing that," Carmen continued firmly.

My eyes darted between them like watching a tennis match.

"I'm not stupid." My friend pushed herself back in front of Carmen who reluctantly relaxed her guarded stance.

"Look at it Rani, that's not who you think it is."

But it is me. I'm me. Arlo. Please. I'm so sorry.

Rani's shoulders dropped and she let out a huff of air.

"Arlo?" She looked directly at me and lowered to her knees. I followed her with my gaze.

"Rani..." I croaked.

"It's okay, Arlo. You're safe now." She slowly reached out her hand and gently placed it on my knee. It spasmed under the touch but then my muscles relaxed, there was no hostility in the touch. My breathing settled.

"Rani..."

"Right, that's enough, I'm going to get Marianne and let her know it's awake. Stay away."

"He," Rani corrected, brows furrowed as she glared at Carmen with an abrupt tilt of her head. *Does she need correcting? Am I worthy of that?*

Carmen stormed off and my friend looked back at me with that same sympathetic look she reserved only for me. She worried too much.

"How are you feeling?" she asked calmly, slightly stroking my right kneecap with her thumb.

My fists instinctively balled, straining against the cuffs. Rani followed my movement with sorrow in her eyes.

"It's just a precaution. For your own safety more than anything else. You... you need help Arlo."

I dropped my head and blinked slowly. "I know," I whispered my admission and an aching silence fell between us.

"You are safe now though. Do you understand that?"

"I don't know what I did." Repressed fear manifested in my voice; I had given up pretending.

"I know, I know. But it's okay." Her voice was soothing, kind.

"Is it?" My chest bore immeasurable weight as the words squeezed their way out.

She nodded in artificial reassurance. A delayed promise.

Never in my life had I felt guilt as strong as I did that day, like a criminal on death row begging for help, but to no avail. I was a monster. *Why do people keep saving me?*

"Rani, I..." I needed to know. "Did I kill someone?" The night flickered in inadequate flashes, my mind grasping for consciousness in the midnight light.

Blood. That's all I saw.

"No, no." She stroked my leg. "You didn't harm anyone."

"But the blood..."

She shook her head, though I had little strength to probe any further. The guilt was mauling me alive. I clenched my fists again as if I thought I could best them, as I so often tried on those dreaded mornings where I would awaken in a bout of sleep paralysis and convince myself I was strong enough to force my way out of it. But I'd lost all faith in myself then, or more, I feared my own strength. Afraid that if I pushed too much, I'd lock more of my humanity away and embrace the creature I had become... I just wasn't ready to face that yet.

Instead, I relaxed my body and closed my eyes; another technique learned from the stress and horrors of when my mind was awake, but my body wasn't. It calmed me somewhat, but I knew it wasn't the same — it wasn't even close. I longed for hours of just lying there, aching to come face to face with all the horrible things that had ever happened in my life because none would come close to the painful isolation that came with being strapped to a chair, overcome with excruciating regret that I had done unspeakable damage to *everything*.

When I opened my eyes, my friend had not moved an inch from her spot below me.

"Do you know what I am?" My burning question. My most feared.

Rani nodded.

"I'm sorr..."

"Stop that," she cut me off. "Don't even think about finishing that sentence. You have nothing to be sorry for. Gosh, we're back here again, aren't we?" She stood and straightened out her trousers. "I understand why you hid this from me," she gestured to our surroundings, "and I'm not going to stand here and say I wasn't a little bit hurt at first because I was, I thought of a million reasons why it hurt, but that doesn't matter anymore. I've known you long enough to know that you did all this to protect me and everyone around us. You didn't want me to get caught up in all of..." She gestured with her hands again, "whatever this is. You thought you could keep it to yourself and pretend you were perfectly alright and there was nothing to be concerned about. Well, unlucky for you, I know all about this now and..." She held up a hand to halt my intrusion, "I am well aware of the risks and am fully willing to be part of this world if it means that I can keep my best friend alive for the remainder of my life. Yes, that's you. My best friend. Never forget that."

She clasped her hands over her mouth to smother the hysterical laugh that followed. "Gosh this... I cannot believe this is real."

I watched her thoughts unfold — her hands were shaking. *How long has she known?*

And as if she had just read my mind, she answered. "You know I was concerned about you. You have a lot going on in your head that you never discuss, and while it's not my place to pry, I knew this was something else. You were physically and mentally wasting away in front of me, and I couldn't do anything about it. It all happened so fast. One moment I catch you slicing open your palm and feeding like a lamb, the next I'm hushed and hauled around a corner to face these haunting blue eyes. It was Carmen, and she told me everything." Her pace finally slowed. "I know you maybe would have told me eventually, in your own time, but I believe this way was better. She explained to me how they were looking out for you, and I thought that meant she had just witnessed what I had, but I learned only last night she had just seen you feeding, she didn't know what you were feeding *on*. None of them had any idea what you were really doing, only had the physical evidence you were not using what they gave you. I didn't understand the severity of it all; it was all just thrust upon me, and I had no choice but to accept it and absorb what I could. I could have warned them..."

She inhaled deeply to calm herself, clearly trying not to deter from the main story. "Carmen had briefly spoken to me the day before and I recognised her from around campus. She's the year above us, actually, and so we got chatting, and realised we had a lot in common." Rani had begun to smile, but hid it once she sensed her own reaction, a moment after I did.

"Now I'm not naïve. I instantly pieced together she was only befriending me so she could get closer to you. I confronted her about it and she just laughed in return. 'Of course,' she said, then *winked* at me. I felt betrayed but laughed it off — I mean, I barely knew her anyway, but that's beside the point..." Rani shook her head then sighed. "Look, what I'm trying to say is, I'm glad I found out sooner rather than later because now I can be here for you always and..." she looked at my face, the glistening sheen in her eyes fading. "Oh Arlo, *I'm* so sorry." She leaned in for a protecting hug and I sensed her pounding heart, the weakness of her limbs, yet the hunger never arrived. I was so full. *Oh, god.*

. . .

"Arlo." The voice pulled us apart and we both looked over to the arched entrance where Marianne stood, dressed in generic attire this time: jeans and a jumper, I noted. She strode in with Mars and Carmen at her heels.

"It's been a complicated few weeks, hasn't it?" she joked. No one laughed.

Reading the room, she was more tactful with her next words. Her tone sobered at our stares. "How are you feeling?" Her eyes landed on me.

"Like I should be somewhere else."

She cocked her head to the side, analysing me. "Hell? Prison? A dark room filled with all the people you've wronged yelling at you?"

I nodded.

"Good," she asserted, marching forward and loosening my leather cuffs without another word.

"What are you doing?" Carmen protested.

"It's gone."

Everyone shared a look, a whole conversation passing between the four of them — one I could only assume I understood perfectly.

Marianne guided me up with her arms, pulling my full weight and only letting go once she confirmed I could stand for myself. "You don't have any explaining to do. You were not lying then, but I'm telling you now: if you think you can walk out of here like last time, you've got another thing coming. I am not letting you out of my sight until I know what happened and that this won't happen again. Your friend can stay," she gestured in Rani's direction in a motion almost too quick to notice, then stole an irritated glance at Carmen before turning back to me, "but we're sorting this out once and for all. I won't tolerate any excuses."

No one said a word.

"Right," she addressed the silence. "Why don't we start again? Welcome to our world, Arlo. Let's get you cleaned up."

I VERY QUICKLY LEARNED THIS labyrinth of a hideout was much bigger than I originally thought. A *lot* bigger; quite alarmingly so. I didn't even think Marianne was aware of the scope of it as, several times, I witnessed her changing directions and going back on herself. The building was a maze of crumbling stone archways and rotting wooden doors with stairs leading to nowhere and corridors with no end in sight. Every so often, a crack of daylight peeked through barred gaps in the ceiling: a reminder we were probably not as deep underground as it felt. Rani took this whole thing frighteningly well, though her close connection with Carmen seemed to help. I wasn't quite so sure how I felt about Carmen still. Her stare was intense, and she assessed me like I was an escaped, rabid animal. I couldn't really blame her; she was perhaps the only person there who saw me for what I really was. Everyone else acted as though what happened was just a minor blip that could be laughed off as I would soon be able to manage myself. That wasn't true, and they all knew that. I felt like I was walking on eggshells every time I passed someone, even though everyone in this place could have quite easily ripped me to shreds in a matter of minutes.

I'd mentally prepared for the fact they were going to help me manage my diet and 'get me on the right track,' but something much darker needed to be addressed, and the most terrifying thing was, I didn't think any of them knew what to do because I could see it in everyone's eyes; what happened to me, my *body*, my *mind* last night... they'd never seen that happen before.

What if it comes back? What if I lose control again and I really do kill someone next time? I'm no better than Lucy... I'm worse than Lucy. I'm a real monster.

A sick black shadow loomed over my soul with every step I

took down that corridor and I had no idea how I would come back from it the next time it consumed me. I was on borrowed time — time already stolen from a second chance I should not have been allowed. How could anyone help me?

With minimal words spoken, Marianne showed me to my room. It was a lot smaller than the room I woke up in, though a lot more spacious at the same time. The air was lighter, the furniture brighter and it was equipped with a bed that didn't look like a left over from an abandoned asylum. She ensured I was comfortable and told me she would return in a moment after she sorted a few things. I nodded in acknowledgement and was told Rani was allowed to stay with The Thorns. She informed me that Rani would be put up in the room beside me, for our own familiarity. I had a feeling I would be staying there for a while, but I had no qualms with that fact. I shouldn't have been allowed anywhere else.

"FOLLOW ME." Marianne appeared at my door; her peach-tinged hair tied back from her face. She looked like she'd walked straight off campus, not nearly three hundred years from the past. I'd been left in silence for longer than I expected, but I did not dare move; instead, I used the time to fully digest the reality of what my life would now be, though I did not find being alone very helpful. Maybe she was trying to figure out what to do with me, or maybe she really had other important business to attend to. Maybe both.

I got up and followed her around the maze. We did not speak but the tension was minimal. After all, there was nothing to say.

We arrived at a dark room, the furthest downstairs I had been, which seemed extremely fitting for the impending conversation. Mars sat on a chair in the middle of the room and beside them were two other chairs that had been arranged in a loose circle over the spiral patterned cobbles like a poorly attended therapy group careering down a plughole.

I didn't have to be asked to sit. I chose the seat closest to Mars. Call it instinct.

"So..." Marianne began, as if she hadn't been the one to arrange the meeting.

Mars looked to me, a bead of dampness sat beneath their left eye, a subtle indicator they had been crying.

"I..." I barely breathed my unplanned sentence before Mars interjected.

"It's my fault."

What?

Marianne and I turned to face them, waiting for them to elaborate.

"This whole thing," they continued after a deep breath. "I thought I was helping him, but I actually made things worse. So much worse. I'm a complete idiot." This last part was said solely to me. I didn't know how to respond.

"Mars..." Marianne started sympathetically.

"No." They stopped her, both hands raised in surrender. "I was the one who gave him the bags. I should have thought of the dangers, I should have known truly how far gone he was. I thought it would be okay, but I miscalculated, massively, and I nearly killed him with my arrogance."

"No, you didn't," I choked.

They tilted their head and looked up at me with maddened eyes that wouldn't allow me to continue dismissing their apology.

"I told you it would help," their tone settled.

I did trust them, but the decision was all on me.

"I put you in even more danger, and for that, I am truly sorry."

Marianne sighed. "Well," she rubbed her thighs awkwardly. "I'm not going to get in between you two on this front — what happened *happened* and frankly, I don't care who was more in the wrong. I'm here to deal with the now and the parts to come. I want to get to the bottom of what *did* happen and figure out how to help you," she pointed to me, "and keep these bloody streets safe from any more unwanted attacks. I've been alive a very long time, and if there's one thing I've learned over many centuries, it's that everyone is to blame for everything, and it's a waste of precious time to argue otherwise."

The two of us watched her in stunned silence as she walked over to the corner of the room and flicked on a switch, inviting much needed light into the room. It was only then that I could fully take in the scope of the room. It was perfectly circular and the walls were lined with canvas paintings, each separated equally with mathematical precision. Some paintings I recognised: Hokusai's 'Great Wave', Dali's 'The Persistence of Memory', Munch's 'Scream' and then some other more unsettling paintings that made me increasingly more uneasy as I studied them.

Marianne followed my gaze. "You like art?" she asked.

I gulped. "A bit."

She laughed. I looked up at her, confused.

"Your face!" she snorted. I glanced at Mars with a look that questioned this woman's sanity. They only shrugged.

"I forgot they were here, to be honest. Completely unintended, I apologise," she said, continuing to fail at concealing her laughter.

I was completely lost for words.

"Anyway." Marianne finally calmed down, returning to her seat, her serious façade returning. She cleared her throat. "Last night."

Last night. *Where to begin?*

"Tell me everything you remember, Arlo, and we'll go from there."

Mars adjusted themselves beside me, failing to give me full eye contact.

"Not much." I rubbed my hands between my legs, and picked

at my fingertips, trying to keep myself calm. "Sorry, that's not much help."

"Do you remember the daytime?" she continued.

I nodded. That I did remember, in vivid detail. The morning lecture, my uneventful lunch time, my distressing encounter with Carmen and *the blood. The toilet. I lost myself.*

I didn't mention the last parts, though Marianne had lived long enough to read them through my eyes.

"When did you first feel yourself slipping?"

My breathing increased and heat itched around my collar.

"How long after you started drinking your own blood?"

My eyes widened. She knew. I glanced at Mars. *'Sorry,'* they mouthed.

My head darted between them both as the room suddenly closed in on me.

"Days? A week?" she persisted.

I genuinely had no answer. I had absolutely no idea when I started to lose control because the entire time, I remained adamant that I was never *out* of it.

I shrugged.

Marianne chewed the inside of her mouth. "Hmm, okay. Let's try another approach. When did you first feel this *thing* take over?"

Mars tensed to my left.

That I did have an answer to. I didn't even have to think about it.

"The day I woke up."

NEITHER OF THEM expected that response. I hadn't meant for it to sound quite so frightening though. All I meant was I'd felt different since Mars saved me, as though the 'me' I was before had now removed a part of himself and replaced it with something else. Something darker, that I couldn't even explain. Not in the literal sense of 'now I'm immortal and live off blood,' but something more interwoven than that. Maybe that was how everyone felt though, and it was in fact nothing to do with what happened the night before. But my response felt as accurate as it could be and once Marianne got over the initial shock of my answer, she composed herself and rubbed her chin, switching her crossed legs over before continuing with her interrogation.

"How much do you know of our kind, Arlo?"

I gulped. Not much, not really. But I feared that answer seemed as though I wasn't taking any of this seriously and thought myself above it all. "A bit," I said, not really a lie.

"I explained the basics: the feeding, intolerances, things so he could initially survive," Mars interjected. Marianne nodded intently.

"But that's it?" she asked, turning back to me.

"More or less."

Marianne chewed her lip. I wish I could have heard what she was thinking.

"I can teach him more," Mars offered as if they had something to prove.

"We'll definitely need that." Marianne spoke the words absently, lost in her own mind. "But that's not entirely what I was hinting at here."

Mars and I instantly caught on to what she meant, and my stomach sank.

"You know that we are the product of a very powerful parasite," Marianne began. "One that almost perfectly imitates that of what ancient folklore most commonly likes to call 'Vampires'. Creatures of the night. Though history makes these creatures out to be cruel, sometimes even pure evil, we are nothing like that. Our minds remain our own while our bodies become…" Her eyes wandered in search of the right word. "Other."

I took in a sharp inhale.

"It stops our hearts but keeps our blood flowing, keeping our bodies as stable as they were the day our lives were taken from us.

We are corpses frozen in time, with only one thing needed to keep us alive. Blood."

I shivered, monitoring my breathing.

Marianne continued. "Like most human diseases, we can deteriorate without proper care. We must feed, to remain alive. If we do not, we begin to lose ourselves and our minds until nothing remains of our original souls and... well. Then we really die — in such horrible circumstances too."

I didn't dare glance at Mars, though I felt their stare burning into me. This was my warning.

"On the other hand, some of us were too greedy in life, or perhaps just lost their grip on human morals. Their immortality makes them believe they are above everyone else, above the law, and they simply end up doing what they want. Lucy, as we've all gathered, is a product of this. We call them the Turned. Their cruelty is what we strive to eradicate.

We are lucky our scent of Manipulation has kept us relatively hidden from all of society and I would hate to think what would happen if we were ever truly found..."

"But the main thing is, Arlo is alive. And he's safe now," Mars cut her off and I finally looked in their direction to see them leaning forward on their chair as if waiting for validation. A plea.

Marianne breathed out slowly. "Arlo is alive. Thanks to you, Mars. But we are far from being safe."

At least she was being honest now.

"There's something wrong with me, isn't there?" Marianne's honesty encouraged the words on the tip of my tongue. I glanced back around the room at the unsettling paintings that seemed to track my every move.

"There is nothing *wrong* with you, Arlo, but there is something inside you. Something that may have planted itself the day you died or perhaps lain dormant for years before this. I don't know what it is, and I will not lie when I say it scares me a little, because I don't believe it has anything to do with our kind. But we will find out what is going on and I will do everything in my power to help you."

My limbs grew numb and I bent over myself, a strong wave of dizziness wiping my strength clean out of me. A pained sigh escaped my lips.

Mars was upon me in an instant. Their body sheltered mine, protective but not touching. I did not see the face they threw at Marianne, but I presumed it was one in favour of my wellbeing as I heard a low apology mumble out of Marianne's lips.

I didn't need the truth hidden from me, but I also needed to learn how to deal with it better. I was petrified.

"For now, we have nothing else to go off. So as long as we keep an eye on you Arlo..."

Mars moved so I could face The Thorns' leader, whose face had returned to one of sympathy. "You can go about your life as normal, with our help, of course."

Mars looked to me and asked a question they had asked countless times before, yet this time felt like the first. A fresh start. "Will you let me help you?"

"Please," I surrendered, nodding to the floor.

"He stays properly this time. He might even become quite a valuable member, if we train him up." Marianne joined in the conversation, though her tone was still a little unreadable. There was something else on her mind, something she refused to say.

Mars detected this tone too, and I saw the fear claw across their face as their gaze assessed Marianne's reddened eyes.

Train?

The lights dimmed, or at least they felt as though they did. I didn't think it was possible for mood lighting to be automatic.

"On top of everything, someone is hunting him. Some*thing*. I don't know what or why yet, but this is no longer just a case of stopping the Turned. Gather the others."

CHAPTER TEN

I n less than an hour, I was ushered back into that dreaded meeting room: the spotlight stage, I called it. Significantly more members had gathered this time, indicating the severity of the situation. Once again, I was overcome with panic at knowing the focus was yet again going to be turned upon me, and I yearned to be swallowed whole by the stones beneath my feet.

But this time, I no longer felt like an outsider. While I was by no means 'one of them' now, I was no longer fresh meat. I stepped in with slightly more attitude in my step and stood close to Mars the entire time. I'll admit, Rani's presence, alongside Carmen, filled me with a spiteful mentality that I was in on a secret they knew nothing about. I was certain of my place in all this, which helped me relax, at their unfortunate expense. I snapped out of that mindset rather quickly, but my mind had calmed for the moment it lasted.

In the time between Marianne's declaration and this gathering, Mars had taken me back to my room and we'd spoken on topics completely unrelated to this whole ordeal. Part of me was angry they decided to simply ignore the issue, while another part was glad I didn't have to worry too much yet. My mind needed to focus on the present, so I could function when this inevitable meeting took place.

"Tell me about your dog," was their first conversation piece. It was very much a 'your house is burning, and your parents are dead, but look at me, what's your favourite colour?' sort of condescending crap. I played along. Mars had a way of making things work.

I explained about Bess and shared a few stories that came to mind. In good spirit, I asked Mars the same question.

"My younger sister was allergic to pretty much everything, but when I was very young and we still lived in Caloocan, my grandad had a cat — a tabby cat named Sweet. I used to run around playing hide and seek in the bushes until the sun burned my back and I was dragged indoors by my uncle," they laughed in reminiscence. "I played with her more than I did with my friends, and I wonder why I was lonely."

"Pets are sometimes the friends you need," I said, not really thinking too deeply.

Mars looked at me, shock twisting their features. "But real friends are important too."

"Oh, of course. That's not what I meant."

To be honest, I didn't know what I meant at all.

We talked some more, narrowly avoiding the elephant in the room, and it worked, as the hour flew by.

THEN CAME THE ANNOUNCEMENT.

"THORNS," Marianne addressed us all, stood atop her dais. Her voice carried across the hall and everyone turned to face her. Some faces I recognised: Ben, Casper, Lawrence, as well as people I'd seen around the city and therefore deduced they had been looking out for me too. Many were new, however — a vast array of not so friendly looking faces. They stood in clusters, reminding me of various school cliques: the group not to be messed with, the group everyone loved, and the group everyone pretended to love. One group looked like they stepped out of the eighties, dressed in leather jackets and denim. A trio of girls opposite wore matching outfits — fit for the front cover of nineties Vogue. There were also a bunch of, what appeared to be, children, though I deduced they were likely decades my seniors. I wondered how they went about explaining *their* existence.

I considered where Mars fit into this. They were the most outgoing person I'd ever met, and yet they had a side to them that was not too dissimilar to me. Ben and Casper were the popular boys; everyone envied the popular crowds, though I never understood why. People carried themselves differently around them, as if they thought they were somehow lesser beings to them. Lawrence loved it; a blond woman draped across his lap, toying with the hem of his patchwork skirt. Casper had his arm hooked playfully around Ben's neck, but neither of them focused on their audience; they both stared attentively at their leader. I wondered what it was like to have all that attention, all while pretending it wasn't happening. But I suppose that was my envy talking. They were no different from me, not really. I thought back to the night when Ben was outside my flat and we talked about his faith, his family, his feelings. He was hiding so much, I realised. Then again, weren't we all?

Maybe being popular wasn't all that great after all. It doesn't erase your life, happy or sad.

"I'm sorry to have called you all so abruptly, but this cannot wait any longer." The speech began. Carmen stood at the foot of the dais, and it struck me then — that was the exact position she was in the first time I was here: like a henchman, the human foot soldier.

Mars caught me staring and leaned in to whisper in my ear. "Marianne saved her as a kid. One of The Thorns turned and went on a spree. Marianne had to watch him kill her parents and swore she'd never let any harm come to her."

My eyes widened and shot towards Mars. I had no idea.

Guilt inevitably washed over me, reminding me of every negative thought and feeling I'd had towards Carmen. No wonder she was frightened of me. *What if the killer was just like me?*

Marianne continued: "As many of you are aware, we've been working tirelessly for months to eradicate the threat to this city. We've always managed to keep everything under control, but three human deaths in one month raised significantly louder alarms and has had us all on high alert." Her voice did not falter. "Now, in these last few weeks, they seem to have gone quiet, but that does not mean they are finished."

"I would be lying if I said we are not a single step closer to catching whoever is behind these attacks though. As you are all aware, we have a name. Lucy, or Lucienne."

Multiple eyes burned into my skin.

"It is evident she it not working alone, and two nights ago, the patrol group reported unusual, inhuman activity near the old swimming baths. They returned last night, and we managed to ensure a follow up this morning. I can confirm we have successfully reprimanded two potential suspects, who will be held for questioning later today."

Cheers chorused across the room, the group closest to Marianne began patting each other on the back.

"Did you know about this?" I leaned into Mars' side.

They shrugged. Odd, I thought. I presumed Mars was a highly regarded member of The Thorns and would be in the loop on current affairs. I chose not to press it.

"Furthermore," Marianne continued, pausing for dramatic effect. The cacophony of pride dissipated and she lowered her tone while stepping forward. The room fell deathly silent in an instant.

This was the leader of The Thorns. This woman who held true

power and had done for a very long time. Despite her oddities, she meant business. She got things done.

"We also have a few leads in the city's outskirts, too. A singular vampire attack was stopped before the victim was even aware. Threat neutralised."

Neutralised. I shuddered.

"We do not know if this rogue was working with this Lucy, but we succeeded regardless. Well done everyone."

More cheers followed. I made quick work of scanning the room for faces, searching to identify those not so in tune with the truth laid before us: Ben and Casper were amongst them. Their claps were delayed, and I noticed shame — and *disgust?* — in their expressions.

Marianne did not wait long before she cut everyone off again, her voice low and collected.

"Now that's out of the way, as of today, we will be upping patrols. No more niceties. If you find something, anything that is potentially linked, pursue it. If we have any more deaths, police will begin looking for a serial killer, which could put us all at risk. We've kept ourselves quiet for many years now and we're not about to hinder that. We've looked after each other as a family, hidden perfectly from the humans, and we won't stop now. So, with that said, I have decided to commence training again."

Audible gasps echoed across the floor. Some, clearly only a few years into their new lives, glanced around at their peers in confusion. Mars tensed again, though they didn't look to me this time. Rani joined my other side and crossed her arms, her heartbeat had increased significantly, and I could detect a slight tremor in her hands as she tried to contain whatever fear threatened to take over. I no longer felt in the loop, as much as an outsider as she. She may have even been hiding it better.

"Twelve years ago, we lost our most loyal member to the evil of our kind. I had been blind to the fact that maybe we never had his loyalty at all. Darkness fell over The Thorns and many fled — some turning to join him in this betrayal. I made a promise to the human race, and all of you, and I am willing to do whatever it takes. I want you to be ready for anything."

I watched Carmen's face fall in the shadows, her stature depleting.

"Whilst his threat no longer remains, something new has emerged. Something very different, nothing like I have experienced before. An unknown blackness in this reality that I fear has the potential to become much worse."

I sucked in a breath, and almost simultaneously, two gentle hands hovered over each side of my back. A spark of reassurance from Mars and Rani. I couldn't look at either of them, but I wanted them to sense my gratitude.

Marianne stepped down from her platform and began to weave amongst the crowd as she concluded her speech. She knew how to play this.

"I fear the worst. That some other worldly being has entered our world. Whom this creature is, I do not know, but hear me when I say this is no caution; this is an order: watch your backs. There is no version of this darkness that comes from unity. It seeks to cause harm and to toy with us. It is unclear whether it is targeting specifically our kind or not, but if this is connected to our string of murders — which it very much could be — this is not what we predicted. A great death is in the air."

I shuddered again. *A great death. What does that mean?* Why had she chosen to speak so cryptically? She clearly didn't want to alarm anyone, and thus, she didn't tell them about me, or how it was after *me. Something is after me. Something is in me. Something called for me.*

But I never told anyone that part though, did I?

I remembered a voice. One as smooth as velvet, gliding over my soul.

It needed me.

It was waiting.

My legs carried me out before the rest of my body realised. I was out into the cool corridor, pulling at my collar in a second. Mars at my heels, Rani a beat behind.

"You can't keep doing that!" Rani was the first to speak. "A bit of warning please, I'm out of my depth here." Her tone was light-hearted, perhaps to ease the situation, or perhaps because she had not yet grasped the severity of it all. Maybe I hadn't either. Well, I knew I hadn't.

"Arlo, we know very little about this yet. Marianne is purely speculating; she doesn't know anything for definite," Mars said.

I looked up from my half-slouched position against the wall. "So, you knew it was some sort of creature too?"

Mars placed both hands firmly on their hips. "Well, what else could it have been? I used my intuition." Their shoulders raised defensively.

I returned to looking at my feet. "Something is after me." Not a question, I attempted to calm my manner.

"Not necessarily after *you*. Again, this is speculation," they pressed.

"But in the room earlier, she said I was being hunted. I'm being hunted."

Mars stared at me, lost for words.

Marianne was not guessing. She *knew* it and I knew it.

"But whatever it is, we can stop it right?" Rani began. "I mean, what you are," she gestured up and down at us both, "I'm pretty confident you've been around for a while. And humans, look at our history! We're not gonna just get wiped out one wet afternoon in November."

"Marianne has lived a lot longer than us all. She knows things. Many things she keeps to herself. There's no self-help books or how-to guides lying about grand castles guarded by bats. A lot of it we just pass on. How do you think we manage to never get caught? I know some history here and there but the majority of the time, we just want to live normal lives. Marianne is pretty good at guessing, but she's also very good at dramatising things. She wants us to take this seriously. She thinks an other worldly creature has arrived, suspects it's linked to the deaths in this city, and she wants to stop it before things get out of hand.

"Maybe this does have something to do with you, Arlo. Maybe there is something significant about you, but maybe you were just in the wrong place at the wrong time. You're as safe as you'll ever be under Marianne's watch, and we will get to the bottom of it all. We always do." Mars winked at me and held out a hand to help me stand. I obliged and a weight left my shoulders.

A few people had started leaving the room, though no one looked as terrified as I expected. Maybe I had been blowing this out of proportion. I was still on edge from the previous night, and it was all I could centre my thoughts around.

"Well, that was intense," Rani said, attempting to lighten the mood again. "But kind of exciting."

Both Mars and I glared at her in confusion. She burst into a fit of laughter. "Oh, don't look at me like that. I'm surrounded by a conspiracy theory come true, and now I get to hunt demons." She made a sword-swinging gesture before turning to make her way back inside with a bounce in her step, presumably to find Carmen. She was considerably shorter than the wave of people travelling against her, yet it did not phase her. We stood aghast, both rallying questions in our heads.

"She's truly something, isn't she," Mars said.

That's my best friend, I thought proudly.

THE TWO OF us held back to let everyone past, the swarm of bodies all deep in conversation.

"Mars," I said, once the corridor quietened.

"Yeah?"

"You won't tell anyone about last night, right?"

"No one has to know," they promised.

"I won't let myself get like that again. I won't hurt anyone. I'll help stop whatever is after me and the thing inside me. I won't betray The Thorns."

Mars dipped their head, a small smile forming across their face. "I know."

CHAPTER ELEVEN

"So, the training..." Ben started, fiddling with the cross on his necklace. "Are we talking like hand-to-hand combat with stakes and chains or just, you know, psychological mind games?" He reached down to sip his tea.

After the meeting, Mars suggested a change of scenery to clear our heads. They invited me and three quarters of Forever Red (who I kept having to remind myself were managed by Mars themself) to a quaint coffee shop outside of the city centre, a place I was duly promised neither I, nor the band, would be spotted while my lecture hall absence would be explained by a 'funny turn' in my health. They somehow managed to calm me and promised I would be able to catch up on the missed lecture, insisting I was 'clever enough to miss a few'. That last part didn't really help, but I had no choice otherwise.

Rani opted for staying with Carmen in the hideout so they could, and I quote, 'explore.' While I was definitely not an expert on the topic, the more I thought of the two of them together, the more I began to realise that perhaps this was no longer just Carmen's ploy to stay close to me — the ploy which likely ended the second I lost control and was admitted into The Thorns care. Instead, they only seemed to have gotten closer. The nicknames, the glances, the grins. I'd had brief discussions with Rani before and based on what she told me earlier that morning, she was enjoying the way things were going between them. Of course, they hadn't known each other long but what did I know? I didn't understand a connection like that at all. I could barely manage a comforting hug between friends... Flashes of that night near the boathouse hit me. Lucy. Her icy hand under my shirt, nails in my hair, wet lips on mine. I shook the thought away.

"I'M JUST NOT VERY strong, that's all." Ben began flexing his slender arms, waving them dramatically like a jellyfish.

Lawrence sat relaxed with his back against his chair, picking at the snake ring on his left thumb. Something told me it wasn't his choice to tag along. "If you can play bass, you can snap a neck," he said, not looking up from his paint-chipped nails.

The four of us paused to look at him, stunned.

"What?" Lawrence glanced up through his dark fringe.

"Dude, we're in a *café*," Casper hissed.

"I'm just saying," Lawrence mimicked the whisper, dusting imaginary dust off his skirt. He leaned forward, eyebrow ticked high. "Bass is hard."

That was when I heard Ben mutter something along the lines of: "I sometimes play keyboard now though."

I repressed the urge to laugh.

"Is this all a joke to you?" Mars piped up, head snapping towards Lawrence. Casper looked at me from across the table with a subtly amused expression on his face, as if to say, 'here we go'.

"I don't know, is it?" Lawrence bit back.

"People are *dying*."

"People die every day."

"Not like this."

"Please!" I shouted, underestimating the power of my own voice as the people on the table beside us swivelled to face us. None of us spoke until the outside attention faded.

"I'm just making my point," Lawrence said, getting in the last word before crossing his arms and turning away from Mars.

"So... am I mentally or physically punching?" Ben innocently tried to steer the conversation back to the rest of the group.

Mars took a pause for calm before answering. "Mental, mostly. Hopefully."

Ben sat back and absorbed the answer; I watched his hands return to his necklace and he began to chew inside his mouth. Casper's hand moved under the table to pat his boyfriend's knee. Another sign of affection I wouldn't understand outside the realms of platonic friendships.

"It's not as bad as it sounds," Mars continued; all signs of the petty ex-lover persona had disintegrated. "And it's only a precaution. We may never even need to actually put it into action. Marianne just wants us to be ready for every eventuality."

"I saw your reaction in that room though." I would no longer pretend to be naïve.

Mars looked at me and I watched their throat bob. "It won't be like before."

Before.

"The traitor," I tried.

They nodded. The whole table paused as if waiting for the story to continue. *Have they never discussed this?*

"Isiah Dumont," Mars sighed, leaning to prop both elbows on the table, tone darkening. "Marianne has travelled a lot in her lifetime, but at some point in the latter half of the last century, she picked up a companion. Isiah. She believed him young and impressionable but driven. Marianne saw his potential and they quickly became friends, close friends at that. They founded what became

The Thorns and pulled together a carefully curated group of vampires who all seemingly had the same outlook on life after death — humans should never have to suffer. They mapped the country, establishing domains and removing threats where they could. They were a team that very soon became a family. Every time they left a city, a few were left behind to maintain the peace, and everyone proved their loyalty time and time again. They were unstoppable. Isiah was the one Marianne trusted the most; her right-hand man. Then, out of the blue, he Turned."

Not a single one of us so much as breathed.

"It was just over a decade ago. They'd settled here in Durham and things had been quiet for several years. It was a matter of keeping things ticking over. I wish I could tell you this exactly as it happened, but Marianne will never explain that night fully, and I won't press her. I can't even begin to imagine the amount of betrayal she felt."

We all remained static while the buzz of life carried on around us.

Mars sat back. "He vanished one night, completely out of the blue. Marianne went out to look for him and found him with his teeth clamped around a dead woman's thigh. The woman's husband lay strewn across the bloodied carpet of their home, limbs mangled and face unrecognisable, seconds from his last breath. An eight-year-old girl was found hiding behind the TV in the corner of the room; she was unharmed physically but, well, you would be foolish to assume it didn't have a mental impact on the poor kid."

Oh Carmen. I'm so sorry.

"Now, I can't remember if he directed her there in his final moments or whether she simply discovered it on her own accord, but she found his *stash* under the floorboards of an abandoned church. Bodies, at least a dozen of them, all in varying states of decay. He'd been collecting them during all those years of supposed peace. Still to this day, I have no idea how it was never suspected. I can only assume he must have been taking them from further afield and luring them back to that place as a decoy. But he'd been lying to her; maybe he'd always been lying to her, at least that's what she believes."

"She killed him, of course, right there on the spot of his final kill. She staged the scene as a premeditated murder and covered the tracks so investigators would be none the wiser. Then she took the kid and planned her next move. It should have been straight forward since the threat was supposedly eliminated, but as it turns out, others had Turned too, right under her nose." Mars leaned forward once again and tapped their head. "He got into their minds and twisted them all. He made them lose their way. He'd been planning this for a long time, so killing him ultimately made no difference. The worst was yet to come."

"The massacre," Casper interjected. "I heard about this."

Mars only nodded regretfully. Ben and I were clueless.

"She killed them all."

My eyes widened. *Surely, I misheard that.*

"All?" I repeated, awaiting clarification.

Mars shook their head. "She's not a monster; she didn't just line them all up and wipe them clean out. But she was ruthless; she had to be."

The rest of the table waited for justification, even Lawrence who had recently flaunted his lack of care for murder, faced Mars while picking his nails in anticipation.

"She wasn't going to play the fool any longer. She found out every single one who showed signs of turning and *made* them confess. I don't know how aware you all are of the sheer strength of that woman's mind, but if you think you've been Manipulated, you don't know the half of it. She practically burns into your skull: every corner, every crevice, every cell. The average human wouldn't be able to take it, they would crumble in seconds. But she did what had to be done for the safety of everyone."

We all stared blankly; it didn't take a genius to figure out we were each thinking the same thing.

"But don't worry, she always knows what she's doing." Mars' tone turned almost comical.

"That doesn't help," Ben croaked, at the same time Casper's louder voice asked, "and the training?"

"Well, you can imagine The Thorns were in a bit of a state after that. We had to be rebuilt, create a fresh start. It was less than two years later that I myself was changed. I'll spare you the details on that one," they cleared their throat, peering down at the table for a moment, "but things like that obviously leave you with a few trust issues. So she set about training us up for the eventuality that this would happen again. She strengthened our minds and bodies alike so we would never stray. So that we would be able to defend ourselves and humans alike, if another Isiah emerged amongst us." They leaned back and smiled. "But I know that won't happen." Then they looked at *me*, briefly, but clearly. The sounds of the coffee shop suddenly got louder and louder until I couldn't take a deep breath. When had it gotten so busy in here?

"Hey, hey, Arlo." Mars caught me spacing out and extended their hand. "I mean it. It's not going to happen. The killer isn't a Thorn. We know that."

"Do we?" My head felt tense and my brows furrowed.

Mars nodded, as did Casper and Ben.

"This isn't any different than anything from the past decade. Our kind likes to travel, and we're not all so nice. Just like humans. There are rotten apples in every orchid. Lucky for you, we've got a lot of experience on this turf and you," they playfully tapped my shoulder and an uncomfortable spark shot down my arm. I ignored it as best I could. "You have nothing to worry about."

"And the creature?" Ben asked.

"Is nothing but an idea," Mars concluded.

"Mars, I'm not stupid," I said, holding out my arms to expose the scars beneath my sleeves.

"Oh, I know. But none of us have any leverage to go on. You were vulnerable. A hunter sought its prey, it's nature. I'm not ignoring Marianne's prediction, but I'm also saying we can't fret over things we don't know for certain. For all we know, this creature is just like us — a different strain, if you will. We don't know what it wants, and so all we can do at present is be cautious."

"How can you be so... calm?" I raised my voice, the tremor distinct.

"Because I've spent too much of my life worrying over things that would consume me entirely otherwise. Nothing is going to happen to you; I will die before I let it, and I intend on sticking around until the end of this great place called earth so..."

"They're right," Lawrence added, all sarcasm removed. "Even if this creature ends up being something entirely not of this world, The Thorns will not go quietly, and *they*," his head jolted sincerely in Mars' direction, "always keep their word."

I ALWAYS WONDERED how certain things in history went completely unnoticed; all those snippets and details lost in time and forgotten in ignorance. After everything I experienced in that month with The Thorns, my mind wandered to all those other possibilities. Somewhere out there, someone had narrowly escaped the fate I succumbed to. Somewhere else, another Arlo might exist — another person going through exactly the same thing as me. Maybe they had friends to help them, maybe they didn't. I would think long and hard about what sort of advice I would give them, how to offer comfort while promising things would be alright. But could I say that so confidently? I'd been told on infinite occasions that everything would turn out for the best. There was always someone out there experiencing a lot worse, people would say. It will get better! Don't worry about it! Move on! Smile!

And I did. I smiled in that coffee shop, with Mars' promise and Lawrence's comforting affirmation. For the first time in my life, I had companions. A group of people who would look out for me and protect me. But how many more times could I hear those promises before I no longer believed them to be true?

I felt safer then, safer than I ever had before, and so I blamed myself for my stubbornness. My stubbornness had gotten me into this mess, and once again, I was letting everyone else get me out of it. I could let myself believe that The Thorns were powerful enough to stop the murders, and that maybe, just maybe, the creature who caught me was nothing but another hungry parasite that merely needed to be lured back into its cage. I could believe that. I could believe I was safe with Mars and Marianne and all the others. Yet one question hung over me, no matter what anyone said: were they safe with me?

It called for me.

There was something in me only Carmen claimed to see — something I believed only Carmen *could* see. It made sense now. You don't witness what she had at her age and live the rest of your life basking in fields of flowers and frills. Carmen witnessed that darkness first-hand, and she knew it could never leave. Marianne knew too, though she would never let on.

I was Arlo then, in that coffee shop, drinking tea with four people who swore to watch my back. And I would hold my promise to Mars: I would be Arlo until my head hit the dirt for the final time.

But no matter what I did, and no matter how hard I tried to fight it, the shadow remained locked around my neck, its talons digging into my flesh, biting deep.

Arlo would never give in, but sometimes we don't have a choice.

THE NEXT HURDLE was the simplest. We left the band to attend their recording session and Mars walked me back to my room to help me clean up the mess. I knew it was coming, it was unavoidable, and so I uttered no complaints as I crouched on my knees and began to scrub.

There were flashes, intermittent shots of the night before. All my inner turmoil. *Had it really only been a day?* Less than that, even. I kept it down.

"How are you doing?" they asked me, bending down to my level. They had gloved up both arms and carried an extra bucket full of soap. I had made such a horrible mess. There was blood everywhere, even in places I thought impossible for it to reach.

Why can I still barely remember the events that led to this? How did I let this happen? I shuddered.

"Coping," I replied, scrubbing harder on the tiles at the entrance to the bathroom.

"You know," they found a clean spot and crossed their legs beside me — voice pleasant, "when I first turned, I ran off twice. The first time, I didn't get far, but the second time? It took Marianne three days to find me."

I dunked the sponge in the bucket and wiped my brow. "Where did you go?" An appropriate question, I thought.

"I ran as far as my legs could carry me, which, as I'm sure you're now aware, can be quite some distance."

"Why?"

"Why did you refuse the blood?"

I stared back at the tiles, hit by a memory of tearing one of the bags open with my teeth. "I wanted to be in control."

"Precisely. When we first turn, we think we can rule the world, or so to speak."

"So, you didn't cope either?"

They shook their head. "I told you. I knew what it felt like. We have to look after ourselves a lot more than a human has to. They starve, we *change*."

I flinched at the word.

"Sorry." They looked at me apologetically. "It's probably useless saying this now but it does get better you know. Once you find your feet, you'll be able to go a lot longer without drinking anything. Look." They stood, and I tracked them with my eyes as they stepped over to my makeshift kitchen stand and pulled out two random mugs. Mars walked back over to return to their position. The clattering sound pierced my ears as they set the mugs down on the tiles and rifled through the bum bag around their waist. They produced two small sachets of... well, I knew what it was the moment the mugs were placed before me.

They poured the viscous liquid into both mugs then handed one to me. I took it, reluctantly, and made eye contact, as if waiting for approval.

"Maybe this would have been a nicer approach," they chuckled slightly.

"Maybe."

"Rat blood, sweet and easy to come by."

I looked at them, repressing the urge to vomit as I thought of sewers and subways. The smell coming right to the front of my mind.

"What? Did you think we constantly raided hospitals? We're meant to be looking after humans, not making things worse. We can't catch any diseases or sickness from any blood, so we do what we can."

That was a very valid point, I thought. I hadn't even considered that.

"Cheers," I said and we clinked mugs. Mars took their sip a moment before I allowed myself. I could only bring myself to take the smallest of mouthfuls, letting the smooth liquid slide down my throat. I willed my mind to stay open at all times, refusing to let anything in. Mars studied my reaction closely.

It worked. I felt nothing but that familiar zing before returning to normal. Maybe the monster was further at bay than I thought.

Mars smiled at me. "See, not so bad, huh?"

I let out a deep breath.

"Oh, you've got erm..." They leaned forward and their arm shot out to wipe my lip. Their slender, brown fingers lingered a moment too long before I jerked away and wiped down hard where their touch had been. Mars backed up in a panic, shaking their head out of whatever trance they'd been lost in. "God. Sorry. I got carried away. You... you don't like touch, right?"

"It's not that I don't like *touch*. That's a very broad term and encompasses many things..." I was angry, but I wished I wasn't. A knee jerk reaction.

"Shh, you don't have to explain." They smiled again. "I over-stepped the boundary. Let's start over." They took a long sip of their drink. "Rani seems to be handling all this very well."

"Yeah," I agreed. "Frighteningly so. She's just straight in there. I don't know how she's always that brave." I swirled the blood around a bit before sipping some more. A dull sweetness lingered in my belly.

"It's because she cares about you."

"Yeah, I suppose." My mind wandered.

"A lot," Mars pressed.

I pressed my lips together in hesitation. "We've stuck close by each other these last few months and we knew each other before moving here. Familiarity, you know? I don't think I do well in new places."

"Yeah, I get that. I was seven when I moved over here; I couldn't speak a word of English and I was just expected to blend in as if it's the easiest thing in the world. Well, I quickly discovered it was not."

We both laughed.

"So, have you ever been back then? To the Philippines?"

"Once. It's not exactly around the corner, but it was nice to see my grandparents again. They never change, probably never will. Maybe they're immortal too," they joked.

I never knew my grandparents. They both died either before I was born or shortly after, and my dad's side might as well have not existed at all. I didn't say that though. No need to dampen the mood.

"You mentioned you had a sister?" I probed, just trying to make the conversation flow.

"Yeah," they said absently. "Poppy."

They didn't continue and I feared that I'd already managed to ruin the conversation. "We don't have to—"

"She passed away."

My chest exploded. "God, I'm sorry, I didn't..."

"No, no. You couldn't have known. I don't really discuss it, ever." They downed the rest of their blood. "Don't worry about it. Please." Mars smiled.

But I could only sit and watch as my surroundings fuzzed and warped around me.

"Don't get hung up on it, honestly. It's completely fine. Anyway," Mars gestured with their hands, "let's get this place cleaned up."

"Yeah..."

It surprisingly didn't take as long as I had originally anticipated to get the room somewhat back to normal; in fact, with Mars' help, we were done in no time. I washed the window frame as casually as I could in case someone were to see me from outside.

We worked mostly in silence and I blamed only myself for that matter. I shouldn't have pushed, but I was glad they felt able to share that with me. Maybe we were becoming good friends. Was this friendship? I needed to be kinder to them. As they scrubbed the walls, I kept looking over and watched as they and brushed their hair behind their ears. What was that moment? My lip still tingled from the touch, and I instinctively pressed my thumb to it as though to wipe away the sensation. It was nothing. Just a friend helping a friend. *But what if they...* I shook my head. I couldn't bring myself to think of it. Mars seemed so genuine and kind, and they *were* attractive, but I just couldn't... *do* that. *What is wrong with me?*

Chapter Twelve

I'll wait for him. He will come to me. He always does.

"I had a look into that name you gave me: Lucy, Lucienne. I asked around a bit. No one was willing to give me any information, or more, no one had any information to provide."

It was the following day, and we were back at the hideout. I'd slept in my own bed that night, mostly buried under the covers and squeezing my eyes tight in desperation, yearning for sleep to take me. My room no longer felt like my room anymore. It was beginning to hold too many scenes I would rather have forgotten.

Mars met me in the morning and walked me back to join The Thorns; we strolled mostly in silence, but there was no awkwardness between us. I spent the entire time stealing glances at them and trying to figure out what made me worth all this. They could have all left me — or killed me even, because that's what I deserved, for everyone's safety. But they didn't. If anything, I felt closer to The Thorns now than I had with any group at school. There was this unspoken unity and respect, something I'd so ignorantly turned away from. A family.

MARIANNE WAS PACING as Mars and I sat on the couch opposite her.

"You would think that sort of green hair would be an easy marker, but nope," she continued, hands finding her hips. "Apparently university students had a meeting and decided natural hair colours just weren't cool enough anymore."

"I mean, why not? Uni is all about finding yourself, right?" Mars jested. I forced a delayed chuckle. That had been my plan, to find myself. *Now perhaps I never will.*

"We're sure she's the one doing the killings though?" I asked, though it was half a question, half a request for confirmation to ease the darkness in my mind. I already knew the answer, I just needed to ask one last time.

Marianne twitched. "Most likely. But like we've said before, she can't be doing this alone. Even the youngest of our kind know it would be stupid to enact so many close public killings in such a short space of time. No, she's with others. How many, we do not know, but all we have to go off is your description and..." She gestured to the medieval style door to our left, "those two."

I'd almost forgotten about the two captives.

"What are we waiting for, then?" Mars stood up eagerly and headed over to the door. I watched them go, confidence and impatience radiating from every stride. Marianne looked as if she was about to stop them, but held her tongue.

"I'll get them talking," Mars said, fishing out some keys and preparing to open the door. "If you had told me they were here all along, I'd had done it a lot sooner." I sensed some bitterness in their tone, and one glance at Marianne confirmed my suspicion.

"Now, now, Mars... there's a reason I—" The creak of the door cut her off as Mars was already heading down the stone steps and into pitch blackness.

She sighed, pinching the bridge of her nose before heading down after them, leaving me with no choice but to follow.

I'D SEEN plenty of action films to have a clear idea of what a secret holding cell looked like, and this was a perfect example. There were no lights except for two burning torches on either side of the walls, and a tall iron cell sat right in the centre. Mars was already inches away from the bars, scraping their keys across the iron to attract the attention of the two figures in the corner. Their backs were hunched as they turned to face us, yet their dark clothes made it difficult to decipher anything about them.

"Well, you can hear me alright," Mars started; impatience laced their tone.

Not a peep.

Marianne pulled Mars by the shoulders. "Come on, step back," she said, but Mars shrugged her off, refusing to budge. In fact, out of sheer stubbornness, they took a step forward, so that they were practically pressed against the bars. They grabbed at the poles and pressed their face in between. "I'm talking to you. It's rude to ignore people, you know," they shouted, voice echoing into the void.

"Mars!" Marianne yelled.

"What?" They spun around sharply, the 't' harsh on their tongue with a scowl fixed into their usually friendly face.

Marianne lowered her tone. "Safety. Please, Mars."

I tried to think of a way to intervene, but decided against it. Yet Mars listened to Marianne that time and walked towards me in a sulk, brushing past a concerned Marianne in childish defeat. "Do it your way then," they muttered.

This tension between them had nothing to do with me, though I stood still when Mars came to my side, and I flashed them a sympathetic smile, which they half-heartedly reciprocated.

We then watched Marianne's attempt. She glided over with an air of grace and professionalism. Her voice angelic — hauntingly so. Even Mars sensed the shift, and I watched their shoulders straighten as they watched their leader.

"You will tell us what you know about the recent killings here in the city." Her Manipulation was so compelling I found myself wanting to confess my own deepest thoughts. The sheer strength of this woman petrified me.

"Nice try," one of them muttered into the darkness, a low gravelly voice.

That didn't phase Marianne at all. "I was just getting started," she said, proudly. I felt her grin from across the room. "*Tell me.*"

A ruffle of clothes and a scrape of metal echoed against the stone floor then one of them stood, turning into the light and stepping forward to face the leader of The Thorns. A young woman, or so it seemed, with soft ginger curls and the purest of faces. She could have been ancient for all I knew, but then Mars gasped, and I turned towards them.

"Jade?" they questioned, stepping closer. The creature behind the cage stepped to one side to peer over Marianne's shoulder, her cold expression loosening into a grin.

"Well, well, now *this* was most unexpected." She licked her lips, fangs flashing in the amber glow. "They got you too, huh?"

I didn't see Mars' reaction but Marianne turned around and faced them with remorse. "I did say..."

Mars knew this person. Most likely from when they were alive — someone significant enough for Marianne to have also known them. *A friend? Ex-partner?*

"It's been a while, hasn't it? Still masquerading as a student or have you moved on from that now?" Her tone adopted a patronising edge. "I didn't last long doing that; people are a lot more observant than you think, aren't they?"

Mars stayed silent.

"I bet you feel good seeing me like this though. It's what I deserve, right?" Her brow quirked up and an evil glint shone in her golden eyes. This was no friend.

"Got a new pal?" Her gaze jolted towards me, making me involuntarily gulp. Definitely not a friend.

"Shut up." Marianne snapped back around. The woman — Jade — staggered back with force.

"We're not here for a catch up. You don't deserve that." She made a brief glance to Mars then turned back. "Tell us what we want to know. Now."

Her words shook the room, and the other assailant stood to face us as well. A much older looking man with a scar across his nose stood, easily a foot above Marianne, but she did not cower an inch as he walked up to the bars and glared down on her. Instead, she repeated herself, one final time.

The man seemed to be holding back words, attempting to maintain composure and dominance. Finally, he released a heavy breath and stepped back slightly. Jade glared at him in annoyance. "Fine," he said. "We'll tell you what we know."

"Lovely." Marianne clasped her hands. "I knew we could come to an arrangement."

"A group who call themselves The Torches started making the rounds a few months ago," Jade said as she started to pace; still acting in power. "They were young, newly formed, and misled. We managed to stop them multiple times, but then things got out of hand."

"They go after people who wronged them in life," the man started.

"Petty revenge," Jade added.

"We have nothing to do with the deaths though, so you're wasting your time there." He squared up to Marianne again.

"I even tried to intervene. That night, when you caught us stalking what you presumed was prey, you got it all wrong. We were stalking The Torches. You missed the mark completely." Jade smirked.

Anxiety began to creep in again. *We nearly caught the culprits, then we let them get away?* I thought. *They're all still out there. Still lurking.* I bit my tongue.

Marianne stayed calm. "But you could lead us to them?"

Both of them nodded in unison. "Right this very second," Jade added, her pitch heightening with ego.

I didn't buy it. Something felt off. Mars' body language indicated the same, but there was no way they could outsmart Marianne. Neither of us said anything as our leader slipped over to the lock and began to open the gate. The two took a slight step back to let the gate swing open. *We're doing this now then. Finding the ones responsible for everything. Finding Lucy.*

But instead of letting them out, Marianne stepped into the cage, closing it behind herself in silence. Mars ran over in a panic of realisation, but it was too late. I didn't move, frozen in place while Mars shared woeful eye contact with their leader and desperately rattled the door. Marianne didn't face them. I was rooted to the spot, watching the next scene play out as if it were a dream, where even running wouldn't take me from where I stood.

Marianne, who was significantly smaller than the two captives, strode over to them with solemn grace. Both of them looked between each other in silent conversation. I saw a flash of silver born out of Marianne's swift wrist movement, then watched as in the space of a second, she slashed out, causing the man to fall to his knees, the dimness of light hiding the violent act. Jade had no time to react, as in a stroke, Marianne danced so delicately around the fallen body and slashed a gaping hole across Jade's neck. The wet crunch sound of snapping bone and cartilage echoed through the room as the light left her eyes almost instantly. Jade grabbed at the easily fatal wound while Mars rammed themselves into the bars in terror. My eyes were fixed only on the death dance that unfolded in front of me. It was like a work of art, if the devil could paint.

Marianne knew this routine inside out, stepping out of the way of monstrously grasping arms and leaping onto the back of the maimed creature, repeating motion with her knife before twisting herself off like a feather. The monster, three times her size, crumbled to the floor with a thud, head barely attached.

Mars continued to shake the gate until we both simultaneously realised there wasn't a single drop of blood on Marianne. She wiped sweat from her brow, hair slightly displaced, and eyes a cold, bloody blue. Carelessly, she dropped her weapon into the heap of corpses below her, then stepped over their bodies with fire in her eyes. She waited for Mars to move away so she could exit, and I realised at this point that I had somehow made my way closer to the cage, perhaps having stumbled over in a trance. Marianne unlocked the door between us and let herself out, without muttering a word nor taking a glance at either of us.

"What—" I managed before Mars overpowered my voice.

"What was that for?" they screamed, arms outstretched and brow scrunched so tightly.

Their tone had no effect on Marianne, who carved her path between us and headed towards the stairs. We turned to face her in unison, exasperated and afraid.

"They were lying," she finally said so confidently with her back to us. "None of it was true. No such thing as 'The Torches', they know our name and attempted to mock us. They killed the first victim. "

"Then..." Mars started, seemingly breathless.

"They were under a much stronger mind control than I thought. Something so strong that I've not seen in a very long time. Something ancient, and I'm not talking about this creature following Arlo, no. I know this. I've seen it and it looks like I'm outmatched here. This is a lot worse than I expected. I'm starting the training tonight. Gather the others, Mars. We're preparing for war."

· · ·

"WAIT! PLEASE." I chased them up the stairs, Mars having inevitably stormed after Marianne, demanding more information.

I was still replaying the scenes in my head, shocked at how this petite, charming woman was capable of such cruelty and violence, but then I recalled the story Mars told me earlier that day about the massacre. Her wrath.

"Wait!" I shouted again, but they'd both already made it through the door and back up into the central compound. I paused to take a breath, glancing back behind me into the pitch blackness, where I knew two bodies now lay strewn across the bloodied floor. *This is my life now.*

I was sick of people babying me, acting like I couldn't use my own brain and had to be force fed information in small, sugar-coated amounts. There was something after me, and yet everyone was acting as though it was something mundane like a trial fire alarm. Innocent humans were being murdered in the streets and we were no closer to finding the rest of the culprits, and I was being thrown into the deep end of this whole historical mess, with a ring to keep me afloat but no legs to swim with. Not only was I distressed by what I'd just witnessed, I was infuriated and confused.

I finally caught up to Mars who was shouting at Marianne, words marked with elaborate hand gestures. I caught the tail end of it, or more, I provoked it.

"...and now we've got to protect *him* from something clearly far worse!" They jabbed a hand in my direction, accompanied by a scowl of anger.

I stopped dead, arms dropping loose by my sides. I'd never heard Mars that angry before. And this was... *my fault?*

"Now, now, Mars. You're frustrated and upset and I under-stand that. I didn't tell you about Jade to protect you. You would have done the same." Marianne's tone was casual and relaxed like always, as if the last twenty minutes had never happened.

"This is *not* about Jade!" Mars snapped.

We'd reached a main corridor now where a few people milled about and turned to face the commotion. Upon realising it was their leader, they turned back to what they were doing, acting as though they hadn't heard a peep.

Since I began my stay, I was growing increasingly more aware of how much of a status Marianne held within The Thorns. She was a born *ruler*.

"Hall. Now. Everyone," Marianne shouted over Mars in complete dismissal. I watched their face drop.

The five people in front of us started to move and Marianne barged past Mars to get to the front, leaving them with no choice but to give up.

At least we were in the same boat now.

Mars looked at me but I dared not speak after that. Their face cooled and eyes drooped downwards with a sigh. "Sorry," they said, genuinely.

I was caught off guard, still reeling over the events in my head as I tried to figure out where I went wrong. Words failed me.

"I... seeing Jade triggered me. She, well... Huh." They shrugged, brushing a hand through their hair, pushing back stray strands. "She made my life hell."

I simply nodded in understanding; I figured that was the case. I tried to picture a younger Mars, more shy and reserved perhaps, with their innocence stripped away from them.

"Then when..." they looked over to where Marianne had been moments before, "she did *that*, I dunno I just... I wish..."

"She'd been more honest?" I suggested.

Mars nodded slowly, then their expression morphed into one of realisation and guilt.

"I guess that's how we've all made you feel lately. Out of the loop. Truth watered down."

I shrugged, but they were right, of course. "For my safety, right?" I didn't mean to sound patronising.

Mars' eyes glistened, a partial huff of a laugh erupted from them. "I suppose."

"I just hope she knows what she's doing," I said, staring off into the distance.

"I hope so too."

Chapter Thirteen

"We're putting an end to this." Marianne stood before a handful of us, adjusting her hair with a stern look on her face. More of The Thorns filtered through after a while and I started to recognise many of the faces. This community. *My community?* I still couldn't remove the memory of how easy it was for Marianne to kill. And she was our leader.

"Something happened. I can tell something happened," Casper announced as he and Ben found their way over to us. "She's got that look on her face."

"Death look," Ben added in a much lower tone from behind his boyfriend. He was playing with his cross again.

Mars explained the past hour, albeit briefly. I stood silent, playing it out in my head as Mars spoke. I watched the shift in expressions over Ben and Casper's faces. Casper took it with a serious nod, like he'd seen it all before. Ben blinked multiple times. Three to be exact. I glanced back to Casper, who at that exact moment, looked to me. His seriousness softened. "I'm sorry you had to see that," he said. I hoped my expression was one of acceptance as I didn't really know what to say.

The room was significantly colder than it ever had been and I tugged at the sleeves of my jumper — a habit I couldn't get rid off.

"Some of you have done this before, most of you will think I'm patronising, but all of you need to listen regardless." Discussions in the hall dissipated as our leader's voice carried.

"Manipulation."

Blood sprays across stone.

"Our kind's greatest gift."

Light leaves her eyes.

"Our most deadly gift."

Body thumps to the floor.

"We think because we ourselves have mastered it..."

He cries out.

"That we are immune."

A guttural screech.

"But we're not."

Thud. Thud. Thud.

"Do you want to end up like those two?"

My mind snapped and I looked up. Marianne stared straight at me, eyes trapping my very soul. Everything else blurred around me. *She's coming for me. I'm next. This is it.* White noise. Static. Buzz.

I squeezed my eyes shut. Tight.

A clap.

A screech.

Then the sounds stopped.

I finally let out a breath as my lungs relaxed.

Looking back up slowly, I found Marianne sat on her chair in the middle of the room. She wasn't looking at me; in fact she was barely looking at any of us, which was when I peered around the room and noticed every single person was standing, mouths agape in horror. Some rubbed their eyes, while others rubbed their throats.

I turned to Mars, who simply stared straight ahead, but I

noticed their hands were clenched tightly into fists, knuckles white.

My eyes wandered to Casper and Ben. Both staring forwards too, almost as though they were in a trance. A single tear trickled down Ben's freckled cheeks.

I wasn't imagining it then.

We *all* were.

Manipulation.

"Lesson one, you all need to work on your mental guards."

THE NEXT HOUR that ensued was most unpleasant.

I decided, in one of the brief moments when my mind was *not* being attacked, that Marianne would make a terrible school teacher. I nearly laughed at my own joke if it were not for someone else invading my head and bringing me to my knees, which, by that point, were severely bruised.

I scanned the room frantically for whoever had infiltrated my mind and at last locked eyes with what appeared to be about a seven-year-old girl, hair in pigtails. She winked at me, yet we lost eye contact as someone was thrown between us.

It was getting very loud in there.

"What's your biggest secret?" Someone — Lawrence — demanded. Though it wasn't directed at me, something dripped from the tip of my tongue. I stopped myself. And apparently so did Lawrence's opponent because his request elicited no response and he repeated his question in frustration.

"Excellent work, Matthew." Marianne's voice carried through the crowd as she leaned over to pat Lawrence's opponent on the back. I was still on my knees and struggling for a breath when she noticed me and shook her head, but not through disappointment.

"Get up," she said. And I did. Quite easily. *Too easily.*

"Face me." Another demand. Behind me. Casper? I didn't have time to try and block the demand.

I turned to face Casper who grinned, his smile then moulding into a laugh.

We were the same height, but I don't think I'd noticed that until now. His deep brown eyes met mine. "Hit me." The words left his lips so casually.

I went to raise my hand, but then... *no.* I stopped. *I can't do that...*

Casper frowned and tilted his head. "Why did you stop? I said hit me." He spread both arms out wide in encouragement.

But I didn't. I couldn't. I lowered my hand, coming back into myself.

"Good," Marianne said, and I spun back around to face her. She was clapping.

Casper came up behind me and playfully patted my shoulder. Leaning in close to my ear, he said: "Well your morals are intact," he laughed, but I felt dizzy.

"You can do this, Arlo. Don't give up." Marianne smiled the same smile from when we first met. My shoulders relaxed somewhat. *I can do this.*

"Ben, kiss me." Casper backed away from me and skipped over to his boyfriend who crossed his arms with a frown. "That's cheating, you know I'd do that anyway." Casper leaned in and bent down to meet Ben's softening face, the pair shuffling into the shadows and into each-other's arms.

I'm so... huh...

Marianne's hand on my shoulder startled me, and if I had a working heart, I know I would have passed out by now. Stressful situations like this *hurt.* I struggled to know whether I was coming or going.

"Urgh, lovebirds. That won't help them in a fight though,

would it?" Marianne whispered, slowly gliding her arm around me to capture my full attention.

She took me by the hands as if initiating a dance and then I was being dragged through the sea of people as if we were lovers on a secret escape, the world disappearing until it was only the two of us.

Marianne pulled me to the opposite corner of the room behind her makeshift throne. It was quieter there, so my brain could somewhat relax and I could regather my thoughts and my surroundings.

"You would think they all would have learned by now. It's not the first time I've done this. I bet half of them can't even remember."

Her bluntness sent an uneasy shock down my spine. A lot of things this woman did unsettled me, and it was becoming increasingly clear why she was the leader above everyone else.

"You Manipulated everyone?" I asked, brow tensing.

Marianne shrugged, her copper-blond ponytail slipping over her shoulder. "They need to be prepared for this world."

"And that's how you go about it?" Anger burned through me, mingled with confusion.

"After earlier? I wish I did it more."

"But our minds, shouldn't they be ours and ours alone?" I lifted my chin in feigned confidence.

"Our minds..." She reached up to delicately catch my head between her hands. I twitched at the sensation but then relaxed into her touch, comforted by the strange warmth emanating from her. "Our minds are never just our own. But we *can* take control."

I didn't follow.

"I know all too well the power of Manipulation. Isiah..." she trailed off, but her soft hands remained at my temples. "The only way I can prepare you all is to expose you to your vulnerability."

"And you think it will work?" I breathed.

"Most certainly."

I swallowed hard. I was so vulnerable — we all were.

Marianne gently removed her hands, and I straightened my back. "We will find Lucy and put an end to this."

She didn't need to Manipulate me; she knew I would agree with her.

"And the creature?" I inhaled.

"Destroy it."

I WAS PUSHED BACK into the crowd and it was like I was falling. Marianne's face faded from my eye-line as I plunged back into the void of mind stealing, but her words from before stuck with me. *I am not weak.*

I took a few deep breaths to catch my bearings — or I tried to at least. I felt high, almost floating, with my feet above ground. Voices echoed all around me.

I attempted to look for Mars, Rani, Carmen... *are they even here?* I thought I spotted them earlier but then I wasn't so sure of anything anymore. I couldn't believe anything that was happening. *Our minds are never just our own.*

But I did see Lawrence, who in turn, spotted me. He prowled over to me with a haunting grace and wrapped his arms drunkenly over my shoulders. Very quickly, it became apparent there were multiple substances in his system, eyes unfocused and jaw slack.

"Let me try this," he whispered. His breath tickled the nape of my neck, messy brown curls falling across his face in a hot mess.

A shiver rumbled in my gut.

"Love me," he grumbled. I tensed, waves of heat passing through my body. I forced myself to stay put, hands firmly by my side.

Lawrence frowned in expressive over-animation, his arms remained flopped around my neck.

"Aww, you're getting better then," he smirked before twirling around my body in one fluid motion, coming to a stop behind me.

I followed his movements in what felt like slow motion; he was at the crook of my collar now, leaning in so close I smelled the stench of cigarettes and alcohol on his breath. "Come on. You know what they say about guys with big feet." He jabbed his knee into the back of my legs and my nerves reacted. I instantly lost balance and coughed with the dizziness of how hard he tried there. The drugs clearly weakened the level of Manipulation he believed he had. Or maybe I just...

I saw a flash of his mesh skirt before a familiar figure stormed towards us: slender legs in leather trousers, striding over in confidence. I looked up.

Mars.

They didn't even look at me before their fist plunged into Lawrence's abdomen and they pulled him close with protective aggression.

"Leave him alone," Mars demanded through clenched teeth. Their fangs lengthened as they held a startled and delirious Lawrence by the scrunched fabric of his shirt.

I watched all this unfold from the ground, my palms flat on the cold stone.

Mars loosened their grip once they sensed they'd subdued Lawrence enough. They brushed off invisible dust from Lawrence's shoulders with a firm and sarcastic touch. "Do whatever you want to me later, but you leave Arlo alone."

Lawrence was then sent on his way with a push.

Finally, Mars' attention shifted to me, all anger leaving their body as they reached down to help me stand. I was too startled to speak at that moment.

I held onto Mars' hand for a second longer than necessary, grounding myself before dusting my trousers as I finally stood straight.

Reality flooded back, and I rubbed my forehead. "You..." *Don't pry. It's none of your business.* "You meant that... that last part?" *What did I say? You never listen.*

But Mars wasn't phased by the question. "He won't remember a thing in a few hours. I could have said anything."

"Oh. Right."

At my response, Mars cocked their head. "Would that bother you? If I meant it?" they quizzed.

Panic inevitably took over. "Oh, god. No. Not at all... it's none of my business, really—" I shook my hands frantically as I tried to explain myself.

Mars narrowed their eyes but softened a moment later. "I didn't mean it."

"Oh, right. Okay... good..."

"Good?" Their brow raised. I couldn't read their face, sweat dampening my brow.

"No — not that. I didn't mean..." Words betrayed me.

Mars finally shook their head in a laugh. "You're so funny."

I am?

"I—"

A gut-wrenching scream broke the moment. Everyone's attention swung to the scene unfolding in the centre of the room. A crowd had already formed in front of me but my height advantage allowed me to just about make out what was happening.

Over the commotion, a glint of silver shone as a bloody arm raised up into the sky. Multiple gasps blended with the wet crunch that followed as a knife plunged down into someone's chest.

CHAPTER FOURTEEN

The room erupted into chaos. A few people screamed in horror but most simply stood frozen in shock. It was fairly obvious someone had just Manipulated someone else into killing — or at best, maiming — another. But regardless of the circumstances leading to that point, someone was bleeding out horribly on the cold, dead floor and someone else was armed.

Marianne came into swift focus, shoving her way through the crowd to reach the centre. Mars pushed themself past my shoulder; Marianne's second-in-command knowing exactly what to do. They reached out in force for the attacker, who was now stood in shock, eyes glassy in a fresh state of realisation. Mars disarmed them and pulled the assailant's arms behind them in a firm restraint. They didn't resist.

I was close enough by that point to be able to watch as Marianne and two other Thorns tended to the victim, who as I noticed once I glanced down, was left lying in a sickening, bloody mess of their own body. Their entire chest cavity looked to have collapsed inwards; exposing shredded fabric and what could have easily been broken ribs. A steady flow of red pooled their body.

Marianne supported the head and didn't even flinch even

when the victim coughed up blood and it sprayed up into her face. She remained calm and collected as if this was a mess she had cleaned up countless times before. Another Thorn pressed a piece of cloth, torn from their shirt, at the victim's throat to try and slow the arterial spray from the lacerations. Someone retched then began to vomit behind me. Ben.

Casper was instantly at his aid, supporting his boyfriend's posture and I caught the soft assurances beneath his breath. "It's okay, Ben. Marianne will save her. You know she always does."

Ben appeared to be reliving something, and I paused as the words sank in. There was still so much I didn't know about these people: their lives, their pasts. I perhaps should have been glad I did not understand why this had triggered him.

My gaze wandered back around to the horrific sight before me. I thought, rather morbidly, how peculiar it was that it was possible for that much blood to be given off without such thing as a beating heart.

I was undoubtedly in shock. My mind had a tendency to wander when that was the case. I felt separate from my body, like I was astral projecting and not physically present.

Mars had since dragged the danger away, to where I did not know, but my only focus was on the body before me.

Someone caused this.

Was *I* capable of such a thing?

'Your morals are intact.'

No, of course not.

But that night.

What would I have done if I had not been saved?

THE VICTIM'S name was Elise, a girl I learned had been turned not long before Ben and Casper. Another vaguely put result of 'being saved by Marianne'. I had learned to never push for further details because my mind always filled in the blanks. This particular case was easy to deduce, merely from the whispers painting the room.

I was sitting in a side room with Ben and Casper, who had ushered me away from the scene once we knew Elise was going to survive. (How, I will never quite fathom, but it was a relief none-theless.)

"You see, this was what I was afraid of," Ben piped up, his voice pitched a little higher than I remembered it. "This fighting amongst us. How can we ever know who to trust?"

Casper sighed, seeming unsure of how to respond. "I guess we just don't." He brushed his hand over his shorn red curls.

"What was she trying to achieve anyway?" Ben snapped, raising his hands in frustration.

"She needs to know us." Carmen's voice slipped through the doorway and I was relieved to find an unharmed Rani loitering behind her. My friend sped up once she saw me and instantly joined my side, her eyes silently searching mine for a reassurance that I was okay. I believed I was, at least on the surface. I nodded.

"She needs to get to the very bottom of who is a Thorn by *soul*," Carmen continued as she entered the light, crouching to sit cross legged on the ground in front of us.

I couldn't help but feel like she was directing that statement at me. A habit I appeared to have developed over the short time of knowing her. I tried not to make eye contact.

"By getting us to kill each other?" Ben's voice rose. "I thought these lessons were to help us work *together*, you know, for the 'greater good.'" He emphasised the last part with his fingers, while Casper's hand stroked his leg in comfort. They looked at each other in mutual sadness.

"She's trying to strengthen our minds to prevent another

attack like Isiah's." I didn't hold back, blurting my thoughts out into the open. "She thinks someone very powerful is behind this, and after what we saw…" I realised then that Mars wasn't in the room with us and my voice and confidence dwindled. Everyone was looking straight at me in alarm. A thousand eyes. My chest stung.

"I think what he means is…" Rani broke the silence in my defence. *God, I love her.* "Marianne understands the power she's seen over her lifetime and she's worried now that we're not prepared for what she thinks is coming. It was all a test to see what she has to work with."

I looked up at her the same time that she looked at me. "Thank you," I mouthed.

Carmen's tense manner softened a tad and she looked to Rani with… pride? I didn't really understand it, but my mind calmed at the gentle look they both exchanged.

"You're strong enough, Ben," Casper continued, still comforting his boyfriend.

"I know, and I know I'm maybe overreacting, and I know we should trust her, but I just… I don't like it." Ben hung his head low, hands going back to his cross. I turned away in respect when Casper then leaned down to kiss Ben's worried hands; it felt too intimate of a moment for me to be present in.

"You should all try practising with each other, but not in unruly groups like that. Work on each other, instead." Carmen gestured around to the room's occupants, and we all nodded in slow agreement.

"Arlo, you can practise on me."

My eyes widened. *I must have misheard.*

But no.

Carmen was speaking directly at me with an air of confidence filtering over her quickening pulse. She was frightened of me, that was undeniable. But she didn't want to show it and she was doing an excellent job.

"And me," Rani added, moving closer to Carmen so I could look at them both clearly. Ben and Casper remained silent until all I could hear were heavy breaths and the syncing heartbeats in front of me.

I scare them.

I never meant for this.

I never meant for any of it.

"Okay." I swallowed my words.

Rani nodded and Carmen reached up for her hand, squeezing it tightly.

I was suddenly hyperaware of how unintentionally but obviously alienated I was in that room.

⚜

I caught Mars coming out of a stairwell as I stepped out into one of the many corridors making up The Thorns' home. They were evidently distracted, and I noticed as I let my focus wander, they had blood on their hands. The corridor was badly lit but I could smell the sweetness of it. *What did they do?*

"Arlo." They turned to face me, stunned by my presence. Their face glowed under the torch on the wall. Their tone was a mixture of shock and relief.

"What have you done?"

Mars frowned, confused. "Done? She'll live. Elise, the girl, she's going to be okay."

Realisation kicked in.

"That's..." I studied their hands and they raised them up to the light.

"Elise's blood."

Elise's blood.

"What about..."

"We locked him up, Marianne is with him now. He'll be guarded all night."

Good. I let out a deep sigh of relief and brushed my fingers through my hair.

"Don't worry too much, Arlo. I know that was pretty horrific, but trust me, Marianne has dealt with much worse. She'll sort this out."

"Will she...?"

They shook their head. "She won't kill him. Not unless she really has to. She's not a monster, Arlo, but she does what needs to be done to keep us all safe. She'll make the right call, she always does."

I ran out of things to say. I was anything but reassured, but once again, I felt like I had no option but to go along with things. I accepted there and then that I would always and forever be out of my depth.

"You okay?" Their tone softened and their head tilted slightly in focused sympathy.

I took in a deep breath and nodded. All I could manage.

"Want to go for a drink?" Mars suggested. "The alcoholic kind," they added before I had a chance to ask for clarification.

"Very much."

"Good. I know just the place."

It was a tight squeeze, accompanied by extortionately overpriced drinks, but of course, Mars knew the owner. A quick handshake, an inside joke and a free whiskey measure upon arrival secured our seats right by the window. I took off my long coat and rubbed my hands together for warmth. Mars followed up with a question on what my preferred drink would be and then informed me — much to my disapproval — the evening was to be entirely on them.

The whiskey had already warmed my insides by the time Mars

sat back down with our drinks. I'd been spending the last few minutes looking out of the petit window before me, eyes dancing over each twinkling Christmas light. People passed by at an array of speeds, each person with a clear destination in mind, all displaying varying expressions and carrying various quantities of bags. Kids dawdled, teens laughed, grandparents sighed. Everything was so... normal. So human.

"Good choice, by the way." Mars' voice tethered me back to myself.

"Oh, thanks." I picked up my glass and swirled it around a little as Mars took a sip of their own drink.

"I never understood the hype around Christmas." Mars was looking at the same lights I had been focused on moments before. "I get the whole religious aspect, obviously, and families coming together yada yada, but I swear Carey's been wanting me for Christmas since the end of August, and I'm thinking she should have taken the hint by now."

I snorted into my drink and Mars' face glowed, a smirk forming like they were testing the waters of my sense of humour. At least I understood that joke.

I wiped the embarrassing dribble off my chin. "I fucking hate that song." I don't know why I felt the need to swear.

"I can probably list a grand total of two festive songs that don't make me want to stick a knife into my ears."

"Go on then." I turned to face them, smug, my legs dangling off the high chair and my hands clasped together.

"Right, now don't judge." They raised a serious hand.

"I haven't even opened my mouth." I was grinning.

"Last Christmas."

I paused, considering. "Okay, I'll give you that. Halcyon days."

"It's the only one my grandad knows all the words too; he sings it to me on FaceTime every year without fail."

My grin shifted into something more genuine. I tried to

imagine a much older version of Mars in a party hat, all jolly and expressive, imbuing pure love into every line.

"Okay and the second?" My smile remained.

"You have to promise you won't laugh at this one."

"You saying that is only going to make me want to laugh more."

Mars rolled their eyes and took another large sip of their cocktail.

Then instead of naming the song, they started to belt: "The boys of the NYPD choir..."

My initial reaction was the typical introverted embarrassment that a scene was being caused around me but the alcohol in my system let me laugh. I was still slightly embarrassed at the fact Mars was drawing attention to us in such a small and cramped space, but a quick glance around told me everything I needed to know, because a second later a woman behind us continued, in full volume, and by the end of the chorus, the entirety of the bar was singing or laughing or raising a glass. I looked back at Mars, who was looking at me too, and I'd never felt so light.

We ordered another round. Then another. More whiskey. More cocktails.

The edges of my vision quickly softened, and my head started to feel weighed down, but I needed this. And Mars was just as bad, if not worse.

We avoided all topics relating to The Thorns for a long while.

No mention of Marianne.

Or the creature after me.

Of Lucy.

Nothing.

But of course, we eventually ended up circling back to that night.

Four rounds deep I asked, "Why me?"

After their fifth shot and a wink they replied, "Why not."

My seventh shot. "I wasn't worth saving."

"Oh, you fucking were."

I was still very much present and in control, but my filter of modesty had skewed.

I leaned in. "Tell me why."

Mars' face seemed off. I couldn't make out the freckle I thought they had on their cheek. The one shaped like a heart. I was so close, but my eyes couldn't focus on it.

Mars leaned closer still so our foreheads were practically touching. They reached out to grab the back of my hair so that our heads collided. Their fingers knotted through the overgrowing waves, hand heated and clammy. I had no desire to move away or untangle myself though, I was looking directly into their blurring eyes.

"Because..." their voice rolled, and before they had a chance to finish the sentence, their grip loosened and they fell off their chair, falling to the floor with a thud and causing several customers to startle around at the scene. In my drunken haze, I followed them down, laughing uncontrollably as I attempted to pick Mars up off the ground. But when I heard them snort and figured out they were laughing too, my legs gave way, all semblance of strength leaving with my voice. I too was then seated and bruised in a heap on the floor. I hiccupped and Mars laughed even more, then I pulled my coat off the chair in an attempt to help myself up, but it fell directly over my head and the next thing I knew, Mars had crawled under the jacket too, their face flushed.

"Peekaboo!" they shouted, then hiccupped, then in a second their expression faded. Their eyes rolled and their face dropped, and I was suddenly propelled backwards as Mars darted upwards and raced towards the toilet, holding their mouth. I followed as quickly as I could manage, catching up to them in the toilet cubicle and offering in a blinding haze to hold their hair as they began retching into the toilet. We were still laughing the whole time, babbling about how we fell while badly attempting to reenact what had just happened, multiple times. The two of us, then staring into the cubicle mirror, tried to compose ourselves but continued falling into fits of hysterics when we both acknowledged how drunk we were.

"You're so tall," Mars managed to say as we stared head on into the mirror. They raised their hand up and patted my head with an audible 'bop' sound before hiccuping again. Neither of us were able to contain ourselves.

"Well, what if you're just exceptionally small?" I recognised the drunken slur of my words and the delay of my blinking, but it did not phase me in the slightest.

"How dare you insult me?" Mars folded their arms, puffing out their bottom lip like a stroppy child.

I immediately panicked and apologised multiple times, my hands flying about as I tried to explain that I didn't intend to be rude but then Mars' seriousness left them entirely and they grinned. "Your face! Ha!" They patted my nose twice. "I was only joking. My sister was five nine."

Sister was — past tense. Poppy.

Mars gave me no time to dwell — I was already being dragged out of the cubicle and back into the bar. I stumbled back over to retrieve my coat and down the rest of my drink (a dangerous mistake), and then Mars had me by the arm and we left the bar with a childish skip. I just about managed to catch the eye of the bartender, who must be used to seeing Mars like this, and I waved a bleary-eyed thanks. He put down the glass he was polishing to wave back, throwing me a thumbs up as we stepped out into the cold, late November night. Mars was spinning around, arms wide and tilting their head back to catch the snow on their eyelashes, as though in a movie. All composure left me, and I found myself running after them — or stumbling to be more accurate — falling into them and hugging them into my arms.

"Thank you," I said into their hair. I meant it deeply.

"For what?"

"For saving me."

· · ·

THE NEXT FEW hours were what I could only describe as fluid. We swayed from one motion to another as a wave would caress the beach on a calm evening. We had no control over any of it — or at least it felt that way. We stumbled back to The Thorns base, and I, without considering the fact that Mars would inevitably follow me, made my way towards my room. In my current state, however, everything looked the same. Lost and confused, we passed a lot of 'shhh' sounds to each other as we stumbled through the corridors and attempted to suppress our laughter. We found it eventually, Mars swinging from the crook of my elbow as I pushed open the door and we both collapsed onto the bed, creasing the sheets terribly and scuffing our dirty boots across the covers.

We weren't thinking. I wasn't thinking. *I don't feel this.*

In a rush, Mars pulled my coat off — and I let them. I didn't even watch how carelessly they threw it to the ground — it didn't matter — nor did I stop to consider how this entire situation was making me feel. I didn't stop at all.

Through a fuzz of black and white and static, Mars took my head in their hands, and we shared not even a full breath between us before they took my lips in theirs. I was numb, aside from the tingle shooting over my lips and tongue, but I didn't pull away, I don't even think I knew how to. Instead, I stayed close as Mars kissed me again, whiskey and mint hot on their breath. I believed I was kissing back, though I wasn't sure what that was supposed to feel like. Hot. Passionate, maybe. I eventually reached out to mirror Mars' movements, threading my fingers through their soft hair, and accidentally pulling it out of style, but they didn't appear to be bothered at all.

What am I doing? I couldn't even answer my own question.

Mars adjusted themself on the bed so that their hands were at either side of my body. I instinctively leaned back, their body parallel to mine the whole time until my head hit the soft pillow beneath me, and Mars was leaning on top of me. My breathing grew shallow as they slowly leaned down, body lying flush with mine. Their face blurred, and they kissed me again and again and again. Deeper. Faster. Our teeth clashed and I thought I heard them laugh a little. I laughed too, deep down, somewhere.

In the heat of the moment, my body became weighty, and I sunk into the sheets. The air felt damp and sticky, and Mars shifted their body over to one side as their left hand began to toy with the collar of my shirt. I watched them play around with it, brush it between their fingertips. We were both slightly out of breath, the only sounds in the room coming from our mouths, and the occasional ruffle of our clothes against the sheets.

"Can I take this off?" Mars asked heavily. They were talking about my shirt. *They want to take my shirt off.*

I nodded. A radio fuzz of blind sensations.

And so it began.

Whether it was the alcohol induced state or the mere weight of what was about to happen, I'll never know for sure, but Mars took their time. As if they were working in slow motion. They unbuttoned right down my chest until they had to pull the rest out from under my trousers. They tugged at my shirt until they could brush it over my shoulders, the cold air hitting me rather unpleasantly, but my limbs were way too heavy for me to shield myself as a sober me might have done.

Mars caged over me then, lowering their mouth to my throat, along each collar bone, and down over every inch of my chest. I let out a sound somewhere between a moan and a gasp, but I couldn't fathom why. *I don't feel this. Not like I should.*

Mars paused.

Eyelids heavy, I lifted my head up to look at them, but I could only make out the outline of their body. Mars pushed a finger to their lips, then leaned back on their knees and climbed off the bed. I struggled to keep my eyes open, but the last glimmer of curiosity allowed me to watch in the blue haze of midnight light while Mars tip toed to the end of the bed and began to undo my shoelaces. I was too weighted to help, but they managed perfectly fine on their own. They bent down to remove their own shoes then waltzed over to the corner of the room; the light filtering through the crack in the door outlining their curves. Reaching the cabinet fridge, they pulled out a wine bottle of sorts, and without even realising it, I had somehow managed to sit up fully and I reached an arm out for the bottle in Mars' hand. I could smell it, the sweet bitterness of blood. I needed it. Craved it.

Mars took a dramatic gulp in the shadows, using their whole arm to wipe the stain from their lips.

I barely managed to make an audible sound, but Mars seemed to understand and passed me the bottle. Upon grabbing it rather greedily, I tipped my head back and savoured the taste as it slid down my throat. I swallowed once, twice, three...

"Enough! Don't waste it all!" Their voice had gone all deep and gravelly which oddly made me chuckle as I was overcome with a strong wave of confidence.

"Come here," I begged, clearing my throat.

I begged?

They crawled back over the bed frame to straddle me again, kissing me instantly. This time, the lingering saltiness of blood left their lips and my senses heightened, forcing me to inhale deeply as my eyes burrowed deep into my skull.

Too much.

I grasped for their face — something to ground me — then rolled our bodies over so that I was on top of them, looking down to their pretty face and protruded canines, exposed in a lazy grin.

"Can we?" they started, tilting their head and peering down at my neck.

"Can we..." I mumbled in repetition. It wasn't a question; my mind just didn't go there —*couldn't go there*— no matter how hard it tried.

They answered themself by reaching down to my belt.

Oh.

I pulled back, my full weight sitting over their thighs. Mars' hands danced over the hollow dip under my ribcage, down over my abdomen, and to the fine hairs over my lower belly.

I nodded.

I nodded.

"Yes."

"Yes."

BREATHS. In and out. Hands. Touching. Heat. Touching. *Oh.*

I AWOKE as the mattress shifted slightly beside me and opened my eyes to a pool of jet-black hair and the smooth brown curve of Mars' back. I didn't dare move a muscle, and instead observed the sight in front of me. I could just about make out three identically shaped moles dotted down their back and I related them in my head to that of Orion's belt.

Pretty, I thought.

Alcohol and blood still shrouded my system, and I drifted off again.

I WILL POSSIBLY NEVER BE able to fully explain what possessed me that night, mainly because I was slowly beginning to realise I could never picture myself with someone, whether it be romantically or sexually. The idea itself just wouldn't compute in my brain. Fade to black. I believed it to be a fault, dodgy wiring of my brain, something that had to be fixed, and I thought that night with Lucy would cure it. But if I had control of my own mind in that moment, I would have never agreed to it. If I'd known to shield my mind, then my whole life would have turned out different. But as it stood, this was my life now. My world. And I had no choice but to be part of it.

The two of us, Arlo and Mars, in an equally drunken state,

sought comfort in one another that night. That's the only way I can describe it.

But lying in my bed in the dark, head still spinning with Mars beside me, fast asleep with the bedsheets slowly rising and falling with their every peaceful breath, I only felt guilt.

I could never love like that.

WHEN I AWOKE the next morning, the opposite side of my bed lay empty, the sheets having been tucked back into place as if they'd never been touched at all.

Perhaps I had dreamed it all. Mars' hands on me, the kisses, the sweat, the heat of our bodies.

But I knew I hadn't.

It was real. Whatever that meant.

Chapter Fifteen

I lay in my bed, unmoving, for nearly an hour. My thoughts were the only things to keep me company as I fixated on what we did. What I allowed myself to do. *How could I do that to Mars?* I didn't know how they felt about it, or if they actually wanted it — if they even enjoyed it. How did they feel about *me*?

I had lost track of how much we'd had to drink. At the time, I thought it was what we needed but I'd never before let myself get that drunk; that out of my head.

But what I did.

Knowing I couldn't connect that way.

How could you?

How could I face Mars now? Tell them the truth?

I LAY STATIC. Paralysed. My eyes wandered to the cobwebs on the wall and down to the mess of clothes I expected to see... except they weren't there. My floor was spotless. I frowned, darting my eyes around the room for any sight of them, but then I noticed my jacket hanging up on the wardrobe and knew fine well that was not where I left it. My boots were neatly tucked under my desk, the space where I normally like to leave them in my dorm room... My chest ached.

Mars cleaned up.

I flopped onto my back and rubbed my face, noticing the dried blood on my hands and on the sheets.

Mars cleaned up.

I needed a shower.

IT WASN'T until I heard the knock at my door that I was shaken out of my trance of watching blood trickle and swirl down the shower drain. I quickly dried off, noticing the array of towels I'd been left with. I threw on my trousers and jumper from the night before and ran to the door as the knocks intensified. If my heart still worked, it would have been pounding in my head.

If Mars was on the other side of the door, I would not have known how to act or what to do — at all. A million scenarios and responses played through my head all at once, making me dizzy.

But it was Rani, smiling, with a mug of tea cupped in her hand.

"Oh. *Oh.*" Her eyes widened as she gave me a quick once over.

My jumper was on back to front, my hair stuck in all directions.

Her eyebrow ticked up.

"It's not—" I began to defend myself, but she cut me off.

"You don't have to explain," she winked, "boys have *needs.*"

My laugh came out delayed as my brain processed what she said. It was just a joke, nothing to get worked up over, but... *that's not me. I'm not like that.* I didn't have *needs.* I'm just *me. A little bit broken.*

She read my face and sighed. "If it makes you feel less embarrassed..." she leaned in and whispered, "I had some fun last night too."

I took a deep breath. "You did?" I tried to stay calm and take the focus off myself. "Carmen?"

Rani responded with a head flick that indicated she wanted to come inside. I pulled the door wider upon instinct, darting to make my bed and to cover up the blood as she entered. I panicked at the sheet's lack of cooperation, and instead opted for crumpling it all into a ball in the middle of the bed where most of the stains were. It was too late and too obvious to do anything else.

Rani didn't sit down like I expected her to, though. Instead, she strode straight through, throwing her arms out and forming claws with each hand. "Oh, that *woman!*" she passionately shouted out to the room.

I stood awkwardly by the door, jumper still reversed.

She turned to me, eyes like headlights. "Oh, Arlo, I think I'm in *love.*"

I made a 'heh' sound in my throat and fiddled with the silver ring on my finger, an attempt to act casual.

"You two are... together then?" I asked.

At that, she flopped herself dramatically onto my pillows, and I took that as an indication the conversation could only properly continue if I went over to join her. I strategically laid over the remaining blood stains.

"Well..." she started, exasperated. "Not like *officially.* But..."

"You're happy?" I suggested.

She turned her head sharply on the bed to face me, eyes still so full of life as she bit her lip. "Happier than *ever.*"

I smiled at her then as her positivity radiated off onto me.

"I'm glad." I wish I said it with more meaning, to truly show how happy I was for her.

She playfully punched my arm. "So what about you then?"

My lungs constricted and I averted my gaze, eyes drifting up to the ceiling. "Oh, we don't need to talk about that."

A moment of silence followed. Rani propped herself onto her

elbows. "Oh, don't be shy, your secrets are safe with me, my guy."
She tapped her nose.

While I knew she wouldn't embarrass me or do anything to
intentionally make me uncomfortable, I just couldn't — on any
level — bring myself to talk about it. How could I possibly explain
it? It wasn't the fact I didn't *like* Mars: Mars was great, and they
saved my bloody life, for goodness' sake. It didn't, *couldn't* make
sense to not want what we did, but *I just didn't want it.* Out of
everyone, Mars should have been able to fix me, and instead I felt
like I had used them. *How could I have been so cruel? So heartless. So
numb...*

"We don't have to talk about it if you don't want to." Rani's
voice grew solemn but sincere.

"Thanks."

AFTER DRESSING PROPERLY, I headed out for some breakfast
and didn't bump into a single Thorn. A blessing.

At some point between returning with Mars and the rise of
dawn, the snow had melted, and then heavy rain must have fallen,
freezing over parts of the pavement. The smell of mildew and wet
stone hung in the air. Mist mapped tendrils over the tops of
buildings as the cathedral ominously consumed the horizon.
When I was a child, my mother used to tell me that fog couldn't
possibly be scary because it was the spirits of loved ones coming
to check in and watch over us. It didn't help, however. I think I
cried.

I bumped into two girls from my course in the queue, who
smiled in a way that said they recognised me, but hoped I didn't
start up a conversation because either they couldn't remember my
name, or they could, and they thought that nothing I would say

would interest them. I knew this because it was a passive smile, one I frequently experienced.

I returned to the base, walking past my apartment complex in the process and stealing a second glance at my window — hit with a flash of *that night.*

What if the creature is watching me now? What if it's always watching me?

I wanted to know what singled me out from the others.

I'm always here.

I turned around with a shiver, hunching my shoulders to brush off the fog, and picked up my pace.

"HAVE YOU HAD YOUR MORNING DRINK?" Marianne was sitting in the social room when I walked in, which wasn't a surprise. I think I subconsciously expected to find her there.

We weren't entirely alone, two long haired girls sat on a bench to our left; deep in conversation.

I sat myself down opposite Marianne, nursing the cup of tea I brought back with me. "I take it you're not talking about this," I gestured to the polystyrene mug.

A quirk of her brow was enough of an answer.

"In that case, no," I swallowed. "I have not."

Last night.

In reply, she pushed one of the two mugs before her into the centre of the table, until it rested between us, not a subtle gesture by any means, but an apparently normal one given our environment.

The mug wasn't as full as I expected, almost half the size of the ones Mars would provide me with. This was a normal portion, I presumed. One for the average vampire. Post teething problems.

"We can work on this." She nudged for me to take it.

I slowly dragged it the rest of the way across the table towards me, cupping my hands around the porcelain in tense consideration as my grip tightened.

"Two of these a day is more than enough, a healthy amount."

Just two? I thought back to how much I must have been consuming of my *own* blood. How obvious my path of self-destruction seemed. The beauty of hindsight. *Fool.*

I thought about adding it to my current drink, it's what I suspected Marianne was expecting me to do. But I wasn't about to ruin a perfectly good cup of tea.

"I'll take it later." I pushed it away slightly.

"That's what you promised Mars, wasn't it? That you'd take it. They trusted you and for weeks you chose to destroy yourself instead."

The skin on my inner forearm tingled, and I gulped down the lump forming in my throat.

"I won't let that happen again."

"And can I trust that now?"

Can she?

Out of spite and sheer stubbornness, I grabbed the mug and tipped my head back, downing it all in one gulp. My canines ached and I closed my eyes, relishing the taste. Bliss.

Marianne watched me tentatively, though I couldn't read her expression.

"We'll work on it," was all she said.

She looked as if she was about to leave, but then her eyes drifted over my shoulder, and I sensed another presence in the room. She relaxed back into her chair as footsteps wandered over behind me. I already sensed who it was.

"The guys on patrol said the streets were surprisingly clean last night. Nothing negative to report." Mars, who still faintly smelled of mint, sat themself down beside me, directing their message at Marianne.

"Excellent news. Gives us some extra time."

"You want me out tonight?" *They haven't even looked at me.*

"Perhaps," Marianne considered the proposal, then her gaze shifted between us both. "You could take Arlo."

A long pause hung between the three of us.

"I could." Finally, they turned to face me. But instead of a seething glare, I was greeted with a smile. "I promised I wouldn't let you out of my sight."

And with that, they stood back up to leave, but not before bending back down, stray wisps of their hair tickling my cheek. So very quietly, they whispered, "I'll wash the sheets."

I didn't turn to watch them walk away. In fact, I didn't move at all. Marianne fixed her gaze somewhere between the two of us, her face calculating. Mars could have sent the message telepathically and Marianne still would have heard.

Heat rose to my cheeks and my palms clammed up. I cleared my throat and licked the last remaining specks of blood from my teeth. "I best be off," I said, rubbing my hands over my trousers.

"Stay."

I raised my brow.

"Just a moment."

I slipped back down into my chair, anxious as to what Marianne could possibly have to say after witnessing that. She most certainly wasn't deaf and had been around long enough to read between the lines. You could cut the tension with a knife.

"Mars will look after you, you know that?"

I subtly nodded. "I do."

"They trust you, a great deal and they've taken a clear liking to you."

I know, but why?

Mars was ten years older than me, yet I was aware Marianne's perception of age was much different to mine. To her, I must have been but a child.

"I'm sorry we left you for so long."

Oh.

I inhaled and exhaled as a response formed in my head. "It's…" I lowered my gaze, damning myself. "Thank you."

She looked at me with that same sympathetic look given to those deemed naïve and immature — someone who didn't know any better, despite wishing they did. The pity look.

"I did some digging." At this, she leaned in closer, quieting her tone. "I analysed the blood samples left on your shirt from that night and I confirmed my suspicions. That was not the blood of a vampire. In fact, I barely recognise its origins at all."

I didn't know why she thought to bring it up at that very moment in time, but for the first time since I joined this world, I was thankful my questions had been answered without me having to dig tooth and nail to get them.

"From what we could salvage, the murders are purely the typical works of our kind, or at least two of them are, though I am fairly certain, given all the circumstances of these occurrences, that all three are closely connected. It is obvious this Lucy is involved somehow, though she may not be directly responsible for them all. Whoever she is with also holds great strength. It might be this creature, or it might not."

The back of my throat dried and my eyes welled up uncontrollably.

Hold it together, Arlo.

It's all so overwhelming.

I had of course figured out her implications, that the creature pursuing me could very well be Lucienne's leader, which meant that I, for whatever reason, was chosen specifically — *but why?* I wasn't special in any way, there was nothing about me that stood out. So why? And why only now? I'd been dead for almost a month at this point. None of the puzzle pieces fit.

"I do not know why she spared you, if she even realised she did at all, but..."

Sweet dreams, Arlo.

Marianne breathed out a sigh. "I'm conscious I've said this before, but I need to know you hear me. We'll find Lucy, that is a promise. We will stop *everything* that puts this city in danger, and we will *not* stop until I am satisfied we have done so. You're safe and you will never, ever be alone again. Welcome to The Thorns, Arlo. I have a feeling you'll go far."

CHAPTER SIXTEEN

Human kind are so simple, all following the same cycle, the same steps.
When I first took this body, I wondered how long I would last. But I quickly concluded that it is not their bodies that age, but their souls.
They do not allow themselves to live long enough to fulfil their purposes, and oh, how sad it is once they realise this.
For millennia we have existed, and for millennia we will survive.
I know we made the right choice, and soon we shall be united once more in all our glory. Unstoppable.
Like gods.

I caress his shoulders as delicately as a lover may, and encourage him to ease his mind. He works himself too hard, slips away and forgets himself too much. His poor human mind is still too stubborn to let go. A testament to his soul, it seems. So old.
He raises a ringed finger to signal me to stop, his auburn mane tumbling from my hands as I release him. Enough working for today, he says. He is tired.
I lower my head in mild frustration, but I do not mind entirely. There is still plenty of time.

So, I leave him be, and wander off into the daylight.

"It just doesn't sound right. You know? The key just feels a bit off."

I had gone to find a quiet room to study and stumbled across Ben hunched over an electric keyboard that was balanced awkwardly over his crossed legs, while Casper sat in a reclining chair under a reading light. He seemed only half engaged in the conversation his boyfriend was trying to coax out of him, whilst the rest of his attention was on the book in his hands. He looked very studious in reading glasses, I noted — an entirely different image from what I was used to. They both looked up as I entered.

"Sorry, I'll go somewhere else." A rush of embarrassment hit me as I stood there with my arms full of textbooks.

The two of them glared at me and then, in perfect unison, told me to 'not be daft'. I was always welcome to join them, they said. I was taken aback by how welcoming they were, yet they were always like that.

I sat down and organised my sheets, pulling out my own reading glasses. Out of everything this bizarre parasitic death had blessed me with, it could have at least corrected my vision.

"You'll probably be better company than him," Ben mumbled, barely looking up from the keys as he worked his fingers and muttered his concentrated thoughts.

Casper peered over his glasses, flopping his paperback over one knee. "I'm looking for lyric inspiration, if you must know."

Ben huffed. "That's Francesca's job."

"Not always." Casper shrugged in subtle annoyance.

Ben finally looked up at his partner, his face halfway between a laugh and a smile. "And when was the last time you wrote *any* of our songs?"

We sat in dramatic silence as the two of them fell into a

staring contest. Casper broke first and at the same time Ben's face went smug and I watched his brow raise under his dark curls.

"You got me." Casper rolled his eyes.

The book was discarded, as were the glasses, and Casper finally made his way over to his boyfriend to aid their collective musical block. I noted the movements: the way Casper so comfortably and casually slipped behind Ben, arms brushing over Ben's shoulders and head resting against the top of his partner's head. So much gentle contact. I marvelled at the way Ben subtly melted into Casper's embrace — letting his back relax into his boyfriend's chest.

Why can't I be normal?

Last night, with Mars... Why didn't I want it? What is wrong with me?

"You like music, Arlo?" I realised Casper was trying to keep me involved in the conversation.

"Oh... yeah. I suppose."

"He hasn't heard of The Cure," Ben chimed in.

Casper's eyes grew theatrically wide, light reflecting off his golden, dangling earrings.

"That's not true! I have!" I argued, leaping to my own defence.

Ben's brow sarcastically quirked again.

"Boys Don't Cry?" I tried, my brain panic-firing suggestions.

Casper's reaction said all I needed to know about the situation. It's funny because I actually did have some, albeit limited, knowledge of that band, but I was put on the spot, so my thoughts malfunctioned.

"That just won't do," Casper exaggerated his Louisiana accent, beckoning me over.

"He's studying!" Ben playfully back handed his boyfriend's chest as I stood up.

"To hell with studying! He's got eternity, ain't that right, Ben?"

Eternity. That notion clogged my throat, but I wasn't given enough time to dwell on it. These two were very persistent.

I was encouraged to sit down on the chair next to Ben where Casper then pulled out his phone and handed me Ben's headphones. My skin crawled at the proximity, but it was a calm discomfort, the attention merely a foreign sensation. I could manage it this time.

A song started playing in my ears, and Ben leaned over to see which one Casper had picked before winking and nodding and the two of them turned to face me like parents on Christmas morning.

It was good. I liked the melody. It was a little weird, but *good* weird. I started to show my reaction and slowly nodded my head along to the beat. Ben and Casper were quite a few years my senior — most of The Thorns were — but these two were the closest thing I had to older siblings, and while we hadn't been acquainted for long, we clicked in an indescribable way that made me smile inside and out. Friends. Family.

Ben began nodding along with me, despite him not being able to hear it and then we were all feeling the music in this silent room, all swaying to the rhythm and grinning and I was... happy.

WE WERE there for about an hour. Casper asked me how I was finding university, I responded with a generic 'it's okay' answer, but the response didn't satisfy him.

"I got a culture shock," he said. "I was very excited to come to England, but y'all were another level of mean."

"Southern snobs in a northern land." Ben finished off Casper's sentence.

"Quite." Casper nodded, head flicking back to me.

They had a point. I had noticed the divide, almost immediately. I knew I'd be entering into some level of classist society with the university having the reputation it did, but there were times when I was dumbfounded with the sheer audacity on some people.

It was quite frankly frightening sometimes — hence why I always tried my best to blend into the scenery.

"Mummy and Daddy's money." Ben sucked in his teeth.

"Avoid the societies and you'll be fine. You play the character well," were Casper's final words on the matter.

I MISSED ANOTHER LECTURE, though the longer I spent in the hideout, the less I seemed to care. I still wanted to do well; after all, there was no point in me wasting all that money to come here and *not* succeed, but I reminded myself that I still had time to figure stuff out — or so I kept telling myself.

I wasn't sure where Rani went that morning. It worried me how comfortable she was surrounded by all these *vampires,* creatures that could leave her for dead in a back alley in a second, just like me. But as much as I hated to admit it, I figured she was in the safest hands with Carmen — the only other human buried in this mess. If Carmen could manage, Rani could tenfold. I'd never met someone so at ease with every situation they found themself in. Rani had the ability to just *blend in*, regardless of circumstances and mould herself to suit every predicament, even when she was completely out of her depth. And as I came to think of it, it should have been The Thorns who were afraid of what *she* might do. How could *they* be so content in their trust in a human who could expose their existence at any moment. I would have thought creatures like us should have understood the dangers of letting in an outsider into their own ranks. Our kind had been so unbelievably *un*documented throughout noted history, we really were living on thin ice every single day of our existence.

But it was the lack of stories about us that reiterated the

shocking strength of the Manipulation: the gift all of us were capable of. A single look, and no one would ever remember us.

I wondered when Carmen would call me for our training and my gut clenched. Trust is a complex thing.

"HEY, ARLO."

I was stunned mid walk on my way back to my bedroom. I had planned to reorganise it to make it more my own — a task to keep my mind from wandering and perhaps gain some understanding and closure as to what transpired the previous night.

I glanced behind myself to see the origin of the call, the tone unfamiliar, but I was greeted with an empty hallway, the torches and lamps not yet lit.

I scratched the uncomfortable itch at the base of my neck.

After a moment of staring, convincing myself that I had not in fact heard anything and piecing together a rational explanation of wind and stone cracks, I turned back around to commence my walk, having an expression battle with my own thoughts.

The next corridor was probably the highest point in the hideout, the closest to the surface it would take me. Light crept through the slits of stone where the wall met the ceiling, not large enough to see through but enough to light the hallway naturally during the day. I adjusted my bag on my shoulder and paid no attention at first to the fact that one of the cracks was blocked.

"Arlo."

There it was again. Louder, closer that time. Not a wail of the wind or a crack underfoot. My ears pricked, and... my jaw ached. I instinctively stopped to massage the spot just to the left of my nose. My canines.

I smelled blood. Rich, thick, blood.

I spun, panic stricken, to face the only place where the voice must have emerged, for no one could have followed me this route without making themselves known.

I couldn't tell exactly what shape shadowed the light, but it spanned the entire width of the crack, leaving no room for even a single light particle.

All awareness of my peripheral surroundings faded as I looked up.

I did not speak. There was no need to.

But my breathing faltered, and my head tightened.

"Thank you, Arlo," it spoke again, the voice more recognisable: low but not harsh, more like velvet.

Thank you for what?

"I'll be seeing you in time. Do not be afraid."

"How could I fear you?"

"ARLO! ANSWER ME!"

All sensation returned to my body as I was violently shaken into the present. My neck flopped down holding dead weight, and I shook my head violently to let my vision regain focus. *Mars.*

"Arlo, what on earth are you doing?"

"I..." *have not got the faintest idea...*

"What are you looking at?" They finally unhanded my coat and brushed their hands against their hips a few times.

"The..." *Come on, brain... what just happened? Spit it out, Arlo.*

"Is someone there?" They turned to the crack I had fixated on, the very same that was now open once again, light and dust filtering through in a peaceful glow.

"I..." *can't get the words out.*

"Arlo, please tell me what you were looking at, you're scaring me." They turned to look back at me, eyes brimming with concern.

My mother often enjoyed telling me of a habit I had as a child, long before I could speak. I used to stop paying attention to my mother or aunt and instead focus on the corners of the room where three points met at the ceiling. I would begin to smile and sometimes even beamed and giggled. She was adamant I was seeing something she couldn't, and I always found it amusing in the past.

Finally, my voice returned to me. As did my mind.

"I think the creature just spoke to me."

IN MERE MINUTES we were outside, Mars charging ahead. They'd thrown open the door that released us into a side alley, and we headed up the cobbled pathway until we reached the other side of the wall. A few people were walking obliviously in the distance, but the square itself was empty. The perfect place for us to stay hidden, or so I thought.

Mars' head jolted around frantically, no time wasted before they pointed to the crack and asked, "Here? What did it say? How do you know it was the creature?" Their tone was hostile, and my brain grasped for a moment to catch up, ears burning. I didn't know how best to react.

"Arlo?" their voice softened, breaths steadying to an even pace. "Sorry." They lowered their head.

"I just knew," I said.

Their eyes said a thousand words, breaths tired and uneven. "Okay."

"I had a feeling it was following me earlier, but I dismissed it as paranoia. There is no way something could have hidden itself in plain sight. Right?"

"I've only ever seen humans and creatures like us. I have no idea what to even picture. It might not even be humanoid... It might not even be from this earth." They had their hands on their hips, glancing around with wary eyes. "God, what am I saying?"

I cleared my throat. "It was a strong sense. I'm normally good at these things." I was bewildered by my own direct honesty.

"It very well could have been then..."

"You believe me?"

"Always."

What a funny thing to say to someone. That you will always, no matter what the circumstances, believe what they say. I don't think I could have ever been that trusting, even if I tried.

"So, what now?" I sighed.

"The only thing we can do."

"Which is?"

Mars tilted their head up to face the greying sky as rain spat upon us. "We wait for it to come back."

"WHAT DID IT SOUND LIKE?"

A valid question — perhaps the only valid question, given we had nothing else to go off. At all.

We sat in my most frequented café with Marianne before us, (which was difficult to adjust to, as up until that point I had only seen her in inconspicuous hiding locations, and presumed those were the only places she dared attend. Someone of her age and stature seemed too important for mundane locations like this). She was tentatively sipping on her coffee whilst Mars queued for our drinks.

"Deep. Smooth. Like it was whispering into my soul." That was the best way I could think to describe it.

Marianne nodded and let out a low 'hmm' before taking another sip.

"A familiar voice?"

I shook my head. I would have remembered hearing a voice that prominent before, hence my frightful deduction.

"I don't have any real knowledge on this creature, believe it or not. As I'm sure you're well aware by now, we ourselves don't tend to write much down. It would be disastrously foolish, as you can imagine. But I have always been cautiously aware that if *we* exist, then there may be a plethora of other beings roaming around undetected too. Just like you will have heard vampire stories growing up, during my lifetime, I've had various verbal accounts passed to me involving unnatural goings on that have never been resolved. I believe this might be one of those moments." Marianne spoke in a hushed tone, despite us being the only people upstairs.

"Young vampires like yourself are extremely impressionable, just like young children. They do not know their own world yet and can easily be led astray." She shifted her chair, a not-so-subtle nod to my handling of my first few weeks it seemed. "If there is anything else out there, it would not be unusual to hear of them taking advantage of the innocent, but that's why groups like The Thorns are so important. We keep you safe and on the right path." Sympathy crawled back into her voice. "And so, I've decided I'm going to join you and Mars tonight. I'll keep my distance, but not be too far. If anything attempts to contact you again, we will know of it."

"How do you propose you deal with it? Surely you can't just run up and pounce from behind?" The question felt too humorous for the situation, but it was an honest query.

"We will approach with caution, of course. First, we must decipher what it wants and then we can move forward to looking at... solutions."

I nodded. I was still partially unsatisfied with the plan, but I couldn't offer a better solution so kept my mouth shut.

At this point in the conversation, Mars appeared at the old, sunken doorway, carrying a tray of drinks and three cakes. My heart smiled.

"I wasn't sure which cakes you like best, Arlo, so I'll let you pick first." They set the tray down on the table and sat on the cushioned bench beside me.

I slid a plate over with what appeared to be a type of lemon drizzle cake then looked to my company for consent.

"Good choice," Marianne said, leaning back into her chair and straightening out her blouse.

"I had a feeling he would go for that." Mars nodded to themself, grabbing the pecan slice while leaving Marianne with a giant wedge of carrot cake.

I struggled to get used to the fact that we *could* still eat. Blood wasn't our only source of energy; it fed our infection, but our bodies still needed human energy from time to time.

I definitely always struggled with food, for as long as I could remember, but was never able to pinpoint why. Perhaps it was my need for control, or perhaps because I was always so focused on something else, I never made it a priority.

But over these last few weeks, amidst my... *addiction* — could I call it that? — I was growing increasingly aware of my rapidly dropping weight. My trousers hung from my hips, my ribs protruded from my chest — even more so than before — and my face was gaunt. I frightened myself when I would look in the mirror. That wasn't me looking back.

I looked down at the cake before me, then noticed Mars' gaze tracking my movements so I picked up my fork and picked the cake apart, forcing down a mouthful.

"You don't have to eat it if you don't want to," they said, calmly. After a beat, they added, "have you..."

"He had some this morning," Marianne answered for me.

"Good." Mars playfully nudged our shoulders together.

I feigned a smile and took another mouthful before pushing the plate away, guilty at the waste.

"We can work on things, I have promised."

I glanced up in acceptance of Marianne's claim.

"We'll be okay, won't we, Arlo?" Mars confirmed.

"Yes. Thank you. For everything."

. . .

MARIANNE LEFT us once we finished our drinks and the room filled up for the lunch time rush.

Awkwardness overwhelmed me again. The smell of Mars' hair, their arms, and their face brought back broken memories of body heat and blood and the dim light of the room. My breath hitched.

"I suppose we should talk about what happened," Mars initiated the conversation. "Last night."

So it was on their mind too. Relief moved through me that they were the first to address it, as I would have held off the topic until it shattered me completely.

I cleared my throat. "Yeah."

"We didn't... you know."

I looked at them.

"Have sex," they finished.

"I... we didn't?" *We didn't?*

Mars shook their head confidently. "I know we were both very drunk, but that cancels out consent. Yes, we started things, but even in that state, I was aware something felt off. You weren't really responding; it was like you weren't really present. So I didn't push it and instead we just... fell asleep."

Mars had no idea the flood of the relief I felt in that moment. The one thing that had been eating me apart all morning — the worry that I'd somehow taken advantage of the situation by doing something so intimate and personal with another without actually feeling any true desire to do it.

"I got the sense you didn't really want to do it," they continued.

"I..."

"And that's okay!"

"I'm sorry."

"For what? Arlo, what have you got to be sorry for? We had a good evening, didn't we? And if anything, it's me who should be sorry for being so *forward*. You've never done that before, have you...?" they cut themself off with a shake of their head. "Never mind. It's none of my business, or my problem... God, sorry, just ignore me — sorry." They kept shaking their head then started to fidget with their teacup and saucer and spoon. I watched every frantic movement before reaching out and grabbing their hand, urging them to stop. Skin to skin contact: warm on cold. I inwardly winced at the action, yet I *chose* to do it. I let go again and wiped away the sensation harshly onto my trousers.

They looked back at me, pained and clearly confused. *Are these mixed signals I'm giving? I never meant for that...*

"Sorry."

"Arlo, stop it."

"Sor..."

"ARLO."

I jumped, though they hadn't been particularly loud about it, only firm enough to put an end to the conversation. No one else turned to the scene, too consumed in their own conversations to care.

Their tone hushed as they leaned in. "Please accept my apology and leave it. Don't think about it. You've never once needed to apologise to me. Everything that has ever happened between us has been *my* fault. Ever since I found you that night... you were so..." *Are they crying?* They were crying. "You looked so helpless and sad. Your eyes were *unseeing,* your jacket was bloody, and your shoes were scuffed and... Your pale skin, your shaking hands you... *I* brought you into this world. I let you struggle. I didn't do *enough.* I never do *enough.* I've tried so hard to keep everyone safe and yet I'm so *blind. Poppy...*"

What does Poppy have to do with... oh. Oh.

Mars was properly crying, and I was unable to absorb the fact that they were describing the details of my own death. Instead, I looked straight at them and choked up at the sight of their weeping face, and their sorry eyes. I scanned through every suitable reaction to offer some comfort until I settled on pulling them into a hug, letting them lean into my side. With my chin atop their head, I wrapped my arms around their whole frame. I held them there for a minute or so, as the dampness of their tears soaked into my jumper.

After everything, I do remember what I said that night as we left the bar.

Thank you for saving me.

CHAPTER SEVENTEEN

My first night of patrolling could be summarised as uneventful. I don't quite know what I was expecting to find but I thought there would be more to it, given recent events. I'd spent most of the day with Mars, so I remained by their side until we were once again joined by our leader in the evening.

Marianne was swift in her explanation of the plan for the evening. The mission that night was to explore the area around the abandoned swimming baths — a location that was deemed to be of high interest for rogue vampire squatters and where most of the sightings had been. Marianne had made it a staple that every night, without fail, at least two Thorns were placed on watch there.

Tonight, it was my turn.

I'd always been interested in abandoned buildings — especially those with a vast, complex history. The more reclaimed by nature, the better. In the past, I'd dabbled in a bit of urban exploration and photography myself, though I sacrificed that hobby once I realised how difficult it was to get into places without being arrested and regardless, I was not one for taking risks or deliberately getting myself into unsafe and unpredictable environments. Thus, after my most successful visit — a trip with my then best friend to an old industrial warehouse where we encountered out of place, rusted medical equipment and heard multiple unexplained sounds that indicated rooms surrounding us could possibly be occupied — I quickly decided I was not cut out for this hobby and hung up my exploring boots.

But I didn't hesitate when Mars informed me of where we would be visiting that evening because I knew that with those two, I'd be safe.

THE PLAN: Mars and I would explore inside while Marianne would patrol the outside, and then we would eventually reconvene in the early morning to discuss our findings.

Marianne met us at midnight, dressed in all black with her hair slicked back and nothing but a small pouch strapped to her side. She directed us around the side of the building, through the gate to the disused car park and we climbed over a wall to arrive at the only visible entrance through a low, slate roof. I'd been warned beforehand that my usual outerwear might not have been very practical and therefore had elected to wear layers of jumpers under one of Rani's oversized bomber jackets (she insisted I took it, regardless of if I ruined it or not). I took extra care regardless.

We were prepared for broken glass and other sharp and potentially dangerous objects lurking in the pitch black. We clad our hands in thick gloves and the two of us equipped ourselves with the strongest torches we could find. A scene replayed in my head that on the other side of every door was either a police officer or a drug addict, but I let Mars take charge and stride ahead — they had been here many times before.

After safely manoeuvring into the main swimming pool area, my skin began to crawl as despite our whispers, our voices echoed, and the vastness of the room unnerved me. Perhaps this would have been quite enjoyable in the day, with the torches illuminating graffiti covered walls — the floor to ceiling tiles bludgeoned in colour. But at night, I felt trapped in a real-life video game simulator, waiting to turn and shine my torch on a figure behind me.

"Keep the torch pointed at your feet otherwise you'll trip," Mars aggressively whispered close to my ear, treading carefully around the debris surrounding the empty pool. I'd been distracted by my thoughts, waving my torch in every direction, stupidly not considering the fact that the centre of the room was essentially a death pit. I had searched for images of the building's layout beforehand and concluded that we had entered through the shallow end, though even then, it would still have been a rather hefty fall without the buoyancy aid of water.

Much to my relief, I heard nothing out of the ordinary, even with my heightened senses. The deeper we walked into the building, the more confident my footing became. Mars must have heard my breath falter on multiple occasions and reassured me that as long as I kept my voice down, we'd be virtually undetectable. A bold statement for them to make but this time I allowed their exaggerated optimism to pass me by without a worry.

"Will we even find anything if we've already cleared this place out?" I asked, nearly stumbling over a plank of nailed, rotting wood. I caught myself inches away from a full fall, with Mars swiftly turning, ready to catch me if necessary. They laughed.

"It is one of the few places in the city where people can hide for quite some time without being detected, human or otherwise. Even once you scare them off, they'll always come back eventually — usually after a month or so when they think you've given up. We're not here for humans, as you know, so if we stumble across a squatter, no we didn't. They won't remember anyway. You'll know what we're looking for when you come across it, a vampire scent, that I'm sure you're aware of now — something a vampire has touched, sat on, or held. They give off a lingering trace that is undeniably easy to detect. We've found things here before, there is a more than likely chance that we shall discover something again."

I nodded and kept my head down as instructed, torch lighting my limited path, moss sticking to my shoes. I think I subconsciously started taking in deeper breaths to hunt for a scent, but all I could smell was mould and rot and occasionally, gagging upon detection, human waste.

Mars sped up a little as we edged along the side of the pool, their footsteps squelching ahead as they appeared to have a destination in sight, though I myself could not see nor smell anything out of the ordinary.

"What is it?" I rasped in the loudest whisper possible.

Mars shushed me with the waft of their hand. In the brief moment my torch cast a light upon them, they looked to be in a low crouch. I heard a rustle of movement and Mars cleared their throat.

"What?" I asked again, this time a barely audible whisper, but more to sate my own confusion.

After a beat, Mars stood back up to their full height. "Human blood."

What?

They waved a full ball point pen under my nose, and I shone the torch directly into their eyes by accident. The smell was obvious then. It crawled all the way to the back of my nostrils, burning my throat with sweetness.

"The pen?" I asked.

"Look."

I was urged to shine a light down onto the object Mars now held in their hands, and as they slowly twisted the pen around, I realised that the blue lid and base did not correlate with the thin slither of red-tinged ink concealed in the centre. Blood. Fresh and very human.

"Why?" was all I managed to ask.

Mars shrugged. "We all have our means of storing blood for long journeys. Not a choice I would have opted for but it's far from the weirdest method."

"But that means they've been here, recently. Don't we patrol here every night?"

"Indeed we do. This was left today. A scent that strong is unavoidable for us, can't have been missed. If you'd stepped but an inch closer, you would have found it too."

I suddenly felt like I was being watched, as if the empty rooms and corridors behind us were swimming with eyes like we were not, and never had been, alone.

"Will that help us?" I questioned.

Mars shrugged. "Anything could be evidence. It's not much, but it may end up being of use. Anyone with but a spec of their human conscience left, will avoid drinking the blood of a human, especially that fresh. This blood has been extracted and stored very, very recently."

Another victim?

"I'll keep it safe and see what we can do with it." Mars then turned and we continued our full circle of the main pool.

As I said, this turned out to be a rather uneventful evening. Except for a few areas where a vampire scent still lingered — a couple of changing room cubicles and the raised balcony floor that surrounded the pool — we found nothing else that would have been of use to us. Not even a group of human squatters that I'd prepared myself for.

After hours of the two of us scouring the buildings from top to bottom, mildly dissatisfied with our lack of findings, we found it a safe enough time to call it a day and returned to what I described in my head as 'the surface', despite us already being above ground level.

Mars slipped on the way out, catching their leg on a piece of metal and laughing that it was a good job they couldn't catch human infections. We quickly bandaged up the wound and continued out into the moonlight, Mars staying ahead of me the entire time.

JUST BEFORE WE exited back out into the open air, through whatever possession I felt, I turned back around to face the building, just for the hint of a second. It's something I screamed at horror movies for, vowed I'd never do my entire life, and yet I did it anyway.

In the dim and groggy light, I could have sworn I saw the flash of something large disappearing behind the wall. A gentle gust of wind, the flap of fabric.

Wings.

He's here.

Chapter Eighteen

arly December gave us some of the coldest days yet. This particular evening was significantly icier than the last, yet the city always looked so cozy once the sun had set. The orange lamps cast the bridges aglow while crowds still bustled around well after the shops had closed.

It had been a couple of weeks since my first patrol, and our unsuccessful searches were beginning to feel rather tedious. While I'd accepted the fact we'd be unlikely to find anything, likely ever, I refused to admit defeat.

For my fifth patrol, running on about twenty hours of sleep for the entire week, we waited once again until midnight rolled around and we would, like always, be out until the sun rose. My previous university schedule and routine had slowly been disregarded, much to my dismay. But this was important, I had to remind myself. Necessary, regardless of... everything I was sacrificing.

"Are you warm enough?" Mars asked me, answering their own question with a deep shiver and rubbing their hands together before folding them tightly into their puffer jacket.

"Enough," I replied, wrapping my deep green, woollen trench

around myself. I had my thickest scarf doubly wrapped around my neck and three pairs of socks shoved into my winter boots. A little excessive possibly, but my nose was already threatening to drop clean off my face.

We waited for Marianne outside the cathedral as planned. I took in its grandeur as I passed between the gravestones, pacing back and forth to keep my limbs from seizing up entirely. I'd still not been inside, though I vowed to change that once all this had died down and life returned to normal. If that was even possible.

I spotted a mildly overdressed Georgian era figure approaching from the bottom of the lane. Marianne had seemingly taken to the theatrics again. *So much for being discrete.* The red velvet frock coat she wore most definitely could not have been hers in those days. If my history knowledge taught me one thing it was that women were never allowed to be practical — in any sense — which made her wearing the coat now feel so... *right.*

"You got a dagger sheathed in thy thigh, madame?" Mars joked, bouncing on their toes for warmth.

"Yes. Two," came the deadpan response.

"Good." Mars then looked at me, biting their cheek with wide eyes.

"Where do you want us then?" I asked, bringing the seriousness back to the conversation.

"Anywhere and everywhere." Marianne neatened out her trousers with heavy handed brushes. "I've got plenty of Thorns on general watch tonight so for you two, I would suggest going back to the area you heard the voice again and the surrounding river area. Pay close attention to any and every sound. It's been a suspiciously long time since this creature made itself known to you, and though I doubt this *thing* would be stupid enough to stay in one place, given what has happened thus far, it is clearly constantly aware of where *we* are. In fact, it is likely not too far from us right now."

A chill rushed down my spine. I hadn't prepared for this.

"I have no idea if it will show itself, or if it intends to show itself at all, but the best we can do is stay aware of its existence, always. Stick together. Communicate. And Arlo," Marianne's eyes found mine as I looked up from the ground, "if you get *any* sense at all that something is *off* or that you are being watched or anything of the sort, tell Mars and then you *call me.*"

"And the other threats?"

"Like I said, I have people on that job already."

I nodded, thinking myself a fool for not listening properly.

Mars nudged me to get started, and I crossed my arms tightly against the cold.

"And guys..."

We both turned back to our leader.

"Keep your minds locked away."

"Roger," Mars said, with only a hint of humour.

"Stay safe. I'll be close all night."

WE TRUDGED through slushy mud and grass, down onto the streets. Bars and restaurants had closed up by this time, but we passed a few groups, mostly students, none of whom paid us the slightest bit of attention.

"You know, I think you fit in remarkably," Mars said, skipping ahead slightly and turning to walk backwards to face me.

"In what sense?"

"Look around you; look at the *costumes,*" they laughed playfully.

"You're saying we all dress the same?" *Of course they are.*

Mars shrugged. "Not *all* of you. But the vast majority of Literature students, especially in old cities, do have a tendency to look as though they thrifted their entire personality from a battered Shakespeare play."

"I take it that wasn't a compliment?" I tried not to seem

offended since I myself had already figured this out. I was just somehow disappointed my cover had been blown.

"Oh, *come on!* Look at you all. Is the term saturation even in your vocabulary?"

I tried to keep a straight face, but their playfulness was rubbing off and I gave in.

"Okay, you have a point! But, in my defence..."

That earned me a raised brow and folded arms. "Go on, *Richard.*"

I gasped in theatrical offence, wagging my finger. "How dare you call me that name! Now *that* is a serious offence."

"Okayyyy then, *Bun—*"

"You haven't actually read that book, have you?"

They raised their arms in surrender, their mouth dropping wide open. "Have you heard yourself?"

"Stop it!"

"Make me." They started to run off and I picked up my pace to follow, clutching my long coat against the wind as my mind swelled with laughter.

We reached the main square, dotted with proud statues on horseback. On weekends, the square was filled with market stalls, and I actually got my coat from there, and my jumper... *oh dear, I am insufferably predictable, aren't I?*

"We'll head down there first," Mars pointed down the narrow-cobbled path that led to the riverside walkway at the base of the cathedral. "It's a bit quieter, easier to spot anything out of the ordinary."

I followed their lead, watching my step and trying not to slip down the steep descent. I couldn't understand how easily Mars walked in these conditions...

I was led down the narrow stairs squished between two over-hanging buildings, resting my hand against the bricks to steady myself.

We were now out of the way of people, after all, this path was not intended to be walked along in the dark. I wouldn't have even entertained the idea of walking down here alone — before *and* after my fall.

Mars remained in charge, pushing aside tendrils and branches creeping in from all directions. Their steps did not falter, nor did their confidence.

We started to talk as we walked beside each other — simple things, innocent things — while watching our footing along the narrow dirt path that bordered the river. I kept looking down to my right to watch the water rippling over sludge and fallen branches, old tree roots protruding from its depths. I moved slightly inwards to avoid tripping and falling in.

I found my mind wandering back to the second victim: the poor man, walking alone across these very same pathways. What was he doing here by himself? My head snapped upwards at the snap of a twig, mind overly alert and on edge. Mars didn't flinch — *I'm overreacting.*

In the few weeks I'd been on patrol, mostly with Mars, but occasionally with Casper or Ben or both, I'd use this time to ease my mind. A time to converse and take a breather from the daytime stresses. I was searching for this *thing,* but the less and less successful we became, the more I had allowed my mind to switch off.

Tonight felt different.

"WHAT SCARES YOU THE MOST?" Mars was still pacing a few steps in front of me.

My vision had since adjusted to the dark, so I could see their outline and the vibrant red of their coat. I spotted the moon up above, too, completely unobstructed and burning in full view.

"What scares me the most?" I repeated.

"Yeah. Like things that really make your skin crawl."

What scares me the most? Everything. Everything terrifies me. Life.

"I'm not really sure."

Mars slowed their pace somewhat until they finally fell back in line with me. "Nothing? Really? You can't think of anything?"

"Not really." I shrugged.

"Okay, I'll go first then. Rats. Rats bloody terrify me. The *sound* they make and the way they scurry." They let out a giant shiver to prove it.

Oh, so we're just talking about mundane fears?

"Okay, well I suppose I'm not the biggest fan of ghosts."

"Ghosts? You believe in ghosts?"

Did I believe in ghosts? I wasn't sure if it was possible *not* to believe in things anymore, not since my whole life had become a fictional story all in the space of one evening.

"I think I saw one once. Normally, I can tell if it's just my imagination or just a trick of the light or sound but still to this day, I have no explanation for what I saw." This was true. I'd always been one to stand by the fact that seeing was believing and that science was proved too strongly for the existence of such supernatural things to be confirmed. *I say as a walking reborn immortal.* But that one night when I was about twelve years old, my mother and I had just returned home from seeing my aunt. It was dark and late and cold, and I wanted nothing more than to just flop down onto my bed and drift off to sleep. And that I did, my mum sleeping in her room down the hall. But something woke me that night — a tapping noise from downstairs. Not the usual creak of pipes that came with living in an old stone chapel, nor was it a dripping tap. This was much louder, and much more present. To this day I will never comprehend what compelled me to investigate. I was such a timid child, and I had not long started secondary school: a big boy at the big boy school. I was brave and confident; I had to force myself to be, or I'd be eaten alive.

I climbed out of bed and greeted the pool of darkness as I

descended the stairs. I followed the intermittent sound that was growing stronger with every step I took. The sound seemed to emanate from our small kitchen at the back of the house, directly next to the glass door that led out into the yard. My mum hadn't had time to close the blinds, so the light of the street lamps lit up half of the room, casting a blueish glow across the countertops. I stood at the base of the stairs, hand gripping to the banister. I heard one last tap and my head jolted to the unlit part of the room where our kitchen table resided, and despite the poor lighting, I saw a figure sat there. A shadow of what I could only assume were horns silhouetted against the wall, but the shadow was out of focus and *off*, so it could have showed anything. I was looking for obscurities. But this *thing* had an inhumanly long arm extended over the table, one that ended with a sharp and pointed black nail. I couldn't make out any features, if it had any at all. But I just stood, heart thudding horribly in my chest. I hated that sound so much.

I remember my first thought being: it was my dad, finally deciding he wanted to meet me and reunite with my mummy. I expected this *thing* to fully emerge from the shadows of the kitchen, and there Jerry would be, smiling that same beaming smile he wore in all of mum's photos. He would extend his arms and say something like 'come here, son' or maybe apologise and *explain*. But the shadow didn't move.

After staring frozen for a while, somehow knowing it wasn't going to move anymore, I sprinted back up the stairs as fast as my legs could carry me and dove under my duvet, curling into a foetal position and feeling my chest throb into the mattress. The sound ceased to continue, and once my heart had settled, I remember cursing myself for even caring about my dad. I had mum. She was more than enough. He didn't deserve us. He didn't deserve us. He didn't deserve us.

But the shine of that white grin in the pitch dark of my kitchen will always be woven into my mind like a vine of death.

And that morning, when my mum asked me why she heard my

movement that night, I lied straight to her face and said I was thirsty. She smiled at the time, but she knew I was lying. But boys don't cry, or at least that's what my first bully said. The second told me to stop being so soft. I was a man, after all.

Over time, I told myself the claws were a trick of the light, and the more I thought about it, the more the memory of the figure merged into something normal. A cold figure, but with an echo of humanity.

A ghost.

As I said, it was an old building.

"So, ghosts then. I get that. Maybe it was a guardian angel — my mum always goes on about them. Someone sent to watch over you." Mars was still swinging in step beside me.

A guardian angel. Maybe.

To our left, we were coming up to the base of the cathedral, and from that angle, it was hard to really appreciate the scale of it all. But it was there, and I could feel the weight of it all. The overbearing presence.

Another snap sounded and this time I turned around. Mars noticed.

"What? You hear something?" they asked.

I stilled for a moment; head fully turned as my eyes scanned the darkness.

"Nothing. Paranoia."

"You've got to tell me if you get a sense of anything though. You promised."

"I know. I'm just a little hyperaware at the moment."

"Understandable."

We continued walking.

. . .

We were a little further along the riverbank now, having reached the clearing where the path widened out past the old mill and the riverbank boat house. I could breathe clearer, knowing we were more exposed now — free from the shadows. Now all I could hear was the river and Mars, who started to run out onto the grass under the willow tree that stood weeping its branches into the riverbank.

"Cool at night, right?"

Do they just not feel fear?

Why would they? Nothing is after them.

"That's one way of putting it. Lonely, perhaps. *Dangerous* being another way you could describe it."

"We're not going to find anything in a crowd of drunk students."

"You never heard of hiding in plain sight?" I tried to suppress my mildly rising anger and the sickening fear that had arisen within my body as I looked out into the vastness with my hands firmly tucked into my pockets.

"Yes, but from what we've gathered, this thing doesn't *hide*. It shows itself whenever it wants to."

"Only to me."

"We don't know that for sure.."

"You didn't see it, though."

"And you did?"

My shoulders dropped in defeat.

"Maybe you should leave me alone for a bit then," I said, surprised at my own suggestion. But if we were going to do this *there*, we might as well have taken advantage of what Mars was claiming. *Be a man.*

Mars tilted their head in consideration. "Okay then."

"I stay here. You walk away. You come back in an hour."

"An hour? You'll freeze."

"Are we going to find this creature or not?"

"Okay," they sighed, stepping away. "Only an hour."

"One hour."

"And you call me if you feel in the slightest bit of danger. Promise me that. Promise."

I nodded. I trusted Mars at this point. Perhaps I always had done.

With one last look, they lowered their head and disappeared back onto the path and under the shelter of trees.

A FEW MINUTES passed where I allowed myself to stand and take in my surroundings, alone with my thoughts. The rush of water flowed all around me and the soft, proud glow of the cathedral buildings peeked through the copse of trees that rose up the bank. It put my mind at ease, and I focused on my breaths, and how they came out as little clouds in the midnight temperatures. I put my gloves on, despite the cold damage having already been done, but I felt it was the least I could do to maintain some body heat. The whole concept of preserving body heat as a vampire was utterly beyond me, but that was another question to add to the never-ending list that would continue for the rest of my life. *If only we'd been studied.* I scowled at the silly thought, its reasoning answering for itself.

Another five minutes passed, and I began to pace, walking as close to the riverbank as I dared. I looked out upon the other mill house on the opposite side. No lights on as usual. I sighed, not really knowing what I was expecting to happen.

I strolled over to the stone throne just to the side of the willow tree and sat in it for a moment. From the front, it looked like a grand but simple chair, yet during the day with light cast upon it, you could make out the cluster of misshapen gargoyle heads that burst out of the back like moles out of molehills. Strange in any context.

Staring out onto the bridge arches in front of me, I pondered on the different shapes I could make out in the dimmed lighting. Then I closed my eyes and took in a deep breath.

A further ten minutes passed. Perhaps I drifted in the chair. Nothing changed.

Then it did.

"I was wondering how long you were willing to wait."

The voice — *that voice* — came from behind me, as it always did, and everything melted again.

My breathing quickened in a panic. I dared not move, though I was compelled to do so regardless.

I was about to meet this *thing,* yet I couldn't escape the sensation we had met before. Had we?

I could have sat there and waited for it to reveal itself, or stand and walk around to meet it. Oddly, I chose the latter.

There it stood: a silhouette in the blackness, with leaves and tendrils curling around its body.

My creature.

Though the creature was merely... a man.

Upon seeing me, he strode over to me as a friend might; one you had not seen in a while but shared a long history with. A close friend.

One might have looked at him and seen a student, barely older than I: Long, biblical, white curls flowing down his back and over his shoulders, a lengthly black coat not too dissimilar from mine hung over a tailored, pin striped suit, one that was tie-less and opened deep at the collar to expose his pale collar bones and smooth, unmarked chest. A thin gold chain poked out from underneath the material — highly inappropriate for this time of year, but his unfazed manner told me all I needed to know. He was otherworldly.

I glanced down to his smartly polished shoes and watched as they reflected the very moon. Then his face. Grinning, again, like an old friend.

There was a fakeness to his cherubic cheeks, an emptiness to his gaze, and foxglove poised between his teeth.

And there he stood before me.

He tilted his head and his chains jangled. "Are you not happy to see me, Arlo?"

I couldn't speak. Whether he compelled me or not, no words came to mind.

He shook his head, disgruntled. "I told you not to be afraid."

Still no sound emerged.

I thought of calling Mars, felt my hand reach into my pocket for my phone, but I stopped. For whatever I might have done then, may have sent him away again.

I mustn't send him away.

What?

"Have you lost your voice?" he asked, voice soft like velvet. *Always velvet. The only way I can think of describing it.* It paralysed me.

"Why do you look so concerned? Are you not pleased to see me again?" He sounded almost *wounded.*

"You're here." At last, my own voice sounded, my head tilting in disbelief.

He smirked. "I'm always here, silly."

Like a friend.

Family.

My head was swimming, as if I'd been sedated and I was slowly losing consciousness. *This was a bad idea. Call Mars.*

"What *are* you?"

He rolled his eyes in such a human manner. "What do you think I am?"

"A demon?" It sounded comical when I said it out loud. Demons are reserved for comic books and stories. Ancient texts I didn't believe in.

"Do I look like a demon?" He performed an open armed twirl on the grass, as if to prove... *what?*

"I'm not a *demon*. How insulting!"

"What are you then?"

"What are you?"

I don't even know anymore.

"Just Arlo." *Am I a child?*

He laughed at that. "Well, *just* Arlo. I'm *just* Michael." He stuck out his elegant hand and bowed slightly so that we were no longer the same height.

"Is that supposed to be a joke?" I looked down at him, unimpressed.

He straightened up and dropped his hand. "Maybe. Maybe not. It's ironic really. Are you religious?"

"Not particularly."

"Then shake my hand. I don't bite."

So, I did. His hand was oddly warm, angelically soft, and his touch delicate. Even through my glove.

"There, that wasn't so bad, was it? Pleased to be of your acquaintance."

Call Mars.

"You were waiting for me to be alone," I said, standing my ground.

"Not necessarily."

"But you don't care about anyone else." Not a question, but he considered for a moment.

"Correct."

"Why?"

"Why not?" He laughed as if it was obvious.

"Not an answer." *Call. Mars.*

"You interest me." Suddenly, he appeared taller. Or maybe he was always that height.

"Why? Why me?"

"Perhaps I see myself in you. A much younger self. And I seek to guide you."

Yes.

He's lying. What did that even mean?

"I don't need any guidance."

"I thought you might say that." He shrugged, acting defeated. "But you might be remembering things wrong. You see, if *I* remember rightly, which I always do, I saved you that night."

You did.

I was struck cold. It really was him. It always had been.

Having read my expression, he threw me a look of pity. "So, you agree with me, don't you? If I had not been there to *aid* you, who knows what you might have ended up doing?"

"I drank your blood."

He smiled fondly. "That you did."

"You're like me?"

A shrug. "Not exactly."

Then what are you? And why does my head hurt so much? I was going to vomit.

"Don't look so horrified. I did nothing but look after your health. You will thank me later."

I'm going to be sick.

I ran over to the river's edge, beneath the willow petals and fell to my knees, vomiting up my insides into the stream. Even in the dim light, I watched as thick blood effervesced in the water, staining the stony edge a deep crimson.

A tight grip tugged on my coat collar, and I was aggressively hoisted back onto my clumsy feet. "Oh dear," he said over my shoulder, an angry tinge of disappointment prevalent in his tone. "I didn't think this form would weaken you this much. Maybe I chose wrong. Hmm."

You didn't.

I'm not weak.

"Have you fed tonight?" he asked, still pressing close behind me as I looked out hazily across the moonlit water. His breath was warm and sweet smelling.

Fed.

I had. I had a dose before we left, as did Mars. We did it together. *Call Mars.* **No point now, what will they say?**

"Can't you keep it down?" He shook his grip loose, forcing me to lose my balance slightly.

I didn't turn back around. "I can." *I'm not weak.*

"I suppose you'll learn." His voice settled, and he dusted off my jacket, forcing me to turn around so that he would stop touching me.

His face mirrored mine, emulating one of confusion. "Oh dear," he said again.

What now?

He grabbed me by my collar once more, this time his firm hand snaked around to hold my neck still as he came up close. I didn't have enough time to register what he pulled out of his pocket until a cloth pressed over my mouth, and he wiped away the excess *blood.*

His eyes were crystal blue, so clear they were almost pure white. This was no *vampire.* He wasn't like us. He may have looked human, but he was nothing of the sort. What he was was no parasite or infection. His mind and soul were not of this earth.

I stared, limbs unmoving and slack by my side.

"How they have let you down."

"What do you mean?" I yanked myself away finally, shocking him.

"Your potential. Don't you realise what you are capable of? Have you not figured out what you are now?"

My potential.

He isn't making any sense. I'm just me. Just Arlo.

"Great things, Arlo. Unimaginable greatness. I chose you for a reason. You were never meant to be like them."

What does he mean?

"You have the power to do whatever you want now. Your life is limitless. You can be *free.* Forever.*"

Like a god.

"If you just let me guide you. You will find yourself."

Guide me. Help me.

"I won't treat you like a child. You are so much more than they all realise."

I am not weak.

I am not weak.

His mouth tilted upwards in pride as he watched something unlock within my consciousness at the same time I felt it happen. The thing that laid dormant in me since the day I died.

His doing. Not Lucy.

"Now," he said after a beat. "I'll be seeing you again shortly. Ponder that proposal will you, Arlo? You know I'm right."

He started to retreat. "Oh, and remember Arlo, you can't trust them all. They all hold such dark secrets."

MY BODY DIDN'T MOVE an inch and I watched him slip away as quietly as he came.

My body doesn't move an inch and I watch him slip away as quietly as he came.

I LET the next thirty minutes pass me by, returning to the chair.

Mars was not a minute late. "Have you really just been sat there for a whole hour?" they asked lightly. "Anything then?"

"Nothing."

They chewed at the inside of their mouth. "Oh well, it was worth a try. Let's get you moving again. I'll update Marianne and we'll head back up."

I nodded.

"Are you sure everything is alright?"

"Always." I smiled.

243

CHAPTER NINETEEN

I need to learn patience. It is, I'll admit, my downfall.
But he has now realised what must be done.

I awoke with a skull splitting headache. It was well past noon, so my watch showed, and I was still with The Thorns. Heaviness overcame my limbs as I sat myself up and swung my legs over the side of the bed. I couldn't for the life of me remember what had happened the night before, a common occurrence by this point. Outside was deathly quiet, which only added to the disorientation.

A call came from outside — Mars — and the door burst open a second later, no regards for privacy.

"God, you're awake! Finally. I heard movement." They were almost out of breath.

"You were waiting outside for me? Since when?" I was suddenly aware of the fact I was sat in my pyjamas while Mars was fully dressed up in a winter coat and boots. I really had overslept.

"Not long, I'm not a psychopath. I figured you needed the sleep, though. You've still got to get used to it."

I shrugged; unfazed for once.

"Anyway, now you're awake, I think Rani and Carmen were wanting you to test them again. Well, that's what I overheard them saying over breakfast... which you missed. Everyone was there, talking Christmas decorations and favourite festive drinks — all that jazz." Mars trailed off on one of their tangents, expressive with their arms as usual. However, their energetic glow faded out as I pinched the bridge of my nose and took a deep breath. I didn't intend for it to come across as *rude,* but I swiftly realised it was impossible to do that in the company of others and *not* seem the slightest bit ignorant.

"Last night really took it out of you, huh?" Their eyes squinted, assessing me.

I only managed to nod.

"You'll probably not be too fond of the fact that Marianne wants you to go back out again tonight then." They clenched their teeth and stared at me awkwardly, awaiting my reaction.

I looked back up at them, a flash of leaves and foaming water shooting to the front of my mind.

The patrol... that's right.

"She thinks it's helping," Mars added, still not budging from their spot in the centre of the room, their duffle looking a size too big.

"Right." I heaved myself off the bed and headed over to my wardrobe, conscious of Mars' following eyes.

"A little privacy?" I turned back to them.

Mars' eyes widened. "Right, yeah, sorry." They spun around on the spot with their arms out, landing firm-footed like a figure skater preparing for their next move.

I haphazardly jumped into yesterday's cords and chucked on one of my many short-sleeved shirts. I liked them better that way, despite the weather. Long sleeves get all itchy and weird...

"Done," I announced, not giving them a chance to analyse my outfit before heading out of the door, a destination still calculating in my head.

"So," Mars started, skipping to catch up with my strides. "The creature was a no-show last night but..." they prolonged their pause, enough for me to look at them to continue, "two other patrollers caught another Turned and we've held them for questioning. They didn't seem as confident as the other two so Marianne might actually be able to get some useful information this time."

Good, that's good.

They sighed at my non-verbal response. "I told you that last night, but you were completely zonked out."

My nose scrunched. I couldn't remember.

"You can tell me if it's getting too much you know, I can talk to Marianne if you think it's getting in the way of your studies, I know how important that is to you and how hard working you are. You are, after all, meant to be living your life as normally as possible. We did promise that..."

"No, no. It's okay. I'm okay, Mars. Promise." I flashed a bright smile to reassure them, but it didn't work.

Mars' tone shifted, growing even more solemn. "Look, I'm just going to say it. It's been reeling through my mind all morning. I feel like something happened during the hour I was gone and you're not telling me."

I genuinely could not recall what they were talking about. I wracked my brain, scrambling around for something, anything.

"Arlo?"

"No, no." *Think of something.* "Everything was fine. Like you said, I'm just not used to being *nocturnal.*"

They sighed again as we turned a corner, descending the narrow steps to the main hall. "You promised to stop pretending everything is fine, yet now you're acting exactly like you were weeks ago. It's called denial."

Their harsh accusation made me stop in my tracks.

"What do you mean?" I snapped.

Clearly, they were surprised by my abruptness, and to be truthful, so was I.

"Arlo, you know exactly what I mean. The blood, the hiding, losing control... we said we could help you, but it takes all of us to cooperate in this. You clearly don't seem to even want to try. I know I sound like a stuck record but please, I'm still young, as Marianne always reminds me, but I'm not stupid. I didn't push last night because you were too tired, but I'm pretty good at reading people, *especially* friends. So please, I'm begging you, tell me what happened."

"I can't remember!" I shouted, my throat spewing the words out right from my gut. Someone startled ahead, staring over in both concern and annoyance.

Mars stopped talking and spun to face me, and I faced them. My confession brought with it a tear. *I don't remember a thing.*

"What do you mean you don't remember?" Mars asked, trying to stay calm, pulling me to the side and out of view. A stinging phantom imprint tingled over my forearm. I flinched.

"I mean I don't remember what happened last night." At least I was being honest this time, surely Mars could see that.

"Shit."

"What?"

"What was the last thing you *do* remember?"

"The riverside." I tore through my brain as hard as my mind would let me, taking a gulp at the inevitable struggle as I filtered through the memories.

"Walking past the cathedral?"

I nodded.

"Do you remember our conversation?"

Another nod. Then I shook my head. *Do I?*

"What am I afraid of?"

"Rats." *I do remember.*

Something in Mars' face relaxed momentarily, but they clenched their jaw and looked to the side. "But you don't remember that hour, do you?" Not a question.

"So, what does this mean then?"

Sad eyes caught my own. "It's like a few weeks ago, when I had to snap you out of that trance."

"What are you implying?" My hands grew hot. I knew.

"The creature. It came for you."

"And I don't remember..." I finished off the inevitable.

"Shitshitshit." Mars flashed their sharp teeth and slapped their legs, pacing in a circle.

Panic overcame me. What did this mean? Was it making me forget? Manipulating my memories? Or something worse? How many times could it have seen me and for me to simply forget? *What if it wasn't quiet the last few weeks. What if...*

"Don't tell Marianne," I cried out, reaching out to stop Mars from their incessant pacing since it was only making things worse.

"I have to. She'll know what to do."

"No, Mars, please," I begged, practically falling to my knees. "I can't have her think I can't look after myself. Everyone already thinks there is something wrong with me..."

"Who said that?" they cut me off.

"No one... I just know. I can sense it and can't stand it. I need to fix this, but I don't want any more attention. Help me, Mars, but please don't tell her. It will only make things worse."

They considered my plea — one I meant with every fibre of my being. If Marianne found out, she'd never let me out of her sight and I'd be stuck in these walls for who knows how long, any remnants of normality would be destroyed.

No, I wouldn't have it.

"Okay."

I let go of their coat. "Yes?"

"Yes. I promise I won't tell her. But on one condition. You tell *me* everything and you let me stay close as much as possible. Even if you don't think it's significant. Maybe we can both prove to her what we're capable of." They threw me a semi confident grin, eyes looking up at me through their dark brows and I was once again shocked at our height difference.

"I promise."

And I did promise; I owed them that much. We would figure this out together. The less people who knew, the better. We'd find my creature and we'd put a stop to it. Prove to Marianne that I was not weak. I could hold my own, but properly this time. No more hiding away, alone and ashamed. No more losing control. Mars would guide me, and I could guide them. Perhaps the first team-work effort I could be proud of. Things would work out with Mars by my side.

But despite my confidence and pride, something felt off. The look on their face right then — I'd never seen that before. I couldn't think of what specifically *felt* odd but then it clicked, and I didn't know how I managed it, but I couldn't shake the feeling that I'd just Manipulated the very same person who saved my life. I'd walked them right into a trap I hadn't even intended on setting, and I'd taken away their autonomy. Would they have even noticed? Would they have even agreed to my proposal?

But the worst part of it all? It felt *good*.

MARS KEPT THEIR WORD, of course. We spent many days and nights retracing steps whilst I pointed out anything that might indicate me *not* being myself. Though I never felt my creature's presence in that short amount of time, I was no less sure of my desire to catch him. Marianne still aided on that front, strengthening patrols and narrowing down possibilities. Sharing her theories when she could and her bold sense of dominance never dwindled; we would come to a conclusion, she insisted.

The fear of not telling her what happened slowly crawled its way to the back of my mind the more time passed, to the point where I barely even considered it anymore. And she was none the wiser — I was happy to keep it that way.

I was so *sure* of myself.

After very little time in the makeshift dungeon, the captive was released. I was relieved by this, until I learned that Marianne had quite literally *'shattered his mind'*. Two days later, he was found dead at our very door — a death by his own hand. His bloody knuckles still twitched from the rapid pounding at the hard oak, unable to bear returning to his clan. He was weak, she explained, the complete opposite to the previous captives. He held nothing of importance other than the pride of his involvement in the murders. Naturally that was enough for Marianne to snap, though we had ultimately reached another dead end. The fool didn't even know who he was working for, he simply enjoyed the thrill.

I completed all my assignments, much to my own surprise, but the incessant late night and early morning studies between patrols and meetings were paying off. Maybe I was going somewhere after all. Rani didn't let any of this business get in her way either, scoring excellently in all modules of study. She even received a commendation from her lecturer for her 'open-mindedness'. I was proud of her. She deserved it all.

Carmen, I'll admit, kept her distance, but only as far as being attached to Rani would let her. I helped them train, as they requested. Holding back a little more with Rani than with Carmen but only, as I reminded myself, because Carmen was older and more experienced. She could take more, so I gave more. Rani would learn in time, as she always did. She always leaped over every hurdle coming her way, and in many ways, I was starting to under-stand why those two enjoyed so much of each-other's company.

Both so strong willed and equally stubborn. Maybe they had found a good match in each other. Maybe that's what it was.

I spent a lot of time with Ben and Casper too, and even warmed to Lawrence. He apologised for his drug induced 'forwardness' and vowed to never try that again — with anyone. Casper explained Lawrence's history with 'going too far' and claimed if he ever did attempt another escapade, he would be kicked out of the band. No questions asked. While I assured him that level of extremity would not be necessary, he wouldn't have any of it, shaking his hands in my face to end the conversation.

I was finally properly introduced to Francesca, Forever Red's lead guitar player and front of the band, though I quickly learned she preferred keeping herself to herself and rarely attended group meetings. That alone gave me the impression we'd probably be great friends in another life.

The opportunity arose for me to attend a stage test of one of their upcoming performances, though I could do nothing but laugh at Mars' managerial skills.

"You're so severe," I joked and they shooed me away with hands, adjusting their clunky headset.

I planned my trip home to see my mum and Bess over Christmas break. Rani wished to return with me, and both Mars and Carmen promised to visit us both.

To put it simply, things were working out. Or so it seemed. It was hard to truly gage what the bright side looked like when you'd spent so long in the dark.

⚜

"PICK THE PEN UP," I demanded. Carmen stared coldly, half at my face, and half at the space just to the side of me, dividing her full attention. She held her breath for a few moments, heart rate increasing and fist clenching, but she didn't touch the biro I placed on the table to her left. She had mastered this over the last couple of weeks, this technique of only half listening at all times.

Rani clapped, perched on the steps in the corner of the room. Carmen threw her a thumbs up.

"Great work, Carmen." Marianne stood at the doorway. I recognised she had been there for a while, though it was evident only I sensed her.

"He wasn't trying hard enough."

I believed Carmen meant that as a joke, but in hindsight, I wasn't too sure.

"Arlo is still only a few months turned. Some of us have strength triple times the power of his young, immortal mind." Marianne entered the room properly, hands on hips and brow tighter than usual. "You'll need to start trying to work with some of the others."

I didn't say anything in response to that, acting as though I wasn't actually present.

"She still did well," Rani chimed in, standing up and heading over to take Carmen's space; the two of them sharing a silent conversation and blushed grins in passing. My friend then turned to look at me head on, shaking her arms out in preparation and brushing her curls to her back. She grinned, stance tensing. "Gimme all you got."

I took a deep breath, catching eyes with Marianne before I began. It was always easier to try it out on Carmen because we didn't share any memories or connections. There was a mutual, unspoken hostility between us at all times, regardless of our situations, which helped ease us both. I couldn't blame Carmen for any of her feelings, but with Rani, I always had to pause.

Marianne stepped in before I opened my mouth.

"Now, Rani dear, close the gate. You're still radiating too many signals."

We both turned to The Thorns leader, confused, but Carmen glanced at Marianne and lowered her head in agreement.

"I'm not sure what you mean. I've done alright so far," Rani said, loosening her stance.

"You're focusing too much on focusing. It cancels out. Your mind is wild and that's too dangerous with our kind. You'd let anyone right in."

"I'm trying." Rani sounded embarrassed, but she had no need to be. Like she did with everything, she was trying her best and I loved her for it.

"Okay then, Arlo. Command." Marianne stepped back as if introducing a stage scene and I stared at my friend, whose expression had now shifted into one of confidence. Over the week, I admit I may have been too easy on her, without even meaning to. It was as though I just had this inability to control her. Even thinking it hurt me, the thought that I could so easily take advantage of her that way. She never deserved that, never will.

Yet Marianne watching this time sparked a shift in my judgement. Like I *wanted* to impress her. Show her my strength. My control.

"Sit down," I tried, and not a breath after I finished, her legs collapsed beneath her and she sat cross-legged on the hard stone, face aghast.

"Oh," she said, absorbing her new position.

"Sorry!" My hands frantically threw out to accentuate my apology. I didn't know if the landing hurt her or not, but it looked as if it had done.

Carmen rushed back over to aid Rani with Marianne at her other side; both of them working together to help her back up. My friend looked entirely disorientated.

Rani's face looked flustered, and she dusted off her trousers. "It's okay... I think I know what he did differently that time. I felt it." She looked back at me, her smile still strong, with only a slight hint of uncertainty. "Again."

Differently?

With my leader backing up but still silently observing, I tried a different approach; something I knew I wouldn't normally be able to change her mind on because of a recent conversation we had. I knew I never would have said this to Rani really. She was allowed to do whatever made her feel comfortable. But that was why I tried it. I was pushing myself in that moment, and that moment alone. **"You know, you really don't need to wear make-up, you look lovely without it."**

Maybe I did mean it a little, but I regretted it the moment the words left my mouth. It didn't sound like me... *Oh.*

Without a second for a breath, Rani's eyes were no longer her own, they grew inhumanly wide and glassy in exaggerated realisation and she began to frantically rub, *scrape* at her face, faster and faster. Her nails digging deep into her skin, eyes hauntingly stuck to my own face as her skin turned raw and mascara streaks leaked down her cheeks. I began to panic and my whole body went into shut down mode. I was pushed to the side and stumbled backwards, losing my footing and falling to the floor as Carmen grabbed ahold of Rani, trying to pull her hands away from ruining her face and restrain her. Marianne leaped over and pulled Rani's poor head into her hands, whispering words and tugging their foreheads close. Carmen let out a sound of desperation as Marianne worked.

I couldn't breathe. I could barely even see anything; blackness clouding my vision.

What am I?

What have I done?

"ARLO!" A piercing scream ripped its way into my skull, tethering me to reality as light filtered back through my eyes.

Marianne hovered like a shadow above me, blond curls glued to her reddened brow.

"Arlo, can you hear me?" Her voice was not kind.

"Get up." Hands grasped at my collar and hauled me up in one swift motion. Despite her small stature, none of it mattered; her strength was enough to pull me into a stand and more. I had but a second before I was slammed against the stone wall and pinned in place, her arm to my throat.

I clocked Carmen cradling Rani in her arms, my best friend's eyes closed and her body still: face bright red and makeup ruined. My gaze was abruptly pulled back to face Marianne's stern, blue eyes. Breath left me, and I was momentarily winded as my eyes struggled to stay pinned to hers.

"Where did you learn that?" Her canines flashed through her chapped lips.

"I..." *Where did I learn that?*

"You answer me now, Arlo. *How?*"

"I'm sorry, I'm sorry, I'm sorry." I couldn't take a deep breath, my eyes wandering back to where my friend lay. "Is she okay? Will Rani be okay?" I begged to know.

Marianne's eyes softened a little then, and her grip on my throat loosened, no longer crushing my Adam's apple.

"She's fine," she said, her tone much softer and threat free.

"I had no idea that would work." I gulped. "That wasn't normal, was it?"

Marianne took a deep breath and shifted her gaze, peering over my shoulder instead, a far less intimidating gesture.

"Not at all," she answered hoarsely.

"I didn't mean to do that, I swear." I continued to try and explain myself. I genuinely did not expect it to work, but even the tiny part of me that *did,* had no idea how strong the Manipulation would be. I expected her to at worst, agree, and ask for a makeup wipe perhaps, or at best, laugh and prove to me that I *couldn't* control her. I didn't want to control her, ever, so I didn't for a second believe she would start mindlessly *tearing* at her face.

I made a retching sound, and Marianne retreated quickly

before I vomited onto the stone. If Carmen reacted to this, I wouldn't have known; instead, my gaze was fixed on the blood before me. I hoped, in the rush of panic, that the dimness of the corner of the room would hide the fact that parts of my vomit was black.

Black.

Michael.

"Arlo that was... strong. Too strong. You didn't even have to *try*..." Marianne's body sheltered me in the corner, hiding our conversation with a hushed tone.

Is that not a good thing? That I'm learning fast?

What? No... No, that wasn't me. I didn't think that. Please. Please. No.

Is it not?

Please.

"You are seriously worrying me now, Arlo. To do something like that at ease takes decades of experience, at the very least. *Decades*, Arlo, not mere *weeks*."

"I won't do that again. I won't... I won't. I'm so sorry."

Marianne's look was hesitant, but I needed her to believe me. I would have never done that on purpose.

It wasn't me.

I know that now.

Arlo didn't do that.

I had lost my awareness.

I stood up again, but this time, my head split with pain. "Please Marianne, you have to believe me, I will never, ever do that again. I can't... I couldn't... I frightened *myself* there." That was the best I could manage without choking up.

Get out of my head.

Marianne leaned in closer, Carmen sat, unmoving, focusing solely on Rani. I thought it odd, however — I expected Carmen to be ripping me to shreds for what I did.

"I wiped their memories," Marianne whispered. "They don't

remember those last few moments. Just the training, and you challenging them, but this time Rani fainted — just fainted. Nothing to do with your mind games."

Wait...

Then she stepped even closer, an inch away from my face. "This will not happen again. If it does, you know what I will do. You understand what I am capable of. I will not hesitate to keep them all safe."

RANI STIRRED and Carmen propped her up in her arms. Bleary-eyed, Rani looked to Carmen, as if slowly beginning to process her surroundings.

"You passed out, I was worried," Carmen said, ruffling Rani's hair.

Marianne finally rejoined the scene, throwing a brief and cautious look my way. "I think that's enough training for today." She stepped in and took Rani's hand to help her up.

"But we're only just getting started with the hard stuff!" Rani released herself from the leader's grip; determined and convincingly unafraid. "I've just not eaten enough today, I'll be fine."

The lie Rani believed sounded so convincing and plausible, and to anyone else would have sounded perfectly valid, but a lump grew in my throat until it blocked my airways.

"Marianne is right," Carmen interjected, patting Rani on the back. "We both probably need some rest. This can wait for another time."

"Actually, girls. I don't think I want you to continue this training." Marianne stopped them, biting her lip in concentration.

Carmen scowled as if she thought she'd misheard her. She had not, of course, and I was glad of Marianne's decision.

"A vampire standoff is no place for a human anyway. This has all just been for fun."

Carmen had seemed to be well and truly on Marianne's side,

until those final words; then her allegiance changed, and she shifted back to Rani's side. "*Fun?* What do you mean? You're not letting us help? You're not letting *me?* Have I not proven myself?" She was angry, and I understood her fully. Carmen was more than capable, but after seeing what I could do, Marianne's executive decision was the right one, for the sake of us all.

"Carmen, don't. Please." Marianne maintained composure, ushering the two humans towards the wooden door. "We will talk about this later. Please understand me. It's for the best."

"For the *best*?" Carmen persisted to protest. "After *everything?* You're changing your mind just like that? Because Arlo's stronger than he should be? Was that not always *expected?*"

"Carmen! Enough!" Marianne growled, her teeth exposed.

It wasn't Manipulation, it wasn't needed. Marianne, the ever soft-spoken Englishwoman, never raised her voice like that unless something was seriously wrong. I'd seen her do this twice in the space of ten minutes now. And it was all my fault.

She wiped their memories.

"I'll be out in a second," Marianne said, not letting Carmen get the last word in.

Rani's eyes caught mine as she shuffled out, then she glanced to the floor behind me. Confusion mixed with something else that I couldn't decipher had painted itself over her face. She saw the blood. She didn't comment on it.

What have I done?

CHAPTER TWENTY

Frost coated the ground the next morning; couples gripped onto coat arms, laughing when one or both inevitably slipped.

I'd spent my morning in the university library, finishing up some last-minute studies before preparing some reading for the following term. My lecturers had barely even noticed my considerable absence over the past month or so. I'd explained my reasoning of course and proved I'd still done the readings as much as I could. With jarring nods and heads tilted slightly to the wrong side, they claimed that as long as my grades remained consistent, my self-study time must be paying off. It shouldn't have been that easy and I should have been penalised — should have been a lot of things. It was constant now.

Most of my bags were packed, ready for me to leave for home in a few days as everything seemed to be winding down for the winter break.

Who would have thought studying was the only thing that could truly keep me distracted now. The only thing to keep the creeping thoughts at bay, the thoughts that had eaten away parts of me over the last month.

Marianne was acting strange around me, stranger than normal. She would no longer smile at me in the motherly way she once did and was much more direct with her questions and requests. It was inexplicably clear that my newfound *ability* had frightened her, overwhelmed her perhaps. The entire concept of Manipulation had baffled me right from the start, but it was slowly unfolding to be quite clear. We had power, our kind. And it was up to us how we chose to use it.

For the record, I never willingly went into a situation with the desire to control it, but it was growing increasingly harder for me to comprehend my own mind as it was not, perhaps, fully mine to own anymore. I didn't know what was happening, but that *voice,* those thoughts that sprung from nowhere... There was something inside me. Something else. Something I now knew no one seemed to know the severity of; no one other than *him*. Michael.

What was I capable of?

Great things.

Since the incident with Rani, and the pain devouring me ever since, I'd felt entirely unlike myself. So I studied, sought distraction, and did what made me happy.

I think, anyway. It was hard to tell. I was becoming a shell.

I FINISHED up my writing and added a note for a poem idea, but then scribbled it out and cursed myself for even thinking it would work. My own projects would have to wait.

Heading out into the late morning sun, I precariously watched my footing along the uneven streets as I strode up past the cathedral for my daily meeting with Mars. I was a little early, as per usual, so I bought a hot chocolate and doubled it up as a hand warmer as I stood beside the doorway to someone's home.

I wondered if Marianne had told them what I was.

An abomination.

A headache was brewing, and I wiped away a single tear that had somehow crawled out. I blamed it on the cold, lying to myself.

While I wasn't particularly paying close attention to my surroundings, every now and again, out of habit, I would look up and around to see if I recognised anyone. I rarely did, it was a fairly big city, and I was still only a few months into calling this my new home, but I would always scan crowds regardless: a desire for a sense of familiarity in this foreign new life.

Two minutes passed, my drink finally cooling to a drinkable temperature, and I looked up again to the alleyway leading up to the side of the cathedral, and maybe it was just a trick of the light or a mixture of greenery and shopping bags but I could have sworn I saw *her*. I shivered, and not from cold.

Lucy. The woman I'd all but convinced myself must have vanished from existence.

But her hair was unmistakable, and she had on the very same outfit she had when we first met... I was losing my mind, surely.

"Earth to Arlo." A hand in a fingerless glove wafted in my face, obstructing my focused squint on... nothing. There really was no one behind the headstones. How silly of me to even think that.

"Lawrence." I landed back into the present.

"I just saw you standing there with eyes like a cat planning its next attack. Who are you looking for?" His eyes dramatically wandered across my line of sight. He'd dressed himself like he'd just returned from some sort of spiritual retreat in Iceland; woollen stripes and laced up layers, his trademark skirt trailing the ground.

"Just Mars, they're running a little late." I flicked my eyes to my watch, a gesture to make this encounter less awkward.

Lawrence chewed the inside of his mouth. "Ahh, of course. I should have known." He didn't say it to be condescending, though perhaps he knew something I should have already known.

"What's your situation then? Dare I ask?"

My cheeks flushed. "What is that supposed to mean?" It came out regrettably more defensively than I intended.

Lawrence rolled his eyes, again, not to judge me but more perhaps at my naivety. "You know what I mean, Arlo." As if it's obvious. "You and Mars. Are you seeing each other? Are you..." He flapped his hands to finish the sentence while I stood, dumbstruck.

"Well?" he added while we waited for my brain to finish computing.

"No," I said firmly. "We're not... *together*. We're not like that. At all."

"Ahh. I see." He raised an eyebrow in feigned belief.

"What?" *Am I stupid? Why can't I read this?*

He sighed and this time I was aware he considered me to be inexperienced on the matter.

"Okay then... I'll shoot my shot." He stepped a tad closer than I usually like people to stand around me, fresh tobacco with a hint of animal blood warm on his breath.

"I know this is probably inappropriate to ask, considering what I did recently, which, for the record I am still *morbidly* embarrassed about, and I seriously don't expect forgiveness for it, but... would you consider grabbing a coffee some time? Just the two of us." He held his head in an unsure manner, preparing for a slap of disappointment.

I tried my best to hide my utter embarrassment at this conversation, my body verging on panic mode.

"Oh, sorry, Lawrence. I'm not... I don't..." I wasn't even sure what the ending of these sentences were meant to be, I was just trying, and failing, at *'letting him down gently'*.

"I promise sober me is *nothing* like that other me." He tried to twist it to reassure me. "And the other me is only like that when I take too much gear, which I vow to stop, I really do..."

"Oh no, it's not that... it's..." *It's what, Arlo?*

"I get it," he said finally, shrugging. "You're not into guys."

I held up my hand in protest. "No, it's not that."

"You prefer girls?" he continued to quiz.

"No, I... no."

"All the beautiful things in between? You know I'm..."

I shook my head, and this time, he stopped.

"You're confusing me, Arlo... who *do* you like?" He tipped his head as though the answer should be blindingly obvious. "You don't like men, you don't like women and you don't like anyone in between, so which is it?"

I didn't know — I'd never known, and possibly never would. If I had to try and label my feelings, I'd say I wasn't really *anything*. Yet I always had this strong urge to constantly reassure people I wasn't straight.

Lawrence sighed before I could respond, then looked over my shoulder towards, as I quickly guessed, the approaching Mars.

"Here they come. Listen, a word of advice? I've seen the way they look at you. The way they act around you and how they worship the ground you walk on. They don't act like that around anyone else, and I don't know how you've done it, but you've entranced them entirely." Lawrence patted my back as he readied to depart. "Please don't hurt them." And with that, he strode off in the opposite direction, and I turned a moment too late to watch Mars' face fall.

"What was that about?" they asked, a tad out of breath.

"Oh, nothing." I smiled.

My dead heart broke at their face.

MARS INFORMED me during our brisk walk that Marianne had hoped to meet with me, alone, which they stressed profusely, to 'discuss' some things. They reassured me they hadn't opened their mouth about what happened between me and *Michael*, but suggested maybe it was about how to deal with what Mars described as my 'scary talent'.

So, she did tell them then. Of course she did.

"You know, then." I wasn't asking.

Mars nodded, their manner fading to seriousness.

"I swear I..." I began to defend myself, but Mars cut me off with a harsh shake of their head.

"No. No. Arlo don't. Please."

"What?" My chest grew tight, and my shirt suddenly lost its comfort. I couldn't figure out if they were mad at me or pitied me, and the not-knowing made my hands twitch and flex into fists.

"I wasn't there. I didn't see what happened."

"But Rani..."

"She's perfectly fine; I spoke with her this morning."

"You did?" I was relieved. "When can I speak with her?"

Mars shook their head again. "Arlo, you know what Marianne asked. Just leave it until tomorrow now, please."

I knew they were right. I needed to spend some time apart from Rani and Carmen, just for the time being. For the good of everyone.

I swallowed the reality down hard, head nodding to the beat of realisation.

"I didn't mean for it to happen."

Mars didn't respond in the way I hoped. They didn't respond at all, just continued on the walk and changed the subject, pointing out the emptiness of the café we were headed to.

MARS WAS RIGHT, of course. Marianne greeted me outside my student accommodation at half-past five and explained she wanted to take me for a stroll. I obliged and followed her down the path.

"Are we finally talking again?" She initiated the conversation, though the comment struck me as odd in many ways. *She* was the one who was behaving differently around me. Or had I not even realised that it was *me* who was the problem. *Was it me?*

"I appreciate anything you say to me, so I would very much like to hope so." It felt like a good response.

"You're a shy young man, aren't you?" she observed as I fell in line with her step.

"I suppose." It was a remark I'd heard all my life. Nothing I did could change that, it seemed.

"You're not comfortable with getting close to people either."

Again, her deductions were correct, though the direction of this conversation remained a mystery. I waited for her to form her point.

"I fear I may have approached things... *carelessly*," she continued, her tone warm and protective. "And that's had quite the impact on you, detrimentally so, and I apologise for that."

"You've been doing your best. I understand my head is a little complicated sometimes. Even I don't understand myself half of the time, so really, it should be me who is apologising." I threw her a compassionate grin, but she didn't reciprocate.

"We're losing you again, Arlo."

That comment was not entirely unexpected.

"I'm trying." *So hard.*

"I know you are, son. I know." Marianne sucked in her lips until they formed a fine line of misery. "I'll be honest, I've met very few people like you in my life, and even though I claim to have experience in *most* things, I still don't always understand the best way to go about everything."

I wanted to thank her for her honesty, but something inside stopped me.

"You're a boy who sees the world through a very different lens than the majority of us, and I now see how that has affected the way you navigate things."

That was a new one. "How so?" I tucked my hands into my coat pockets.

"I forget what it is like for mortals to live in this world. Carmen, bless her soul, has helped me keep track here and there but even she has spent so long surrounded by us that she's not the best representative anymore."

"So, you're saying you don't know what it's like to be human anymore?"

She answered with a low shrug and a sigh of laughter. "I suppose I denied it for far too long."

I mumbled my understanding as we continued our walk down onto the riverbank, the distant drilling and groan of machines drifting through the air as we approached the bottom of the steps.

"I can help with that, maybe?" I tried to suggest. I'd never been good at comforting and offering assistance or solutions, but I was ever the people pleaser.

Marianne smiled distantly at this, but I deduced that wasn't necessarily where she intended on going with the conversation.

"Your friend, Rani, exhibits it so well. She's the most human person I've ever met, even when I once was one."

"How do you mean?"

Rani.

"She reads people, so intimately and in detail. She adapts and she understands, even when she doesn't think she does. She has a heart of gold, and she always speaks her mind, regardless of her surroundings. That's such a lost talent in our world."

I smiled fondly. "She is one of a kind."

"You're lucky to have her."

"I am."

"She helps Carmen in many ways too, which I'm sure you've noticed."

"I have."

We crossed the bridge over onto the narrower path, manoeuvring around fallen thorn branches.

"I know Carmen can be difficult sometimes, and I apologise for the way she acts around you."

"She has every right. She watched her family die in front of her, dead by the hands of someone you so openly welcomed into your community. Someone who was trusted and admired and doted on. Even *praised*. Someone who should not have held such evil in their nature and yet still succumbed to the urges." I brushed under my nose discretely. "It sounds all too familiar if you ask me."

The shy Arlo Marianne obviously thought she knew held back no longer; I had nothing left to lose, so I voiced what I'd been thinking for a long time.

Marianne sighed. "And that's what has been worrying me. You are *different,* and it scares me. I can openly admit that. The whole story around your rebirth... Lucy, if that even is her real name, she's behind this, she has to be, and then you were *chosen* by something else entirely."

It hit me like a gut punch, but it was true. *Did she know the whole truth, though?*

"Mars saved you and hates themself for leaving you alone to fend for yourself without actively intervening, and I hate that I let them. We forgot you were still so very human. You still are, in a way."

"You think so?"

Her eyes widened. "Oh, I know so. You yearn for purpose and a future and *control* of your own life. You struggle and you let yourself, even blame yourself, yet you strive for greatness and are frustrated no one can truly help you. At least, that's what you convince yourself. The self-doubt... those are not the traits of someone who knows they have eternity to do whatever they want. Cling onto that, Arlo, and never let it go."

Her brutal honesty astounded me, and my chest ached at the *truth* of it all. She was right, and I was relieved. *She understands. She understands and I didn't even have to explain myself. I can never truly explain myself.*

I let my eyes wander over to the illuminated bridge and castle to our left, tears rising and threatening for release.

"We invited this creature right to you. Let it have open access. We left you helpless," Marianne's pitch rose, and only then could I tell she was also trying not to cry. *Why does she care?*

"Marianne, I..."

"Don't you dare apologise. You do that too much. Too much, Arlo. You have *nothing*, I repeat, *nothing* to apologise to me about, or my Thorns. You are no burden, just a boy who was trying to live his life to the fullest before being *dragged* into this world headfirst and forced to keep above the raging tide of an endless ocean."

She was beginning to sound like Mars. Or maybe Mars sounded like Marianne. Maybe they both had a point.

I was crying. Not how I thought this evening would have started.

"I won't hug you because Mars and Rani have made it very clear you do not like that."

They did? My breathing hitched.

"But I will protect you and I want you to be happy. I want you to live this life the best way you can, and I will use every last drop of strength to guarantee that."

A sense of déjà vu overcame me then. I'd heard this kind of promise before — many times in my life, in fact — to the point where I could no longer be certain of its validity.

"If I can help you understand yourself in any way, I would love to try."

Too many emotions had pent up in my chest and they all emerged in one shaky laugh. "You can fix my brain if you want. Explain to me why emotions are so impossible to understand."

She smiled at that. "See, you are still very much yourself, I know why Mars cares so deeply about you."

They worship the ground you walk on.

Mars.

"That's where I'm confused," I eventually said. *Why did I say that?*

Marianne didn't give me the weird look I expected however... in fact, she appeared to understand exactly what I was about to say...

"You think Mars likes you in a way you can't reciprocate."

"Yeah." I breathed it out as a deep sigh.

"But you don't think it's a problem with Mars."

"No."

"That's a perfectly normal reaction... even *I* only understand love to an extent," she chuckled to herself. "Here's where my maternal instinct kicks in."

Love.

"Arlo, I'm going to ask you a very personal question, but I hope you'll hear me out because I actually think I *can* help here."

"Okay."

"Have you ever been in love?"

"Never."

She nodded her head. "Understandable. You're only what, eighteen, nineteen?"

"Nineteen."

Another nod. "But do you find yourself wanting to be in love? Answer me honestly."

"No." A sudden weight fell from my shoulders.

"And do you ever want to be in a relationship? Do you want — forgive me if I sound cheesy — do you want romance?"

"I don't think I do, no."

"And do you think there is something wrong with you for thinking that?"

I... how does she know this?

"Arlo, have you ever considered the fact that this is an entirely normal thing. That there are people out there, many in fact, who feel exactly the same?"

I was stunned. Of course, I'd come across the term *asexual* a handful of times, and some related terms, but I'd never given myself the time to look into it. The world around us was so inherently sexualised that my brain always drew the same conclusion: that these poor people must be very lonely, and I pitied them. *How could anyone not want love like that?* I would think, despite never looking at myself and what I wanted. What I didn't want.

"Is that it then?" I asked.

"It may well be. I can't answer that for you, but I can sense when I'm right." Marianne flashed a smile. "You understand that it is perfectly normal and very human in fact to *not* want these things? You know that, right?"

I said nothing, overwhelmed with the giant, thousand-piece puzzle in my head that was coming closer and closer to completing itself as she spoke and...

"I'm ace."

"Seems like it."

"And... *aromantic*, is that the word?"

Marianne nodded.

"And so..."

She smiled again. "So, do you understand that you are not broken?"

"I'm not?"

"Arlo, my dear, do you want to know something? It took me over two hundred years to figure out that I wanted nothing to do with sex and romance and all those icky feelings that came so naturally to everyone else. It took me over two hundred and *fifty* years to learn that there are many different types of love and that they are all equally important. They all have a role in our lives and that *not* feeling some of them does not diminish the strength and power of the other types, and in fact friendship..." she took a deep breath, still shaking as I was, "there is nothing more omnipotent than friendship. And you, Arlo, will never, *ever,* be alone. You are loved in so many ways and don't for one second think that because you don't want romance that it makes you any less of a man or a human or even a goddamn being on this planet."

She calmed herself. "You owe the world nothing. You are perfect just the way you are. Never forget that."

I grabbed her and pulled her into the tightest hug I'd allowed myself to give in years. It took Marianne a moment to absorb what just happened, but then I felt her arms tighten around my back and I was grounded, more than I ever had been in my whole time in this city.

I am not broken.

"DOES THAT FEEL BETTER? Figuring that out?"

We recommenced our walk, my rib cage unweighted, and the burning confusion in my mind had finally flown free. One less thing off my chest. *It's fine. I'm fine. I'm unbroken.*

"I think I've always known... just not *realised* I've known."

"That makes perfect sense. We know ourselves more than anyone else ever could, even if the world doesn't give us the eyes to see it."

"So, you're like me then? You don't want, you know... stuff? It doesn't feel right?"

She released a pleasant laugh. "Yes. I'm aromantic asexual, if I want to put a label to it. I don't want *stuff.*"

"And you don't wish you were different?"

"Not at all. For a time I believed I should wish I was different, but then I quickly learned that it had nothing to do with me... it was merely an issue with everyone else not wishing to take the time to understand."

We stepped through the narrowing path as we crossed under a bridge, and each step I took, the more I realised how much I'd let the world manipulate *me*. It was like I'd spent my life in a trance and only now was I finally waking up.

"Be proud of yourself," was Marianne's final comment on the topic, followed with a gentle pinch to my coat sleeve.

"WHY DID you really want to walk with me?" I asked, skirting alongside the black, iron railings between the path and the river, keeping my coat wrapped tightly around me. I knew this would shift the mood, but no matter what we discussed, it would always come back around to this.

"You've probably already guessed that, Arlo."

"What I did to Rani."

A nod indicated my correct assumption.

"I suppose we're at a point now where I have no choice but to be honest with you and explain why it scared me."

Worry drowned my senses. I suspected she was about to bring up Isiah and indicate how my behaviour displayed parallels to him — something that crossed my mind frequently.

"I had a friend once, a very long time ago. Well before everything. In fact, you could say he was my best friend. We'd both been around a very long time, had seen and experienced the same things. We drifted after a long while..." she waved her hand dismissively, "but that's beside the point. This friend was unmatched, possessing skills on all levels. We argued and started to fall out a lot. We disagreed on how we saw the world and ultimately, I left him because he *scared* me. I ran away, wanting nothing more to do with him or the perspective he watched the universe from. His strength was terrifying, to the point where I hold him wholly responsible for why I do what I do now. I protect people; vampires and humans alike. If I'd been experienced like I am now back then, I would have killed him, no hesitation. But instead, I ran away. Despite having horrific encounters all my life, I'd never felt *that* level of fear until I watched a newly turned crawl so deeply into the mind of an innocent as effortlessly as the flow of water and not even realise the extent of what they had just done."

"It didn't feel *difficult*." That frightened me.

"And that's my issue. It should have. It's one thing to encourage a thought, an entirely different thing altogether to watch her eyes go blank, as if her entire soul had been exhumed from her body."

I never even noticed.

"If your ability falls into the wrong hands, if you are misled in any way, you will fall into a hole so black and so vile, there will be no hope for redemption."

Michael. She's talking about Michael. Can I even call him that? Does she know?

"So, I wanted to ask for your permission to do something. It's not something I enjoy nor *want* to have to do, but I fear it's the only way to keep you safe."

I looked at her, anticipating the worst.

"I want to put a lock on your mind and halt this ability so that you cannot use it, even if you try."

"Can you do that?"

"I've done it before. It's not... pleasant, and not something I *want* to do. It leaves a pungent smell..."

It took a few swallows to remove the lump in my throat. "If that's what you think is best."

"Good. I'm relieved you understand."

"For how long?" I asked, controlling my breathing to calm my nerves.

"As long as necessary. Until we remove your direct threat and I can train you properly."

"But I'll still be me?" My only concern.

"Of course, nothing will change, you will just be... safer."

You are going to let her take control of your mind?

I rubbed my eyes with the palms of my hands. "Okay. Now?"

She pointed up ahead to a building where there was a viewing point with a metal bench. "It won't take long."

I could sense she was trying to Manipulate me there. The same way I was still so very self-aware after a few drinks — the way I *knew* how everything functioned, but didn't have the capacity to care. So I gave in trying to deflect it.

Weak.

"Okay," I said again.

Then we were facing each other on the path, overlooking the oak buried cathedral and the dancing lights over the water, and she took my head in her hands, thumbs pushing gently above the crooks of my eye socket as she closed her eyes in concentration. I managed one deep inhale then in an instant I fell to my knees, as if my spinal cord had been ripped right from my back, but she held me steadily until I could breathe again, and I was looking back up at my leader, and she smiled like she always did, cupping and brushing my chin with her hands.

"It can't get you now," she whispered. Her hands returned to my head and blackness consumed every crevice of my mind.

Of course she knew.

CHAPTER TWENTY-ONE

I will never tire of watching things unfold. Of observing the inner workings of every train of thought, every reaction, and every response. Humans are such pitiful things, even those long beyond their humanity. They still think in such a linear format, clinging on to the possibility they might have won against whatever it is that keeps them up at night.

It would have saddened me if he could not remember our meetings, but I kept them hidden so far back in his sorrowful mind that her efforts made little difference. He doesn't remember all the incredible work we've accomplished, or all the imperative ideologies we have explored. He still scurries back to his friends believing he can be rid of me, yet he can't even remember why he wants me gone anymore. He just tries too hard to find his purpose that he is oblivious to the fact I've already shown him.

I was floating. Arms outstretched; ankles soaked in soothing warmth. Miles and miles of vast blue ocean churned beneath me; above me lay an infinity of white. My eyes were scrunched tight, yet I could see every colour and every shape that held itself before me. It was so peaceful; I could have lain here for all eternity.

"Arlo, we're going to be late," Rani's voice called out and my eyes shot open. I was stood in my sandstone room, facing the wonky landscape painting in the corner with my back to the door.

I looked down at my feet before I reacted to anything else, ensuring I was grounded. Awake.

A knock. "Arlo! You're not still asleep in there, are you?"

I waited for the rest of my body to awaken, and once it did, I turned to my bed and pulled on the jacket that lay out ready for me. *How did I get here?*

"Carmen has the engine running. Are you going to let yourself be late? That's not like you!"

My body finally followed the voice to the door and I swung it open, smiling at my friend on the other side.

"Ready?" she asked.

I nodded.

"Good, because it will look bad if we turn up late. We promised Ben and Casper we'd be in the front row."

Ahh, the concert. What day is it?

THE NEXT THING I knew I was in the back of a three-door car, neck bent forwards with my back almost pressed against the roof and my legs drawn in until they were inches from my chin. We were driving to a small gig venue on the outskirts of the city. Rani was in the passenger seat, Carmen directly in front of me. We shared a limited conversation, unwilling and stubborn from both ends before Rani turned the music up and reminded us for the seventh time that we were going to be late. All the while I was blinking and shaking my head, trying to get my mind to wake up and for me to remotely feel present. I felt as though I'd been asleep for days.

We didn't have to queue; Mars greeted us at the back door, and we avoided the growing line of attendees. It was pitch-black outside, and I realised as I looked around myself that I hadn't missed days and days like I'd originally believed. Only yesterday was I walking along the riverside with Marianne. *Where did she go?*

Rani held Carmen's hand as a child would their mother. She looked at Carmen with such joy, the emotion and energy reciprocated. I walked behind them and lowered my head, still disorientated and believing I was missing something.

We were ushered through the stage side entrance in the dim rehearsal light and Mars left me and Rani in the dressing area whilst Carmen followed them, picking up her camera and wrapping the strap around her neck.

Rani propped her bag on the table beside her which was littered in wine bottles and a vibrantly multicoloured lace scarf which undoubtedly belonged to Lawrence.

"Living the lavish life here. Does this make us groupies?" Rani's eyes were pools of delight and it made me laugh out a smile.

"I suppose so."

"I never used to listen to this sort of music, as you probably already know, I tend to stick to my upbeat playlists, but the *lyric* work and Francesca's guitar?" She pressed her hands to her lips in a sign of a chef's kiss.

I couldn't deny their talent. The four of them playing together just *worked*. I was happy I was there, again, regardless of my confusion.

Casper waltzed in a moment later with a hoodie on. "Ahh, friends!" he said, putting on a funny accent and welcoming us with open arms.

"Are you playing *'Stars for Alex'* tonight?" Rani rubbed her hands together in excitement, one brow raised in anticipation.

"You'll just have to wait and see." Casper winked at her. "Is that your favourite?"

She nodded and blushed.

"Well, in that case..." He strolled over to the worn leather sofa and flopped down into it, "we might just be playing it."

"God, I sound like I've never met you before," Rani burst out an embarrassed laugh.

"I like Moon Brats." I integrated myself into the conversation. The sudden attention it gave me made me a touch self-conscious, afraid I'd somehow mispronounced it or misread the title, or that it was perhaps what the band believed to be their weakest song.

"Yeah? That's cool." Casper grinned proudly. "Ben wrote that all by himself. All parts." The pride in his face was so prevalent. They loved each other so much. *You're not broken.*

"Are you getting up there with us tonight then?" When Casper asked initially, I was completely disengaged from the fact that he was directing that at me. Then it hit me, and I remembered...

"He played piano for you didn't he," Rani guessed, her mouth wide open.

Oh, god. I completely forgot about that.

I played a piece for Ben and Fran one afternoon not too long ago, after I let it slip that I played piano. They both insisted I showed them, and asked me to play it again while they recorded it. Ben must have shown Casper, now I sincerely hoped he was joking. I couldn't just get up there and *play*. I could barely play my own doodles for an audience, let alone someone else's music, without rehearsing.

"Ben played me what you created. It was beautiful," he continued.

"I... thank you. Wow. But I can't..."

Casper chuckled to himself, reaching for the half empty beer can he must have been drinking earlier, taking a long mouthful before slamming it back down onto the chipped table. "Not tonight, but we're getting you in the studio. You're really talented, my friend."

Rani mouthed 'I told you so' then looked back at Casper. I blushed. I would never get used to people complimenting me, but I needed to accept that and stop hiding. Times like that were what made me feel invincible.

WE WERE ALLOWED FRONT-ROW ACCESS, though we were early enough into the room to be close to the front regardless. Carmen was their stand-in photographer for the night, and I watched her move around in front of the stage, crouching and turning the camera at different angles — the band engaging with her movements as their set commenced. Francesca screamed close to the lens and even climbed down off the stage at times. I caught glances between Ben and Casper during songs, eyes glistening in true happiness. Lawrence channelled all his energy into his guitar-playing, Francesca joining his side to duet in a passionate rendition of the band's most popular song.

Mars' shadow loomed to the side, their head nodding to the beat whilst the audience bounced, dancing and thrashing magnificently to every single song.

I was so lucky to be there.

So lucky to have these friends.

I was surrounded with such an overwhelming sense of *love*, and I never wanted it to end.

"WE'LL JUST BE OUTSIDE," Rani informed me as she and Carmen followed the crowd out of the fire exit, and I walked the other way to the toilet. I nodded in acknowledgement and pushed open the toilet door, letting it swing shut behind me and block out the excess rowdiness. I sighed as I could finally hear my thoughts again, and headed over to the wall in what I believed was an empty room...

"Ahh, finally. Some peace and quiet."

I startled and whirled around to the mirrored sinks, where a glamorously suited man sat with one leg over the other, resting one hand against the sink's edge, the other ring-clad and raised as he inspected his nails. Long, curly blond hair cascaded down to his narrow waist and in the reflection of his back — and *only* in the reflection — sat two dove-grey, feathered and bird-like wings. *Wings.* The tips trailed slightly over the porcelain counter.

"Michael."

Everything came flooding back as he grinned a pearly grin and shifted his weight to the other arm. All our meetings. Over weeks. All our conversations. All my emotions. Everything we did...

I could see him now; his true form. His fingers extending to blackened claws and his wings stretching out into full view. His eyes too white for any human.

"Did you enjoy the concert? It sounded pleasant enough." *Velvet. Velvet. Velvet.*

"You followed me again." My heart sank.

"You should surely understand by now that I am *always* following you. That was a waste of a question."

How do I stay calm?

"I need to leave."

The creature let his bottom lip pout and his glassy eyes drooped. "So soon?"

I turned to leave but then I was stopped in my tracks as the back of my mind opened up and his icy fingers crawled their way in, yanking me backwards. *No.*

"Please don't run away from me, Arlo. You know I hate that."

No. Please. Please.

Anything for you.

"Lovely. Right. Now I have your full attention. I'm correct in believing your precious Thorns leader tried to block your mind, yes?"

She tried.

He scoffed.

Please stop.

"Oh, don't cry. She failed. She's nothing compared to me. Though she does get points for effort." He elegantly slipped down off the countertop, and stepped over to me, wiping away a frozen tear. *It's so crowded in here.*

"It's frustrating how hard you're still trying to fight this. Why can't you simply embrace all I've opened up to you? All the knowledge I shared, and all the freedom I have promised. Are you not relieved?"

Of course I am. You gave me air to breathe.

Stay, Arlo.

"What are *we*?" I begged, pleading for answers.

"We? Oh, that's more like it. You know your place." He circled me like a vulture. "We, my boy, are everything. The infinite possibility of *everything.*"

"Gods?"

He moaned, thinking up a response with a heavy eye-roll. "We are not *gods*, but we are the closest thing to the idea. Can't you feel that? Why won't you let it in?"

"My mind."

"Oh, don't worry so much about *your* mind. You are but a host. You only need to worry about *the* mind."

My mind.

"You will get nowhere by fighting it." His long fingers danced across my shoulders as light as petals as he glided past my back, his feathers dusting over the floor to his side.

I am but a host.

"Who *were* you?" *Stay present. Ask and stay present.*

Michael scoffed. "Irrelevant. Michael was no one. It was such a long time ago now anyway."

"And me? Am I no one?"

His smile chilled my very core. "Oh. Oh, no. You are very much *someone*. That is why I chose you."

I was chosen after all.

"It was always you. And the three of us united on earth again will mean the new beginning. Finally."

"Three of us?" Tears fell uncontrollably from my eyes.

"Oh yes, don't forget. We are three."

"Who is..."

"Ah ah ah." He waggled a bony finger in my face, and swooped around me, prancing like a court jester. "All in due course. I want to see how this story plays out first."

What do you mean?

I thought I was finally in control.

Where am I going?

Where is my mind?

"I'll let you keep this memory this time. I trust you won't go divulging this information. You've done a marvellous job so far." His cold smirk brushed my skin.

"Enjoy Christmas." He was so inexplicably close to me, and I wanted to scream. I could not move an inch. Paralysed. The light buzzed above us, sounding seconds away from exploding. His phantom claws squeezed and dug in so tightly into my mind. Arlo flickering in and out of reach. Then the toilet door swung open with a careless bang and two men walked in, eyes widening in embarrassment, thinking they had walked in on something else. Our connection dropped then, and Michael turned swiftly on his heels, pushing his way between the two men. "Apologies, gentle-men," he said as he disappeared out of the door, releasing me in the process.

Let's go.

I wiped away Arlo's final tears.

CHAPTER TWENTY-TWO

M y first term ended on a questionably sunny day. All signs of frost had melted away while the rainfall earlier that day allowed a faint rainbow to appear above my accommodation.

Lecturers sent out their generic 'stay safe and enjoy the holidays' emails, undoubtably grinning at themselves with relief knowing they were student-free for a handful of weeks.

Yet it seemed many students were staying, with a lot of international travellers electing to remain in the city.

I'd planned well in advance that I would be returning home. I owed my mum that much.

Rani promised she would help me stay 'normal' so my poor mother wouldn't suspect her child had been murdered in a back alley during his third week of term.

In my first few weeks of my new life, if I let myself linger too much on the reality of the matter, I would make myself spiral, so whenever the topic arose in conversation, Mars and the others would always keep it light and positive. Now though, my mind forbade itself to wonder.

When I was still most myself, late at night, I would cry myself to sleep. But then I'd awaken and judge my older self for being so pathetic. I'd never felt more alive now thanks to Michael. Though I knew that was not his real name, it never had been.

I straightened my collar in my mirror, tousled my hair and adjusted my silver ring which oddly felt more a part of me now than it ever had done before. I'd never taken it off since my mum gave it to me. Yet now I wore it with pride, for whatever reason.

Time to put on a show.

"You don't mind if I possibly follow you out in a day or two, do you?" Mars appeared at my doorway — I had forgotten I'd left it propped open.

I turned away from my mirror as if it was never there. "What, come to the Lakes?"

"Unless you were planning on *not* visiting your wonderful mother and instead had a secret rendezvous planned that none of us knew about." They crossed their arms and leaned sardonically against the door frame.

"You want to come home with me?"

"Just for a few days. To, you know... keep an eye out."

I brushed my chin, pondering the proposal. I had considered asking them before, after my incident. But I was more than content with my routine now. I was taking blood morning and night, and they should have known by now that I told them everything. ***Almost everything.*** I shook it off with a smile.

"That's a no then? Or was that just a twitch?" Their tone held a hint of humour.

"No, no. Yes." I rubbed the hairs on the back of my neck. "Yes, I'm sure that would be fine."

"Yeah?" Their brows rose.

"Yeah," I confirmed. "I'd quite like you to meet my mother."

"Good because I've already packed."

It was my turn to raise my eyebrows. "You would have come regardless, wouldn't you?"

They winked and shot finger guns at me as they backed out of the doorway. "Melissa will love me."

THE TRAIN JOURNEY would have been insufferable if not for Rani's wise choice to travel in the late evening — the quietest and cheapest time to travel — so we could sleep, or at least try to. We couldn't go direct, but the changes were smooth enough. Of course, Mars tagged along with the excuse that they weren't used to travelling alone, which was hard to believe, and they felt as though they would be putting my mother off by arriving late and not, for convenience's sake, accompanying her son right from the start.

For a brief moment, realising I wouldn't be able to drift off as Rani had so easily managed, I pulled out my notebook and began to summarise some thoughts. My shaking pen and the presence in my mind made it too difficult to concentrate, so, after noticing Mars was trying to steal a glance in the window reflection, I tucked it back into my pocket and closed my eyes.

Finally, I slept.

I open my eyes as our fourth table seat is loudly occupied by another traveller. He apologises for waking us and hauls a stiff, leather duffle bag onto the overhead racks before throwing himself into the seat beside Rani. She doesn't stir. In fact, neither does Mars beside me. Their chest gently rises and falls, face flopped to the side to face me. So the apology was just for me...

"Yes, I was talking to you, Arlo."

"Michael? I thought you weren't joining me. You said you had business to attend to..."

"That I do. So, you are correct, I am not joining you. I just wanted to wish you safe travels." His toothy grin is too sharp for a

human, nor is it that of a vampire, and as I look to his reflection, low and behold, there are his wings. Cramped behind him on the chair, they look much darker this time.

He catches me staring.

"Like what you see?" He lifts his heavily decorated neck and pushes against the headrest.

"You have wings."

"You are so perceptive."

"What are you? What are we?" I ask, as I always do, though I never quite receive an answer.

"I've told you before: we are everything. The Sun, The Moon and The Star."

The more he answers like this, the more he begins to make sense. Nothing he does seems to scare me anymore. But a tiny flicker in the back of my cramped mind shivers. It cannot bear the weight of this reality. I shut it off.

Good.

"Drink up!" He nods towards the flask I unknowingly hold in my hand now. I peer down to its contents, filled with a thick black liquid. I look back up to question him, but the seat is empty, and his bag is gone.

"Tickets please." I blinked to watch a lady in rail company attire sauntering down the aisle, clipping her hole punch in one hand, a scanner in the other. The train wobbles to the side a bit and she holds out an arm to steady herself on the empty chair beside Rani.

Mars unveiled a slightly bent paper ticket from their pocket and after a few more waking breaths I prepared my own ticket, as did Rani.

With the lady satisfied and moving on, I slapped my face to confirm I was no longer dozing.

"Did she startle you there?" Rani yawned and laughed at the same time. "Should make that my alarm," she joked. A moment later she frowned. "What have you been eating?"

"What do you mean?"

Mars was now looking at me strangely too. "Your lips are black."

I pressed my fingers to my lips and rubbed a little, removing my hand to see charcoal-coloured tips.

I drank it. Again.

"Oh, that. I had some of those boiled sweets, you know the liquorish ones that are more E numbers than anything natural." I laughed it off and watched them both nod intently as if they knew exactly what I meant and didn't even remotely suspect that I'd just told them a complete lie...

Their eyes...

They stopped nodding in unison and blinked.

Oh.

I spent the remainder of the journey saying as little as possible. Neither of them questioned me. *I'm so sorry.*

My home was the next village over from Rani's, so we parted ways and arranged to meet in a couple of days. Mars followed me to my house, and they were quick to bring up the sleeping arrangements. Mars was adamant that I should remain in my own bed and that *they* would gladly take the couch, but I refused, and I contacted my mother in advance with the decision. She would have never allowed a guest to stay in anything but a freshly made bed.

The taxi crossed over the stone bridge; misty lamp-lit gardens and paint-chipped fences being our only view through the headlights. In daylight, you could make out hills for miles, and watch the village rise up into the mountains; church spires and telephone poles standing side by side amongst slate roofs and smoking chimneys. All of this was invisible in the dark.

It had been raining heavily that day and we stepped out straight into a drain puddle. The taxi driver hopped out to assist, joking to us that we would probably have preferred staying in whatever city we came from. I faked a gentlemanly laugh and thanked him.

The clock tower opposite us was illuminated ominously as usual, despite the door below it having been bolted for years. The air was damp and smoky, just as I remembered it. It was as if I'd never left.

Mars walked ahead after I told them where the front door was. The sensor light triggered, then seconds later, the living room was aglow, and we were greeted by a barking Bess.

"Cool house," they observed, staring up at the chapel windows on the side.

"It's tiny on the inside. If you look there, you can see it's actually divided up into four." I pointed with my free hand to where the neighbours rose-covered fence began.

"Still, a lot of history there."

"Definitely."

I had spent most of my life inventing scenarios of things I believed might have happened within those walls. People around the village would always tell us ghost stories about it, with my mum deducing that they were probably just trying to scare her off since she was considerably younger than most other residents when she first moved in. I used to sometimes exaggerate these dramatic stories with whoever wanted to listen at school, using it as a way to make friends.

"I'll let you go first." Mars held back and dropped their bag on the gravel driveway. I turned the corner to the garden gate, the gush of the stream sounding out the back. Neighbouring kitchen lights glowed behind the trees on the other side. Everything was the same as it always was and I smiled inwardly, rummaging for my keys.

A loud bark came from inside again, and the door opened before I was successful in locating my own keys; Bess pounding outside and diving straight over to me. I dropped my bags and bent down so she could leap up and lick my face, muddy paws clambering up my mac. My Bess. I missed her so much.

Bess stayed for a few seconds, then backed away suddenly. Panic shot through me. *She knows,* I thought, but she then made her way over to Mars and welcomed them the same way she would any stranger. *So, what's different?* **You know the answer to that.**

My mother stood in the doorway, tears brimming her eyes. She was dressed in a white knitted jumper, one she normally only wore for special occasions.

"Come here, my boy." She stretched out her arms to me and I stepped over to embrace her, bending down so she could tuck her head into my shoulder. I leaned into her warmth, and she pulled me away slightly, beaming as she gazed at my face. She pulled me back in again so she could smother my face in kisses. I would have been embarrassed, but after hearing about Mars' own relationship with their mother, I knew they wouldn't care.

"Oh, come in, come in," she ushered us both towards the doorway. "It's absolutely freezing!" And with that, she moved aside to let me through, then slipped outside to retrieve Bess who was excitedly jumping over Mars' legs, rooting them in place.

"See, she loves me already, Arlo," Mars shouted, unable to move. They looked at my mother, grinning. "It's lovely to meet you, Miss Everett. Thank you for letting me stay with you!"

We invented the excuse that Mars had always wanted to visit the Lakes as they were an 'avid walker'. Their 'just a few days' would inevitably turn into a week, and, if Mars felt necessary, the entire two weeks I planned to stay.

"Pleasure to meet you too, Mars. I've heard many great things about you," she reached down for Mars' dropped bag, "and please, just call me Mel."

Mars mouthed up to me with a smirk, "*many* great things?"

I shrugged, my mum may have been slightly exaggerating, as usual.

"Oh, please, I can carry my own bag!" Mars patted my mother away from their bag in the politest way I've ever seen anyone complete that action.

Once we were all inside, with Bess still focused more on Mars than myself, my mother busied herself with boiling the stove kettle and I told Mars to make themself at home in our tiny living room, big enough for the two small sofas, a box television and a tragically blocked up fireplace.

They made no hesitation in flopping down onto the nearest couch. "I tell you what, that was a much longer journey than I expected. Are you sure we're only just across the country?" they said it loud enough for my mum to laugh from the other room.

"And I was the one who told him Carlisle would be much easier. I went to Cumbria, and I turned out alright," she piped up, slamming the fridge door shut in three attempts. *Still faulty then.*

"I didn't like the course!" I shouted back.

"Isn't English Literature English Literature *everywhere*?" Mars added, playing devil's advocate.

I stared at them. "I'm not going to answer that."

"Mars, milk and sugar?" my mum called.

"Just two sugars please, black!" Mars answered, crossing their legs.

Bess had settled into a bizarre routine of weaving around the chairs, sitting down briefly then wandering off. She would normally be all over me, but as I sat myself down and attempted to encourage her up beside me, she ignored me and pattered off into the kitchen.

"She'll be able to smell the shift in your scent," Mars said in a hushed tone, having just observed what transpired.

"Hmm."

"She'll get used to it, don't worry. It's not what she's used to. She's never met me before so wouldn't know what to expect."

I nodded but said nothing.

"Your mum won't suspect a thing. I promise."

I continued nodding slowly, melting back into the fabric of the chair and propping an ankle over my other restless leg.

My mother shuffled in, expertly carrying three mugs. I jumped up to save her from the struggle, and she ruffled my hair, joining me on the same chair.

The conversation flowed exceptionally well; Mars, ever so confident, asked all the right questions and listened for the appropriate amount of time. In between thoughts, I would glance to my side to stare at my mother. Think about how I'd missed her and how sorry I was that I would forever have to hide so much from her, despite everything she had done to protect me.

I was going to make a difference in this world now though. She'd be safe. *Indeed.*

Mars caught on to my wandering mind and brought me back into conversation. "So, Arlo is a budding poet it seems."

They were *reading my notes.*

My mum rubbed my leg, clearly forgetting my unease with abrupt contact, but I kept my mouth shut and relaxed as much as I could. "Oh, he always wanted to be. Have you read his stuff?"

"I don't really like—" I was cut off.

"He's got a real talent for it." My mum stood and told us to wait whilst she went to dig out 'The Arlo Archives.'

Mars' smile stretched from ear to ear, and I begged for the ground to swallow me up. This wasn't how I wanted the evening to go, or any evening for that matter.

"The Arlo Archives. I'm going to cry. She's so cute."

"I didn't realise she kept stuff." I honestly didn't.

"Mummy's boy," Mars teased. I slapped them on the leg with the scarf that I'd left draped over the arm of the chair.

A few minutes later, my mum returned with a battered, cardboard shoe box filled with—*oh no*—photos.

She joined Mars's chair this time, Mars looking more than happy to slide along to offer her ample space. I stood quickly to join them in my own horror.

The box contained letters and school projects and hand knitted baby shoes, and she rummaged through it proudly.

"Sorry, son. I'm allowed to embarrass you." She glanced at me briefly, scratching my chin with her warm hands. Mars exaggerated a nod of agreement and pressed their hands between their thighs in anticipation.

"Ahh, there it is! Arlo's entry for his first poetry competition!"

I remember that day vividly. Out of the entire primary school there were only 3 applicants. I was ten, and my teacher encouraged me to enter since I spent every play time in her room either reading or writing. I had a few friends, but I didn't like the intensity of the school yard and never understood why no one *else* preferred staying indoors.

I won, but only because the other entries were from reception children who scribbled pictures as opposed to writing. The following day there was an assembly expressing the sheer disappointment at the fact that no one entered and what an utter disgrace it was that we all preferred playing computer games than '*god forbid, reading a book for once!*'

Reading lessons became mandatory at the beginning of every afternoon, much to everyone else's dismay, and I had to mask the fact that it became the only reason I wanted to actually turn up to school every day.

My mum read the poem out to Mars, who looked as if they'd already read through its entirety in their head because they peered up at me with puppy eyes before my mum had finished.

"That's beautiful, Arlo. Wow." Their voice was so genuine that I was no longer embarrassed. *Really?*

"How old were you when you wrote that?"

"Ten. Year five."

The two of them both stared at me then. "That's my boy," my mum said. "I always said he would go far."

The photos came next. My mum apologised for embarrassing me so early in our visit, but Mars' heavy interest won her over, and I gave in trying to stop them both.

The year 2000: Christmas in Edinburgh with my cousin, Maia, holding my one-year-old self like an offering in front of the ugliest tree ever, my face bright pink and confused.

My first cave trip aged four with a helmet drooping over my eyes and a cheese and tomato sandwich squeezed tightly in my excited hands.

My mum and I in Whitby eating fish and chips on the beach, two minutes before a seagull pooed on the blanket we were sat on.

Me wrapped up in too many layers, walking our first dog for the first time through the park.

Our first holiday abroad; my mum squeezing my shoulders and grinning as I stared down, wide eyed at my melting ice cream.

My first day at school.

My last day of sixth form.

My whole life in a box.

Arlo's life. His humanity. The boy I will never be again.

But look at who you are becoming.

I tore at my hair and squeezed my eyes shut, crying out in pain.

"Arlo! God, baby, what's wrong?" The box was thrown to the floor in an instant, my mother's arms wrapping tightly around my body.

I sensed Mars following suit, but I didn't open my eyes. My spine ached and my shoulder blades flexed unnaturally, toes curling. My head was so very crowded.

I started to convulse; my body hitting the floor. I couldn't keep it out.

My mother hugged me from behind, supporting my head to keep me from hurting myself anymore. I tucked myself into a foetal position to try and relieve the pain; Bess was barking madly somewhere in the distance—a cry for help.

"Arlo, breathe. Can you breathe? Sweetheart," she cried out into my back. My eyes were threatening to roll right back into my skull. I couldn't do *anything*.

Help me.

"Call an ambulance," my mum demanded. Mars' feet hurried over to their bag, and I heard them curse under their breath, unsure what to do. I wasn't human anymore; I couldn't fall into the wrong hands.

I could barely breathe — barely move. A million voices warred in my head, on and on and on.

"**Stop.**" I commanded out of nowhere. My mum released me and I heard a phone drop onto the hard wood floor. I uncurled myself and stretched out, finally finding my feet. "I'm okay, I'm alright. It's nothing to worry about. Those photos were just bringing back... memories." I turned to my mum who sat, mouth agasp, on the floor. "Just happy memories." Then I looked to Mars, frozen to the spot. I'd done it again. *I've done it again.*

"Mars, I'm fine. Don't worry about it." I brushed myself down.

The second hand on the kitchen clock ticked behind us.

"Good, because I was worried there!" *Not Mars.*

"What a relief!" *Not my mum.*

"Anyone want another cup of tea?"

I SAT ALONE on the sofa, having bid my mother and Mars goodnight. Bess opted to sleep with my mum, so the downstairs was deathly quiet, the tower clock my only light source as I kept the curtains open.

The radiator clicked and rain trickled down the window. A car drove past, crossing through the sodden tarmac.

Michael had been right. Marianne had failed to block my mind. For my own good, she had tried, yet for my own good, she had *failed*. I didn't know who to trust; hell, I didn't even know who I even was anymore. This *darkness* kept on growing and growing, but I didn't want it to stop, did I? *What am I to think this? It is not a darkness; in fact, it is the only true light.* I didn't know why I couldn't *see* properly, yet then I felt I was seeing too much. My mind was *open.* Opened to greatness and power. Open to *more. So much more,* Michael said. The creature, my creature. *We are not gods.* But our potential? Who was to say we couldn't be... **He is everything.**

I *wanted* to follow him, to see all he had promised — to be in the light. Yet I saturated my pillows with Arlo's tears, muffled his cries into the sheet, and banged his fist over and over and over in silent pain as I knew — he knew — things would never be the same again.

I knew my purpose now.

MARS GOT ALONG EXCEPTIONALLY WELL with my mum, and I awoke the next morning to the two of them already sat at the kitchen table, discussing their favourite artists then laughing into mugs of tea over references I would never have understood.

In the week that followed, I would watch them washing dishes, helping with groceries, walking Bess with us. They blended in so well, made it seem so easy.

· · ·

"MARS WAS TELLING me they manage a band?" my mum said one night once we were alone. I had since migrated back into my room, having made a makeshift bed on my floor beside Mars, but they opted for much earlier nights than I did.

"Yeah, Forever Red. They're really good; I'm friends with some of them." *Arlo is friends with some of them.*

"They seem too young to be something like that. How old did you say they were again?"

I hadn't. "Twenty-nine."

Her eyes widened. "Wow. Now I would never have guessed that. Wow." My mum was in utter disbelief, and I would have been too, if I hadn't met them under the circumstances in which I did. They looked my age, because their body *was* my age. And I would never age either. *Never.*

"This might be a bit forward of me, and maybe I've got it wrong, but..." she reached her hand across the table. "Be safe. I know you're a sensible boy, and I trust you implicitly but with older people, there's a maturity imbalance... and I'm sure Mars means well—"

"Gosh, mum, no. We're not like that. Mars isn't my *partner.* They're my friend. Just like how Rani is my friend. We're not... I'm not into them like that, or anyone, for that matter."

She released a sigh and tapped her hand on the counter twice. "Good. They genuinely are very sweet, and I know these age gaps sometimes work out, but I'm just looking out for my boy."

"I know, mum." I smiled.

She continued asking me about my term in detail, expressing how she was excited to properly meet Rani the following day, but my mind wandered.

Arlo's mind always flicks back to her, but he will learn what is more important in time. Once his first life passes, this one will be all but a blur.

297

Chapter Twenty-Three

"I'm just saying, how can no one have ever figured out you exist?"

We were sat in a triangle formation in my room: Rani leaning over the back of my chair, me on my bed and Mars resting against the wardrobe.

"The same way no one believes in the tooth fairy — no one *actually* goes looking for us. Governments don't waste time and energy into researching the existence of tiny forest people with wings. We don't leave behind ancient texts that say 'hey, by the way, some humans are immortal!' The Manipulation helps of course," Mars answered.

"The tooth fairy is real?" Rani perked up.

Mars just rolled their eyes.

"Hey, I saw that," she laughed at herself.

"I'm sure there are humans out there who *are* aware of our existence as it would be dumb to believe otherwise," they straightened their back, "but imagine what would happen if they released that information. Imagine the chaos that would ensue. The mass panic. It would be like the witch trials all over again, but with the internet and science and powerful, ignorant men with big red buttons. We've gotta fight for ourselves a bit."

"Now, you've got a point there," Rani jabbed her finger in Mars' direction. "Conspiracy theories are terrifying as it is."

"I don't particularly want to become a science experiment. I wouldn't wish it on my worst enemy, but that's why The Thorns exist, and its why I guarantee you there will be internal organisations across the globe doing the same thing. The right thing. Keeping humanity safe without making a big deal about it."

The tone of the room shifted.

"Carmen thinks it's going to happen again, you know. She thinks one of you will turn and go behind Marianne's back — behind *all* your backs — and do something much worse than Isiah."

I looked at Rani, ***Arlo's friend***, and said plainly, "she thinks it's me."

"Don't say that, Arlo," they both said in sync.

"Tell me I'm wrong."

Rani's arms dropped to her side and sat up straight, glancing to Mars for reassurance; they didn't oblige.

"She wants us to find this Lucy person, and whoever else is behind the murders. And then, obviously, that will lead us to whatever is after Arlo. It's those people we need to worry about, I believe." It was an attempt to shift the topic away from the elephant in the room, backtracking as best she could.

"You believe the two are connected, too?" Mars piped up, ears pricking.

"Well, it's obvious, isn't it? You're all part of a pack, she's part of a pack. Good and evil, if it were."

"It's not that clear cut though, is it?" I suggested.

Rani's head snapped towards me, Mars instead taking their time to slowly look up, but both of their faces read the same.

"What?" I asked. ***Was that out of character?***

"Good and evil. Yes, it is clear cut. We protect people; she, or whoever is in charge, *doesn't*. I don't see how that's hard to understand."

Come on Arlo. Fix it.

"Sorry, I didn't mean it like that. I just wish it *was* that simple, and that we could be the heroes in this, but it feels like we're always walking towards a dead end. She's strong, a difficult match for even Marianne. So, even if we do find her and we are able to prove she is behind everything, what sort of opponents will we be? What is her motive? How big is her army? Will our training be enough?"

I'm sitting in a dark room. No lights, I can't see my own hands. Do I have hands?

Enough.

My mind slams shut.

"We'll have to be ready." Mars stepped over to the window and pressed their palms to the sill, staring out in deep thought. "We have no choice."

"You really think there's going to be a *battle?*" Rani's voice trembled.

"Maybe. It's not as if it hasn't happened before. Marianne has fought many battles over her lifetime, and she is yet to lose. I don't see what makes this time any different." They looked to me. "You saw what she did to Jade. She's *powerful* — frighteningly so. I wouldn't want to get on the wrong side of her."

My mind wandered back to her threat to me after what I did to Rani. *Poor Rani.*

"We'll win, you'll win. And then everything can go back to the way it should be." Rani clapped her hands together and half smiled.

I admire your optimism, human.

"And Arlo will help us succeed." Mars nodded in my direction **— is that pride I sense?**

"And me and Carmen will shake our pom poms from the sidelines." Sourness laced Rani's voice.

Mars' eyes turned to her with pity. "You do understand it *is* no place for humans, right? The Thorns won't harm you, but it is in our nature to hunt. The sheer resistance it takes to *not* attack humans is a lot harder than it seems. In a violent setting, everything will be out of our control. It's hunt or be hunted."

Rani rested her chin in her palm in a sulk. "But our training was going so well! And we have Arlo to protect us. Arlo has helped me so much — Arlo and *you* and Marianne. You'll be unstoppable!"

She's so foolish.

She's strong.

False hope.

"Lucy *killed* Arlo!" Mars snapped, their fist hitting the wardrobe door. Rani stared at them in horror, making them rub their hands self-consciously, then mouth an apology.

"But he's not human anymore... she won't be able to do it again." Her voice grew quiet, less confident.

"Exactly my point. We're *not* human and *you* are." Their tone settles somewhat. "I would hate to see anything happen to you and your girlfriend."

"I..." Rani ran out of words.

"I just... have a feeling we're getting close, that's all. And yeah, I suppose I do feel a little unprepared. It's not exactly how I saw the end of the year panning out." Mars strode over to join me on my bed, curling their hand around the base with a sigh. "I'm just so fucking tired."

"Everything will be fine." My eyes wandered to them, then to Rani who looked ready to up and leave. "You've got me." I smiled.

It's so easy.

RANI ENDED up staying the night and the three of us decided to watch a movie. A mundane thing.

She also stayed in the room when we took our evening dose, much to Mars' protests.

"It heightens our senses you know? We prefer not to do it in front of vulnerable people," they said, pulling out the cooled sachet from their bag. (We had to catch and drain rodents this day, much to Mars' discomfort. Not a pleasant activity, but no one suspected a thing.)

"I know, but I trust you both. I need to get used to these things, to normalise it."

Mars shrugged in effortless defeat. "Fair enough. Don't flinch then." They poured out a portion for each of us and the two of us stood in the centre of the room, Rani between us on my bed, staring intently. Arlo would have been too embarrassed at this. It was too private a venture.

"Cheers," Mars joked, lifting their mug. We clinked and drank; the soft liquid sliding down my throat in less than a few gulps, and my head tipped back in elation. I gasped and wiped my mouth with my sleeve, eyes all seeing, and body rejuvenated. I sensed Rani's presence so much more vividly and I turned to her, her eyes having never left me throughout it all. She was trying not to look horrified, and it was like the realisation had only just kicked in. We were *not* human.

"Wow," she finally said.

"Not ideal, but it's our safest option," Mars stated, placing their mug down on the table and stretching their back out, rubbing their gums.

"So, you do this every day? Morning and night?"

"Would you rather we used people?" Mars joked lightly, without scaring her.

She threw her hands up in protest. "God no, it just looks... unfortunate."

I was hyperaware of her still. My mind craving more. That wasn't going to be enough tonight; after all, I had two minds to feed.

I think Mars knew what I was going to do before I moved. Saw my eyes perhaps, followed my senses. Their arm shot out to hold my body as it leapt out in Rani's direction. She threw herself back onto the bed in terror, face instantly drained of colour as she pulled her legs up to her chest. *I'm still hungry.*

"Easy, Arlo," Mars asserted into my ear, strong arms pulling me back. I tried to break free from their grasp, but they were exceptionally strong. But so was I.

I strained a little harder until their clasp broke and I prowled free, diving for Rani. Mars reached out and grabbed my legs as I growled in frustration that I still. Couldn't. Reach.

"Rani, out! Now!" Mars screamed, Manipulation in their voice. She backed into the wall, then managed to scramble out. A knee drove into my back, and I fell to the floor. I doubted she looked back as her feet clambered down the stairs, my mother's startled and confused voice calling out from underneath the floor. She'd be coming up in a few seconds, wondering what's going on. Confused why her son's best friend is running from her house in tears. Wondering in horror why, when she enters my room, she sees Mars straddling my back and holding my arms back in arrest. Why were my eyes red? My neck strained, and my teeth a little too long for my mouth? Why was there fresh blood on my lips? She'll want to know why she can't remember the reason she came up into my room in a second because Mars will reassure her and tell her to go back downstairs and enjoy her quiet time as they open up another bag and force me onto my back, pouring the blood into my mouth with their knee firmly on my chest. I will gag and choke on it, but welcome it as it warms my insides, and I am sated. Mars will then scold me and tell me how worried they are for me. Express how they don't think I can control myself still and that I'm weak and pathetic and—

"You're staring at me Arlo." I was still standing beside Mars, Rani still comfortably cross legged on my bed. An empty mug in my hand.

"Sorry." I put my mug down beside Mars' and scratched my head.

303

"Still getting used to the feeling, aren't you?" Mars laughed.
Yeah, something like that.

CHRISTMAS CAME AND WENT; Rani and Mars spent the days leading up to it ensuring I didn't slip up and do anything *out of the ordinary*. They promised me I was doing amazing, and no one would ever sense anything was different. The woman at the corner shop was adamant that I had grown even more in the few months I'd been away, and never failed to remind me of how much I looked like *Jerry*. The old Arlo got so overwhelmingly annoyed, I had to let him at least roll his eyes and thank her for the groceries but leave swiftly. *It hurts mum to be reminded.*

Every day I thought I saw him — *Michael*. Whether it be a feather fluttering past my window, the clang of jewellery amongst the trees, or his voice soothing my mind by the stream. I knew it was unlikely he had followed me, my trip was not important to him, but it brought me comfort to think that he clearly thought of me.

I was washing dishes when my phone rang. My mother was out; Mars lounged on the sofa, flicking through random channels on the TV while muttering to themself in Tagalog.

It was Marianne. The first contact I'd had with her since that evening...

"Hello?" I picked up, curious as to why she was calling.

The line was muffled for a brief moment, but then I heard her voice. "Arlo, are you there?" She sounded *worried*.

"I am. Yes." Mars looked over at the seriousness of my tone, muting the TV and mouthing 'who is it?'

'Marianne,' I spelt out slowly with my lips, holding the phone from my ear momentarily.

Mars got up and wandered over, hovering beside my shoulder. "Marianne?"

"Arlo, is Mars with you?" Her voice was intensely unsettled.

"They're beside me, yes."

"Good. I need you both to come home right now."

I can't just up and leave. I put the phone on speaker and held it between the two of us.

"What's wrong?" Mars shouted into the phone, casually leaning on the head of the kitchen chair.

"I need you both here as soon as you can."

She sounded *terrified*.

"Marianne, is everything okay? Is anyone hurt?"

"Lucienne Dumont."

It took a few seconds for it to click in my mind but Mars knew instantly. They looked up at me, eyes wide with all casual glimmer gone.

"Lucienne Dumont," Marianne repeated. "That's her name. Dumont. Mars? Mars are you hearing this? Lucy is Isiah's sister. *Twin* sister."

What?

"How do you know?" Mars started making fists with their hands; knuckles going stark white.

"I didn't. Not at first. He never mentioned a sibling. I never suspected it. But after seeing how strongly controlled their minds were — Jade and the others — I couldn't shake the hunch. And I finally found records. It took me a while, but I did it. I proved it. I found them..." she choked up and the line went fuzzy.

"Marianne?" Mars shouted.

The line cleared, and it sounded as though she was rustling papers. "Isiah and Lucienne Dumont, born on the twelfth of February 1801 in Versailles, France. It's her. Mars, she's here."

"And she's out for revenge. Come to finish what her brother started," Mars finished off, staring out the window, clearly unsure of what to do next.

"How could I have been so stupid." It sounded as though she was crying. Understandable, though, given the circumstances.

"We're coming. We'll be with you as soon as we can." Mars left me, already heading for their bag and shoes.

"We can't just…"

"Yes, we can," they called from the hallway. "We can and we will. Leave a note, your mother will understand. You've got commitments. You'll see her soon. You're very sorry."

"Mars. You can't Manipulate me."

"I know, but I mean it regardless. Marianne needs us. She needs *you.*"

She needs me.

"Okay." *I need to go. Please.*

"I'll sort the train; you go and pack…" they trailed off then looked down to their trouser pocket where their phone just buzzed.

"Shit," they said, eyes on the screen then locking onto mine, face horror-stricken.

"What? What is it?"

"Casper. He… Ben didn't come home last night. He's not answering his phone. No one knows where he went. Arlo… Ben is missing."

It would have been too much of a coincidence for it all to be connected but I knew — all of me knew — that this was undeniably linked. Just as it all had been from the start. It was as if I was somehow seeing the world through her lens, Lucy's lens. She'd known where we were the whole time. And what would I do to tease out the murderer of my sibling? I'd strike when they least expected it. Strike right in the heart.

Ben is missing.

Act 3

The Star

CHAPTER TWENTY-FOUR

Michael

We have watched a million lives pass by; observed a billion pasts, and an infinity of futures. We have seen things one could only dream of. We have been here since the dawn and will live on through the night.

If everything had gone my way, they would already be beside me; ready to conquer everything. Watching as worlds turn and life cycles on and on. The Sun, The Moon, and The Star.

It took time, you see. Joining a world anew is no easy feat, even for forces like us. I found him — Michael — trailing the dusty streets of Amsterdam as a hopeless young artist. Lost but driven. For years, I followed him and watched him grow; I analysed his every move. He was the one; I'd known the whole time.

As he was the first, he had nothing to consent to. It was a choice made for him, but I found he was too lonesome to fight back, so we melded easily as one, as easily as fire melts ice.

The wings were perhaps his last conscious decision, yet a necessary addition, after all, we were more than human. Adapted.

One of his final creations in life had been that of the archangel — his namesake. He always believed that one day he could be grand and above humanity, perhaps even using himself as a muse for the piece — an ego of the gods, some might have said, but all I saw was pride. Pride and ambition, buried deep inside his sorrow.

I was always the decision maker; we three preferred it that way, and thus, a mere two years later at a drug induced mania of a summer festival, I found my Moon. He was not to know of my realisation, not for many years to come, but once again, we knew he was the one. We would make this world perfect, the three of us, just like we always dreamed. Once again, we were one step closer.

I left him be, analysing his mood and his steps as he traipsed the globe. You see, having a body this time meant I had to act as such. I had to approach him and entice him. He too was broken and helpless, but where Michael had had no say in his fate, I allowed this man a chance. Where Michael was merely human, this man was something else. A vampire, the humans called them. Creatures who fed off the blood of others and survived poisoned, eternal lives. So surprisingly similar to our kind, only not quite. He had lived a long life, and he was so very tired. The solitude corpse of a once regal man. So, I granted him the life he wanted. It was remarkably easy to drain the innocent and have them switch places — to revive him like a new creation. And once it was done, I sent him on his way. He craved a human life, to find love and to grow old as everyone he knew once had. After spending so long in the shadows, he so desperately begged to see the light.

When he was first taken from me, I mourned for some time, believing I was foolish to have set him free. I did not entice him enough. I held the essence of my Moon in my claws. Yet it was not long before I learned he would come back.

When we finally met again, he was not the same. Greater, perhaps; corporeal and grand. But limited. A thing of greatness confined to the body of a helpless soul. Fickle, he feared his ageing: the thinning of his hair and the click of his knees.

He was happy for a while; from a distance, I had watched him as he believed he was living. He indulged himself in the petty desires of human men, ones he had never fully enjoyed undead. He thrived, but all I saw was the shell of what once was, while The Moon grew restless. Eventually, he felt it too. The longing for more. He watched as his mortal hands departed from his static youth, his joints stiffened, and his breath shortened. A healthy rate for a human. Nothing inhibiting, not yet. Though he saw the inevitable, for even his human self had lived too long as another that he had forgotten about his true humanity, he did not care for it. So, he came crawling back to me, returning to his loyal companion in life and beyond, begging for his deathless soul back. I was not to waste my time finding the now aged vampire we had created. He needed The Moon.

"Why have you chosen me, might I ask? I'm no one special, and you should know that having followed me around for the better part of two decades," he asked me on the evening he ran away from his new life.

If only I had a simple answer, but alas, I did not. I cannot explain what is meant to be. My Moon needed a host.

"Once we find a place for The Star, it will all make sense," I would repeat as my only reply. "Then we will be at full strength to tackle this dreary, mortal world."

I slashed his throat then and there, watching his final essence of humanity stain the dirt beneath us and gazed in admiration as he breathed in for the first time again. The Moon had risen.

And then of course, it was not long before I found The Star.

When I found *him*, he was but a child. The Moon had no say in this discovery, he did not need to know anything yet. I thought to surprise him, instead.

I almost revealed myself to the boy too soon, my eagerness getting the better of me. But I waited and waited until that fateful night, many years later, when *she* found him and brought him into *her* world, unknowing of what she had done. They almost beat me to it of course, those stupid, stupid creatures. I should have expected us to have more in common, those of us who were not mortal, and had the power to control the simple mind, but even they would not be able to grasp what needed to be done.

When his body breathed again for the first time, I was sickened to see him fall into their thorny hands, but I had managed just long enough to feed him The Star and then all I had to do was wait.

I do not entirely blame her, his sire. She was blinded by rage, furious about the death of her brother. And now that she realised she had finally led herself straight to the door of his killer, she grew unstoppable. I thought once that perhaps if time had been different, she would have made a perfect host over Michael. My mind changed though, once I witnessed hers.

I kept her from my Star as much as I could, she had done enough damage and I needed him safe in my arms. Bonding two immortal souls together proved a much heavier feat than I thought, but he managed. I fed him my blood and whispered into his mind until he was strong enough to take over. His body was stubborn, from time to time, but that was to be expected, knowing who he took after. In a way, it made me proud that both my Moon and my Star found themselves wound up in such unassailable vessels.

I could feel the end of the old time coming, sensed the desperation and frustration on both sides, knowing I needed not do anymore to aid it, my work was done, for it was only a matter of time.

I WOULD HAVE PERHAPS NOT CHOSEN her ways in the end, but I had to remind myself of her lingering humanity, no matter how evil it seemed.

· · ·

SHE TOOK the black-haired boy in the middle of the night. Chose him at random, she told the others, but there was a method to her madness. She knew this one in particular would stir enough commotion so they would all have no choice but to come to her, begging on their hands and knees, and drag them from their hiding place to face her at long last.

She stole him from the alleyway meters from his house, his cigarette still alight on the cobbles as she dragged his unconscious body to the rotten church and bound him to a post until he roused.

Bait, that was all he was in the end. Innocent and helpless *bait*.

"Do you know why you are here?" she asks him, hands clasped behind her back. She flicks her head at the mindless guard, a reminder to remove the captive's mouth rag.

"It's you, isn't it? Lucy. Your green hair."

He seems so small, so fragile, and so afraid. The runt of the vampires. What a sorry excuse for their kind. I tut from the rafters, bored already, and she looks to me briefly, then to my wings dangling over the beams, but doesn't acknowledge me entirely. Lucy doesn't really know who I am or why I'm here, but I'm in her head enough for her to not care.

"Arlo really did remember me after all. Talked about me. I'd call that a successful date, wouldn't you?" She winks at the boy, but he remains quiet.

"So this is how it's going to work from here. You don't have to speak if you don't want to, I don't need any information, I already know everything I require. I'm simply going to keep you here until they come looking for you. Perhaps tease them if it takes too long." She leans in towards the boy, he in turn backs away as much as he can. "How long do you think they'll take? Your precious Thorns," she whispers with malice.

He says nothing, but I watch as he glances down to the chain at his neck. A cross, I observe. Hmm. Interesting.

"I tell you what, we'll give them a head start. I've run out of patience," she laughs maniacally, making me wonder just quite how unhinged she must have been in life. She reaches around to undo the boy's bound hands and pulls them towards her. Her guard holds the boy's body in place from behind and shoves his rag back between his teeth.

"Right. Let's see. Which one will you miss the least?" She pulls his trembling, bony fingers close to her face for inspection, his own eyes widening in visceral fear at the realisation of what is about to happen.

I have no interest in her sadism, but I admire her methods. They will be sure to come for him in no time.

I fly away just as the first of the gagged screams rings out into the night.

CHAPTER TWENTY-FIVE

Arlo

W e were back in the city by noon the next morning, not even stopping to drop our bags before heading to the hideout. Marianne met us at the door and frantically shooed us in, slamming it behind us. We hurried into the main hall where a reasonable handful of The Thorns already stood. Some looked more shocked than others, with faces buried into hands. Prayers and mutterings of hope marked the silence.

I scanned the crowd for Casper, though he was nowhere to be seen.

The entire journey back, Mars wouldn't stop speculating the worst; biting their nails until they were red raw, unable to sit still in their seat. Arlo sat on his knees in the back of my mind, banging his fists and begging to be let out to comfort and reassure them, so I tried my best to do as he asked, raising no suspicions. I patted their back, and they looked at me strangely. Maybe Arlo wouldn't have done that. I forced a sympathetic smile saying, "I'm sure he will return." Though that was very much a lie, since I truly had no idea if he was even still breathing.

"MY THORNS," Marianne didn't even try to hide the hurt in her voice. Her makeup had run tremendously down her face; her eyes bloodshot and afraid.

"Ben wouldn't just run off like that," someone shouted.

"We've been out all night and he's nowhere. He can't have gone far, it's not possible," said another, heavily in denial.

"Ben would never leave without telling us, we all know that." Everyone perked up as Lawrence entered the conversation. Francesca beside herself to his side — she'd been crying too.

"It's obviously connected," Mars blurted, looking to Marianne for confirmation.

"I hope for the sanity and safety of us all that you're wrong," our leader answered, rubbing her eyes in distress.

"But I'm right though, aren't I," Mars said: a statement, not a question.

Marianne's lips pursed and she closed her eyes, inhaling deeply. "She's a Dumont."

The name was supposed to mean something to me, though Arlo never saw what Isiah did first hand, only heard of the so-called 'atrocities'.

"Just as I think we've bested her, she's already one step ahead."

"Perhaps she was always one step ahead," Lawrence said bluntly. Honestly.

Marianne dragged her hands roughly through her hair, clearly avoiding the flinch of annoyance her body was about to make. "She wants us to bring the fight to her."

"We're not falling for it though, right?" a smaller, blond-haired boy piped up. He only looked about ten.

"Excuse me?" This was Mars, lashing around in shock.

"We're showing her it will take more than that to get at us, right?" The boy's confidence did not falter.

Mars charged over, and by the way the child acted, it was evident he was a lot older than Mars.

"So you are saying," Mars shouted in his face, "that Ben's life doesn't matter? That the concept of him possibly being in serious danger *isn't* enough?"

The boy didn't flinch.

"What constitutes as *enough* for you?" Mars pressed.

"He is just one person," the confidence rolled off his tongue: fearless. And to Mars' surprise, a few others joined in with nods.

Mars gasped, glancing around in disbelief at the others, Lawrence stood in the same state of shock with his arm around Francesca, her heart thundering in anger.

"How can you say that?" Mars' voice turned helpless and unsteady as a tear formed in the corner of their right eye.

"Enough," Marianne asserted herself. "We're not going to debate this. Don't think it's relevant? Then leave. I won't stop you. But Thorns don't leave each other behind and rest assured I will remember this. When the time comes that you," she looked at the boy and the crowd that had formed around him, "find yourself in difficulty," her eyes narrowed, voice deepening, "I will never forget."

The room fell silent. No one dared argue against her.

After a long minute, the blond-haired boy stood and walked head-high from the room. A handful of others followed slowly and possibly reluctantly, but it was difficult to tell.

Mars glared at them in dismay. Marianne's expression mirrored theirs. How could her own Thorns still be so careless after everything she had done for them?

"Casper is still out there, isn't he?" Francesca asked quietly once the room emptied slightly.

"He's been out all night, I just got back from helping him." Marianne was pacing; shocked at what had transpired. I breathed in her scent, noted with the pungent smell of guilt. She was so easy to read.

"He thinks it too, doesn't he?" Lawrence asked the room.

"Oh, he knows it. He knows Ben better than anyone in this world. Knows his scent like the back of his hand. He won't rest until he finds him."

Love does things to you, doesn't it? What a shame Arlo will never feel what that is like.

But I do. I ignored him.

"He's been back to the site where we last saw Isiah... the abandoned church. He said he smelled him and that he was not long gone," Marianne confirmed.

"Which means she *was* there. She knows the significance of that place," Mars added.

"She's messing with us." Marianne.

"She's going to hurt him, isn't she?" Francesca said, biting her fist.

Coldness swept through the room. No one confirmed nor denied her statement. Truthfully, no one knew what to say.

WE SPLIT INTO GROUPS. Every remaining Thorn was willing to help. Marianne had chosen her crowd wisely and allocated each group a certain area of the city so that collectively, everyone covered as much ground as possible. The streets were oddly quiet for that time of year, and if anything, it made the search more difficult because people didn't hunt in packs through streets in broad daylight. Our Manipulation helped us to fall relatively unnoticed, but every now and again there would be an odd passerby who would throw us a funny look or smile at us, possibly assuming we were participating in some sort of treasure hunt or a school trip.

Not knowing Lucienne didn't help either. Marianne and some older Thorns had an understanding of how Isiah had worked his way around the area, but as far as any of us were concerned, Lucy wasn't from here. Hadn't been here long, so she could realistically have been anywhere... If she was even still in the city at all.

"SHE WOULDN'T HAVE LEFT. There's no point." Mars paced through the woods around the river, their usual vigour fallen to that of a solemn puppy. "If she wants us to come to her, she should be right in front of us. She obviously knows exactly where we are, otherwise how could she have found..." their voice trailed off as they seemingly choked up with emotion.

"Ben," I finished. *Shut up, Arlo. You are above this.*

Mars looked up at me, something lost from their face.

"You've gone so cold."

I squinted my eyes a little before rubbing my hands together. "It is very cold," I confirmed.

Not a good enough answer, apparently. "No, Arlo. You know that's not what I mean."

"I'm afraid I don't." We continued to walk while Mars searched for signs.

"You. You're not yourself. You've been acting funny lately and I can't really put my finger on it..." they sighed. "Well, I *couldn't* until now... you just don't seem to care about things the way you used to. The Arlo I met cared so deeply about everyone and everything; he always wanted the best for people and tried to stay positive, yet now..." They stopped and glanced upwards, asking the sky whether they should speak their mind, it seemed.

They did.

"Do you even care about Ben?"

He's like the older brother I never had.

Pathetic.

I acted surprised, placing both hands firmly in my trench pockets. "How dare you say that! Of course I care about him! I'm out here helping, aren't I?"

Only that wins me a greater look of disappointment. "You see,

that's exactly what I mean. Arlo wouldn't say that, he doesn't
word things like that, he always talks so... sweetly. Even when he
doesn't mean to nor realise it. The Arlo I *saved* wouldn't have
questioned why we had to leave in such a rush. He wouldn't have
questioned why we couldn't have waited for the later train. He
wouldn't have complained why we had to go straight to Marianne
once we arrived..."

"I didn't."

Another sigh. "Your eyes did." Mars stopped and turned to
face me. I didn't know how to react. Shocked? Surprised? Oblivious? I wasn't used to acting human.

Reaching out their bare hand, they cupped their frozen fingers
around my cheek, thumb pressing gently under my eye. I leaned
into the touch, eyes falling hazy. Bare branches nodded around us
as the distant hum of the river flowed from behind the trees. I
closed my eyes as their thumb stroked across my skin.

I slowly exhaled through my nose.

Mars took a step closer to me, so that we were almost touching
entirely. "The real Arlo," they hissed, thumb pressing in harder to
ruin the peace, "would never have let *anyone* do that."

The next thing I knew, I was shoved to the ground; my hands
landed on the icy brown sludge beneath me. Arlo's blond head was
mere inches away from a hidden, jagged rock. Mars looked just as
surprised at their strength as I did, though I suspected they were
more alarmed at the fact that they had nearly seriously injured
someone they claimed was their closest friend. We both stared at
each other, wide-eyed, while Mars panted out clouds of cold air.

After a moment, my energy seeped back and a grin crawled
across my face; encouraging Mars' eyes to widen even further, and
they stumbled back in sheer fear. Of course, their Arlo would have
never reacted like that.

"I had dreams," they started, slowly retreating towards the
path while failing to hide their fear. "Recently, I've had horrible
dreams which always end the same. You being taken over: your

mind and body. You let it inside. The creature..." their voice shook as I held their stare. "You were Manipulating us all, fooling us. That Arlo..." they gestured up and down to my body, "was all but an act." Their eyes glazed over in a sheen of sadness.

I said nothing, expression still holding.

"When you asked me to help you find the creature... I went behind Marianne's back for *you*. I kept quiet as I thought it was for the best." They clapped their hands to the side of their thighs in surrender, holding their head back slightly to prevent falling tears. "You were seeing it, weren't you? The creature. The *monster*. You kept meeting it and you didn't tell me. You *promised*. We had a deal, Arlo...." They looked towards the bank where the trees were bare and parted enough to see right through to the other side.

"Tell me I'm right." They faced away from me. "Tell me I understand and that you Manipulated me. Manipulated all of us. Tell me I'm correct and that I know Arlo too well. Please. Give me this. I can't... I tried so hard. Was that still not enough? Am I doomed to forever lose *everyone* because of my own *blindness?*"

I watched the shake of their shoulders as I listened to the agony lacing their voice.

"Tell me I'm not naïve. That I *get* it. That I tried. I *tried,*" they cried out across the open water, too far away now for any human to sense their rumbling, roiling emotions. Oh, poor Mars.

They snapped back towards me before I was allowed even a breath of a response. Their feet charged across the mud; their eyes red and inhuman, fangs showing. I didn't have time to stand back upright, my hands still sinking into the dirt.

"Tell me!" they growled, reaching out and grabbing me by both my coat collars, dragging my limp body out from the earth. "Arlo is still in there, right? He's still alive. After everything, tell me he is still alive." Their fierceness reverberated through me, I was still too stunned. ***I never expected this. Why didn't you warn me of their strength, my Sun?***

"Arlo is... resting," I managed to say, despite being shaken.

Not good enough, apparently. I was pushed back down to the ground, and this time, Arlo's soft head cracked against the rock it so narrowly missed the first time. Even in this form, my eyesight blurred slightly as his head began to bleed out beneath me. Again, Mars seemed appalled at their own strength. They must have noticed the bleeding but something in their eyes proved it was intentional. I caught on to what they are about to do a second too late.

Mars ripped off their coat and rolled up their sleeve, exposing their slender, brown arm. Holding it up to the sky, their other hand unsheathed a pocket-knife, and in one swift motion, they slashed across the tendons of their bare arm, their boot firmly cementing me into the soil. Mars leaned over me and let their blood trickle down onto my face. At my unwillingness, their free hand dropped the knife and pulled at my jaw, nails digging into my gums as they pried my teeth apart.

"This better fucking work," they muttered from behind their gritted teeth. "Come back to me Arlo."

I had no choice but to release my jaw, letting their warm blood trickle down my throat, their grip too strong for my failing body.

My limbs had grown numb. Arlo's — *my* blood — flowed deep into the roots of the ground.

No. Not now.

Mars.

Please, Mars.

I choked on it and spluttered a spray as I sat up. Mars relaxed their pressure slightly in anticipation of the outcome of their relatively reckless experiment.

No.

Mars...

I'm crawling. Crawling through this spiralling tunnel, grasping for the light. My hands are torn and bloody, tears dried to the cracks of my face. I can breathe. I am breathing. The light grows bigger and bigger as I scramble forwards. Not looking back, never looking back. Please Mars... help me.

As if they could hear my plea, Mars crouched down to my side and wrapped their free arm around my body, helping me sit up properly, and they forced their wounded arm back in front of my mouth. Fierceness vanished from their eyes as they said: "Take what you need to be free."

I bit down and started to drink, Mars flinched and bit back a cry, but kept their arm firm as I latched on deeply.

"Please work," they muttered again, arm strong behind me. "I can't lose you, Arlo."

I'm right here.

I'm almost there, I can feel the heat of freedom as I take those last few steps. Flashes of my friends and memories. My mum. Bess. Rani, Mars, Casper... Ben.

Ben. The first person who made me feel accepted in this new world. The idea that maybe I could find myself was planted with him. His cheery outlook on everything. His chipped, black nail polish and his long baggy coats that were always one size too big. His passion and energy. His smile and innocence. The way he looks at Casper and the way Casper responds. The world doesn't deserve him.

Casper, with his confidence and pride. The way he protects everyone around him, so selfless and loyal. Someone to lean on, someone who is always there to listen. I feel so safe with him.

Rani, my best friend. I wouldn't have made it this far without her. She made life worth living. Brought the sun to the storm and held away the tide with her might. She grounded me. Set my roots deep into the earth of humanity. I love her for that. She'd laugh if she heard me say that aloud.

I'm so close. So very, very close.

Mars. Wonderful, beautiful Mars. My saviour. Mars who would sacrifice heaven and earth to protect the ones they loved. Do they love me? Am I worthy? Of course. Mars has always proved that, and I was always too blind.

I'm not blind now though.

I'm there. Can feel the edge. My hands cling over the side of the hole, light dazzling my eyes, burning my face. I made it. I really made it. I'm close enough to haul a leg over the edge, pulling myself up with every ounce of strength I can muster. It hits the grass, everything so bright. Clouds hanging so low. The sky angelically white. I use both hands and leg to pull my final part of my body out. Just as I'm inches away from standing, I feel something tug my ankle and without thinking, I turn to face the abyss before me...

I pulled away once Mars' strength began to falter. I focused in on their face, now gaunt and ashy.

"Mars," I gulped down.

They collapsed backwards; head lolling forward, only just managing to catch themselves from full fall with weary arms. They landed into my chest, panting for a full breath. I'd taken too much.

"Mars," I said again, this time in worry. I leaned forward to hold them steady, feeling the back of my head tighten as it healed itself. *I took so much.*

"Arlo." They fell into my grip, letting me hold them up as their head fell backwards. They forced out a smile through chapped lips, eyes weary. "I... I was right."

"Yes," I said, pulling them close to my forehead. "You were right, and you saved me, Mars. You always save me."

Their smile turned into a laugh, but one of relief and disbelief. A laugh of masked pain. Coughing, they leaned forward again and forced our brows to touch. I didn't pull back. Instead, I allowed us to sit there for a moment with my hand wound through their hair. "You did it." I smiled. *I'm free. Mars, how can I ever repay you?*

"I did it," they sighed, voice hoarse and faded.

We shared the same breath for what felt like a lifetime.

"Can you stand?" I asked once I became aware of how exposed we were. The blood surrounding us, on the back of my head, down my front. I moved to retrieve Mars' discarded coat from down the trail of leaves and branches, and I helped them cover up.

I made sure their arm was healing itself enough to stem the blood flow.

I aided them in bending their arms through the sleeves and let them rest their head on my shoulder as they did so. I helped them up slowly, holding their arms with delicate care. Even standing for me, despite being full of my new free strength, made me give in to a brief dizzy spell.

"Arlo," was all they said again, still resting against me for support.

"Yes?"

Our eyes met once more.

"Let's go and save Ben."

CHAPTER TWENTY-SIX

Michael

I feel the shift as he pulls away, we both do. The Star, gone. I don't know how he managed it. I was elated to finally reunite us all, and I do not doubt that I still will, but this was... unexpected.

I sit at the foot of my Moon, resting my head over my overlapped hands, with my wings trailing across the stones of the cathedral. He sits forlorn atop his chair, idly fumbling with a ring in his hand, his mind distant. He has not spoken in a while, instead his eyes wander around the room, and I watch them, trying to read their signals. He is growing restless, for he still has not met the body of our final source. But I have reassured him he will get his wishes, that I will grant them when I can. So that we can all achieve our greatest desires.

"Why the delay?" he asks, eyes refusing to meet mine.

I adjust myself against his robed leg. "Minor inconveniences, that is all."

That minor inconvenience being Lucy; her plans greatly interfering with ours. If it had not been for her, we would be well on our way to having everything.

She's fuelled by pure rage, something I know all too well. But where I see a way out, she cannot. Another trait I am above. She believes the only way to find peace is to seek vengeance, no matter how bloody. But revenge only opens up a jar of worms and leaves chaos in its wake. Maybe that is what she wants; after all, she has lived long enough to see beyond human comprehension. Beyond morals and ethics. She's driven — I will give her that — but unfocused. Why didn't I just end her when I had the chance?

"Will you be ready?" I ask him, fingers curling to trace the hem of his amber garments. "For the end of old time?"

He shrugs, looking off into the distance. He believes himself to be past that, too great for such petty work.

"Oh, but my dear Moon, this will be fun. Don't you want to witness it? Watch it all unfold. For old times' sake?"

His head snaps down at me and I halt my hands under his gaze. "I do wish you would stop calling me that. You know we coexist. I am no more your Moon than I am myself."

"You are right. I am sorry if I overstepped."

He gets like that sometimes, when he lets his mind wander and lets his old self back in. Nothing I can't quickly rectify though; it does not worry me. I play into it, let him believe what he wants.

"You should know by now. Neither of us want to be stuck here," he says.

"I know, I know. I am sorry, Jerome."

I watch his lips flicker slightly, content with his name being spoken aloud. Hmm. Now *my* mind wanders. Even after all these years of trailing the earth together, he still has so much to learn.

THE BLACK-HAIRED BOY CRIES OUT, his pain seemingly infinite. Even as I stand, having never been in a true human state, I will never understand why she pushed this far. The boy had done nothing to her, so why did she waste her time with such brutality? She expects a grand audience, this is plain to see. And a grand audience she will receive.

In the night, I watch over him. This night, my form fills out the doorway as I look at him, a worn-out mass, curled in a foetal position across the cold, hard floor. Clothes barely covering his back. He whimpers into his hands, spine and ribs exposed. He does not notice my presence, not even as I step into the lightless room, candle in hand, and place it at his feet.

You see, the trouble is, I know who he is. I know of his significance. I won't interfere with her actions — it is, after all, nothing to do with me directly, so I can't let myself get too involved.

I slip over so that my body shadows his and I watch his shallow and rushed breaths. His bloody and bandaged hands are not empty. In them, he holds onto that silver cross: his remaining fingers fumble over the feeling of each point as he mumbles inaudibly. Hmm. I have never understood religion.

Slowly, I reach a hand down to brush aside his mop of black curls, and only then does he flinch with the realisation he is not alone. As he turns to me, I startle back onto my hands, body catching my wings between my back and the ground so that I slip to the floor with a thud.

"Who is it?" his voice cries out, sorrowful and edged with agony. I go to speak but all I can do is stare. I stare and stare at the two raw and hollow pits that once held such vivid green eyes and the jagged, almost clown-like, bloody scars slit down his cheeks.

What has she done?

I think back to watching his lover scour the city on his own for hours — days now. He's probably out there right now, hopelessly traipsing and searching for any sign of him. I think of my family, for they are a family of a sort. My Moon, my Star. How I would move time itself to keep them safe.

Is this me growing sentimental? *Never.*

"Please," he continues to helplessly cry out, "I'm not telling you anything else. I've given you everything I can. What more can you possibly want from me?"

I flee before he speaks anymore.

So this is the true capability of one who seeks revenge.

Arlo

"STILL NO LUCK?" Rani entered the room with Carmen at her tail, the two of them flustered from the cold. Mars must have contacted them once we left, I had no memory of even *considering* getting in touch. My head *ached.*

We had spent the rest of the afternoon and well into the night searching. Yet we found no clues. I kept Mars by my side, allowing them to lean into me as we continued through the trees. I could not wrap my head around how quickly they laid down their life for me, without even knowing for sure if they would help, and yet they still tried. I kept catching a glimpse of their deathly hollow face and weary eyes. A pang of guilt pierced my throat.

I caught them through their stumbles; held them back when they pushed too hard. Not once did they look at me, but I couldn't blame them, and part of me was grateful. We continued through the sludge in silence.

My head continued to throb. The back of my head ached from the crack while the front felt heavy, a sign of Arlo's — the true Arlo's — waking fatigue.

Rani sat herself onto the nearest chair and wrapped her scarf even further around her neck. She exhaled, breathing out clouds of cold air, her nose bright red. "We checked around the train station. I know it's not much and there realistically isn't anywhere there that we could find anything, but I couldn't *not*." She folded her still trembling arms, feet trapping together. "I mean, it's *Ben*. He's..." her voice dropped. "I don't even know.... I just can't believe it."

"She has to be teasing us. They'll be constantly moving." Carmen came up behind Rani and rested her hand on the back of the chair, standing as tall as she could. Maintaining her last remaining essence of composure. "If I had to guess? She'll deliver him right to us before long and blame us for not trying hard enough."

For a while, no one responded.

"You might be right," Mars piped up. After we returned, Marianne didn't even stop to question why we were both covered in blood. She simply looked at me with understanding eyes and ushered Mars into a separate room. My head was looked at by someone and Marianne came back out before long, telling me I didn't even need to explain, and that she was just glad that we had sorted things. She didn't elaborate and I didn't even think I could have if *I* tried.

Now Mars sat wrapped in a blanket, still devoid of their usual energy, but looking a lot less... ill.

They stared at the floor when they spoke. "Or she'll bring us directly to them. Pick her spot. Make a scene." They sipped their drink: an apparent concoction of blood and herbs, given the smell. "That's what Isiah did."

Carmen stiffened at the mention of his name. She knew, of course, that Marianne had figured out the relation. But seeing her react in person shifted something in me. Isiah was the sole reason this was how her life turned out, and now he had returned in the form of his sister. It was like watching history repeat itself through her eyes.

Rani rubbed Carmen's wrist, which now firmly gripped the

chair head in a claw. They looked at each other, reaching a silent understanding between them.

"I wish we could just *know*. I feel like we're stupid for not being able to figure this out. It's not *that* big of a city; there are hardly infinite spaces for a vampire and her *captive* to hide," I piped up with whatever hung on the tip of my tongue. It also just felt good to hear myself talk... to feel my voice match up with my mind.

"If only," Mars spoke again, still staring at the stone ground.

At that moment, the door burst open and Casper swooped in... his face gaunt and cracked from tears. His gloveless hands were clenched into fists and his long coat — *Ben's coat* — frost-bitten and mud-dragged.

We stood in utter silence, no one strong enough to look him in the eye.

After he finally caught his breath, he collapsed into the chair opposite the fire and leaned forward, pressing his lips between his fingers in mournful contemplation. The embers cast a glow against his face, his eyes glassy and wet. He swiftly brushed his face through his hands, pulling down on his lip as he sat back. "Anything?" he sighed out, not looking at anyone in particular.

I shook my head after a beat, and in time with Mars. Rani bit her nails, one elbow against the chair arm, eyes distant. Carmen stood looking off into the fire, hand now on Rani's shoulder.

I watched Casper's head turn to fully face the flames, a tear welling in his left eye then naturally dripping down his cheek. He covered his mouth with his hand and took a deep breath.

How long had he been outside looking? He looked physically *exhausted*. Drained. Lifeless.

Mars quietly stood and let the blanket fall, slipping over to Casper's side and sat beside him, looking towards his eyes. Casper finally acknowledged them directly. Mars' reaction was a clear indicator of what we all feared.

"He's just... gone," Casper muttered a cry then leaned down in defeat. Mars caught his head against their chest, wrapping their arms around his neck in comfort.

"It's okay, it's okay, I know, I know," they muttered as they began to stroke his back. *Ben's coat.*

My mind flashed back to the night I ran from my room and out onto the streets where I found Ben, a cigarette in hand, that coat drowning him out. At the time, I was frustrated none of them would leave me alone, but less than two minutes of speaking left me at ease, and I knew right then that I had found a real friend. I began to think about all the bands he recommended to me, and how I couldn't remember their names, and the fact I never did listen to them even though I really meant to, and now I'll never remember. He was so excited about his interests.

He had told me about how Marianne had saved both him and Casper. I never did push the conversation further, but I always wondered in the back of my mind how they both ended up joining The Thorns. What really happened to them for them both to end up here together?

I zoned back into Casper and Mars on the sofa. I'd stepped closer without realising. Casper wept while Mars closed their eyes, continuing to soothe him.

"He's my everything. He can't just *disappear.*"

"We will find him," Mars tried to promise, though they were just as doubtful as the rest of us.

Rani joined my side, Carmen by hers. My friend slipped her still gloved hand into mine and I obliged, the two of us exchanging a brief glance of reassurance.

"He's my everything," Casper muttered again, all force lost from his voice.

Mars tilted their head back as if to halt tears. They'd known each other a lot longer; worked together, lived together, experienced years of the world I wasn't even here for.

We were all breaking.

Not a single full heart in that room.

"We are not going to give up," Rani promised. "We will all stick together and win. That's what The Thorns do."

And it was when Casper finally jolted around to face us, that we could see the coldness of his features.

"How can you say that though?" he wailed through tears. "I've been out looking for two days, and I've searched *everywhere*. I've not slept, and I *never will*, not until I find him."

He pulled away from Mars' grip entirely, pushing himself back against the chair so that he faced us all. "If he is harmed in *any way*, I swear, I don't care about our *policies*," he glanced sideways at Mars, throwing up his arms, "I will tear her apart and everyone else that tries to stop me."

Mars didn't even dare protest. They understood this feeling — they'd felt those emotions before. *Poppy*.

Casper abruptly stood and pulled his glasses out of his pocket. "I've got to go back out there. I can't waste another second." He started towards the door, Rani and Carmen parting to let him through until Mars shouted for him to wait.

We stared back at Mars who now stood, an orange glow outlining their body. "We're coming too."

⚜

THREE WHOLE DAYS PASSED. We walked on an endless cycle of paths, through endless alleyways and tunnels. Nothing. Not a scent nor a sign. It was as if he had simply ceased to exist. His keyboard and bass lay untouched in their music room. A discarded eyeliner pen sat beneath one of the chairs in a side room, and I knew fine well it could only belong to him. Lawrence and Francesca followed us out on walks and shared stories of their time in the band together, both happy and sad.

Casper never stopped looking. After that day we all left

together, returning in the early hours with him refusing to follow, we'd not seen him at all. Our only contact being the occasional phone call, usually to either Mars or Fran.

"I don't know if I should tell his parents or not," I heard him saying to Mars one morning.

"Wait a few more days. We don't need to worry them if it turns out to be nothing," they replied, turning away from me slightly.

If it turns out to be nothing. It had been five days now. *Nothing.*

I was prevented from hearing the rest of the conversation, but I believed it ended with Casper shouting and Mars trying to remain calm.

Later that day my mum called, as she had been doing every day since I left, to check in. I reassured her with my most eloquent lie; sending my love to her and Bess then tucking my phone away and ignoring it for the rest of the day.

On the final day of the year, Mars put out a brief statement for the band, which explained Ben was taking some time off for health reasons, but the band would be back in the new year. 'Thank you for supporting Forever Red this year. We would not be where we are without all of you.' It read, mimicking Casper's words. 'Happy New Year everyone.'

It was met with an influx of comments from the band's growing fanbase, wishing Ben a speedy recovery, and checking in on Casper too since their relationship had very much been public knowledge these last few years.

That evening, Marianne led us all to the top of a hill to a house she owned; it had an upstairs balcony and an uninterrupted view of a large portion of the city. A yearly tradition, I was quick to learn.

I sat, bulked out in layers, huddled between Rani and Mars with hot chocolate in our mugs. We gazed out over to the blues and golds of the city, to the stone turrets and slate roofs. To the city I now called home: the city buried in invisible blood.

Mars shifted beside me and moved their legs into a more

comfortable position. To my right, Rani linked her arm with Carmen's.

Marianne stood with her arms perched over the side of the balcony wall. She watched over her city as a ruler would. A protector; her face emotionless.

Five minutes to midnight I heard footsteps in the doorway behind me. I didn't turn, no one did, but we all knew he stood there, Casper — his presence reflected in the balcony glass. He stood in silence, eyes a river of pain.

I felt Mars' arm link under mine, and I let them, tucking our arms warmly to my side.

We all looked up as the cathedral clock chimed and the first fireworks shot into the sky.

Red, gold, green. A cacophony of sound and colour. Someone to the house to our left set off their own fireworks while someone in the house to our right cheered. I felt the presence of both my friends by my sides. So alive.

The last firework was a bittersweet red and Mars turned to me, planting a swift kiss to my shoulder.

"Happy new year, Arlo."

When I turned around, Casper was gone.

CHAPTER TWENTY-SEVEN

W e didn't acknowledge the dawn of a new year the way everyone else would have. We didn't wait for miracles or new beginnings.

A solemn shadow hung over The Thorns, even those few who deemed Ben's disappearance as insignificant. Eventually, they came crawling back in sympathy.

My headache dampened, and I felt clearer than I had in weeks. I sat on my bed, staring at the cold, hard wall. Mars knocked then waltzed in.

"How are you this morning?" they asked, joining my side. They'd asked me the same question every morning since they freed me. Each day my response had been the same: 'Okay, but could be a lot worse.'

Today, however, I smiled at them and tapped my temple, "Great," I said. Over the weeks and months, I had crafted a new definition for that word, but it still held the same meaning, I just reevaluated how it stood against everything I *now* experienced.

"Casper came back this morning," they said, looking down at their nails.

"He did? How is he?"

"Great," they echoed back my own words, looking up at me with a sarcastic brow.

I leaned back. "Sorry."

"Aren't we all."

"What is he going to do?"

"He'll never give up, we all know that. There is only so much searching one can do without driving themselves mad."

I thought about Casper traipsing the streets every hour of the day for a whole week. *'I'll never stop.'*

Flopping back onto my bed, I fixed my eyes to the cracks in the ceiling. "Do you think *she* will give up?"

"Not give up." Mars slid down the mattress so that they mirrored my position; hands pressed against their abdomen. "But I believe she will get impatient. Probably give us a clue to try and mock us."

Lucy's unnatural green hair flashed in my mind and my neck tingled, right where she had bitten me. I instinctively rose my hand to scratch the area and Mars looked to me as if my thoughts had been projected out above us.

"It's maddened us all, how easily she has gotten away with everything. Right when we were meant to protect everyone."

I was about to make the 'we're only human' excuse, though I halted in understanding that that phrase could no longer stand.

Instead, I sighed and stared straight ahead. "Do you think he is still alive?"

A pause.

"I do."

I wasn't sure which response I expected, but maybe every other answer would have sparked the same reaction.

"Because she would love nothing more than to inform us otherwise."

I thought back to my date, which seemed to be many moons ago now, and my growing discomfort I felt as the night progressed.

The way she forced herself against me. I hoped she didn't try anything like that with poor Ben. *Oh god.*

"He proposed, you know," Mars added to the silence.

My chest constricted. "Casper?"

Mars shook their head. "No, Ben did. The night he went missing. Christmas day."

"Oh." I imagined it: Ben gleefully falling to one knee.

"He asked me for advice." A laugh was hidden in their words. "Me, of all people, being asked for proposal advice."

I was unaware of the true ins and outs of Mars' dating history, nor was it my business, but from what I gathered, it consisted of a handful of very different types of people with a multitude of personalities. None were ever serious though.

"I helped him pick the ring, bless him," they continued, reminiscing.

I fell sick to my stomach with sadness. Poor, poor, poor boy. He was almost a decade my senior and yet I always saw him as a younger brother whom I needed to protect. I think everyone saw Ben that way.

"She will pay for what she has done," I stated through gritted teeth.

"Oh, I don't doubt that for a second."

As it turned out, Mars was exactly right. Ben was still alive.

Less than an hour later, Marianne called us in tears she no longer tried to hold back. She hauled us into the hall and tossed a crumpled piece of paper in our direction, Mars grabbing it from her and biting the back of their hand after reading it. They threw it to the floor in a fit, stomping their foot and pacing. I picked up the discarded letter from the floor, the smooth parchment mocking me as I held it in my hands. Right there, in fountain ink: a satire of formality.

Dearest Thorns,

It saddens me that you have made no effort to find your most valued player. He sits and begs for you, and yet you do not come. I have informed him of your attempts, or lack thereof, and he is deeply saddened by this. He longs for his partner, or should I say fiancé (my congratulations), but this long distance is taking a toll on him, poor boy. Do they not wish to see me? He wonders at night. Hmm. It appears you do not. Disappointing.

Yours most dearly,

Lucienne Dumont x

My FIRST THOUGHT was *I wonder if she thought she was revealing herself here?* But my second quickly became that of Ben, lying on a cold dark floor, calling out helplessly for Casper — or any of us for that matter.

"That fucking bitch," Mars growled and kicked the nearest wall.

My hand hand fell to my side, note still tight in my grip. I did not speak.

"There's one for you too, Arlo."

I looked to my leader, another less crumpled note residing in her outstretched hands. Still in its envelope, though the seal had been broken. I hesitantly pulled it from her hands, looking deep into her eyes, searching for some understanding of what I was about to read.

Mars turned to watch me open it, coming up close beside me.

Sweetest Arlo,

How is death treating you? My apologies for not having written sooner. As you can gather, I am a busy woman. Things to do. But fear not, for I have always kept you close in mind and heart. I hear you have become closely acquainted with my dear Michael? He is quite a handful, isn't he? Has he told you of his plans? He is quite the secretive sort but I trust he knows what he is doing with you. Though I must say, he doesn't seem to like me very much. I wonder why? He and his 'Moon' were so welcoming at first. Oh well, some friendships are not meant to last — I'm sure you understand all about that, don't you?

And oh, say hello to Marianne for me. Though I'm sure she will be reading this before you so I suppose I could say it myself! Hello! Isiah spoke so highly of you. Such a shame you had to cut him down. Will you ever learn our true purpose? Or will you forever be trying to cling on to every scrap of your humanity? Such a waste. Tut tut.

Anyway, Arlo I hope this letter finds you well, I look forward to hearing from you very soon.

Love, your sire x

I LET Mars read the whole thing over my shoulder; there was no point in hiding anything now. Marianne already knew everything anyway.

Mars made a stubborn 'pfft' sound. "Your sire? *Bitch*."

"I knew she would do this. It's exactly like before. Isiah. His *teasing*." Marianne wiped her still damp cheeks, blackened makeup smeared below her eyes.

"This means he's alive though right?" I tried, completely glossing over my own personal letter, which was now perhaps the least personal thing I owned in this room.

"I fucking hope so!" Marianne shouted at us. She was no leader anymore, just a tired woman; exhausted from holding up this front for so long. For the first time since I met her, she sounded how she looked. Like a young woman who had bitten off more than she could chew. Finally the mask was slipping.

"He's alive?" A quiet Louisiana accent floated through the door. I turned to see Casper standing at the threshold; coat sodden from rain, and his face damp. Marianne must have called him.

"Let me see the letter," he begged, striding forward and pulling it from my hand. I had since pocketed my own.

Casper's deep brown eyes scanned the document, his breathing hard, and a lone droplet of water still hung from his cupid's bow. Both his hands gripped tight to each side of the letter.

Mars tried to pull it back. "Casper, don't."

Casper didn't respond, but simply wiped his lip, sniffling and turning his body away to stop either of us from retaining the paper. His golden earrings swung from his lobes.

"So where is he?" he finally demanded once he had finished reading. "WHERE IS HE?" he screamed at us all, eyes wide and shoulders trembling; his pain drowning each of us.

Marianne flinched the most. Her face having still not recovered from her initial reading. "I don't know," she said, almost inaudibly.

Casper shook the letter violently in the air, pointing towards our leader. "Is this no clue?" he cried. "Did nothing else come with this?" His energy was draining fast.

Marianne shook her head and Casper whirled to face me and Mars. His eyes pools of desperate pleas.

"She clearly doesn't want us to know yet," Mars said, closing their eyes to avoid any of our reactions.

"I'll kill her." Casper backed up, panting. He hunched his back as if he were surrounded by hostility and was preparing to flee. "I will kill her."

"Casper you can't just..." Marianne's words halted and she inhaled deeply, pinching the bridge of her nose.

Casper didn't react, not immediately, but his breathing grew shallow as we waited for her to finish.

"We can't act rash, we... we can't start a war. I can't put any more of you in danger."

"That's easy for you to say when it's not *your* partner."

I don't know how he hadn't completely snapped yet.

"You don't think I've lost people?" Marianne straightened her back and raised her chin. "Do you think I haven't had to fight before? That I haven't had to watch those I love be taken away right from under my nose?"

It was only then that I noticed the echo in the room and Marianne's voice grew larger than life.

Casper stiffened, hands forming fists at his side while his eyes turned crimson.

Marianne stepped towards us so that we were all but inches apart. I wanted to step back but I didn't.

"We will find Ben, through any means necessary, but I cannot justify any more bloodshed. We will *not* be taking any lives unless it's clear they plan to sacrifice us."

Marianne was the smallest of us all, by far, but her voice rose ten feet above us. No one dared to move.

The room grew cold, as if a draft had found its way through every crevice and crack in the walls and floor.

I looked up at Mars, their eyes were locked onto mine. Instantly, I knew that we were both thinking exactly the same. The cage. Jade.

I thought Mars was about to open their mouth, and I glanced at both Marianne and Casper, but they were cut off as Casper stood to full height with his brow furrowed into a deep scowl.

"You're such a hypocrite," he spat before turning on his heels and storming out of the door, Ben's worn, old coat billowing behind him.

How long can one wait? If you've set out with the intention of doing something, how long is it before you concede? I speak as though this was an art and crafts project, perhaps my novel I so dutifully neglected at the start of the term, or the bundles of poetry I crumpled to the bottom of my bag. Maybe that could have been something I couldn't hold my tongue about, if I'd had the confidence. Something to be proud of. But not this. No, this was malicious to the core. Having us chase around like wild dogs, hunting for a scent that was never left in the first place.

She waited a further two days, let us wallow in shame, before she sent her second note.

She knew where we resided, and likely had known for quite some time, yet how long exactly, none of us could tell.

The package was dumped at the door right at the point when Rani and I were walking past the entrance, as if she was able see our every move and calculated the prime time. Or maybe it was *Michael's* doing. After all, he always knew where I was.

I couldn't bring myself to speak his name; the name I so adamantly knew was *not* his real name — if he even owned a name at all. His voice had grown quiet since that evening in the woods, but I knew he would never be too far. A small flicker of otherness still burned in the back of my mind. My darkness. Just ticking away until the time was right.

I refused to let there ever be another time.

"DID YOU HEAR THAT?" Rani turned to me, her face startled.

"I did." I barely looked at her, my attention already focused on the exact point of the sound's origin — the front door, barricaded up as it always was.

"Someone's outside," she guessed, and she followed me as I stepped closer.

I placed my palm flush against the oak and pressed my ear to it. Closing my eyes, I let my senses do the rest.

"Anything?" Rani asked after a handful of seconds had passed. She extended a cautious arm in my direction.

After a few minutes of utter silence, I motioned for Rani to stand back. I carefully removed the metal bar and latches to one side, slowly creaking open part of the door, just enough to see that there was in fact no one there, but a lone brown box sat on the pavement below. I was at first hesitant to do anything, but my brain was beyond being cautious by that point. If it were to bring us immediate harm, I would have thought it would have been executed much more professionally.

I scraped the package, which was much lighter than it looked, across the ground and onto the other side of the door, swiftly closing it behind me and locking it back up.

"What does it say?" Rani crouched down to read the cursive black scrawled across the top.

She traced her finger across the words then looked up at me, sucking in her lips. Her eyes said everything I needed to know.

"'For Casper'," Rani read slowly.

I crouched down to her height to inspect it further. It was indeed addressed to Casper, and though I had not spent too many months around them all, my gut knew it to be true — it was Ben's handwriting. Shaky and unsure, but the curl of the 'C' was unmistakable.

Rani stood back up and headed for the door.

"No." I held her back, but I knew I was trying to reassure myself more than her. Rani wouldn't have been so stupid as to go outside now, but I perhaps might have been.

Her eyes flashed to me. "What are we going to do? *What's inside the box?*"

I paused, lowering my head; hair falling in front of my eyes. *What are we going to do? We can't give it straight to Casper, but shouldn't we? Seeing Ben's writing will comfort him, right? But what's* inside?

I carefully picked up the box, its weight suspicious.

"We can't just give it to him. What if it's..." she stopped herself with a hand cupped over her mouth in a gasp.

"It's light," I said, putting it back down on the floor.

"And that's supposed to be, what? *Reassuring?*" she snapped.

"I don't know." *I honestly don't know.*

"Maybe we should just get rid of it? He doesn't need to know," Rani suggested, crossing her arms firmly across her chest, as if to hide the fact that she was now shaking. I could sense her fear. "It's clearly another teaser, and she expects us to open it, to fall for the trap. If we *don't* then we win, right?" She was not sure at all.

"Or we could open it," I said, not quite liking the idea as it came out of my mouth, but I didn't revoke the statement anyhow.

"Did you hear a word I just said?" Rani's eyes widened.

"I did, but I think we should open it."

Rani gulped, heart hammering.

"Well?" I waited for her to agree, the only thing that would have gotten me to follow through.

"We need to show Marianne," she finally suggested.

After everything, we probably should.

"Okay," I agreed, standing up with the box in hand. "Okay."

· · ·

"DEAR LORD."

I rested the box before Marianne, who we found in the painting clad room, pacing. She'd been out all night with the rest of us. We were never giving in.

"I don't want Casper to open it alone," I said. Rani nodded beside me.

"I understand that." Marianne bent down and lifted up the package. She held it above her head and analysed the base before shaking it a little — something I was too anxious to do.

Something shifted and rattled inside, but it offered no clear indication to its contents.

Setting the box down again, Marianne traced the font with her finger.

"That's Ben's handwriting." She pursed her lips deep in thought.

"Meaning he's still alive, right?" I asked hopefully, as if she knew the answer.

Marianne looked back at me, then briefly to Rani. The next instant, she swiped a sharp nail across the tape seam and ripped open the flaps on either side of the box. The two of us instinctively backed up, as if preparing for a jack in the box, but as Marianne pulled away the silky, black material used to pad the contents, we watched as her hand reemerged with a small silver tin. She held it by the tips of her fingers like it was scolding hot, the ornate container was made from the purest of silver. She grimaced.

"Ben's okay, right?" Rani asked, less confident now.

Marianne didn't acknowledge her, instead lifting the box to her nose. She pulled an unsure face.

I had no idea what to expect, but my mind drew the worst conclusion.

Setting it down onto the table beside her, Marianne leaned forward. The tin, no bigger than one used to hold cigars, rested perfectly at her eye level.

Her next movement shocked us more than anything had that

day. She jumped up and ripped off the lid, but it was only when she staggered back and tripped to the floor that my insides lurched and I gasped at what fell out and rolled to the floor...

An eyeball: sloppy and fresh, the optic nerve still dangling from it.

Verdant and unseeing.

Ben's.

Rani gagged beside me and grabbed my sleeve, turning away and crouching down, free hand over her mouth.

I was the only one left standing up right, and suddenly the room felt a thousand times bigger. All eyes fixed to what lay before us.

All I could think to do next was charge over to tip out the rest of the box's contents. And so I did. I shook it in front of me, my legs unsteady, and watched as the rest of the silk glided to the floor along with a small white note.

You didn't see me coming x

CHAPTER TWENTY-EIGHT

I had no words. Standing there, the room froze over. Rani choked up behind me as Marianne rose to her feet and shook herself off, stepping ever so slowly towards the *gift*. Wiping her face, she sniffed, and then used the lace to clean it up off the floor. Dropping it back into the box, she sniffled again before replacing the lid.

She stood there, back to us, speaking in a hushed tone, "I don't know why she is doing all this when it's really *me* she wants." Marianne's hands gripped the table, knuckles white.

Rani took another stifled breath, and I was struck yet again, at my severe *lack* of emotion. Or more, my inability to show it. Static in both mind and body. Only the clenching and unclenching of my fists reminded me that I *could* move.

"*Why?*" Rani turned to look at me, and then to Marianne who did not face us, her voice hoarse.

"Why not?" Marianne's answer was brutal as she finally turned to us. "When you've lived this long, why not try a little *evil?*" The unhinged twang of sarcasm made me shiver. Marianne's eyes were wide with distress.

"So that's it then? He's gone. Lucy wins." Rani finally gathered the strength to stand back up.

"Never," Marianne snapped.

I didn't know what compelled me to return to the note, but I did... Picking it up, I turned it over, both sets of eyes on me.

A date, time, and location.

The abandoned church.

I looked at Marianne. It didn't take her long to deduce what I had read.

"We'll be ready."

I hope so.

WE INFORMED the rest of The Thorns as best and as quickly as we could. Tomorrow morning at sunrise. She'd be there.

We gathered Lawrence and Francesca, and Mars hugged them both close, pressing their heads together in a promise of hope.

Carmen wasted no time in arming herself to the teeth, refusing Marianne's safety advice. "I will not fucking *stand by,*" she said, pocketing another knife.

Casper was inevitably the hardest to inform. He didn't even let Mars finish the call before he hung up. Less than half an hour later, he stood in the room with us, covered in snow.

"I need to see it," he demanded, his whole body restless. The wobble of his voice oozed endless anguish.

Marianne shook her head as I looked at her.

"I need to *see it,*" he insisted, his feet shuffling and banging against the floor as his legs threatened to give way.

"I can't." Marianne's eyes were full of sympathy, like that of a mother; who she really was to them all.

As Casper let his knees fall to the ground, Marianne was there to hold him up, petting his shoulder in protective comfort.

His guttural cry consumed the entire room. He started to

pound a weak fist against her breastbone, fingers grabbing at her jumper.

"Please."

"I can't. I can't. I can't," she whispered into his curls, kissing his head.

A twinge rose up the back of my neck and my cheeks burned. I watched this tragedy unfold in front of me and I couldn't take it. I could not let this happen. *I can't.*

It's nearly time.

I hoped Lucy knew what was coming.

I stand sheltered by a tree, some meters away from where she stands on her own, her back resting against the crumbling walls. A flurry of snow starts to fall, the sky an ashy coal. She moves in a shiver before lighting a cigarette in impatience.
I smarten my bracelets.

WE WAITED FOR EMPTY STREETS, before the world awoke. Some of us armed physically, but all of us fortified with our mental guards.

We may have looked like an army, but one filled with terrified soldiers sent into the jaws of death, *wanting* to fight but afraid, nonetheless.

Once we hit the woods, the snow dissipated under the shelter of the gnarling branches. Torches on, the weight of it all started to pull on my shoulders and Mars slipped by my side, throwing me an unreadable glance. No one spoke, the crunch underfoot created the only sound around us for seemingly miles. There was no true path, either, yet each of us had the sense to stick close together — all hyperaware of the slightest crack, or intake of breath.

Marianne led us, her Thorns, her step refusing to slow. I wish I could have understood how she was feeling in that moment, but her fast pace left no room for hesitation. I gulped down the lump in my throat at least six or seven times, as it returned with each step. I kept my hands in my trench pockets to hide them away and stop them from exposing how I really felt — utterly terrified. This woman hurt Ben. *This woman killed me.*

A further twenty minutes finally spat us out into the clearing, the church mere yards away from us. The surrounding trees formed a perfect amphitheatre for battle.

Marianne had prepared us to be ready for anything, her slowing steps and glancing back at us set our first plan into motion. *Do not startle. She will not be alone.*

From our vantage point, and the still dead sky, the abandoned building seemed entirely neglected. Nothing but the crawling ivy and window-piercing brambles hugged it. Our many searches of this land still give it a sense of familiarity in the faded light, but this time it was different. We had no scent, no sight, just sense. She had to have been there already. *But where?*

"Watch your backs," Marianne called.

A boot clicked beside me and I looked over, realising I was standing almost eye level with Casper; red rage in his mourning eyes.

I lowered my head in acknowledgement, and he in turn, did the same. A silent understanding.

A twig crack startled us all to our left. Nothing but dead woods, blackening into an endless abyss. Something creaked from above and a large bird flew outwards in a frightened manner. Even the cold air now seemed to be whispering to us, but there was still no ground movement.

Seconds passed.

"We're here," Marianne broke the silence with a sturdy shout. "Just as you wished."

A few Thorns behind me exchanged a frightened look with one another, as if silently asking whether our leader had a death wish. The rest of us knew we could wait no longer. In my pockets, my nails bit into my palms.

Nothing. Then, a laugh. *Lucy.*

And so, it begins.

From out of the shadows, her figure emerged. My fists made a tear into my skin, and blood welled in my palms. Casper was ready to lunge forward, yet Mars and two other Thorns held him back from all sides. He bared his canines in a hiss of discomfort.

The figure started to clap as it prowled forward through the knee-high blades of grass and shrivelled weeds.

She came in view fully, green hair flowing elegantly over both shoulders. I recognised her outfit. The same one she wore the last time my heart beat, the one that adorned her body as she gleefully lowered me to the ground and wished me sweet dreams. The clothes only I would recognise: a direct address to me.

Her claps slowed; she believed she had the upper hand. *She does.*

A toothy grin.

Marianne straightened her back, giving her but an inch of height on Dumont.

Lucy cocked her head. "Well, hello all," she greeted us.

None of us dared open our mouths, instead, we waited for Marianne's next signal.

Marianne's sigh was dramatic and impatient, and she folded her arms firmly. "I don't want a fight."

Lucy laughed as an insult then threw her arms out wide. "Do I look armed to you?"

The woods shifted around us. *We are not alone.*

"Look at you all. All rallied up for war. You would think I had *killed* him!"

Ben's alive?

Casper took advantage of the loss of grip, slackened from shock, and charged. Shoving past Marianne, he caught Lucy by the throat, and practically lifted her from the ground.

"Where is he?" Casper's voice was icy, fingers pressing in hard around Lucy's delicate neck. It was not enough to rattle her though. The rest of us tried to pull him back, but Lucy's wide eyed grin grew into something more sinister. Even in Casper's grip, she found room to laugh.

"Calm yourself, boy," she coughed, then glanced behind herself. "Ben dear, do come out. You've got company."

Casper's grip loosened as he and the rest of us looked over to the church where movement began.

Two figures appeared, the one in front was significantly shorter than the other. The figure in the back rammed its clumpy foot into the back of the smaller one in front, sending him to his hands and knees.

Ben.

In an instant, perhaps even before the rest of us even realised what was going on, Casper was running over to the figures and dove straight for the fallen one, pulling him into a deep and protective hug. *He's alive.*

"Come," Lucy waved her arm. "See your precious pianist."

We ignored her patronising tone, but slowly and hesitantly made our way over to them while Lucy followed casually behind so that, as she clearly planned, she could block us off from the back.

As we approached, I heard Casper's tears. In his arms lay a frail, black-haired boy. A few fingers bound in fraying bandage cloth, clothes torn and skin exposed, with a bloody blindfold pulled tightly over his eyes. *Eye?*

But he was alive. Battered, but alive.

Behind the two men stood a monster of a man: a muscular face and arms of steel. *Lucy's guard?* I couldn't help but notice the blood and scratches up his bare forearms — ones that corresponded with the remaining exposed, bloody fingertips on Ben's trembling hands that now gripped so tightly to his fiancé's coat.

Some of his fingers *weren't there.*

What did they do to him? Why Ben? Why? Why? Why?

"You're safe now. You're safe now. I've got you. I've got you," Casper chanted into Bens curls.

Marianne moved over to them now, joining Casper on her knees and reaching her arm around to pat Ben's battered back, his clothes barely covering it. I observed the deep gash wounds that had badly scarred over his exposed abdomen and chest. His breaths were shallow and fast.

Casper tried to remove Ben's blindfold, but Ben's cracked hands frantically gripped on tightly to Casper's in protest.

"No. Please," he croaked. "You can't look."

He can't see. She took them both.

Bile rose to my throat.

Ben reacted to one of us moving, his startled head turning in my direction. *Does he know I'm here?*

"You brought them. They're not safe," Ben panicked. "I'm... I'll hurt them."

Carmen and Rani. I looked to them both, and they looked back at me, the two of them stepping back and hiding amongst the group.

She starved him. I think. *He can sense them.*

"I'm..." he coughed and turned back to the familiarity of Casper's warm body. "I'm sorry," he said. "I didn't tell her where you were, I promise." His voice was so painfully strained, it almost didn't sound like him. "She already knew. I'm sorry Casper. I'm..." he looked as though he was running out of breath. His head tilted back slightly as his muscles relaxed unnaturally. "I'm sorry, everyone."

"How touching," Lucy interrupted from around the back of us. We all watched her pace around to stand before us once again.

Marianne squared back up to her, standing inches away from her opponent. "Take one of my Thorns again and—" her threat was cut short.

"—What? You'll murder me? Like you did my brother?"

Marianne tensed. "So this is truly what it's all about then? An eye for an eye." She stepped closer. "How long were you waiting for this day?"

"Long enough." Lucy flashed another soulless smile.

"And you thought to bring my Thorns into this, why?"

"Am I not allowed to have a bit of fun? You really have forgotten yourself in your old age. You killed Isiah. He was only living his life how he wanted, he hadn't harmed *you* or any of your precious Thorns. He was hungry, as are we all. Humans are insects to us, yet you escalated it. You brought this on yourself, Marianne Ashtown. All of the dramatics over one man. I thought you would have learned how to handle your emotions better, especially after *Jerome.*" She clapped her hands twice and the silent monster at her disposal reached down to pull Ben away from Casper, holding his weak body and limbs tight against his monstrous chest. One arm squeezed under Ben's arms and over his ribcage, restricting his breaths. Casper pawed for grasp, but I watched the light leave his eyes as he froze in motion, then as if being rewound like a video tape, he returned back to his knees, face relaxing. Ben ceased trying his best to struggle, and his limbs grew dead. Even the beast that held him froze, too. We all turned back to Lucienne — Marianne's eyes widening. *She said she was powerful. I had no idea how strong.*

"No," our leader breathed.

All Lucy did was grin, but in an instant, Marianne's fist collided with her face, and green hair fluttered into the air as the force of the punch threw Lucy backwards. Two more Thorns joined in and then chaos ensued.

Carmen was the first soul I noticed take a real slash at Lucy with a knife. It failed, Lucy too quick to leap backwards and protect her throat. Someone screamed and once more, Lucy laughed above all other sounds; her choppy fringe askew and hair covering her face as she ran backwards.

Bodies, dozens of them, eyes glowing and teeth elongated, emerged from the trees surrounding us and they all closed in one by one.

"You're probably going to wish you brought more of you," she cried.

I watched it all unfold from the second they entered the woods. Of course, I only care about him. My focus fixed to his ever-changing emotions as they make their way through the trees, apprehension high.
I watch his sorrowful face as she reveals the boy, face bound and joints weak.
But what stands out the most is when he notices the Manipulation at work. She had no need to even move her lips. And why did that frighten him the most? He's been away from me too long. He knows what he is capable of.

IN THE CROWD, I frantically searched for Rani as bodies shoved and lashed out without any sense of direction. The morning sun beamed through the cracks in the trees, blinding and hindering my ability to tell everyone apart. I pushed around, and someone's back was thrust into my side, knocking me sideways. Somehow, I was able to keep myself on my own two feet, and then I saw her. A fierce looking man, twice our age in human terms, was lashing out with iron knuckles that she so narrowly managed to dodge.

"Rani!" I screamed. She whirled around in my direction, dropping her defence ever so slightly at the recognition of my presence.

Her opponent looked back to me too, giving her the chance to regain advantage, and allowing her to thrust a knee between the older vampire's legs. He crumbled backwards, giving me the opening to pull at him from behind and snap his neck — the body crumbling to my feet. I had not killed him, it would take a far deeper wound to end our kind, but I had at least relinquished our immediate threat. I stood panting a little, making eye contact with the startled Rani. She'd just watched me do that.

"You need to get out of here," I said, trying to stay calm.

"I can't leave you all." She didn't give me a chance to stop her before she ran off back into the heart of the battle and I lost her almost immediately.

Shit shit shit.

My next move was to run back to Casper, to free him from his trance. I got half as far, his frozen form in the same position it was moments before. Ben was still held firmly in the arms of Lucy's henchman, but a knife was now pressed to Ben's exposed lower abdomen. The three of them were paused in time as if waiting for an audience before resuming.

But before I could get any further, a cold breath kissed the back of my neck and a long, slender hand slid over my mouth and nose.

"Shhhh."

I felt a sharp stab to my neck — realising a moment too late what was happening. Once the black blood started to mix in my system, my eyes grew fuzzy, and as the plunger was released and thrown to the ground, I too collapsed to my knees.

Michael.

The Sun.

No. No. No.

My eyes grew hazy as I grasp at the ground. My legs failed me, failed Arlo. I crawled as best as I could over to Casper's blurry form and pulled myself up by his shoulders.

"Casper." I tried to shake him awake. I tugged on his body a further two times before—

I'm back in the light, my arms pulling my body up out of the hole. At the last moment, something grips my ankle and I turn back around into the abyss. What looks back up at me is a mirror, or more, my reflection. That thing inside me, lying dormant until once again it can swallow me whole. It has no real form, but it is part of me now. Forever.

And consume me it does. Pulling my body back down until I am falling, falling, falling, into an endless pit of darkness, as if thrown into an icy ocean, the rippling light growing smaller and smaller until I run out of breath and my consciousness fades, once again.

Welcome home.

CHAPTER TWENTY-NINE

Marianne

A ll my life I had done what I believed to be the right thing. I lived whilst everyone around me moved on or died. I watched the very world fall apart, but I had always done what my gut told me to. Protect people, no matter who or what they were. We all deserved a chance at redemption and freedom, but some just never listened.

The minute the church came into view, it was twelve years ago again. Beaten and bloody and high from his death, I rattled the door open to see his sinister work. Bodies upon bodies buried in plain sight. His *pride*.

I hadn't even suspected it. He'd been doing this right under my nose and I'd been blind to it. *You didn't see me coming.*

Sometimes, they say evil wins. Sometimes, no matter how hard you may try, there is just no stopping such cruelty, and this world stands testament to that. But I thought I'd won that time. I thought he was the worst threat we'd have to face.

I was naïve, even with all those years behind me. I let my guard down and started a war from my own stupidity.

Maybe I let my personal rage get in the way, this was *my* lapse in judgement, after all. Ever since I found Isiah in Carmen's house, my world tipped itself on its head. Learning to trust again after something like that is something I admit maybe I've never been able to do.

And of course Lucy knew about my life before. That name, *Jerome.* I had not heard that name in decades. He was all but a ghost story to me now, but she knew how to push me over the edge. She knew I had faltered time and time again. That I was weak.

And now, once again, I led my Thorns into hell and all I could think to say was *sorry.* Sorry for not being who I believed I could be. Who I always used to be.

SHE THRASHED AT MY NECK, a swift blade of nails. How did I never know of her existence? And why *now.* Had they been planning this together all along? Killing and killing forever and ever until they were the only ones left? What had they been doing before, together? How many people had suffered because of them?

"Surrender," she hissed her demand as I managed to trip her, causing her to stagger back, eyes never leaving my face.

"Never." I lunged forward again, and her teeth latched onto my arm. Foul play, just like her brother. I grimaced and released my wounded arm, throwing it behind me, defending with the other.

She was behind me now, and I turned to block another bloody bite.

It was at that moment when I spotted Carmen, staggering up stealthily from behind Lucy. *She shouldn't be here,* I thought. I would never forgive myself for putting her in danger after all I did to protect her. But she would not have it. She never would. It was out of my control.

Part of me wanted to Manipulate her to turn back, but then what would that make me?

So I distracted Lucy as best as I could and prepared myself to be ready for what was to come.

"You will never win this," I spat as we sparred around, waiting for one of us to strike next. I kept her in line with Carmen as best I could. "I've killed your brother, you will be no different."

"Oh, but my brother was always the weakest of us — begged me to turn him in the end. He was never like me."

"That means nothing." I was lying, but I just regurgitated whatever words first came to mind, as the next second, Carmen pounded up onto Lucy's back and with all her might, plunged a blade into her chest, screaming out every piece of anger she'd saved up.

But she missed the heart; it did not go in deep enough, and in the next instant, Carmen was thrown to the ground.

I saw my chance to strike, leaping up and pushing a wounded Lucy to the sludge of the earth and I pushed down, watching the blade sink deeper and deeper as the blood oozed out from her sternum. It was nowhere near her heart, but I did what I could. Her eyes grew wide in pain and she lashed out with her arms and *mind*.

I worked quick; barricading Carmen's open gates as best as I could. Keeping her down on the ground and semi-unconscious.

'*Protect her.*' Alvin Wood's final words to me as he lay a mangled corpse on the floor next to his dead wife. His daughter clung onto the arm of the sofa, nails biting down and eyes as wide as headlights. Protect her — a promise I could never break.

"Oh, you're no fun," Lucy gargled up at me as blood pooled in her throat and began to seep through her teeth and flow out onto her face.

You will never win.

For a moment I believed I had her. Her eyelids fluttered and her mind faltered, arms slackening from around my arm and neck.

Then her voice rang out and I thought then, that I would

forever remember those two words. Words that bit down into my very soul and tore me apart from the inside out.

"KILL HIM!" she cried in a ferocity so *chilling* and demonic. *Ben.*

Stunned, my own arm stupidly relaxed for less than a human heartbeat. But enough time for her to remove the blade and *shit.*

I fell back, hands reaching for my now deeply slashed throat, blood bubbling and pooling down my neck, soaking into my clothes.

No.

Arlo

THEY AWOKE: all three of them reanimated at once. **She released them. She has grown weak.** I glanced around to find Marianne with Lucienne Dumont beneath her knee. Then I looked back to the scene before me, Casper scrambling to his knees and running over to Ben who was still held tightly with a blade to his pale, exposed skin.

Casper begged and clawed to free his partner. Ben gave it all he could to reach out, although his arms were pinned down.

Help him.

Shut up.

"Let's get out of here." A hand found my shoulders, and that voice of velvet whispered so elegantly in my ear.

I nodded. This was no place for us anymore.

No.

Everything changed when that voice screeched out across the field.

"KILL HIM!" she demanded. Lucy.

Ben.

I whirled around, the henchman performing his sole duty.

He kicked Casper backwards, the inhumanly strong thrust sending him flying into the sodden dirt, he would not have stood a chance.

The instruction was swift, a clean impale to the abdomen and straight up the sternum through the heart, insides spilling out. The blade in his other hand cut clean across the back of Ben's neck; severing his spinal cord. A fatal blow.

Ben was dead in an instant.

A crucifixion.

No. Please.

I didn't think she would do it. I have spent too long in this realm.
I...

CASPER SCREAMED, birds startled out of the trees and fled in terror. It was as if everything transpired in slow motion. He threw himself forward to stop Ben's body from thudding angrily to the ground. They fell together: one alive, one not. Casper rocked the lifeless soul in his arms, hands trying to stem the blood flow as if it was still possible to save him. Ben's head unnaturally bent over his fiancé's arms, limbs limp at his side, scraping against the ground.

We are above this.

No.

Yes.

My Star. Oh, my Star. I stand behind him and watch as he turns
away. I can feel him. *My Star.*
I need not move.
He is reborn.

Marianne

I LAY on the frozen grass, propped up by my failing arms, head heavy and eyes weary. My throat had already started to clot, and I felt the skin stretching to close together, but I'd lost too much to stand. Lucy's body still slumped before me, the winter sun glowing around her like a mocking halo.

I heard Casper's despair, even from my distance, and my chest seized up. *Ben.*

I could barely lift myself.

The battlefield did not cease entirely, but it is obvious that people from both sides were curious to see what just happened. The *scream* that escaped Casper's lungs. My eyes brimmed with tears. My boy.

I would have never considered myself a maternal person, it was not in my nature, but The Thorns were like my children. My equals. Mine to guide and mine to protect.

I had lost a child.

Sweet, sweet Ben.

And it was all my fault.

I TRIED to keep my arms steady as my view swam into focus. Lucy lay weak in front of me, Carmen not too far behind, standing but exhausted. Everything had stilled, as if even nature itself yearned to mourn.

But then came the fire.

At first I didn't understand what was happening. No one did, but then I saw him.

Carmen jolted around and I knew what I must do. She would thank me after, if I survived.

Run. I told her. And she did. I sent her to find Rani, to take them both to safety. *Run. Far, far away. Hide.* If only I could do so myself.

The creature in Arlo's body strode forward, fire burning in his eyes. I watched from the floor as a few from the opposing side attempted to block his path, but they were met with his unnatural strength which tore away at them all. He stopped for nothing.

The closer he got, the taller he appeared. Bigger. Grander. *A god.*

"Arlo, no." Mars. They ran up to him with begging arms. "Don't do this. Please." They frantically attempted to pull him back. He did not lash out this time, but shrugged them away with great strength. *He's still in there. Just.*

Mars, get out of the way. Please. I beg you. I could not call to them though. I was too weak.

Arlo continued to move. His face now readable, even in my state. His brow was tight and eyes blood red.

Everyone... run.

The blurry outline of a battered Lucy stood up to greet him with open arms, her pride somehow in tact. He took none of it.

I will never learn how much of my life she knew. But there was one thing for certain, and it all hit me at once. She brought up my past for a reason.

Weeks ago, I had been struck with the realisation that Arlo reminded me of someone I once knew, but I brushed it off in an instant, thinking it wholly impossible and near insane. But as he stood before us all now, only one name came into my mind.

Jerome.

My old friend.

The man who first destroyed my ability to trust.

The man I thought I may have even once loved like a brother.

How is this possible?

With Mars still watching from behind, and the fighting stopping entirely so that everyone could turn to the scene... he took his first blow. Struck her down with the back of his hand. I think I heard her laugh one last time before black claws plunged down and removed her jugular *entirely*. Everyone stood frozen in place — his Manipulation — as he hacked away brutally, snapping and pulling and biting; completely ripping her apart. A massacre, and he would not stop.

From his back, I blamed my failing eyes at first, but then there was no mistaking: two tawny feathered wings unfurled and stretched out in the morning sun, extending out to their full span as the light glowed behind him.

Hands bloody and shirt torn, he stood before us in his new form, a cry escaping from his throat as he bared his head back in anguish.

It still sounded like him. His tone cracking ever so slightly into a wail. And maybe he was in there still, pained from the death of his friend. But it was too late. I did all I could to prevent this, but some things are beyond even the powers of our kind.

I caught a glimpse of Mars; their body language reading red.

I had no energy left.

I closed my eyes in defeat, head hitting the cold, hard ground.

I'm sorry, Arlo.

Arlo

HOW CAN I stand by and let my friends die. What sort of pathetic excuse of a human lets that happen? And that's what I am — what I always have been. Never enough.

I think back to his words that night. How I could be so much more...

Is this the only way?

Michael

I TAKE HIS HAND, waiting until he has completed his work before I join his side. A deathly quiet has fallen across the land.

Four dead, all from Lucy's side — well, except the boy. His partner continues to cradle his body in the melting snow. The humans survived, somehow. Both long gone, running as far as their little legs could carry them.

Mars, dear Mars. I stand aside to see how they react as my Star turns to face them in his new form. Long black claws and his beautiful, beautiful wings.

Mars does not — cannot move. Tears stain each cheek, their mouth fixed in a sorry gasp.

They stare at each other for a moment, so many unspoken words channelling between them.

"Come on," I finally say, taking his hand.

Maybe he does still recognise them, maybe he always will. But for now, it is not enough. With one final glance, he turns back to me and follows me off into the light.

The Sun, The Moon, and The Star together on earth.

I smile. My work here is done.

CHAPTER THIRTY

2 weeks later

Marianne

W hen I was a little girl, my mother showed me a painting of an angel.

"Why do they need wings?" I asked.

"So that they can watch over us all and be there for us whenever we need protecting," she would always reply.

I've never been a heavily religious woman; I tended to keep my thoughts and opinions to myself and live my life as *I* saw fit, not the way someone else decided. But I would always think about the human image of an angel. Our guardians.

As I walked towards the cemetery and looked amongst the headstones, I took note of all the stone angels watching down over the fallen and I thought back to my mother's words, and how the wings helped them to be there for us always. I wasn't sure how true that was anymore, not after I watched one do what it had. Angels probably aren't real, but their image came from somewhere.

Not one, but two stood before me in the forest that day, and when they spoke and acted as they did, I was no longer sure what to believe.

I do not consider myself a mother, but I lost two children that day.

WE HAD NOT SEEN him since, of course. Though the weight of Ben's death hung heavy on us all, so we didn't go looking. I blamed myself for everything. And I would not let anyone tell me otherwise. I started this twelve years ago and it may never end. Perhaps this was only the second beginning.

Mars stepped into stride beside me, head facing forward, dressed head to foot in a black suit, shiny brogues at their feet. "I brought roses," they said, holding up a small bouquet of cherry red petals and thorns. "Fitting, I thought."

I nodded, adjusting the black scarf covering my neck and folding my lips inwards, closing my eyes slightly to withhold my emotions.

When we reached the church, we were greeted by the priest and gently shown to our seats.

I had not set foot in a church, or any religious establishment, in decades. Had had no need to. It was not a place I saw myself welcome — not because of my otherness, but for the mere fact I did not believe in the power supposedly held within religious walls. But I felt it that day, in whatever way it chose to present itself to me. I believed it to be the power of love.

We sat ourselves and awaited the service; a frame stood to the side of the altar with a picture of a much younger Ben printed across it. One of him smiling at the camera: close up with his eyes squinting against the sun. A black bass guitar was propped up below it, a red rose woven between the four strings.

Ben's mother and father sat beside each other in the front row, perhaps for the first time in a very long time. Katerina and David sat hand in hand, his mother's lace-gloved hand pressing a pale handkerchief to her face. Sat beside them, taller than them both, with freshly dyed black hair, was Casper. I had seen very little of him or any of the band for that matter, since that day. Casper flew back to America for a few days to be with his family, Lawrence and Fran followed suit and left the city too. I don't blame them for their distance, nor do I ever expect any of them to return to The Thorns. I had hurt them enough. They did not deserve it.

Casper sat with his back straight, his posture failing to falter. His older brother, Jesse, sat beside him. They must have flown back together; Jesse was always his closest sibling. I wished to speak with them, even for only for a second. I did not need Casper's forgiveness, but I did need him to know my love for him. For them all. My Thorns.

I failed them all.

Mars squeezed my hand, sensing my drifting mind.

"Don't think about it," they whispered. Maybe they were right, but there was only so much guilt I could hold before I exploded.

They were lost in their own silent mourning. I knew they missed them both equally. They got to know Arlo more than any of us did, and I think they loved him, in a way. In fact, I knew they did. They would just never admit it, especially not now.

Mars had been as strong a friend as anyone could be, for both boys. Yet they did not cry today. Perhaps they had already mourned them alone, it was sometimes easier that way.

I knew how they always acted in front of me, I've always been aware of how they tried to impress me. I wished they understood how much I trusted them, and how strong I knew they were. That if anything happened to me, it would be Mars who I wished to take over The Thorns. It was Mars who I wanted to lead the future.

I smiled at them in reminiscence.

The murders had stopped. Perhaps that day showed us all, on both sides, that bloodshed would get us nowhere. Or perhaps they were lying dormant — you can never be rid of opposition. I knew that all too well now.

The day before the funeral, I met with Carmen and Rani for the first time in two weeks. They'd gone into hiding, all by my own unavoidable command. They were not angry, and demanded no explanations. They just held my hand as I held theirs and kissed their foreheads.

"He's really gone, isn't he?" Rani asked. She wasn't talking about Ben.

I nodded, and the two girls nodded back in silent understanding.

For now, perhaps. He would not be gone forever though.

And I would await his return.

The Star

It begins to snow on the morning they lower Ben's coffin into the ground. The sky is grey and mournful for humanity's loss.

It was a quiet ceremony, limited to only friends and family.

The media reported he suffered from a short illness and passed away peacefully surrounded by loved ones. No one deserved to know how he fell, bloody and afraid, into his lover's arms. How in his last days, he lay cold and helpless, blinded and alone.

They all stand around his coffin; heads hung low. Casper and Ben's parents are up front with their heads lowered to the coffin below them, hands full of final memories.

I spot Mars first, a handful of red roses gripped between their hands, ready to place before the dirt.

Rani is there too, head resting on Carmen's tear-stained shoulder. As is Marianne, a black, silk scarf crossed tightly over her neck to hide the scar.

I should be there. A friend.

Michael stands by my side as we watch from a distance, unseen and silent.

I cannot let them suffer, my friends. After all they did to protect me. I need to do this. It is the only way.

From beside the grave, as the final biblical words are spoken, Casper steps forward and speaks from his heart:

"Most of you knew Ben as the sweet guy who could play any instrument you threw at him. He had a heart of pure gold — someone you could trust with anything, no matter how big or small. He never talked about it much, but he had a strong faith; he believed we were all put on this earth for a reason and made it his mission to find his true purpose." Casper wipes his eyes, pulling out a small metal chain from under his clothes. *Ben's cross.* He holds the base between his fingers and looks to the sky. "I think we can all agree he left his mark."

Everyone nods in agreement; Ben's mother falls to her knees, and his father pats her back.

"Although he is no longer with us," Casper continues, clearing his throat and sniffing back the pain, "a soul as big as Ben's cannot possibly leave us. He will always live on, for eternity. As we both promised. The Eternal."

The humans hold their hearts at such a touching statement, but The Thorns know the true meaning.

Neither I nor The Sun move, snow dancing onto our eyelashes and wind whistling through our heavy wings.

I am still growing used to the weight of them. The bird-like feathers trailing clumsily across the ground, my fingers stretched and sharp.

I mourn him, Ben. In the two weeks since The Star and Arlo joined for the final time, I learned to accept his sorrow. I would get nowhere without emotion, even if it choked my very core.

It is necessary, what we must do. I cannot let myself waste any more time.

We wait until the crowd dissipates, Katerina the last to leave, her sun halo'd silhouette placing a final, gentle finger kiss to the soil. Her final goodbye to her only child.

"Come," he says, squeezing my hand. "It is time you finally meet him."

Epilogue

From the echoes and shadows in the depths of the cathedral catacombs, far away from human acknowledgement, Jerome sits on his wooden throne, his long fiery hair flowing down past his shoulders, and his chin resting on his jewelled fingers.

When the creature first told him its beliefs, he scoffed and shooed it away. He did not have time for foolish antics. He would not be toyed with and mocked.

Thirty years ago, The Sun promised him the world. Freedom from his undead state and the promised life he had always yearned for. He could live, start a family, be human.

But hundreds and hundreds of years beyond the light had shredded him from his old way of thinking. He could not bear growing old, after all this time.

So, he joined with The Moon.

"Do you ever get bored?" Michael once asked him, not long after they met for the first time. "Being stuck in this plane, restricted to humanity, to this body?"

He had been asked that question before. Jerome's answer was always the same. "Yes, but what else can you offer me? You too are trapped by your desires. You will never leave us now. That was your decision, to walk this earth. I had no choice."

The Sun sulked, folding his arms in defeat. It was, as Jerome grew to learn, always just an act.

"Well?" Jerome would push.

"One day, I will bring you with me, my Moon. When I find a vessel for The Star, we shall be strong enough to do what we were made for, together. It will take time, but I refuse to believe it impossible."

Jerome considered the confession. He never did understand why Michael cared that much about changing a world he was not even originally part of. Jerome had never felt that strongly about anything before. He would move the earth for no one, and there was no one he would willingly spend eternity with.

Until he regained his humanity for ten short years: after a couple of years of childish, teething antics, he met Melissa. Sweet, sweet Melissa Everett.

Years they spend travelling the world, seeing things he could have only ever dreamed of. He *loved*. For the first time in centuries, he *loved*.

It hurt him, having to leave her. He never even let her say goodbye, but it was better that way, he told himself. Better he left her like that so she would forget him. She would move on, find another, and live her life as he wished she could. To the fullest.

Michael, much to Jerome's ignorance, stayed. He stayed in the shadows and learned what came after. He knew. He always knew.

Many years after Jerome came crawling back, Michael returned to that house: the converted chapel at the end of the street, right next to the post office and the little babbling brook that fed out into the lakes. He watched the boy grow. He never let on to the fact that Jerome had left so much behind because he knew: he could sense his Star. Always.

One night, the boy hears him. Maybe he intended for it to happen, no one will ever know. He courageously follows the tap of

Michael's claws, and in that moment, the Star shone through. Long before the host would even know it.

He smiles at the boy, his true form sheltered by the midnight shadows. And the boy smiles back, he beams at the shadow in the corner of the room.

Out of all the forms The Star could join with, life had chosen wisely.

The incident with Lucy was a misstep, but nothing they could not persevere through.

Marianne tried to free him, oh she tried. But sometimes it's never enough. This was too important for anyone to diminish.

Now, Michael comes to Jerome with a different greeting.

"Wakey, wakey." The Sun bends as a jester would, introducing his next act.

Jerome, awake but distant, stirs and looks up, unfazed.

"Oh, don't give me that look. I think you are going to simply adore what I have brought you."

Jerome straightens his back against his chair. "What can you possibly have done now?"

"I promised, and I shall deliver."

On cue, Michael stands aside and reaches an arm out to the flame lit corridor where a new body stands, one Jerome has never seen before. He feels his own dirt blackened wings twitch and stands, a sense of unsure fear crawling up his spine.

"Have you finally brought them?" There's a wary caution in his voice.

"Arlo, come now."

The young creature stumbles and sways his way into the light, unsure of this meeting. Soft, brown wings trail behind him and Michael grins in pride.

Jerome drops his hands as he realises. Walls come crashing down in his mind, his Moon far away as he thinks — Melissa.

Arlo looks up and his face drops. His Star stepping back for a moment, too, as he truly sees who stands before him.

"Dad?"

"My... my son."

Jerome moves first, the boy's face in his hands in an instant. Arlo is stunned in place, allowing his arms to wrap around him. They are the same height, allowing for Jerome to pull Arlo's head to his shoulder.

"My boy," he whispers kisses into Arlo's blond waves.

"Dad." The boy's arms come up to wrap around his father's. United at long last.

The Sun stares at his doing.

"The Sun, The Moon and The Star," he says to the scene. "Reunited at long last."

His family.

"We are going to change the world."

The end.

To Be Continued...

FOREVER RED

Ben and Casper's story is not over.

Forever Red: A Fallen Thorns Novella out Summer 2024

Before The Sun, there was just a band. A band of kids who had the world at their fingertips.

Follow Ben and Casper through their lives leading up to the events of Fallen Thorns and the aftermath as they navigate their passions, relationships, and eventually, their undead life. Told in part interview format, part narration from the boys, learn the story of two kids who lived as if their lives would never end.

FALLEN THORNS PLAYLIST

'La Ment' by The Cure
'Bathrooms' by Wy
'My Lights Kiss Your Thoughts' by Lucy Gooch
'Sanitarium' by Choir Boy
'From Above' by Rae Morris
'Your Rabbit Feet' by Wild Nothing
'Vapor Frames' by You'll Never Get to Heaven
'Sadness is Taking Over' by Flora Cash
'Moon and Moon' by Bat For Lashes
'Angel' by Eganomixxxxxxxx
'Saman' by Kælan Mikla
'Fable' by Grayera, Lady Moon
'Rose of Sharon' by Topographies
'All I Need' by Radiohead
'Televangelism' by Ethel Cain
'So You Wanna Be a Superhero' by Carissa's Wierd
'Dagger' by Slowdive
'not a lot, just forever' by Adrianne Lenker
'Bloodhail' by Have A Nice Life

Acknowledgments

I've wanted to do a lot of things in my life but it always came back around to this... I've only ever wanted to create.

To my favourite authors who inspire me in infinite ways: Olivie Blake, V.E. Schwab, Rafael Nicolás, Robin Hobb, M.L. Rio, Allison Saft, R.F. Kuang, Fonda Lee, Sabaa Tahir, Shelley Parker-Chan and Renée Ahdieh. Please never stop writing.

Thank you to all my fellow author friends who helped me through this process, and a special shoutout to Jade Church, C.J. Merwild and Isabel Agajanian for answering my many, many publishing questions. And to my lovely beta readers: Karnam, Naj, Sy, Benedetta, Shajeda and Maia for being as enthusiastic as possible about my silly little book. You helped me out in the first and most important way.

My utmost thanks to my editor Eden Northover for tearing away at the manuscript and stitching it back with a golden thread. You are a wonder and I cannot wait to work with you again!

Thank you Rebecca for cancelling that one coffee shop trip that time, creating the snowball effect of me actually completing this story in the first place.

Thank you Maia for being the first person to read this manuscript, even before it was edited, and who listened tirelessly to my hours and hours of discussions about my characters. You're now canonically Arlo's cousin.

Many thanks to my family and friends for letting me be me. To my gran, I am proud to hold the Baxter name for you and your stories, I wouldn't be where I am today without a lifetime of encouragement from you. And of course, to my partner who doesn't read but has stood by my side through this whole process. I love you all immensely.

And lastly, and most importantly, thank you to every single person over the last two and a half years who told me they wanted to read this story. I never would have guessed one random 3am scene idea would spiral into what it has become, and it is all thanks to the support and encouragement from you all.

Oh, and a shoutout to The Cure. I need not say anything else...

About the Author

Harvey Oliver Baxter is an author and illustrator from the North of England.

Fallen Thorns is their first published novel.

instagram.com/lastvanillasmile

tiktok.com/authorhobaxter

Milton Keynes UK
Ingram Content Group UK Ltd.
UKHW041031260124
436746UK00004B/181